P9-CSW-722

A FRAGILE DESIGN

Books by Tracie Peterson

www.traciepeterson.com

Controlling Interests
The Long-Awaited Child
Silent Star
A Slender Thread • *Tidings of Peace*

BELLS OF LOWELL*
Daughter of the Loom • *A Fragile Design*
These Tangled Threads

DESERT ROSES
Shadows of the Canyon • *Across the Years*
Beneath a Harvest Sky

WESTWARD CHRONICLES
A Shelter of Hope • *Hidden in a Whisper*
A Veiled Reflection

RIBBONS OF STEEL†
Distant Dreams • *A Hope Beyond*
A Promise for Tomorrow

RIBBONS WEST†
Westward the Dream • *Separate Roads*
Ties That Bind

SHANNON SAGA‡
City of Angels • *Angels Flight*
Angel of Mercy

YUKON QUEST
Treasures of the North • *Ashes and Ice*
Rivers of Gold

NONFICTION
The Eyes of the Heart

*with Judith Miller †with Judith Pella ‡with James Scott Bell

TRACIE PETERSON
AND JUDITH MILLER

A FRAGILE DESIGN

BETHANYHOUSE
PUBLISHERS
MINNEAPOLIS, MINNESOTA

A Fragile Design
Copyright © 2003
Tracie Peterson and Judith Miller

Cover design by Dan Thornberg

Scripture quotations identified KJV are from the King James Version of the Bible.

All rights reserved. No part of this publication may be reproduced, stored in a retrieval system, or transmitted in any form or by any means—electronic, mechanical, photocopying, recording, or otherwise—without the prior written permission of the publisher and copyright owners.

Published by Bethany House Publishers
11400 Hampshire Avenue South
Bloomington, Minnesota 55438
www.bethanyhouse.com

Bethany House Publishers is a Division of
Baker Book House Company, Grand Rapids, Michigan.

Printed in the United States of America

Library of Congress Cataloging-in-Publication Data

Peterson, Tracie.
    A fragile design / by Tracie Peterson and Judith Miller.
        p.   cm. — (Bells of Lowell ; . 2.)
    ISBN 0-7642-2689-4
    1. Women—Massachusetts—Fiction. 2. Women textile workers—Fiction.
3. Lowell (Mass.)—Fiction. I. McCoy-Miller, Judith. II. Title. II. Series:
Peterson, Tracie. Bells of Lowell ; v 2.
    PS3566.E7717F7   2003
    813'.54—dc21   2003002569

In memory of my mother,
Gladys E. McCoy. Thanks be
to God for the blessing of a
godly mother.

—Judy Miller

TRACIE PETERSON is a popular speaker and bestselling author who has written over fifty books, both historical and contemporary fiction. Tracie and her family make their home in Montana.

Visit Tracie's Web site at: *www.traciepeterson.com*.

JUDITH MILLER is an award-winning author of five novels and three novellas, two of which have placed in the CBA top-ten fiction lists. In addition to her writing, Judy is a certified legal assistant. Judy and her husband make their home in Topeka, Kansas.

Visit Judy's Web site at: *www.judithmccoymiller.com*.

CHAPTER 1

Canterbury, New Hampshire
March 6, 1831

Arabella Newberry raced through the woods, the fallen leaves crunching beneath her feet and the echo of her footsteps beating the message *Hur-ry, Hur-ry, Hur-ry*. Darting through the timbers, she hastened by a grove of rock maples and onward toward the sheltering heavy-needled pines. Her breath came hard as she edged her agile body between two of the prickly green trees, the needles now poking her arms as they punctured her gray woolen cloak. She forced herself to breathe more easily, then leaned forward and listened. All was quiet, save the occasional chattering of a squirrel or the scampering feet of a frightened rabbit.

Without warning, a hand clamped around her arm and pulled her from the bristly nest. A sick feeling churned in her belly as she twisted to free her arm.

"You're late, Bella!" Jesse Harwood stood beside her, his cloudy gray eyes filled with recrimination.

She expelled a ragged breath. "Only a few minutes. I couldn't manage to get away from Sister Mercy. She asked me to assist her with one of the children."

Jesse's look softened and he released her arm. "I'm sorry. I was beginning to fear you weren't coming. I think I've worked out a plan for us."

Wisps of straight blond hair had escaped from under her palm-leaf bonnet. She automatically reached to tuck them out of view before giving Jesse a tentative smile. "I'm listening, but we must hurry before I'm missed."

"We'll leave tomorrow night, after the others have gone to sleep. We can meet right here and make our way toward Concord under cover of darkness. If we can't find your relatives in Concord, we'll continue on to Lowell. Pack only as much as you'll be able to comfortably carry, and I'll do the same. Be sure to bring some food."

"What if I awaken one of the Sisters as I'm preparing to leave?"

Jesse's eyes flashed with concern for a moment. "Say you're ill and can't sleep—that you don't want to bother the rest of the Sisters and you're going to make some tea and sit up for a while."

Bella shook her head back and forth. "But that would be a lie, Jesse. I can't lie to one of the Sisters."

Jesse gave a quiet chuckle. "We lie to the Sisters and Brothers every day when we fail to tell them of our love for each other."

Her brow furrowed at his reply. "Jesse, I'm not sure what I feel is the kind of love that need be confessed to the Society. If we merely love each other as brother and sister, we've done nothing wrong."

Jesse took her hand and looked deep into her eyes. "The love I feel for you is one that requires confession, Bella. And I hope the love you feel for me is much different from what you feel for Brother Ernest or Brother Justice—or any of the other brothers, for that matter."

"You know I care for you more than the other brothers, Jesse. But we have little knowledge upon which to base the love between man and woman. I feel no guilt in not confessing our friendship, but I would feel guilt if I openly lied to one of the Sisters."

Smiling, Jesse continued to hold her hand. "You'll soon realize that what you feel for me is love—the love that binds husband and wife together for a lifetime. If you're concerned about lying to the Sisters, I suppose we'd best pray that they remain sound asleep." He looked out into the quiet. "We should return soon or someone will miss us. You go first, and I'll follow in just a bit. Until tomorrow night," he said, pulling her hand to his lips and placing a kiss upon her palm.

Bella's face grew warm at Jesse's boldness. She quickly withdrew her hand and rushed back down the path. Slowing as she reached the children's dormitory, Bella removed her cape and attempted to casually walk toward the east door, which led to the side that was occupied by the young girls. Opening the door as quietly as possible, Bella made her way into the large room where the children were napping.

Daughtie Winfield glanced toward Bella as she slipped into the room. "Was I missed?" Bella inquired as she brushed a stray wisp of blond hair under her cap.

"No, but I was fearful for a short time. Sister Minerva walked with me until we reached the entrance of the dormitory. Fortunately Eldress Phoebe summoned her away before she had opportunity to inquire of your whereabouts. Did you meet Jesse?"

Bella nodded as she lifted one of the toddlers to her lap. "We're leaving tomorrow night, so this will be our last opportunity to visit, Daughtie. I transfer to the kitchen tomorrow. I'm sorry we'll not be together on my final day, but if we must be apart, I'm pleased I'll have some time with Sister Mercy before my departure."

Daughtie began to wring her hands, a nervous habit that brought constant remonstration from the older Sisters. "Are you sure you won't reconsider, Bella? Do you understand that you are leaving the safety of the Family? Won't you miss your Shaker Brothers and Sisters?"

"I'll miss you, Daughtie—and Sister Mercy and the children, of course."

"And your father?" Daughtie ventured.

"My father? You forget, Daughtie. Among the Shakers, I have no earthly father. Besides, Brother Franklin wishes his life to be separated from mine. How can I miss something I haven't had since my father—excuse me, Brother Franklin—convinced my mother four years ago to join the United Society of Believers in Christ's Second Appearing?"

"He cares for you, Bella. It's the rules of the Society that forbid him to show his affections," Daughtie insisted.

Bella stared out the window. The naked trees surrounding the house were forming small buds, awaiting the touch of a springtime sun before finally bursting into fragrant blooms. Like the trees, Bella waited. She, too, needed warmth before she could fully blossom, the warmth of knowing she was loved by another. The child on her lap snuggled closer. Bella turned and looked at Daughtie. "If my father cares for me, why did he push me away when I went to him seeking comfort after my mother's death? What kind of father does such a thing to his child? I don't believe the Shakers have correctly interpreted God's plan for our lives, and I can't remain among people that force parents to separate and withhold love from their own children."

"But your parents knew the rules when they signed the covenant—and so did you, Bella," Daughtie added hesitantly.

"I signed because I knew not doing so would cause a further breach between my father and me. Besides, Daughtie, what was I to do? What choices did I have at such a young age? But now I do have a choice, and I choose the world over the Shakers. You can come with us, Daughtie. I know that Jesse wouldn't mind, and you have no reason to stay here." Bella lifted the sleeping child and placed her in bed. She turned toward her friend with a surge of excitement. Why hadn't she thought of inviting Daughtie before this moment? "Say that you'll come, Daughtie," Bella pleaded.

Daughtie's mouth went slack as she gazed at Bella, who had now returned to the rocking chair. "You're running off to marry Jesse. Where do I fit into that arrangement?"

"I'm not running off to marry Jesse. I'm not even sure what love for a man is supposed to feel like. I'm leaving this place with Jesse because he knows the way to Concord and Lowell. It will be safer traveling with Jesse, and he's determined to leave the

Society. I've not pledged my love or my hand to Jesse. The world has so much to offer, Daughtie. I know you've been here among the Believers since you were a tiny child, but there's more to life than this protected existence. Don't you ever long to know more about the lives of the people who come here on Sundays to observe our worship service? Don't you want to see what lies beyond this acreage?"

Daughtie was thoughtful for several minutes, obviously weighing her friend's words. "I can't say that I haven't felt a tinge of envy since you first told me that you were planning to leave."

Bella clapped her hands together and leaned forward in her chair, hoping to draw her friend into their scheme. "There's no need to be frightened. You know the Believers will welcome you back if you decide against the world."

Daughtie nodded. "Yes, but I'd certainly never be considered faithful enough to become an Eldress if I left and then later returned."

"Is becoming an Eldress what you aspire to, Daughtie? For if that is your heart's desire, I'll say no more. But if you're merely using the hope of achieving religious rank as an excuse because you fear any change in your life, then I'd say, 'Be brave, dear friend.' The three of us will learn how to survive in this new life. There's much I remember from my early years living in the world. And Jesse knows much more about the outside world than I do. With his weekly visits into town to sell and barter goods with Brother Justice, he knows how to talk and act among the world's people. He assures me we'll be able to work and support ourselves. Will you at least consider going? You have until tomorrow night."

Daughtie gave Bella a timid smile but said nothing.

"Why don't we both agree to pray about the decision to leave and see what happens tomorrow night? Would you agree to do that, Daughtie?"

Her friend gave Bella an enthusiastic nod. "Yes, Bella. And if I believe that God is leading me to leave, I'll accompany you and Jesse."

Slumber came in short spurts throughout the night, and when the first bell rang at four-thirty the next morning, Bella was already awake. She sat up and swung her legs around until her feet touched the pine floorboards. After waiting for Sister Mercy to finish, she padded across the floor and took her turn at the washstand. The familiar waking sounds of muffled voices and quiet footsteps could be heard next door and across the hall as members of the Society prepared for the day. Bella dried her face and hands, then exchanged her loose cotton nightwear for a plain blue cotton and worsted gown. She fastened the dress and then with long, even strokes, brushed her long ash-blond hair before deftly twisting it into a knot and tucking it under her white starched cap. After carefully fastening a kerchief across the bodice of her dress, Bella pulled back the bedcovers, neatly folded them over the foot of her bed, and went about her other chores until her sheets were properly aired.

"You appear tired this morning," Sister Mercy commented as she patted Bella's shoulder. "Didn't you sleep well?"

Bella gave the older woman a smile. "I'm fine, Sister Mercy. And I'm looking forward to helping you with the pies later today."

"And I'm looking forward to your company, also," Sister Mercy replied while pouring additional oil into one of the lamps. "We're low on oil. Would you kindly remind me to ask the Deaconesses for more?"

Bella nodded her agreement as she quickly ran a cloth over the windowsills and built-in drawers. The second bell rang, and the Brothers could be heard leaving their rooms and walking down the steps as they headed off toward the barn. Without a word, Bella, Daughtie, and two other Sisters moved across the hall to clean the rooms of the Brethren before returning to complete their mending.

Absently retrieving a sock from the willow basket by her chair, Bella pushed her needle in and out, darning over the spot until the hole finally disappeared. She glanced over at Daughtie and wondered if her friend had made a decision. This would be the last morning Bella would sit in these familiar surroundings mending socks and stitching initials onto clothing—of that, she was certain.

The breakfast bell sounded, breaking Bella's reverie and the early morning silence. She moved along with the rest of the Sisters as they joined the Brethren in the hallway and made their way down the separate stairways. The two groups converged in the rectangular dining hall that was now filled with long trestle tables laden with heaping platters of sausage, biscuits, and eggs, and gravy boats filled to the brim. They filled their plates and ate in silence, then rose to leave.

"Any decision yet?" Bella questioned in a hushed tone.

Daughtie shook her head. "I'm still praying, but I do need to talk to you."

Bella smiled broadly and gave her friend's hand a quick squeeze. "I'll see if Sister Mercy will permit me to come to the children's dormitory after we've set the pies to bake. Be thinking about what you want to take with you."

Daughtie pulled Bella closer. "I haven't yet agreed that I'm going."

"I know, but it's best to be prepared in case you do decide to come along. I must hurry to the kitchen. Sister Mercy is expecting me. Keep praying, Daughtie, and I'll see you later this morning."

Bella rushed down the path between the laundry and syrup shop, skidding to a halt as she entered the kitchen.

Sister Mercy gave her an apple-cheeked smile. "You best not let Eldress Phoebe see you running about with your cap askew."

Bella grinned as she adjusted her cap, then grabbed a knife and began paring apples while Sister Mercy mixed enough dough for thirty pies. "I have a favor to beg of you, Sister Mercy," Bella said.

The rotund sister chuckled while setting her rolling pin to the stiff pie dough. "And what good deed might you need of me?"

Bella continued peeling. "I need a few minutes to talk with

Daughtie. Could I take a few minutes later this morning to visit her at the children's dormitory?"

Sister Mercy wiped her flour-covered hands on the large white apron that protected her woolen dress. "I think I can accommodate that request," she replied with a smile. "You can go see her before the dinner bell rings."

"Thank you," she said to the Sister as she whispered more words of thanks upward.

The pile of apples in the barrel seemed unending. Bella continued to work in silence, attempting to pray as her knife skimmed across the apples, peeling away the red and gold covering to reveal the white fleshy fruit. Each of her supplications was quickly interrupted by thoughts of her father and Jesse, which were occasionally interspersed with a warm recollection of her mother. Jesse seemed so sure of himself and their plan to leave. She didn't doubt the decision to leave; however, she did doubt that she would have the feelings of love for Jesse that he so desired. With love comes trust, and trusting was a dangerous thing. Her mother had blindly trusted her father, and he had ended their marriage by joining the Society against her mother's wishes. Bella was certain her mother had died of a broken heart. And she didn't plan to follow in her mother's footsteps.

"You can go visit Daughtie," Sister Mercy said, releasing Bella from the kitchen. "Be sure you're back here in fifteen minutes, or you'll be late to dinner and I'll have Eldress Phoebe looking to me for answers regarding your whereabouts," she cautioned.

"I'll be on time," Bella promised as she hurried out the door. With her heart pounding, she breathlessly hurried down the path and entered the dormitory. "I have only a few minutes, Daughtie. What do you need to talk about?"

Without waiting for an answer, Bella plopped down in a rocking chair and beckoned one of the children closer. Mary Beth, a chubby two-year-old, waddled across the room and buried her face deep in Bella's skirt. Bella reached down and lifted the plump toddler onto her lap. Giving Mary Beth's cheek a fleeting kiss, Bella quickly turned her attention to the little girl's neck, nuzzling until Mary Beth laughed in delight. The high-pitched laughter brought several other children running, each one obviously eager to become a part of the frivolity. Bella held Mary Beth close to her chest as she leaned down to tickle the fair-haired Genevieve and dark-eyed Martha. "I shall dearly miss these children," Bella lamented. "Save Sister Mercy, most of the Sisters expect them to act like miniature adults. I pray once we are gone they will appoint several young replacements to take our positions with the children. They don't need any more dour faces peering down upon them."

"Who would they appoint? You know there are only a few other girls our age, Bella, and they already take their turns with the children. With the rotation of work among the Sisters, our leaving assures the children additional hours with pinched-faced sisters who would much rather spend their time mending and weaving than chasing after these children. Perhaps we should remain—for the children's sake," Daughtie ventured.

Bella lightly rested her chin atop Mary Beth's head, the child's downy soft hair tickling Bella's face. "You know how much I love the children, Daughtie. And I already know that once I'm gone I shall long to cuddle them in my arms. However, should I remain in this place, I would evolve into one of those pinched-faced sisters we've been speaking of. More importantly, it would be dishonest for me to indoctrinate these children with beliefs I do not embrace and accept as true."

Daughtie's lips curved into a tiny smile. "I know, but if I can convince you to stay, I won't be forced to make a decision. I suppose I'm merely attempting to make life easier on myself."

Bella shifted Mary Beth's weight on her lap. Daughtie's comment brought Bella's thoughts back to her earlier question. "I didn't give you a chance to answer me when I first arrived. What is it you need to discuss with me?"

Daughtie hesitated momentarily. "I was thinking, Bella. Why don't we just tell the Family that we've chosen to leave the Society? It makes more sense—we'd be given funds to cover our journey, and one of the Brothers would take us to board a coach. We could pack our belongings and leave in an honorable fashion rather than sneaking off like thieves in the—"

"I can't do that," Bella interrupted. "I know what you say is true, but the Ministry would bring Brother Franklin to talk to me. If they knew I was planning to leave, they'd suddenly believe it permissible to use my birth father to try to dissuade me. I will not argue my decision with him. Besides, if they knew Jesse was going, they'd accuse us of wrongdoing. And, Daughtie, I pledge to you that there has been nothing inappropriate between us. Besides, the Ministry would not believe us—they'd shame us and encourage us to confess and repent before the Believers. I'll not take their money, and I'll not confess or repent to something I've not done. Please, Daughtie, don't base your decision upon my willingness to seek approval from the Ministry."

Daughtie seated herself on one of the straight-backed wooden chairs and stared at her friend. "I understand, but you must admit it makes more sense to leave with money."

"You're right. It would be easier to have their help, but I'm unwilling to pay the price they'd demand for a few coins and a ride to the stagecoach. It's almost dinnertime, and I promised Sister Mercy I wouldn't be late. We can talk more on the way to meeting tonight," Bella promised as she leaned down and gave her friend a quick hug. She ought not take the time, but she knew she might never see these children again. Kneeling down, she held her arms wide and pulled each child into a warm embrace before leaving the room.

A tear trickled down her cheek as Bella glanced toward the Sisters' Weaving Shop. She exited the dormitory and hurried back toward the Dwelling House. Rounding a turn in the path, she looked up toward the bell, hoping it wouldn't sound until she had safely returned to the kitchen. If detected, it was certain one of the Sisters would question why she was outdoors rather than baking pies. Worse yet, she didn't want to cause a problem for Sister Mercy, whose judgment in permitting such a visit between the young Sisters would be closely scrutinized by the Ministry.

"Just in time!" Sister Mercy exclaimed as the bell began to toll.

Bella met the older Sister's smiling gaze, a keen sense of melancholy suddenly assaulting her senses. The time when she would flee Canterbury was quickly approaching. The thought of never again seeing Sister Mercy, coupled with her good-byes to the tiny children she had helped care for over the past several years, was more distressing than she had imagined.

"Something is bothering you, child. I can always tell when you're troubled. You know you can talk to me, don't you? I love you like you're my own. Many's the time Eldress Phoebe has accused me of caring too much about you."

Bella struggled to hold back her tears. "And what did you tell Eldress Phoebe when she made her accusations?"

"Same thing I'd tell her right here and now if she were to ask me again: It's impossible to love or care too much for a child. We all need as much love as we can get," Sister Mercy proclaimed, her cheeks dimpling as she gave a wide smile.

"That's certainly true. You're a wise woman, Sister Mercy. Had it not been for your love, prayers, and consolation, I don't know how I would have survived those terrible weeks after my mother died. You know you'll always be very special to me, don't you?" Bella asked, unable to hold her tears in check.

Sister Mercy pulled Bella into a warm embrace and lovingly patted her back as if she were a small child. "There, there," she comforted. "Tell me what's caused you such misery. If you'll only let me, surely I can help."

Knowing she must deceive dear Sister Mercy caused Bella further sorrow, yet she could not confide in the woman. Bella knew Sister Mercy would never break a confidence. It was for that very reason Bella would not take the older woman into her confidence. The Elders would surely question Sister Mercy once they discovered Bella's disappearance. The older woman's allegiance to Bella would become grounds for chastisement by the Elders, and poor Sister Mercy's loyalty to a wayward Sister would certainly become the subject of a sermon. Bella could not abide being the cause of such embarrassment for the woman she loved so dearly.

"It's nothing, Sister Mercy. Merely a bout of melancholy," Bella finally replied.

Sister Mercy hesitated a moment. "If you're certain there's nothing I can do, then we'd best hurry along. If we're late, Eldress Phoebe will expect a confession for our tardiness. But just remember, Bella, I'm always here should you need me, and you are always in my prayers."

Bella swallowed the lump that had risen in her throat and nodded. "Yes, I'll remember. I could never forget anything about you, Sister Mercy."

The older woman gave her a strange look, almost as though she realized something was amiss, but before Sister Mercy could question her further, Bella gave the older woman a bright smile and said, "We've made it just in time. Eldress Phoebe will have nothing to complain of this noonday."

CHAPTER 2

"Shh!" Bella's warning hissed through the night air as she turned to face Daughtie. There was a slight chill to the moonlit evening, and Bella pulled her cloak more tightly around her shoulders before readjusting her satchel. She waved her friend onward toward the stand of pines—toward Jesse and their new life among the outsiders.

"Can we talk now?" Daughtie whispered. "I don't think anyone can hear us this far from the Dwelling House."

Bella glanced around the area. "Jesse!" she called. "Are you here?"

They waited in silence. "I don't think he's here," Daughtie offered. "What time was he supposed to meet us?"

"We didn't set a specific time. There was no way to guarantee when the others would be asleep. Apparently the Brothers don't go to sleep as early as the Sisters," Bella replied. "He'll be here soon."

Slowly, minute by minute, the night wore on. "I don't think he's coming, Bella. Let's go back. If we're careful, we can return to the Dwelling House and be back in bed before anyone misses us."

"No! I'm not going back. If Jesse doesn't arrive shortly, we'll go on without him."

A look of fear crossed Daughtie's face. "We can't go without Jesse to lead us. What are you thinking, Bella?"

"It seems I'm always surrounded by men who convince me to trust them and then disappoint me—first my father and now Jesse. But that doesn't change my decision to leave. We merely need to follow the road south until we reach Concord. I copied my aunt's address from my father's journal. I don't know if she still lives in Concord, but we can at least attempt to locate her. I'm sure she'd give us shelter." She reached out and grasped Daughtie's hand. "I want you to go with me, but if you must return, I'll not hold it against you, dear friend. I know you're frightened."

"No. I'll not leave you here to go on alone, Bella, but I believe that returning to the Family is the prudent thing to do. We could return and find out what's happened to Jesse. There's nothing to prevent us from leaving tomorrow or next week, is there?" Daughtie asked, her question filled with the same hope that sparkled from her eyes in the moonlit night.

The hood of Bella's cape fell back as she vigorously shook her head back and forth. "We're ready now. Either Jesse has decided he's not going or he's already left for Concord, thinking we weren't coming. Perhaps he expected us earlier than we arrived and, like us, decided it was best to go on alone."

Daughtie was silent for a moment. "If you're sure we can find Concord, I suppose we'd best be on our way. The longer we wait, the greater the possibility of being discovered."

Bella nodded and took the lead, hoping she could remember all that Jesse had told her regarding the route they would follow. "As soon as we find the road to Concord, we'll rest for the night. Jesse mentioned highwaymen can sometimes be lurking about, waiting for unsuspecting travelers," she advised.

She carefully chose each turn of the path until they finally reached the main road that would lead them to Concord. "I'm certain this is the road we'll need to follow come morning," she told Daughtie. Pointing toward a stand of pines, she smiled broadly and grabbed Daughtie's hand. "There's a place over there where we'll be out of sight and sheltered for the remainder of the night."

———

The heat of the sun as it rose into the eastern sky began to warm their bodies as the girls arose the next morning. Nestled among the small clump of trees, Bella discovered a fallen log and pulled it in front of two maples. "There! I've formed two chairs for us, Daughtie. We can sit on the log and lean against the trees and rest our backs," she said, offering the loaf of rye bread and a wedge of yellow cheese to her friend.

Daughtie tore a piece of bread from the loaf. "Nothing ever tasted so good. I'm famished."

Bella nodded as she stuffed a piece of bread into her mouth. "If we keep a steady pace, I think we can reach Concord in three or four hours and then get directions to Lowell."

"Lowell? I thought we were going to stay with your relatives in Concord."

Bella nodded her head in rhythm with her chewing and then swallowed hard. "I've been thinking about that. I doubt we'll find them. Jesse and I had planned to go on to Lowell if we didn't locate my aunt and uncle."

Daughtie's eyebrows raised in obvious concern. "I certainly think we should try to find them, Bella. Isn't it a long way to Lowell? Do you know anyone there who can help us?"

Bella gave her friend a smile that she hoped was reassuring. "No, I don't know anyone in Lowell, but it's not so far that we can't make it with proper directions."

"Then why not stay in Concord? At least for a short time?"

Bella quickly packed the leftover bread and cheese into her satchel and stood up. "Do you remember the Family discussing the new textile mills in Lowell? There's work for girls our age. You may recall Mary Wiseman that wintered with us at the Village last year."

Daughtie's brows furrowed. "I vaguely remember her, but we never talked. Wasn't she the girl who got in trouble for talking during meals on several occasions?"

Bella nodded in agreement. "Yes, that's Mary. She never did learn to remain silent at the proper times. Anyway, she told me they pay good wages in the mills. We'll be able to support ourselves, but in Concord we'd be fortunate if we found employment as housekeepers or teachers. Lowell is our best choice, Daughtie."

"Unless we find your relatives," Daughtie added.

Leaving their makeshift dining room, the girls walked back toward the road. "Even if we find them, we'll have to find work, and I doubt we'll find anything in Concord that will pay the wages Mary received in Lowell."

"If life was so good in Lowell, why did Mary find it necessary to live off the Shakers all winter? She should have had ample money to support herself if she was receiving those fine wages you speak of."

Bella nodded at her friend. "Yes, one would think so, but Mary spent her money on every new fashion and whimsy her heart desired. She spent her money as quickly as she made it. Then, when she was least prepared for losing her employment, she became ill. With no money and unable to work, she made her way to the Family. The Ministry realized she was a bread-and-butter Shaker and would remain only until she was once again able to make her way in the world. Mary never did indicate any desire to become a Believer."

"I just think it might be safer to at least try and find your aunt."

Bella could hear the worry in Daughtie's tone. "If it makes you feel better, we'll do exactly that. It couldn't hurt to rest up and have a good meal."

The sound of approaching horses could be heard in the distance. Bella grabbed Daughtie's hand, pulling her behind a stand of forsythia bushes. "Keep down!" Bella warned.

Daughtie crouched beside Bella until the last rider had passed. "Why are we hiding?" she asked as they stood.

"The Brethren may be looking for us," Bella replied, surprised by her friend's question.

"They won't come after us—you left a letter for your father saying you were leaving. And you know the Believers have no respect for those who run off in the night. They've probably bid us a 'fare thee well and good riddance.' "

"I suppose you're right, but I'd rather err on the side of caution. Besides, you never know what kind of highway bandit or scoundrel might be on the road."

Daughtie giggled. "Well, a bandit would be sorely disappointed if he sought to enrich himself with our meager belongings."

Bella joined in her laughter, trudging onward, the dust clinging to their cloaks and shoes. Three and a half hours later they rounded a bend in the road. "Look, Daughtie! We've finally reached Concord," Bella exclaimed, pointing to the south.

"And none too soon. My shoes are pinching. I'm sure I'll have blisters come morning."

The girls moved with renewed vigor, the thought of a warm meal and soft bed beckoning them onward.

Bella pulled the folded scrap of paper containing her aunt's address from the inner pocket of her cloak. "We'll stop and ask someone directions."

A kind middle-aged woman directed them to the corner of Franklin and Ridge Streets, telling the girls to remain on Franklin until they reached the fourth house from the corner.

"There it is," Bella announced. "Let's see if my aunt and uncle are living here," she said, walking up the wooden steps to the small front porch. Bella knocked on the weatherworn door.

A large woman with a strange accent opened the door. "They live up there," she said while pointing to the stairs. "Room three. Go on," she encouraged, waving her hand toward the stairway.

Bella led the way up the dark stairway. The odor of strange-smelling foods, mixed with the stench of unwashed bodies, caused Bella to immediately long for a breath of fresh air. Instead, she held a kerchief to her nose as she knocked on the door of room three.

The gaunt stoop-shouldered woman who came to the door

appeared much older than her years. "Ida Landon?" Bella questioned, not sure that the woman standing before her was truly her mother's sister.

The woman nodded.

"It's me, Bella, your sister Polly's daughter."

A look of recognition crossed the woman's face as she opened her arms and pulled Bella into an embrace. "You're all grown up," she said, placing a kiss on Bella's cheek. "Let me take a look at you." She moved an arm's length backward and smiled, nodding her approval. "From the look of those clothes, I'd say your parents are still among the Shakers."

Bella nodded and said, "This is my friend Daughtie."

"Hello, Daughtie. Goodness, where are my manners? You girls come in and let me take your cloaks."

The room was small and sparsely appointed yet somehow appeared cluttered. The walls were sorely in need of whitewash, and the wood floors lacked care. A tiny potted plant sat drooping on the windowsill, a testament of those who lived within. Bella scanned the room, seeking a place for Daughtie and her to sit down. Ida appeared to follow her gaze and hastened to remove drying clothes from the two straight-backed wooden chairs.

"Sit here," she offered, gathering the laundry into a bundle and placing it on a narrow cot. "I'd make some tea, but I'm fresh out," she apologized.

Bella reached into her satchel and withdrew a small cloth bag. "We can use this, Aunt Ida," she offered. "I brought tea with me for just such an occasion as this."

A tentative smile appeared on Ida's lips. "Thank you, dear. You're as sweet as your mother. I want to hear all about her. How is she faring among the Shakers? I never thought she'd stay there. Polly was the one who always wanted a family with lots of children. Guess folks change, though," she remarked, setting a pot to boil in the tiny corner that served as a kitchen. Seating herself on the cot, she leaned back against the bundle of laundry and rubbed her hands together. "Now! Tell me everything."

Bella hesitated a moment. "I'm not sure how to tell you this. I don't suppose there's any way to soften what I have to say, Aunt

Ida, but Mother died of consumption not long after we arrived at Canterbury. I was certain that Father had written."

Ida was silent for several moments. "He may have written, but we left this place for nearly two years. Arthur was sure he could do better in the South. He had a strong inclination to live where it was warm. Unfortunately, we didn't make it any farther than Pennsylvania. He decided if he was going to be poor and cold, he had a greater fondness for New Hampshire than Pennsylvania. We returned the following year and made our way back to this same place. Just our luck that it was still unrented."

Bella looked around, unconvinced that landing back here was a stroke of luck.

"Times have been hard, but Arthur says it's only a matter of time before he finds a better paying job." Her voice was filled with a sorrow that belied the upward curve of her lips.

"I'm sure things will take a turn for the better," Bella encouraged.

Ida jumped up from the cot and took the few steps to her makeshift kitchen. "Just listen to me! Here you've made a long journey with sad news and I'm heaping my problems upon you the minute you walk in the door. Let me pour you girls some tea."

"We'll be leaving as soon as we finish our tea, Aunt Ida," Bella said as she took the chipped cup her aunt offered. "We've a long ways to go."

"And where are you off to?"

"Daughtie and I have decided we'll go to Lowell. We plan to seek employment in the mills," Bella replied, giving her friend a sidelong glance.

"I've heard tell there's good wages being paid down there. But you girls had best spend the night with me. Arthur's gone to Boston on a delivery with his employer. We can make do, just the three of us."

"That certainly makes more sense than sleeping along the roadside," Daughtie whispered as Ida returned to pour herself a cup of tea.

"I suppose we could stay, Aunt Ida," Bella said. "If you're

sure it won't be an inconvenience," she quickly added.

Ida beamed. "It will be fun. Just the three of us—we can visit, and you can tell me all about life in the settlement. I'm surprised Franklin gave you permission to leave the Shakers. It's out of character for him to be so agreeable."

"I didn't seek his permission. Daughtie and I ran away."

"Oh my!" Ida placed a hand on each cheek and stared wide-eyed at the two girls.

CHAPTER 3

An early spring storm refused to let up, and Bella and Daughtie soon found their shoes weighed down with the muck and mire of the roadway and their woolen cloaks heavy with rainwater. Bella grabbed Daughtie's hand and pulled, hoping they could avoid the splattering mud from a passing coach. But her feet wouldn't take hold in the slippery mud, and they both were showered with flying sludge before the coach finally came to a halt a short distance down the road.

"Would you want a ride? I've space available," the driver called down from his perch.

"Yes!" Daughtie shouted.

Bella stepped in front of her friend. "We've no money to pay."

"I wasn't expecting any—ride or walk, it's up to you."

There was no stopping Daughtie. She had opened the carriage door and climbed inside before Bella could reply. "It appears we'll take your offer."

"Good enough. Get in. I need to keep moving."

Bella seated herself beside Daughtie and pushed back the hood of her cloak. "Hello," she said to the other passengers.

Two girls who appeared to be near her age stared back. "Hello," one of them ventured.

The greeting was tentative, and Bella was careful to keep her muddy shoes and wet clothing away from the clean, dry passengers. "I'm Arabella Newberry—everyone calls me Bella. This is my friend Daughtie Winfield. We were caught in the storm."

"That much is obvious," one of the girls said.

"No need to be rude, Sally. I'm Ruth Wilson and this is Sally Nelson. We're going to Lowell—to work in the mills," she added. "I'm from Maine. My family has a small farm where we raise sheep, and Sally's home is in Vermont. Where are you and Daughtie going?"

"From their appearance, they've lost their way. You're Shakers, aren't you?" Sally questioned with a tone of condemnation.

"We've left the Society. We're going to Lowell, also," Bella replied with as much decorum as her drenched appearance would permit.

"Do you suppose the driver will permit us to ride all the way to Lowell?" Daughtie asked, obviously pleased to be out of the rain.

"I wouldn't know why not. So long as you sign a paper saying you're seeking work in the mills, he'll provide you a seat in the coach and pay for your room and board when we stop for the night."

"Really?" both girls cried in unison. Bella couldn't believe their good fortune. She hesitated for a moment. "But why would he do such a thing?"

Sally gave her a look of disdain. "It's his job. He travels throughout all of New England seeking farm girls who are willing to sign on for work at the mills. The Corporation pays the cost of transporting us to Lowell."

"I see," Bella replied. This sudden blessing seemed like affirmation from God that she'd done the right thing.

Sally looked down and made a purposeful show of pulling her feet away from Bella's shoes. "Let's hope it's soon. I'd like to arrive in Lowell without mud on my shoes."

When they stopped at the inn later that afternoon, both

Daughtie and Bella were chilled, and the breeze did little to warm them as they descended the coach. At least it had ceased raining.

"You two willing to sign on to work in Lowell?" the driver called out as he handed Ruth her bandbox and Sally her leather satchel.

Bella and Daughtie nodded.

"Good! Only need to locate three or four more girls and we can return to Lowell. Grab your belongings, and I'll arrange for a room with the innkeeper."

"That means four of us will be sharing a room instead of two," Sally muttered.

"Don't mind her. She didn't want to leave home, but her folks forced her to come along. That pride is all a show. Her parents stand to lose their farm if she doesn't go to work and send her earnings home," Ruth confided.

"And what of you? Why are you going to Lowell?" Daughtie inquired.

Ruth smiled. "I'm going to send most of my money home for my brother's education. He wants to attend college."

"But what of your education, Ruth? Once your brother has finished college and found a position, will he then pay for your schooling?" Bella inquired.

Ruth giggled. "Why on earth would he do such a thing?" she asked as she grabbed her bandbox and entered the inn. It was obvious she didn't expect an answer.

Bella hastened to reach Ruth's side. "Because you're worthy of an education, also. Men and women are of equal value."

Both Sally and Ruth stared at Bella as though she'd gone mad. Sally wagged her head back and forth, then said, "I don't know where you ever got such a notion, but you'd best readjust your thinking if you plan to live in the real world. Short of finishing school, there's really very little available for women. And if you're of a lower class, there's no need to even consider finishing school." Her words were spoken with a harsh tone that suggested Sally had a bit of history with this topic. "Come on, follow me." Several coarse-looking men leered in their direction as the girls wended their way through the inn and up a narrow stairway to one of the rooms above the dining area.

The room was small, dirty, and they suspected even lice-infested, but the girls were weary. Daughtie and Bella quickly removed their clothing and began spreading the garments out to dry.

"As soon as you've changed, come downstairs and we'll have supper. Once we have something warm in our stomach, we'll be so sleepy that we won't notice how awful the room is," Ruth said.

Although the food wasn't flavorful or appetizing, it was hot. By the time they made their way back upstairs, all four girls were longing for sleep. The men in the dining room below, however, were still drinking their ale, with their drunken voices growing louder as they continued to imbibe.

"I miss the quiet of home," Daughtie said. "I fear we've made a mistake, Bella."

Ruth patted Daughtie's shoulder. "Don't make a decision just yet. Lowell is a wonderful place to live. The boardinghouses are clean and the food is good. You'll soon find that working in the mills provides girls with a good opportunity to be independent."

"So you've lived in Lowell?" Bella inquired.

Ruth nodded. "Yes. I worked there for three months last year but had to return home to care for my ailing mother and help out at home. My prayers were answered and she's better now, so I'm off to the mills again and hoping I'll not have difficulty being rehired."

"Why would you have difficulty being hired? The coachman said they needed workers, didn't he?" Bella questioned.

"They do need workers, but each girl is required to sign a contract before commencing work. Among other things, the contract says you agree to stay one year in your position. If you don't give proper notice and gain approval before leaving, they place a mark beside your name and then share that information with the other agents so that none of them will hire you. You're blackballed as a bad employee," Ruth explained.

Daughtie shook her head back and forth. "No wonder you're fearful."

"It's not as bad as it sounds. Most of the time the agents are so much in need of girls that they don't care if you've left without approval. They're pleased to have an experienced worker return. I witnessed them taking back several of the girls who had left without warning, so I'm hopeful for my situation. At least my supervisor knew the condition of my departure. He knew it wasn't for some nonsensical matter. Besides, the coachman said they've opened another mill since my departure, so I'm fairly certain we'll all find employment."

"Tell us about the boardinghouses," Daughtie entreated. "I hope it's not a room such as this that we'll be living in."

Ruth smiled. "You'll be crowded. Two or three girls to a bed and not much storage room, that's for certain. But you'll not spend much time in your bedroom, anyway. We're awakened early and off to work by five o'clock in the morning. We return to the boardinghouse two hours later for a half-hour breakfast, then back to work until noon when we have three quarters of an hour for dinner. Supper is waiting when we return home at seven o'clock in the evening, and we have free time until ten o'clock. That's curfew, and if you're not back in the boardinghouse by then, the keeper will lock you out. The rules are all set out in your contract, so you'll know what's expected before you agree to work for the Corporation."

Daughtie appeared overwhelmed by the concept. "Free time to do as you please every evening? You're not required to attend Union Meeting?"

"They don't have Union Meeting, Daughtie," Bella whispered.

Sally sniggered. "No, we don't have Union Meetings, but I'm told the contract requires church attendance. But from what I've heard about the Shakers, I doubt you'll find a place to attend that will suit your fancy."

Bella held her temper in check. "I don't know what you've heard about the Shakers or their worship, Sally, but I hope we'll be able to find believers among the world's people who are more open-minded than you appear to be."

Sally glared across the room at Bella. "The world's people? Is that what we are, the world's people? Well, you're one of us now, Bella, so you'll have to adjust to *our* life. And believe me, you'd best spend your first pay on some clothes! I'm told many of the mill girls dress as well as society ladies do. You'll be outcasts in those clothes. You can't begin to imagine how the world's people clothe themselves."

"We know how they dress, Sally. There were some of the world's people at our settlement every Sunday to watch us worship. Some of the most prominent people from all over the country—even Europe—have been there. The finery will come as no surprise."

Ruth moved closer to Bella. "Why did they come to watch you worship—if you don't mind my asking?"

"We dance during our worship. I assume they find it entertaining or amusing. Perhaps both. They come to satisfy their curiosity about a people they don't understand. Unfortunately, they leave with little more wisdom than they arrive with, but they go back into the world and tell others, who come to see for themselves."

Sally swung around on the bed. "Dance? I thought Shaker men and women were forbidden such familiarity. Then you and Daughtie should be well prepared for the dances in Lowell."

"Our dances are not the type of which you speak. They are a part of worship, and the men and women don't touch in the manner of the world's dances," Bella replied.

Voices of bellowing liquored men sounded loudly through the floorboards and were followed by what sounded like crashing furniture and then the frightening roar of a gun being discharged. The girls squealed and huddled together on the bed.

A knock sounded at their door. "You girls all right?" the coach driver called from the other side of the door.

"Yes, but what's happening down there?" Ruth timidly inquired.

"Just a bit of an argument between a couple of men. I think

things should quiet down now. You girls get to sleep. We've an early start in the morning."

"Yes, sir," Ruth replied.

Bella blew out the candle and burrowed under the covers. "Everything is going to be just fine, Daughtie," she whispered, hoping the words she spoke were true.

CHAPTER 4

After eight days of crisscrossing New Hampshire, Vermont, and Rhode Island, the horses lumbered up a small rise pulling the damsel-filled carriage as their heavy hooves churned the dusty roadway.

"There's Lowell," the driver called. He snapped the reins, urging the horses onward.

Bella sighed as she shifted her weight to her right hip. "Finally!"

Daughtie nodded her agreement. "I seem to remember the driver saying he was going to seek only two more girls."

Ruth wiggled in her seat. "I think he wanted us to be as uncomfortable as he was."

"If that was his intention, he certainly succeeded," Sally snarled. "But I think he's greedy. The more girls he delivers, the more money he makes."

Priscilla, the newest passenger to board the coach, scooted forward on the seat, her gaze riveted on Sally. "How do you know that?" she asked in an awe-filled voice.

Sally looked down her nose at the girl. "It's an obvious conclusion."

Bella watched as Priscilla shriveled back in her seat. "Don't be upset by Sally's manner," she whispered. "She treats all of us with the same disdain."

"Look, Bella," Daughtie said. "Those brick buildings must be the mills."

Sally leveled a look of contempt toward Daughtie. "You and Priscilla should become fast friends. You seem to be endowed with the same level of intelligence," she remarked as the coach came to a halt in front of the Appleton Mill.

The driver pulled open the door. "Here we are, ladies. I'll escort you inside. As soon as Mr. Gault assigns you to your boardinghouses, I'll deliver your baggage."

The girls dutifully followed behind as the driver pulled a rope hanging over the iron gate. A bell rang and a portly gentleman strode toward them. "Morning, Luther," he greeted.

"Mornin', Mr. Gault. Got a surprise for you. Eight girls when you was only expectin' four or five—all good workers."

"And how would you know?" Sally asked, directing her annoyance at the driver as they squeezed into Mr. Gault's small office.

Mr. Gault took a draw on his pipe. "And how are you able to make such an assertion, sir?" he asked the driver, exhaling a puff of smoke that circled and then floated upward.

The coach driver shuffled his feet and gave a sheepish grin. "Well, I guess I don't know for a fact that they're good workers, but they all signed the paper saying they wanted to come work for the Corporation," he replied, waving the documents in the air.

Mr. Gault nodded, took the paper work, placed it on his desk, and quickly surveyed the girls. "Any of you girls related or friends that want to live in the same boardinghouse?" he asked while looking at Bella and Daughtie.

"We'd like to be together," Bella replied, taking Daughtie's hand.

"I'd like to be with them, also," Ruth added quickly.

"Why?" Bella asked, surprised at the request.

Ruth shrugged her shoulders. "I enjoy your company, and I

don't know anyone else," she replied simply.

"You can deliver the luggage of these three girls to Adelaide Beecher's boardinghouse here on Jackson Street," Mr. Gault told the driver. "The other five girls will go to Hannah Desmond's boardinghouse. They'll be assigned to the Lowell Mill."

The driver began to leave, then hesitated as he neared where Bella stood. He motioned to Mr. Gault. "I was wondering if I could maybe get paid today," he stammered.

Bella attempted to pretend she couldn't hear the conversation, for the driver's embarrassment was obvious.

"Payday's the same for everybody, Luther, you know that. Last Friday of the month. You'll need to line up out in the mill yard with everybody else," Mr. Gault quietly replied. He drew closer to the driver and lowered his voice to a whisper. "If you'll come back later, I can personally advance you a few dollars."

Luther's cheeks flushed a rosy red. "Thank you, Mr. Gault. You're a kind man." Squaring his shoulders, the driver made his way to the door. "Your bags will be waiting at your boarding-houses, ladies. I wish you well." He tipped his hat and quickly departed.

"Ladies, I apologize for my inability to offer seating to each of you, but I will attempt to be brief. Each of you signed this document," he said, raising the documents the driver had given him into the air. "However, there is an actual contract that must be signed prior to commencing employment with the Corporation. Until a full-time agent is hired at the Lowell Mill, I'm hiring for both the Appleton and the Lowell. You girls assigned to the Lowell will, most likely, have no further contact with me. The three of you," he continued while looking at Bella, Daughtie, and Ruth, "will see me from time to time in the mill yard or here in the offices. You will certainly see me on payday," he said with a smile as he handed each girl one of the contracts.

"You can all read?"

"Yes," they replied in unison.

"Excellent! Please read the contract. If you agree to the terms, you will sign here." He pointed to the blank line at the bottom of the page.

There was something about this room that reminded Bella of the Trustees' Office at Canterbury, where the world's people signed their contracts to enter the Society. It wasn't the quietude or formality of the setting, for certainly this place was far from serene. And Mr. Gault's manner, although forthright, held none of the austerity of the Elders as they had questioned novitiates. Perhaps, she decided, it was the solemnity of contracting her life to others, which was a concept she found particularly disquieting.

The girls took but a few moments to peruse the paper work. Bella watched each one sit at Mr. Gault's desk and pen her name and was surprised when no questions were asked.

When her turn arrived, Bella seated herself, folded her hands, and looked up at Mr. Gault. "I have questions."

"Certainly," he replied, smiling down at her.

"How much will I be paid?"

"Three dollars and twenty-five cents per week. You receive your pay every Friday."

"Room and board?"

Mr. Gault smiled. "One dollar and twenty-five cents is your share. The balance is paid by the Corporation."

"And our hours of work?"

Mr. Gault carefully explained that the first and final bells tolled at differing times throughout the year, the workday beginning earlier in the summer and later in the winter.

Bella listened and then mentally tabulated what Mr. Gault had told her. "And so we work approximately seventy-three hours per week?"

The older man nodded, a look of admiration crossing his face. "I believe that would be correct. Any other questions?"

"I'm satisfied," Bella said before dipping the pen into ink and carefully signing her name.

"Should I sign?" Daughtie whispered to her friend before dutifully seating herself.

Bella nodded and handed the pen to Daughtie.

"Now that you've all signed your contracts, I have but a few comments before sending you off to your boardinghouses. I need to advise you of your choice to begin work in the morning or take the day to rest. If you decide you need a day to recover from your journey, you will owe room and board for the day. You are not paid for any day you do not work. However, you will not be charged for your room and board for the remainder of today."

"How very charitable," Sally retorted.

Mr. Gault glanced in her direction. "You have a quick tongue, Miss Nelson. You would do well to remember that it is best to think before you speak. I believe you'll find that piece of advice particularly helpful with your overseer in the mill."

Turning his attention back to the girls assigned to Hannah Desmond's boardinghouse, Mr. Gault offered instructions for locating the boardinghouse as well as where they should report the next morning. He escorted the five girls to the door and then returned to the remaining three.

"Any of you girls have previous experience in the mills?" he asked, seating himself behind the desk.

"No, sir," Bella and Daughtie replied.

Ruth hesitated a moment before replying. "I do."

"Thank you for your honesty, Miss Wilson. I saw your name in my book. It has a black mark beside it, so I am assuming you left before your contract was completed?"

"Yes," she replied, her voice barely a whisper.

"The circumstances were beyond her control. Her mother was ill, and she was forced to return home to help her family. Surely you're not going to hold that against her. I'm sure her overseer would vouch that she was a good worker. Weren't you, Ruth?" Bella questioned.

Mr. Gault grinned and leaned back in his chair. "I appreciate the argument on behalf of your friend, Miss Newberry. However, I'm sure that she can speak for herself. Miss Wilson?"

"What Bella said is true. My family needed me and I was required to leave. I worked at the Merrimack in the spinning room and was tending twenty-eight spindles when I was forced to return home. I truly want to work in the mills, and I don't

39

take my contract lightly. But my family is of great importance to me, also."

Mr. Gault looked down at the page, seeming to consider the black mark beside Ruth's name, then snapped the book shut. "Again, thank you for your honesty, Miss Wilson. You three girls will be working here at the Appleton operating the weaving looms. You may report directly to your overseer, Mr. Kingman, in the morning. For now, you may present yourselves to Miss Addie at number 5 Jackson Street, which is across the street and down the road a short distance. I'll escort you out and open the gate. I'm sure that Miss Wilson can find her way to number 5."

"Yes, of course," Ruth replied as the trio followed Mr. Gault out the door.

The girls patiently waited as Mr. Gault unlocked the gate and pulled back on the metal bars. "Good day, ladies. I wish you well as you begin your new positions."

The clanking of the iron gates could be heard in the distance as the trio walked across the street, with Bella and Daughtie attempting to gather in the details of their new surroundings.

The rows of sturdy brick boardinghouses lay before them, an occasional flower box sporting a few green sprouts, evidence that summer's blooms would soon arrive. A mobcapped boarding-house keeper was busy hanging clothes at one house while at another, the keeper was diligently sweeping her entryway. The scene unfolding before them gave the appearance of warmth and welcome whereas the gated fortress to their rear cast a shadow of detachment and apprehension.

"The mills remind me of prisons that Brother Jerome used to speak of," Daughtie commented, taking one last peek over her shoulder.

Ruth giggled. "Only because of the gate. They close it five minutes after last bell so that anyone who is late must pass through the counting room. The agent and overseers won't abide tardiness."

Bella looped her arm through Ruth's and gave her a warm smile. "The Society believed in punctuality, also. I was pleased that Mr. Gault rewarded your honesty and rehired you, Ruth."

A tinge of pink colored Ruth's cheeks as she nodded in agreement. "Unfortunately, I wavered for a moment, but I'm glad I gained enough courage to tell the truth. I was fearful Mr. Gault would send me home."

"Here we are—number 5," Bella said, pointing to the stenciled address.

A giant white apron covered a matronly woman's ample figure as she pulled open the front door and gave the girls a beaming smile. "I've been expecting you. Come in, come in! I am Miss Addie, the keeper of this house," she welcomed. "I bribed the coach driver with a piece of apple pie, and he carried your baggage upstairs. And believe me, until you've climbed those stairs, you won't appreciate his deed," she informed them with a giggle.

She led the trio into a large room and settled herself on the tapestry-covered settee. "Let's get acquainted," she offered, patting the cushion beside her. "I'll show you the rest of the house if there's time before the others arrive for dinner."

Bella liked the woman's unrestrained laughter and pleasant countenance. She had an easy way about her. Though Miss Addie's questions were sometimes prodding, they somehow seemed unobtrusive, for her manner was gentle, and when the conversation became gloomy, she would pepper the discussion with an amusing anecdote to lighten the mood. It was obvious she was attempting to set them at ease—so dissimilar to the welcome that had been extended to Bella's family when they first arrived at the Shaker community.

That meeting was one she would not soon forget. Inside the Trustees' Office they had been greeted with prying eyes and pursed lips, and by the end of their meeting, the Elders had leveled looks of displeasure and disgust. Bella wasn't sure exactly what had caused their displeasure during that interview. In fact, four years later, she still wasn't certain. Her parents had been honest in their declarations to the Family, had severed all ties to the world, had willingly surrendered their meager belongings, and against her mother's wishes, had relinquished their parental rights to Bella. Miss Addie's acceptance today was as welcome as a cool drink on a hot summer day.

"Would you prefer to see the rest of the house or have your tea first?" Miss Addie inquired.

The girls quickly agreed they would take the tour first and the tea later if time permitted.

The older woman chuckled. "I knew that's what you would choose," she said as she stood up and led them to the stairway. They ascended at Miss Addie's slow pace, finally reaching the top floor. "One step short of heaven, that's how I feel when I finally arrive in this room," Miss Addie said, the words bursting forth in short puffs as she made her way around the girls' baggage.

The three girls glanced around the room, Bella taking note of the personal belongings atop a small chest and clothing strewn about. "It would appear this room is already occupied, Miss Addie."

Addie carefully lowered herself onto one of the two beds and began rubbing her knees. "It's only partially occupied—at least until today. You girls will room with the other three girls already assigned to this room. Three in each bed. You share the chests and what other bit of space you can find available."

"I told you the room would be crowded," Ruth said. "But we won't spend much time up here."

"It looks like someone needs to spend some time up here," Bella replied, retrieving an embroidered glove and satin-bordered sash from the floor and placing them on one of the beds. "It's obvious your boarders aren't particularly interested in tidiness."

"They're up early and busy until bedtime. I fear tidiness isn't their top priority. They'd rather spend their free time at a lecture or visit in the parlor. Not that I blame them, of course."

"You launder the bedding, and we wash our own clothing. Isn't that correct?" Ruth asked.

Addie nodded. "Right as rain," she said with a smile. "I clean the downstairs, but you girls are responsible for your rooms. Some are neat and clean while others are rather . . . shall we say, unkempt?"

After one bump on her head, Bella moved about the room

more carefully, examining what little space wasn't occupied. "And there are no other rooms available?"

Addie shook her head. "You're taller than most of the girls, and I know these sloping walls and low ceiling will be difficult, but this is the best I can offer for now. You will have an opportunity to move downstairs when a space becomes available; however, you'll have to wait your turn. First ones here have priority in choosing if they want to move to another room. Since this is pretty much the worst of it, they almost always want to move," she said while checking the timepiece pinned to her dress. "Goodness, look at the time! The girls will soon be home. You get settled; I'll go down to the kitchen."

Bella met Daughtie's look of alarm with a waning smile. "We can make this better. We'll put pegs on the wall to hold our clothes, and if we move those chests over here," she said, pointing across the room, "it will provide additional space. This bed can be moved against the wall."

Ruth bobbed her head in agreement. "We had ten girls in the room at my former boardinghouse."

Bella glanced at Daughtie. A tear trickled down her friend's cheek. "We're going to be fine, Daughtie. I promise."

Now Bella prayed that God would provide her with the capability to keep that promise.

CHAPTER 5

Clad in a dove-gray cutaway and matching cravat, Kirk Boott stood in the foyer of his large frame home awaiting the arrival of his guests, members of the Boston Associates and the key employees of the corporate operation in Lowell.

Matthew Cheever placed his hat and gloves upon a receiving table as was the routine, then turned to greet his employer. "Good day to you, sir." Matthew knew that as far as Boott was concerned, it would be the very best of days.

These semiannual meetings were a source of pleasure to Kirk. He enjoyed receiving the accolades bestowed upon him by the members of the Corporation. The bursts of applause that occasionally interrupted his reports of progress at these meetings were almost as important to Kirk as the tidy sum he was paid to oversee the paternalistic community created with the Associates' money. As general agent for the Corporation, Kirk continued to receive the complete support of the Associates—except for one or two recalcitrant men who harbored ill will toward him.

Kirk grasped Matthew Cheever's hand. "Glad you arrived early, Matthew. I'm depending on you to assist me during this meeting. I'll remain at the door. You see to their comfort once they enter the sitting room."

Matthew knew exactly what was expected. Matthew would see to the comfort of Kirk's guests, ensuring that their glasses were full, their cigars were lit, and adequate seating was available. Kirk was careful that his servants couldn't overhear business conversations, and it was a foredrawn conclusion that women would not be in attendance. Matthew didn't mind. As the evening progressed, the other men would realize Kirk had also begun to rely upon him for loftier responsibilities.

Taking his position in the large sitting room adjacent to Boott's office, Matthew offered a welcoming hand and glass of port to the gentlemen as, one by one, they began filling the room.

Paul Moody entered the room and made his way to where Matthew stood. He gave Matthew's shoulder a friendly squeeze. "Helping the boss keep his guests happy?"

Matthew nodded as he filled several goblets with the expensive port Kirk enjoyed serving. "If you'd care to help, you can deliver these to William Thurston and Nathan Appleton."

Paul laughed and drew a weatherworn hand across his balding pate. "I'll be happy to deliver Nathan's glass. William is another matter. I have no use for that man. I fear he is a double-minded sort who has only his own best interests at heart."

"He's not one of my favorite people, either, but you can always count on him to be present at the meetings."

Paul nodded. "Exactly! He wants to cause Kirk as much grief as possible. Given any opportunity, he'll be up to his same old tricks this evening."

Matthew picked up the glasses and gave Paul a grin. "Let's hope Boott can hold him at bay. Otherwise we'll be here until the wee hours of the night, and I don't think that would please either of our wives."

"How is Mrs. Cheever? My wife reports there's to be an addition to your family."

"It seems there are no secrets in Lowell. She is doing very

well, thank you. Needless to say, we are delighted with the news."

Paul took one of the goblets. "I'll take this to Nathan. No need to worry about your news. It's safe with me—and I'll tell my wife that she's to keep her lips sealed until you and Mrs. Cheever have an opportunity to spread the word."

Matthew strode toward the other side of the room, wondering how Evangeline Moody knew that Lilly was with child. He offered the glass of port to William Thurston, who stood staring out the sitting room window. "With all those buds on the trees, it appears we're going to have an early spring," Matthew said.

William startled at the words, appearing embarrassed as he turned around. "I was deep in thought. I didn't realize anyone was close at hand."

"Quite all right," Matthew replied. He waited only until William accepted the glass before turning away. He didn't want to be drawn into a conversation with a man he didn't trust—especially this one.

John Farnsworth, the Englishman in charge of the print works operation at the Merrimack, grasped Matthew's hand as he turned. "Good to see you, Matthew. It appears you've got things well in hand for tonight's meeting."

William Thurston glanced over his shoulder, his features contorted into a sneer. "If a mobcap and frilly apron are all that are required to have things well in hand, I'd say that Kirk's lackey is certainly prepared."

Matthew's jaw clenched and he could feel the blood rising to his cheeks. Farnsworth gave a slight nod of his head as he took hold of Matthew's elbow. "I believe there's a more intelligent level of conversation across the room," John said, tugging at Matthew's arm. "Ignore him. He isn't worth your time or trouble, and nobody here values his opinion. That's why he's been standing by himself since his arrival," John said in a hushed voice.

"I know," Matthew replied. "But he's so puffed up—full of conceit. I'd like to take him down a peg or two."

John laughed. "That's your youth speaking, my boy. There

are more effective ways to deal with the likes of William Thurston."

"Such as?"

John gave him a sly grin. "Pray for him. Let God deal with William Thurston. Men such as William want to be the center of attention. He's insecure and angry. A fist won't change his heart—only God can do that."

"You're right, of course, but I'm not certain I want God's grace to shine down upon that man," Matthew replied. "Perhaps you should pray for me, John."

John slapped Matthew on the back. "I'll be praying for the both of you. How's that?"

"Gentlemen, I believe everyone is here. Shall we get started?" Kirk inquired as he strode into the room. There was no doubt Kirk Boott was in command. "We have several matters upon which to report, and then I'll be glad to entertain any questions or new ideas."

The account grew lengthy as Boott reported on the Merrimack, Hamilton, Appleton, and Lowell Mills, carefully explaining the profits and expenditures of each mill. "Of course, the Lowell Mill hasn't been in production long enough to show a profit, but I believe it will do so more rapidly than any of our other mills. I believe Nathan's strong encouragement to expand into rug production was another stroke of genius. Our fine friend and associate Tracy Jackson has given me several contacts for overseas buyers, and orders within the country are burgeoning."

"Hear, hear!" a few men called out, while others applauded loudly.

Matthew watched as Kirk basked in the adulation for a moment or two before continuing. "I'm certain you are all interested in hearing about our latest projects. I believe Matthew Cheever can give you a more detailed report on those ventures," he said while motioning Matthew to his side. "As many of you know, I'm relying on Matthew more and more as we continue to expand."

This was Matthew's first opportunity to speak before the

assembled group, and he didn't want to embarrass himself or Boott. Thanking Kirk, he took his place and told the men that projections were on target for the Middlesex Mill to begin production in the fall. There were murmurs of approval from the group.

"During your tour earlier today, I'm certain you noted that even with a particularly harsh winter, Hugh Cummiskey and his Irishmen have continued to make excellent progress on digging and laying stone for the new canals required to power the Suffolk and Tremont Mills. Those two mills remain on schedule to open in 1832. As our capable agent-in-residence, Mr. Boott, has pointed out, there is great demand for our products both overseas and here at home, particularly in the South. Not only for rugs but many of our other goods, as well. We plan to expand the production of our lightweight Negro cloth for our southern states as well as warmer climates overseas. The demand has been beyond our highest expectations," Matthew acknowledged. "Although the weather sometimes causes us to become innovative in order to continue work on these new buildings and canals during the winter, I think you will all agree that we have prevailed and excellent progress is evident."

Once again, resounding applause filled the room. Somewhat embarrassed by the ovation, Matthew nodded and took his seat. Kirk stood and moved forward, basking in the continuing applause.

At length the room grew silent, and Kirk continued. "We've had a profitable six months, gentlemen, and I trust the next six months will prove even more to your liking. Your vision for expansion has given birth to a thriving community," Kirk complimented. "Questions or comments?"

Tracy Jackson raised his lit cigar into the air. "You didn't mention the Catholic church. I'm sure we'd all like to know how that's progressing, Kirk."

Boott nodded his head. "Hugh Cummiskey tells me the final work should be completed by summer's end. He's looking for an accomplished stonemason before finalizing the interior work. We're planning to invite Bishop Fenwick to come from Boston the last Sunday in August to preside over the first Mass."

"Just what we need—more Irish," William Thurston called out from the far end of the room. "They're swarming into Lowell faster than flies settle on manure, and Boott encourages them. He spends as much time trying to make Cummiskey happy as he does all the rest of us combined."

An uncomfortable silence hung in the air for several long minutes before Tracy spoke. "I hear tell there's been discussion around town in regard to the schools, Kirk. Apparently there are those who think a better education should be offered. . . ."

Kirk held up his hand. "I've heard the talk, but I understand the murmuring comes from only a small faction of townsfolk. I doubt there's anything of consequence to concern us."

"Any issues that impact the community will in turn impact the Associates. We don't want to be caught unprepared. Matters such as this bear watching," Tracy warned.

Taking a sip of the expensive burgundy liquid in his glass, Kirk leaned against his carved walnut desk before speaking. "Rest assured, Tracy, that the best interests of the Associates are always foremost in my mind. I will personally keep abreast of this matter and give you my word that you will be well informed on this and all other matters of consequence."

"Good enough! I can't ask for any more than that. We all know you're a man of your word."

Matthew sighed a breath of relief. The exchange between Tracy Jackson and Kirk had ended amicably. Kirk had spoken in a quiet, even tone, maintaining his deportment and composure, though Kirk's mounting anger at Jackson's comments had been obvious to Matthew. Perhaps the others had not noticed.

"I, for one, would like to get back to the problem of the Irish. If, as Mr. Boott purports, the Associates are always foremost in his mind, why has nothing been done to control their growth in this town?" William Thurston grumbled from the rear.

Nathan Appleton turned in his chair and faced Thurston. "I don't think anyone else in this room shares your intense passion to rid Lowell of the Irish, William. The remainder of us seem to be in accord. We realize that these men fill a need. They work hard, and they're willing to perform the necessary manual labor that no one else is willing to undertake—at least none that we're aware of. We are also keenly aware that the married Irishmen desire to live together with their families. I can't fault a man for wanting his family nearby, although you seem to spend a great deal of time away from yours, William. By all appearances, you spend more time in Lowell than in Boston, which I am hard pressed to understand. Aside from pursuing problems with the Irish population, what is it you do here in Lowell?"

A chorus of laughter filled the room as a crimson-faced Thurston glowered. "Mark my words—one day you're going to regret that you didn't take this problem seriously. One day you'll come to me, hat in hand, apologizing for your shortsightedness." The venom-filled words echoed down the hallway as Thurston made a hasty departure out of the house, the front door slamming with a resounding thud.

Matthew had no idea what might be going through Boott's mind, but his own thoughts suggested that Thurston was a man to be watched. As Nathan Appleton noted, no one was really all that sure what Thurston did in Lowell. His many visits were apparently given to some purpose—but what?

CHAPTER 6

Daughtie pulled an initial-embroidered handkerchief from her pocket and dabbed it to her eyes. "I don't think I'm ever going to become accustomed to the world's ways," she lamented. "You know I'm not one to complain, Bella, but these people move so rapidly. Everything is measured by speed, both at work and at home. I feel like a pig being slopped when I rush to the table for a meal; there's no time for manners or even the slightest civility. Why, just this morning Margaret was so intent on forking the last serving of bacon that she reached across me, her elbow striking my cheek. Even worse, she didn't take a moment to apologize! And the noise—at work it's all the machines, and when we come home, everyone talks at once. There's no peace, no time to reflect or meditate. Tell me—is this how you remember the world? Because if it is, I can't imagine why you wanted to return."

Bella squirmed on her chair and gave Daughtie a pensive look. "Life here in Lowell is very different from what I experienced with my family. But I was living on a small farm, not in the city. Living here is unusual for everyone, not just us. Each girl who comes here must go through an adjustment."

Daughtie's chin drooped and rested on her chest. "I don't think I can adjust to this life," she whispered. "I don't like it here, Bella."

Bella's mind was racing. She didn't want Daughtie returning to the Shakers, for although she liked Ruth and the other girls, they didn't understand her—not like Daughtie. She lowered her voice to avoid being overheard. "Give yourself more time. It's too soon to make a decision. Only yesterday the supervisor said that you and I were already the best weavers on the floor. Didn't his words of praise make you feel good? And I was thinking that we could take some Scripture verses and tack them to our looms. I know the supervisor sometimes frowns upon reading material, but many of the girls have pages tacked to their machines. We can memorize Scripture while we work. It will make the time pass more quickly, don't you think? And we'll spend more time alone. We can go upstairs in the evening when no one else is there and talk quietly." The words spilled out, tumbling over one another in a panicked staccato.

"Please don't be angry with me, Bella. I'll stay a while longer, but I wanted you to know that I'm giving thought to returning to the Society," Daughtie hesitantly replied. "But I do like your idea about the Scripture verses. We can copy some verses tonight and begin memorizing tomorrow." She gave Bella a wistful smile.

"That's the spirit. In time, we might both find Lowell to be exactly what we're looking for."

"But what about Jesse?"

Daughtie's question caused Bella to sober. "What about him?"

"Don't you wonder what happened to him? I mean, you were to leave the Society together. Don't you want to know why he didn't appear—where he might be today?"

"I don't really think about him, at least not much. Like I told you before, Daughtie, I wasn't in love with Jesse. He thought he was in love with me, but if he couldn't even follow through on our plans and leave the village with me, then why should I give his kind of love a second thought?"

A persistent knock sounded at the front door. "Would you see who's at the door, Bella?" Miss Addie called from the kitchen.

"Yes, ma'am," Bella answered. "I'll be right back," she promised Daughtie as she rose from her chair.

Obviously the three girls sitting in the parlor with their gentlemen callers couldn't excuse themselves long enough to answer the door, Bella decided. A prick of irritation assailed her as she glanced at the giggling girls, all too self-involved to be bothered.

Turning the knob, she gave the door a tug. "Yes?" she inquired a bit more curtly than planned.

"Well, good evening to you, too. Apparently I've come at a bad time?"

Bella felt the heat rising in her cheeks. A young man of about twenty years stood before her. A mass of straight hair fell forward over his eyes as he removed his felt hat. Raking his fingers through the blond strands, he gave her a roguish grin.

"Were you going to invite me in? Or do you prefer standing in the doorway?" he quickly added.

Jumping back, Bella nearly lost her balance as she made way for the handsome gentleman caller. "I apologize for my rude behavior, sir. May I be of assistance?" she inquired formally, closing the door once he had entered the hallway.

"Why, yes, thank you," the man replied, bowing deeply from the waist in mock formality as he once again thrust his tousled hair off his brow. "Taylor Manning to speak with Miss Addie, if you please. And you are?"

"Bella—Arabella Newberry of New Hampshire. I'll tell Miss Addie that you've come to call. She's in the kitchen," she replied, turning to make her way down the hallway.

"Good. I'll just follow along behind," he replied. "Miss Addie won't mind if I call on her in the kitchen."

Bella could feel his towering presence matching her steps as he followed her through the parlor, past a wide-eyed Daughtie sitting at the dining table, and into the kitchen. "Mr. Taylor Manning to see you, Miss Addie," she announced as they entered the warm kitchen.

Miss Addie twirled around to face them with damp gray curls clinging to her forehead. "Taylor! What a surprise. It's early—I wasn't expecting your uncle just yet."

"That's why I've come. Uncle John asked that I advise you of the fact that he's going to be detained. We have a meeting of the Mechanics Association this evening—"

"Come in the parlor, Taylor. I don't entertain guests in the kitchen," Addie interrupted as she pulled off her apron and tucked a few stray strands of hair into place.

Taylor hesitated. "I've come merely to deliver Uncle John's message," he insisted.

"Tut, tut, I'll hear none of that. Come along—you, too, Bella," she clucked. "Come along, Daughtie," she said, grasping her by the arm as they reached the dining room. Daughtie took her place behind Miss Addie, the three of them resembling a brood of chicks following a proud mother hen. "Make room, ladies and gentlemen," Miss Addie commanded the girls and their guests already assembled in the parlor. "Daughtie and Bella, this is Mr. Taylor Manning. He's John Farnsworth's nephew and because he has an artistic flair, he's been hired on to work on fabric designs." She looked at each of the young women and then offered, "Taylor, this is Miss Daughtie Winfield and Miss Bella Newberry." The girls curtsied and Taylor bowed.

Taking a seat, Addie nodded for her three followers to sit down. Folding her hands, she rested them in her ample lap and smiled at Taylor.

"As I said, I've come to advise you that Uncle John has been detained. There's a meeting of the Mechanics Association," he said, pulling out his pocket watch and glancing at the time, "for which I certainly don't want to be late. Uncle John has agreed to assist a group of us who will be scheduling some lectures in the near future."

Margaret and Harriet ignored their visitors and immediately turned their full attention to Taylor, both of them obviously besotted with his confident behavior and strapping good looks. Bella found their behavior annoying.

"The other men must value your opinion greatly if you're

assisting with such important matters," Harriet fawned in a syrup-sweet tone.

Margaret nodded. "You must be very worthy of their trust." She batted her lashes and lowered her head in a coy manner. Bella had to admit this was not something she'd had to deal with in the Society. She had to smile at the very thought of Sister Mercy lowering her head and simpering for one of the Brethren.

Taylor squared his shoulders and nodded. "Why, thank you," he replied, tucking away his watch. "These lectures are of enormous value to the men. They aid us in keeping abreast of current topics of importance. There's absolutely no way of evaluating how much good these lectures and the library are accomplishing for the men, but I must say that I'm proud to be a part of this noble venture."

"These lectures you speak of—are they only for the men, or may we attend also?" Bella asked as she perched on the edge of her chair. She'd opened her mouth almost before she'd given herself a chance for thought.

The room grew silent. All of them, save Daughtie and Miss Addie, stared at her as though she'd spoken a foreign language.

"The lectures and library are both sponsored and funded by the Mechanics Association, which is comprised of skilled tradesmen."

Well, I'm committed to this now, Bella reasoned. *I might as well continue.* "The women working in the mills are certainly skilled workers." She tried to keep her voice soft and nonthreatening. "I'm certain many of them would be pleased to spend a small portion of their earnings in exchange for a membership that would permit them to enjoy the valuable services you've so aptly described."

Taylor shifted in his seat and cleared his throat. "You do understand, Miss Newberry, that there is a vast difference between a skilled tradesman and someone who merely passes a shuttle back and forth through a loom, don't you?"

Struggling to keep her temper in check, Bella clenched her hands together in a white-knuckled clasp. Gone was her attempt to keep her voice decidedly calm. "Where I come from, Mr.

Manning, women are treated as equals, given the same opportunity to expand their minds as men, and encouraged to explore all the abilities God has given them. Am I to understand that the men of your Mechanics Association find that an unacceptable ideology?"

Taylor rose from his chair and paced back and forth on the floral-designed wool carpet. "I believe you're twisting my words, Miss Newberry. However, we do not have female members, nor do they utilize our library nor attend the lectures."

"Aha!" Bella retorted, now matching him step for step as he continued pacing. "But you obviously believe women are inferior since you disallow them the use of your facilities and attendance at your lectures. I'd venture to say that if women were permitted to assist with these lectures and the library, you would see an improvement."

Taylor raised a finger and pointed it toward Bella. "So you're saying that women are more enlightened than men, Miss Newberry? What makes you the better in this disagreement? You argue on behalf of women while I argue on behalf of men."

Bella pushed his finger away and stood facing him, hands on hips. "No. I do not argue solely on behalf of women, Mr. Manning. I argue on behalf of both men and women. I believe that opportunities should be available in equal measure."

Taylor gave a husky chuckle. "I hail from England, Miss Newberry, where such a concept would be viewed with disdain. Where in New Hampshire were you taught such principles?"

"Canterbury, where I lived among the United Society of Believers, who not only taught the principle of equality but also lived it."

"Based upon its name and your attire, I assume this society is a religious sect of some nature. I do wonder, though, if you hold their beliefs in such high esteem, how is it that you've come to Lowell, miss?"

The group turned its attention toward Bella, obviously anxious to hear her reply. She hesitated a moment and looked at Taylor. His eyes were sparkling with anticipation; a mischievous grin played at the corners of his lips.

"Both my attire and my reasons for leaving, sir, are personal matters that I'll not discuss with a stranger," she curtly replied.

The group applauded her remark. "Well done!" hollered one of the young men. Soon the others were cheering along with him. When they had quieted, the same young man who had spoken out smiled at Taylor. "I believe she's bested you, Mr. Manning."

Taylor nodded to the group. "Perhaps she has. We'll see how she fares the next time we meet. Please know, Miss Newberry," he said, turning to face her, "that I truly desire to remain and discuss this matter further. However, I must depart or I'll be late to my meeting. In the meantime, you might consider forming a sewing circle. I'm sure you and the other young ladies would find that enjoyable—and I promise I won't attempt to join."

Bella gave him a demure smile. "We would certainly welcome you, Mr. Manning, and perhaps one day you'll be inclined to extend an invitation to me to attend your meeting."

He shook his head at her remark and strode toward the front door with Miss Addie following closely at his heels. "Once the meeting is over, Uncle John will be calling on you, Miss Addie."

Miss Addie extended her thanks and then rejoined the others. "I believe young Mr. Manning was somewhat befuddled by you, Bella."

With Taylor Manning gone, everyone's gaze remained fixed on Bella. She immediately regretted her sharp tongue and quick response. "That wasn't my intent, Miss Addie."

"Well, you certainly managed to gain his attention, which is more than the rest of us have been able to do," Margaret offered, her beau scowling at the remark. "Why don't we walk into town?" she questioned her gentleman caller, obviously realizing her blunder.

Addie, Bella, and Daughtie remained in the parlor while the other girls and their gentleman callers retrieved their wraps and made a hasty departure to view the latest shipment of goods to arrive in the shops and, perhaps, stop for tea and cake.

"While I have reason to regret the hasty manner in which I responded, I do not regret making a stand for the women of this town. I hope your Mr. Farnsworth is a freer-thinking man than his nephew," Bella remarked.

Addie giggled. "I'm not sure that he is. Of course, I'm not sure you'll find too many men in New England who believe women are their equals. However, I must admit that young Taylor has much to learn in his dealings with people."

"I don't believe I've ever seen a gentleman so proud of himself—and for so little. He seems to think that his mere membership in an association gives him reason for puffery. And did you notice the way he was watching Harriet and Margaret? The moment he saw them swooning, he became even more obnoxious."

" 'Tis true the boy's a bit of a rascal, and he's certainly aware that his roguish good looks attract the women," Addie replied. "According to his uncle John, that handsome face and muscular build have gotten him into difficulties in the past."

This was getting interesting. Bella leaned forward, giving Miss Addie her full attention. "What sort of difficulties?"

Addie looked about the room as though she expected an intruder might be lurking in one of the corners. "It seems that young Taylor became involved with the daughter of a wealthy aristocrat. Of course, Taylor comes from a fine family, but certainly not from the same level of society as this young woman."

Bella furrowed her brows in concentration. She wasn't sure she understood the import of Miss Addie's words. "And that creates a problem?"

"Yes, my dear. Crossing social barriers is frowned upon in England—even more than it is in America," she explained. "In fact, the girl's father told Taylor that if he saw him anywhere near his daughter again, he wouldn't bother with an honorable challenge to a duel. Rather, he said he would shoot Taylor where he stood. You must understand, the girl was engaged to be married and the banns had already been read. A duel seemed very much in order to maintain the girl's honor."

Bella gasped and then quickly covered her mouth with one hand. "It's difficult to believe that a member of the aristocracy would exhibit such unrestrained anger," she replied. "Of course, it isn't difficult to believe Mr. Manning would find himself in such a predicament! He is obviously a man who prides himself on getting ahead by using his appearance and contrived charm."

"My! Those are harsh words, Bella. John is hoping that with a firm hand, his influence, and continuing prayer, his nephew will begin to see the error of his ways and perhaps even seek the Lord. Personally, I doubt there are many young men that possess Taylor's rugged good looks who wouldn't use them to advantage," Addie exclaimed.

Bella gazed out the window. "There may be some," she replied.

Jesse had never attempted to influence anyone with his appearance, and although Jesse and Taylor looked nothing alike, Jesse was handsome in his own right. In all their conversations he had been honest and forthright—at least she thought he had. She wanted to believe Jesse had spoken the truth when he had told her of his desire to leave Canterbury. Daughtie's previous questions now haunted her. Why hadn't Jesse appeared or somehow sent word to her by now?

"I find that men are difficult to trust. Their willingness to commit themselves seems lacking," Bella absently commented.

Addie patted Bella's hand. "Now, why would you say such a thing, dear? Has some young beau broken your heart?"

"The Shakers are a celibate society. I've never had a beau, although my friend Jesse Harwood had planned to leave Canterbury along with Daughtie and me. He never appeared."

"And based on that one incident you believe all men are untrustworthy?"

Bella hesitated for a moment. "No. That incident only served to confirm my beliefs. It's my father who demonstrated the inability of men to honor their commitments," she replied in a soft voice.

Daughtie placed her arm around Bella's shoulders. "Bella's parents came to the Shaker village when they were in financial difficulty. Her father decided they should become members of the Society, but her mother was against joining. She wanted to go back to their home near Concord after their first winter with the Believers."

Bella nodded. "But my mother finally gave in to my father's wishes and signed the papers. The three of us lived separately—Father in the Brothers' Order and Mother in the Sisters' Order. I was in the Children's Order until I was fourteen, when I signed my papers and went into the Sisters' Order. By then my mother was very ill and only the physician and the nursing sister were permitted to see her. And so our separation continued. When she died a short time later, I was told that shedding tears was inappropriate behavior. My father offered no comfort nor did he appear saddened at her death. When I asked my father how he could choose to stay with the Believers rather than live in the world with his family, he said the Believers' way was easier."

Miss Addie gasped. "Easier?"

"Yes. It wasn't his deep level of religious belief that caused him to remain but the fact that he enjoyed the lack of responsibility living among the Believers afforded him. He didn't like the commitment of being responsible for a family."

"Dear me. No wonder you've come to such a conclusion. But you must remember, child, that you've judged all mankind upon one man's actions," Addie countered.

A lump rose in Bella's throat. "Two, if you count Jesse."

———

Taylor glanced over his shoulder toward number 5 Jackson Street as he hurried off toward his meeting. The spirited girl from New Hampshire was provoking his thoughts. A pretty young woman—at least she would be if she'd wear some proper apparel and fix her hair in a more becoming style, he decided. He'd never met a girl quite like her. She certainly wasn't afraid to speak her mind. Even when he'd flashed his sapphire blue eyes at her, she'd continued on with her arguments as though she conversed with astonishingly handsome Englishmen every day of her life.

"Amazing!" he murmured, shaking his head as he entered the meeting room.

"What's amazing?" John Farnsworth inquired. "That you're over half an hour late?"

Taylor pulled out his watch and clicked open the gold case. Eight o'clock. He shook his head in wonderment. "Is the meeting over already?" he asked while glancing about the room. There were only a few men gathered reading books.

John nodded. "It didn't take long to decide we needed to acquire more information before scheduling any lectures. None of us was knowledgeable about available speakers, and I didn't think you'd had time enough to gather a list. I suggested that each of us secure a few names and topics and meet again in two weeks. I hope you don't mind; I saw no need to continue waiting for you, and I prefer to spend my evening with Addie," he said, clutching his felt top hat in one hand and walking toward the door.

Taylor turned and matched stride with his uncle. "So you're going to Miss Addie's now?"

John stopped and leveled a look of concern at his nephew. "Yes. Isn't that what I said a few moments ago? Are you sick, boy?" he asked and then continued walking.

"No. I was wondering if you'd mind if I joined you."

"You want to accompany me while I call on Miss Addie? Now I know you're sick."

"I don't exactly want to accompany you while you're visiting. I merely want an excuse for reappearing at the boarding-house."

"What for, pray tell?"

Taylor gave his uncle a sheepish grin. "When I stopped to give Miss Addie your message, I became engaged in conversation with a young lady who is now boarding there. We didn't have time to complete our conversation, and I thought—"

"I should have known this had something to do with another conquest," John replied, shaking his head.

"It's not what you think, Uncle. Conquest, yes—but in an intellectual capacity."

Clasping an earlobe between his thumb and index finger, John tugged on the lobe several times in rapid succession.

"Excuse me? Did I hear you correctly? You want to conquer a young lady on an intellectual level? Forgive me if I have difficulty believing such an avowal."

"This girl is different, Uncle John. She's from New Hampshire. Belonged to some sort of religious sect—the United Society of Believers or some such thing. I admit she's an attractive enough girl, but it's her philosophy that intrigues me," Taylor explained.

John laughed. "I see. And just what is this intriguing philosophy?"

"She believes in equality, that men and women are equal. Actually, it was a discussion regarding the Mechanics Association that detained me. She was of the opinion that women should be entitled to use the library and attend the lectures of the association."

John arched his eyebrows. "That is quite a philosophy. And how did you defend your position, Taylor?"

Taylor glanced down. "Instead of defending my position, I turned the tables on her by asking why she had left her religious group and come to Lowell if, in fact, she preferred their way of life."

"Not an impressive argument on your part," John declared.

Taylor agreed. "That's why I want to return. Perhaps I can give Miss Newberry a worthy reply."

"In that case, I suppose I couldn't possibly turn down your request," John said as he knocked on the front door of the boardinghouse.

Taylor straightened his coat. Since he was a small boy he'd been used to girls falling at his feet. He'd never met a woman he couldn't intrigue and entice with a wink or a smile. Miss Newberry promised to be something of a challenge, and that idea alone was much too exciting to pass up in his otherwise dull world. Memories of his mother's warnings against arrogance and pride filtered through a hazy veil, but he quickly ignored them. Miss Bella Newberry had rather asked for this attention, and

Taylor was only too happy to comply.

The door opened and Bella stood at the threshold with a look of surprise etched upon her face. "Mr. Manning! What brings you back again so soon?"

CHAPTER 7

Bella lay still, not wanting to awaken Daughtie or Ruth before the first bell. Surely the customary clanging would soon begin. She'd wakened several hours earlier and had been unable to once again fall asleep. Her body now ached, protesting the hours she'd remained stiff and motionless, longing to stretch the cramped muscles and throbbing joints into another position. She yearned for the sound of the reverberating toll she normally detested.

"Not yet," Ruth groaned, pulling the covers over her head at the sound of the first bell. "I don't want to get up."

"You'd best hurry or Daughtie will be tugging off the covers to air them out while you're still abed," Bella warned.

Bella was already at the pitcher and washbasin, glad to be up yet aware that she would be exhausted by day's end. However, she wouldn't complain to Daughtie, no matter how tired she was or difficult the day might be, for Daughtie would use such talk as yet another reason they should return to the Society of Believers. Although Bella understood her friend's discomfort with these new surroundings, she was of the opinion they both needed more time in which to make their final decisions regarding the world and its ways.

"You dressed quickly," Daughtie commented as she pulled back the covers on the bed to air.

"I can't find my shoes," Harriet whined from across the room. "Does anyone see my shoes?" She held a candle at arm's length as she scoured the room.

Daughtie shook her head. "If you'd put your belongings in their proper place when you disrobe, you'd have no difficulty finding them in the morning."

"I don't need a lecture, Daughtie; I need my shoes," Harriet replied, her candle illuminating the cross look etched upon her face.

Shrugging her shoulders, Daughtie sat on Ruth's trunk and brushed her hair. "You ought not expect our help. If we give you assistance, we're merely encouraging you to continue in your slothful habits."

"What did you call me?" Harriet shrieked.

Bella stepped forward and took Harriet's arm. "Your shoes—they're over by the window," Bella said, pointing across the room.

Harriet pulled her arm from Bella's grasp and, after one last glare at Daughtie, went to retrieve her shoes.

"You could be less critical," Bella whispered as she handed Daughtie a comb.

Daughtie gave her a look of consternation. "This room is too small for Harriet and Margaret to throw their things about. I'm used to orderliness and so are you. Why are you taking her side?"

Bella pulled the sheet taut, tucked it under the mattress, then pulled up the covers. "I'm not taking her side. I'm merely trying to keep peace. I agree that the disarray makes it difficult, but harsh words among us will make this room seem much smaller than it already is. Perhaps kind words and deeds will go further with Harriet than criticism."

"I'll try, Bella, but she is lazy."

Bella grinned. "Come on. We have time for prayer and a bit of Scripture reading before the second bell. Let's go downstairs and give the others space to finish getting ready for work."

By the time Bella and Daughtie completed their Bible

reading and uttered a brief prayer, the other girls came racing down the steps, their thumping shoes and volubility drowning out the clang of the second bell.

"I wish we could eat breakfast before going off to work," Daughtie complained as they joined the group of girls hurrying out the front door.

Bella hooked arms with her friend. "We did our mending and cleaned the Brothers' rooms before eating breakfast in Canterbury."

"Performing routine daily chores isn't the same as going off to work in a mill before having a bite to eat."

"True, but leaving the mill for breakfast gives us a break and an opportunity to get out in the fresh air," Bella countered.

"And shovel down our meal without the time to properly chew or digest the food," Daughtie shot back.

Bella grinned and gave her friend's arm a squeeze. "It is obvious nothing I say is going to cheer you or change your mind, so I'll permit you the last word on this topic."

Daughtie laughed. "I'm sorry. I sound like Sister Eunice—never willing to cease my arguing."

"You haven't quite reached Sister Eunice's level, but promise you won't make that a goal," Bella said, joining in Daughtie's laughter.

"I'm pleased to see you two so cheerful this morning," the overseer greeted as they entered the room. "We have several girls out sick, and I'll need each of you to tend an extra loom."

"So much for memorizing Scripture today," Daughtie whispered as she patted her pocket.

"But, Mr. Kingman, we've only just learned to manage one of those metal beasts. Surely you don't expect us to capably tend two," Bella replied.

"You'll do fine. Besides, I have no choice. Too many of the operatives are either ill or leaving without proper notice."

Bella gave Daughtie a waning smile as they walked toward their looms. "We can paste them up today. That way they'll be ready and waiting for us tomorrow." At the moment it was as much encouragement as she could offer.

"If we can find time to do even that," Daughtie replied. "I find it appalling they expect us to take over another loom. It's obvious all they care about is quantity. They care little about the quality of their products or the well-being of their workers."

Bella nodded. She couldn't argue with what she knew was truth. These mills were a moneymaking proposition for the owners, who were interested in a handsome profit above all else. On the other hand, the Shakers placed incomparable workmanship above all else. Reconciling the opposing concepts was not possible.

"We'll just have to do the best we can," she replied as they took their places at the looms and awaited the bell's pealing before setting their looms into motion.

Taking up the brass-tipped hollowed-out piece of wood, Bella filled it with a long thread-laden wood bobbin. Lifting the shuttle to her mouth, she sucked in, pulling the bobbin thread through the small hole near the tip of the shuttle and then set the prepared shuttle in the metal box at one end of the race before moving to the next machine and picking up the second. As she sucked the thread through the eye of the second shuttle, the bell tolled and the weaving room clamored to life.

Bella slapped the handle of her machine and watched momentarily as the shuttle carrying the weft thread flew across the race between the shed of warp threads. The reed swung forward, beating against the weft, evenly tightening the latest addition of thread against the already-woven cloth. The beam crashed up and down, raising and dropping the heddles into position as the shuttle, flying in and out of the shuttle box, continued journeying back and forth at breakneck speed. The floor reverberated as she moved back and forth between the machines, repeating her routine: replacing empty bobbins with full ones, tying a weaver's knot when an errant thread snagged, always mindful to watch that the finished cloth was uniformly winding onto the take-up.

Glancing across the room, she took a moment to watch Daughtie moving back and forth between her two assigned machines. Her friend appeared miserable, with her face screwed into a look of anxiety as she stopped the second machine to insert a filled shuttle. A tight fist of remorse formed in Bella's stomach. She shouldn't have encouraged Daughtie to come with her. It had been a selfish act. If Daughtie decided she wanted to go home, Bella determined she would accompany her back to Canterbury. But she would not remain in New Hampshire herself—of that she was certain. Once Daughtie was safely delivered, she would return to Lowell and this new life by herself.

Adjusting to the world's ways would take perseverance, but Bella was willing to accept the hurried meals, the crowded boardinghouse, the deafening noise of the mills, and the lack of privacy in exchange for the freedom to explore her beliefs and make decisions based upon those new discoveries.

Daughtie, however, was not one who questioned anything. Whatever the Society taught, Daughtie believed. But their early lives had been differently formed, Bella reasoned. While Daughtie had spent her entire life among the Brothers and Sisters, steeped in the teachings of Sister Ann and the United Society of Believers, Bella had spent her early years within the nurturing nest of her parents, who had encouraged her inquiring personality. At least until they moved to Canterbury. But unlike her father and Daughtie, Bella and her mother had never completely embraced life among the Believers.

Time moved slowly until the ringing tower bell announced the breakfast break. The machines groaned to a halt, the whirring leather belts ceased turning, and the roomful of operatives raced between the rows of machines toward the stairway.

"Are you able to keep up with both looms?" Bella asked as they joined the throng of workers scurrying into the mill yard.

"I suppose I'm doing well enough, although this day can't end soon enough for me," Daughtie replied. "I only hope those sick girls are well come morning."

Bella nodded her head. "I agree, but it's been easier than I anticipated. I even pasted up the Scriptures on my loom. Did you have an opportunity to place yours?"

Daughtie gave her a frown. "I feel fortunate I was able to stop the looms when I saw an uneven weft row or snag, but I fear I may have missed some imperfections in the cloth. I surely hope not, but I did my best. My verses are still tucked in my pocket."

Reaching to embrace her friend in a quick hug, Bella said, "I know you did your very best."

"It comes easier for you, Bella. I'm not making excuses for myself, but you move among those hideous monsters without fear. When the power comes on and the looms heave to life, I fear that the trembling floors will drop from beneath my feet. The whole room seems synchronized to the incessant rumbling of the looms," Daughtie replied soulfully.

"It will get easier," Bella promised as they entered the boardinghouse.

"I hope so," Daughtie replied as they hung their cloaks near the door.

Bella and Daughtie joined the other girls in the dining room and were soon filling their plates with breakfast fare, passing bowls of oatmeal and boiled potatoes seasoned with chunks of bacon with one hand while forking food into their mouths with the other. There was little time for the formalities of courteous dining. The girls had not yet completed their meal when the tower bell pealed out its warning signal. Chairs scraped, silverware clanked, and napkins were tossed toward the table, a few missing the mark and tumbling to the floor as the operatives jumped up and hastened off to the mill.

Bella remained near Daughtie as they returned to work, hoping somehow the closeness would provide encouragement to her friend. "We can spend the whole evening together," Bella offered as they neared their looms.

Daughtie smiled and squeezed Bella's hand. "That would be nice—if we're not too weary to remain awake by day's end."

The routine resumed in earnest at the clanging of the bell. As the hours began to pass, Bella was able to read the Scripture verses tacked to her loom. She glanced about the room while attempting to memorize the words, enjoying the challenge. Bella smiled at Clara, the young doffer who came running to gather her box of empty bobbins. The child was no more than ten, with hazel eyes and long chestnut brown hair. As Bella nodded, the girl opened her hand to reveal a beautiful glass marble for Bella's inspection.

"It's beautiful," Bella mouthed to the child.

Clara smiled her obvious appreciation for the compliment while pushing the cart of empty bobbins away from Bella's looms. She continued down the narrow aisle, her small stature permitting her to move through the machinery with apparent ease.

Returning her gaze to the Scripture, Bella was beginning to repeat the words aloud when the young doffer dropped to the floor and began crawling through the machines. Bella saw the marble rolling across the floor with Clara in pursuit.

"Nooo!" Bella screamed, her voice drowned out by the perpetual thump and bang of the surrounding machines. She felt as though her shoes were fastened to the floor, her body moving in sluggish, laborious motion as she struggled to reach the young child whose screams now matched her own.

Clara, anxious to reclaim her marble, had reached through the gears of Annie Williams' loom. Before Bella could reach her, the girl's fingers were snapping like brittle twigs. Annie stood frozen, her machine continuing its inhumane torture, the child unable to remove her hand. Shoving Annie aside, Bella grasped the handle and slapped it to the off position. The loom groaned to a stop, yet Clara's screams were unrelenting as Mr. Kingman made his way toward them.

"What are you doing away from your looms, Miss Newberry?" he hollered, his baritone voice resonating above all other noise in the room.

Bella pointed toward the child. "She's injured—her hand . . ."

The overseer scooped up Clara. "Back to work," he commanded before carrying the limp child out of the room.

Bella spun around and retreated to her looms, gazing toward Daughtie as she made her return. Daughtie stared back—a wide-eyed vacant look, as though her mind was unable to process what she had just witnessed.

CHAPTER 8

Lilly Cheever straightened the folds of her lavender silk carriage dress as the horse-drawn buggy came to a halt in front of Addie Beecher's boardinghouse. Her frock wasn't of the latest fashion, but when topped with the double-pointed cashmere-lined pelerine, she could pass the scrutiny of Lowell's fashion-conscious society women. Adjusting her large leghorn hat, she tightened the matching lavender ribbons before stepping down from her coach.

"You may return for me at four o'clock," she instructed the driver, who nodded and tipped his hat.

Lilly walked up the wide step to number 5 Jackson Street. Eighteen months ago, she would have burst through the door without knocking. But that was when she was one of the operatives at the Appleton who boarded with Miss Addie. Nowadays, she was Miss Addie's visitor, so she raised her gloved hand and firmly knocked at the door of what was once her home.

The sound of Miss Addie bustling toward the door could be heard even before it opened. "Lilly! Do come in, dear," the rosy-faced keeper greeted. Her lips were turned up in a welcoming smile that caused dimples to form in each of her plump cheeks.

"I just prepared our tea," she said, leading Lilly into the parlor. "I didn't want to waste a minute of our visiting time out in the kitchen," she explained with a giggle.

Lilly seated herself beside Miss Addie on the familiar over-stuffed settee and watched as Addie filled two delicate china cups with the hot brew. "It's been too long since we've gotten together for a visit," Lilly commented as she took the cup Miss Addie offered. "I must admit, however, that it is still difficult for me to think of myself as other than one of your girls," she observed. "In fact, I still awaken with a start at the sound of the bells and think it's time to get ready for work."

Addie chuckled and patted Lilly's hands. "You'll always be one of my girls, Lilly. How could you not be? Were it not for all of your help teaching me to cook and manage this house, the Corporation would have dismissed me long ago."

"You were a capable student. Besides, you would have learned on your own had I not appeared on your doorstep."

"Eventually. But I doubt any of the girls would have remained in the house long enough to find out. I'm just thankful you came knocking. God was certainly looking out for me that day."

Lilly took a sip of her tea. "Now, tell me, what's been going on with you and John Farnsworth? I've been expecting a wedding invitation."

"I don't think a wedding is in the offing right now, Lilly. I care deeply for John and I believe he feels the same, but we've encountered an obstacle upon which we disagree. Until we're able to reach a resolution that's suitable to both of us, I doubt you'll hear any wedding bells."

Lilly furrowed her brow. "Please don't think me forward, Miss Addie, but dare I inquire as to the nature of your obstacle?"

Addie nodded. "Of course, dear. You know the Corporation built that fine house for John?" she asked.

Lilly nodded. "It appears to be a lovely home."

"John is very fond of it. But I am very fond of this boarding-house and my girls. I want him to move in here when we marry. He wants me to give up the boardinghouse and move into his big house. Accordingly, we reached an impasse. Now that his nephew has arrived from England and moved into the house with him, John seems content to keep our arrangement as it is. There's been little discussion of marriage since young Taylor's arrival."

Lilly gave her friend a thoughtful look. "I'm guessing your decision may have been based on more than leaving the boardinghouse."

Addie glanced toward the floor. "Whatever do you mean?"

"I would guess you're concerned about Miss Mintie and how she might react if you married John and moved into his fine house. You don't want to hurt your sister. Am I correct?"

A slight blush colored Miss Addie's full cheeks. "I know I'm entitled to a happy married life with John, but I won't deny that I worry about Mintie's reaction should I wed. I believe she's beginning to soften a bit—her occasional outings with Lawrence Gault have helped, but he appears unlikely to make a commitment at this time. Mintie tells me his mother is ailing and he feels the weight of responsibility for her care. Even though his mother doesn't live in Lowell, Mr. Gault travels home frequently and provides for all of her financial care."

"Mintie's problems aside, Addie, it's time you thought of your own future. I realize doing so seems selfish to someone of your sweet nature, but John is a fine man who wants only the best for you. I'm sure he doesn't want to see you laboring in this boardinghouse every day, waiting on all these girls when he is perfectly capable of providing a fine home for you. You haven't always lived like this. You were once a part of Boston's upper society. Now, I realize Lowell is a far cry from that, but think of the good you might do. You could have teas for the girls. You could open your home for lectures and such. Besides, what would become of that fine home the Corporation built for him?"

"Speaking of houses, how are you and Matthew enjoying your new home?"

It was obvious Miss Addie was moving the topic of conversation away from her dilemma with John, but Lilly pretended not to notice as she took a bite of her tart.

"This is delicious," she complimented. "Perhaps you'll share the recipe."

Addie grinned. "Now, who would have thought the day would arrive when I could share a recipe with you?"

"Well, it doesn't surprise me a bit!" Lilly exclaimed.

"Thank you, dear. Now, please, do tell me about your new home."

Lilly gave Addie a mischievous grin. "I don't think I will."

Addie's face reflected astonishment at the reply. "What? Whyever not?"

"Because I want you to come and see it for yourself. I'm extending an invitation to tea for a week from Sunday if you're available. I decided upon Sunday afternoon because I'd like you to invite any of your girls to come along who might enjoy the outing."

"Oh, Lilly, that would be such fun. How kind you are to include the girls. But you may end up with quite a houseful when they discover they'll get to see your fine new home."

Lilly smiled at her friend's excitement. "I've not been gone from this boardinghouse so long that I don't fondly remember those special outings that made the routine of working in the mills more bearable."

"Especially the ones with Matthew?" Addie teased.

"Yes, especially those," Lilly agreed, returning Addie's smile. "It will be fun meeting—"

A knock sounded at the front door, interrupting Lilly's remark.

Addie rose and walked toward the hallway. "I can't imagine who would come calling at this time of day," she remarked before pulling open the door.

"Are you entertaining this afternoon?" The words were more of an accusation than a question.

Lilly immediately recognized the voice. Mintie Beecher. Most likely she had spied the carriage when Lilly arrived. From all appearances, life hadn't changed much in the past year and a half. Miss Mintie was still peeking out at the world from behind her drapery-covered windows in the boardinghouse across the street and was still inserting herself in Addie's affairs whenever she pleased. She believed it not only her right but her duty as elder sister to see that Addie lived above reproach.

Mintie swooped into the parlor and peered over the top of her wire-rimmed spectacles while conducting a survey of the room. "Just as I thought," she condemned. "I'm not invited when you have special guests come to visit."

Miss Addie's face screwed into a tight knot at the reprimand, and Lilly immediately came to her friend's rescue. "Please direct your anger at me, Miss Beecher. I haven't seen Miss Addie for some time and requested a private visit. However, we'd be pleased to have you join us," Lilly responded graciously.

Mintie appeared somewhat mollified as she settled onto one of the straight-backed chairs and primly folded her hands. "I see. Well, since you insist, I suppose I could stay for a short visit." Her pinch-faced expression never altered. Mintie Beecher appeared as though perpetually guilty of sucking on sour lemons.

Lilly arched her eyebrows at the reply but said nothing.

"I'll go and get another teacup," Addie said as she bustled off toward the kitchen.

"Has Adelaide told you about her newest boarders?" Mintie inquired with a note of expectancy in her voice.

Lilly shook her head before taking a sip of tea.

"They're Shakers," Mintie continued. "You know, the ones who dance during worship services—heathens, if you ask me. Whoever heard of such a thing?"

Lilly couldn't resist. "I believe David danced before the Lord, Miss Beecher."

The birdlike woman pursed her lips. "That's Old Testament."

Lilly waited a moment, thinking the woman surely had more to say. "And?"

"And nothing. History. David and his antics are history. You don't hear tell of the disciples dancing in the New Testament, do you?"

Lilly stared at her, open-mouthed.

"I rest my case!"

"What case?" Addie inquired as she entered the room. "Shall I pour your tea?"

Lilly turned toward Miss Addie. "Your sister was explaining to me that the disciples didn't dance," Lilly said with a grin.

Addie began giggling and nearly spilled the tea. "You're discussing dancing disciples?" she sputtered.

"They didn't dance," Mintie angrily replied. "And the disciples are not a topic of amusement, Adelaide. What we're truly discussing are the heathen practices of those Shaker girls."

Addie gave her sister a disgusted look. "They are not heathens, Mintie. They belonged to the United Society of Believers and left that life behind when they came to Lowell. They attend church every Sunday, which is more than I can say for some of the girls who lie abed pretending to be ill until after church services. Bella and Daughtie are fine young ladies attempting to adjust to a very new way of life. They need our support, not our criticism."

Lilly nodded her agreement. "Adjusting to the mills and living in a boardinghouse is difficult, even when you don't have faith issues involved. I imagine those girls are struggling on a daily basis to adapt to this new life."

"Oh, pshaw! It's not as though their life in that Shaker community was so different. The men and women live separately— no marriage allowed—and the women live together in big rooms, just like the boardinghouses. They're required to work, and I doubt the transition has been any more difficult for them than for any of the other girls."

"You seem to be quite the authority, Miss Beecher. Where did you gather your information, if I might ask?" Lilly inquired.

"Mrs. Goodnow. She visited that Shaker village up near Canterbury. She said it's the devil's workshop for certain. Those people dancing and whirling about and calling it worship of the Lord. It may be worship, but I assure you it's not of the Lord!" Mintie smugly retorted.

"With all the information you've gathered, I'd think that instead of reviling the girls for having once belonged to that community, you would be encouraging others to help them adjust to this new life," Lilly replied. "Of course, I believe people sometimes unwittingly exaggerate their stories, don't you?"

"Indeed, I do," Addie agreed. "I've spent several evenings visiting with Bella. She's an enchanting young lady who is seeking to find the truth by studying God's Word. Some of the Shaker beliefs are in conflict with what she learned before her family joined the community, and that's one of the many reasons she chose to leave Canterbury. We should remember that most of the young people in the Shaker communities had no choice in their placement. And there's something to be said for a group of people who are willing to assist others when they find themselves in desperate circumstances."

Mintie glanced heavenward before giving her sister an intolerant scowl. "Honestly, Adelaide! Must you always argue with me? I'm sure Reverend Edson would be pleased to confirm everything I've said about the Shakers and their strange habits."

"Really? I've always considered Reverend Edson more of a visionary, a man devoted to seeking innovative ways to win souls to the Lord as opposed to condemning souls who are seeking the truth," Lilly interjected.

Mintie sputtered and turned her attention toward Lilly. "Of course you would take Adelaide's side in the matter."

"I'm not taking sides, Miss Beecher. I am merely stating my opinion," Lilly calmly replied. She had yet to know a visit with Mintie that didn't turn into an argument. Mintie Beecher would brook no opinion that differed from her own.

Mintie placed her cup on the tea tray and announced that she was going home. She was slow in making her departure, most likely hoping that Addie or Lilly would beg her to remain. However, both remained silent, and Lilly watched as Addie firmly escorted her sister to the door.

"She's angry," Addie announced as she returned to the parlor. "But she'll come around in a few days. She always does."

Lilly nodded. "She doesn't appear to have softened so much that one would notice. And I'm quite certain we won't have to worry about her dancing in church," Lilly said before bursting into giggles.

Miss Addie soon joined in, the two women settling down momentarily before once again launching into gales of laughter. Tears streamed down their cheeks before they finally regained their composure.

"Dear me!" Miss Addie exclaimed as she blotted her eyes. "I don't know when I've laughed so hard. I must admit I'm a little ashamed I could find such enjoyment in my sister's displeasure."

"I suppose it isn't very charitable of us," Lilly agreed, "but you must admit that she was set on an argument when she first came in the house. She always is. If she sees something going on without her involvement, she's hard pressed not to thrust herself into the middle of it no matter what."

Addie nodded. "You're right. She's always been that way. I'd think she would tire of the routine, but I remember her being this way even from our younger days. But let's not spend the rest of our afternoon discussing Mintie. I want to hear more about you. I've wanted to ask about your progress finding Lewis's child. Has there been any success?"

At the mention of her brother's name, a lump began to form in Lilly's throat. "No. Matthew has failed me in regard to the little boy," she whispered. "I fear he's satisfied himself the child cannot be found. He conducted a hasty search shortly after Lewis's death. Locating nothing and unable to find any leads, he seemed content with the idea that the child never existed."

"Perhaps he's right," Addie replied quietly. "You didn't have much information to go on, my dear."

Lilly snapped to attention, prepared to defend her position. "I doubt he would have made such a declaration from his death-bed if the child didn't exist. He even spoke of a birthmark."

"I don't mean to offend you, child, but I've heard tell of dying people who sometimes become delusional and babble on incoherently before they finally die," Addie offered. "In fact, you'll remember I told you about my father—the Judge—doing just that."

"Your father's circumstances were entirely different, Miss Addie. He lingered in his illness for a period of time. However, Lewis knew his burns would soon render him dead. He wanted to do the right thing. I believe Lewis told me of the boy's existence because he wanted the child to have proper care."

Addie nodded. "But you may have to accept the fact that even if the boy does exist, you may not find him. Knowing about a little boy with a birthmark doesn't mean that you have a great deal of information."

"I also know that the mother was Irish, so there's little doubt that someone in the Acre knows something about the boy. However, Matthew tells me the Irish are slow to cooperate, especially about personal matters such as children born out of wedlock," Lilly related. "It seems that if Matthew really wanted to find the boy, he would talk to some of the men working for the Corporation. Surely one of them would trust him enough to do a bit of investigating."

"I'm not so sure," Addie replied. "The Irish have learned they have to stick together and look out for their own."

Lilly sighed. "You're probably right. I just don't want to accept the fact that I have no family left in this world."

Addie's mouth dropped open. "Child! You have a husband. He's your family. And what of Matthew's parents? You couldn't ask for finer relatives."

Lilly held up her hand to stave off the onslaught of Addie's words. "Yes, and I love all of them very much. But they're not blood relatives, Miss Addie. I've watched both my parents die, and then just as Lewis and I were beginning to mend the problems of our childhood and build a relationship, he, too, died."

Addie took Lilly's hand in her own. "It's difficult to understand the way of things, Lilly, but if you are meant to have this boy, God will direct you to him. If He doesn't, you must learn to accept the fact that you are not the person intended to rear the boy. Otherwise, you'll become bitter and contentious. And heaven knows I can't deal with another Mintie," she added in an obvious attempt to lighten the mood.

Lilly smiled, deciding it was time to share her secret. "I promise I'll not become bitter—I doubt I'll have much opportunity for such things. You see, I've just discovered Matthew and I are going to have a child of our own."

Addie clapped her hands in delight. "So you will have a blood relative, after all," she responded. "Isn't God gracious? He's giving you your heart's desire, Lilly."

Lilly's eyebrows molded into thinly knit strips as she stared at the older woman. The ticking of the mantel clock resonated in the background, with each click of the tinny pendulum proclaiming the passing moments as she considered Addie's words.

"To be honest, I hadn't thought of this new life in those terms, Miss Addie. It's true that the child will be my blood relative. Yet the fact that Matthew and I are going to have a child doesn't lessen my desire to locate Lewis's boy. I'm sure it will sound strange to you, but Lewis's child gives me a connection to the past, while this child is my connection to the future. One does not supplant my need for the other. I don't want to sound ungrateful, for I realize our marriage has been blessed by God's goodness. However, my prayers remain steadfast: I want to find Lewis's child."

Addie nodded and gave Lilly a cautious smile. "I didn't mean to imply this babe would be a replacement, dear girl. But do remember that living in the past can sometimes thwart a healthy future, not to mention the present. I wouldn't want that happening to you."

"Nor would I," Lilly agreed.

CHAPTER 9

Bella slipped into her blue worsted gown, the normal attire for Sunday meeting among the United Society of Believers. Not that she was attending church among the Shakers—far from it. This Sunday she was attending St. Anne's Episcopal Church with Miss Addie, analyzing yet another array of beliefs. She and Daughtie had listened to the Methodists, Baptists, and Unitarians. Now the Episcopalians would have an opportunity to divulge the tenets of their faith, at least to Bella. Daughtie refused to observe another form of worship, certain she would only become more confused. So while Bella and Addie prepared to attend St. Anne's, Ruth and Daughtie set off for services at the Methodist church. Bella feared her friend's refusal to further explore the churches in Lowell was a harbinger of what would lie ahead. Bella worried Daughtie would soon announce her plans to depart Lowell.

Descending the steps, Bella walked through the parlor and then into the kitchen, where Miss Addie was busily packing items into a large basket. "I thought perhaps you had left without me," Bella remarked.

Miss Addie gave her a wide grin. "Not a chance! I wanted

to get our lunch packed because immediately after church services today we'll be attending the annual church picnic. I wanted to surprise you."

"Well, you've certainly managed to do that," Bella replied. "I've never attended a church picnic. What are the rules for such a thing?"

Addie giggled, her fleshy pink cheeks jiggling ever so slightly. "The only rule is to have fun," she announced. "And I plan to see that we both follow that rule."

"Are you going to carry that heavy basket to church? Surely we don't need all that food for just you and me," Bella protested.

"No need to worry about the basket. John Farnsworth is calling for us in his carriage. And I've packed enough food for four, not two," Addie sheepishly explained.

"Four?"

"Yes. Taylor Manning will be joining us."

Bella sat down on the small wooden stool. The sound of the front door opening and closing, along with the voices of chattering girls moving about the house, filtered into the room and interrupted her thoughts. Bella could enumerate a long list of objections to spending the day with Taylor Manning. Miss Addie was an understanding woman, but she might be offended to hear that the thought of spending a day with Taylor Manning and his outlandish ideas about women was probably more than Bella could bear.

"Goodness, that certainly comes as a surprise. I was thinking that perhaps it would be better if I joined you for church next week, when there are no special activities," Bella ventured.

"Nonsense! The picnic is wonderful fun. That's why I specifically requested you visit this Sunday. And don't you concern yourself about young Taylor. John will see that he's on his best behavior."

A knock sounded at the front door, and Addie scurried off to answer it before Bella could offer any further protest. It appeared there was to be no escape. Bella stewed silently for a moment before standing up and straightening her skirts. Grasping the heavy basket by its handle, she swung it around, nearly knocking Taylor to the floor as he entered the room.

"My leg!" he hollered, grabbing one leg by the shin while hopping around on the other.

Bella dropped the basket to the floor. "I'm so sorry," she apologized hurriedly. "Sit down and let me take a look at it," she ordered while pointing toward the stool.

"No thanks—you've done quite enough already," Taylor replied as he rubbed the bruised leg. "Uncle John and Miss Addie are waiting for us in the carriage. I was sent to fetch you and that confounded basket," he said, grabbing it from her hand.

"Mr. Manning! Please don't use foul language in my presence," Bella ordered.

Taylor stared open-mouthed at her. "What are you talking about?"

"If you think I'll repeat your words, rest assured that I will not."

Taylor's brow wrinkled into deep creases, which caused him to appear years older. "Confounded? Is that the word? *Confounded?*"

His words punctuated the air like a needle piercing cloth. She glared at him. "Stop using that word—now!" she commanded.

Taylor shook his head. "It's going to be a long day," he muttered.

Bella stopped in her tracks. "I share your sentiments. Spending a day in your company is not my idea of pleasure, either," she rebutted before marching off.

"Don't worry about me and my injured leg. I'll be fine carrying this heavy basket," he called, his voice laced with sarcasm as she walked out the front door, leaving him in the wake of her anger.

Addie smiled down from the carriage. "Oh, good, I was beginning to wonder where you were. Now, where is Taylor?" she asked, looking expectantly toward the door.

"He'll be along. He's nursing his injured leg."

"Oh, my! He's injured? John, you'd better go and see to him," Addie fluttered.

"No need, Miss Addie. Here he comes now," Bella said as Taylor limped slowly toward them.

John jumped down from the carriage and assisted Taylor with the picnic basket. "What happened to your leg? You run into something?"

"You might say that," Taylor replied. "Miss Newberry swung that basket into my shin."

Bella gasped at Taylor's explanation while Addie twisted around on the seat, a look of astonished surprise etched on her plump face.

"Bella!" the older woman exclaimed in horror.

"It was an accident, Miss Addie. He came into the room unexpectedly just as I was lifting the basket off the table. As I turned, the basket swung around, tapping him on the leg. Then he began cursing, and when I requested that he refrain from such ill-bred language, he used the word several more times. And that is the truth of what happened," Bella explained. Then she leaned forward and whispered to Miss Addie, "He's acting like a big baby. The basket barely touched his leg."

With John's assistance, Taylor heaved himself into the carriage, making a great show of his pain and leaning heavily against Bella as he adjusted his leg.

"Get off of me!" Bella commanded, pushing him away with all her might.

Once again Miss Addie twisted around in her seat as Taylor gave Bella a dejected look. "I am terribly sorry, Miss Newberry. I wasn't attempting to be offensive, but I'm in pain and needed to straighten my leg."

"Give him a little more room so he can make himself more comfortable, Bella," Addie instructed before turning back toward the front of the carriage.

Taylor gave her a smug grin and then winked. Winked!

"You are no gentleman, sir," Bella hissed. "It's good that we're on our way to church."

"And why is that?"

"Because you're certainly in need of help from the Almighty!"

Taylor gave a hearty laugh. "I doubt you'll find me any more proper after the church sermon than before," he responded jovially.

Bella tapped Miss Addie on the shoulder. "You see? He's laughing and feeling much better already," she said with a look of satisfaction on her face as she leaned back against the leather-upholstered seat.

Taylor leaned close, his hair sweeping down across one eye. "You're out of your element, Bella. I'm more practiced than you are at this type of behavior. They may listen to your words, but they won't believe my leg is healed until I've convinced them."

She stiffened and looked away in an attempt to push down the boiling anger that was welling up inside. If she spoke, her words would spew out the anger she felt for this man. Rather than speak, she shifted her body toward the buggy door and directed her gaze at the passing scenery.

"Don't be angry with me, dear Bella," Taylor whispered, his breath on her neck causing her to shiver. "I want to be friends. Give me just a little smile," he pleaded. Still leaning close, he ran his finger along her cheek.

Unable to restrain herself any longer, Bella slapped his hand away from her face. "Keep your hands to yourself!" she hissed through clenched teeth as the carriage came to a halt.

Bella noted Taylor's obvious lack of pain as he stepped out of the carriage and offered her his hand. "May I assist you?"

"Oh no, I don't need any help. You take care of yourself. I wouldn't want you to hurt that leg."

Miss Addie gave her a sweet smile. "That was very kind of you, dear."

"Obviously Miss Addie didn't notice the sarcasm dripping from your reply," Taylor commented as they sauntered toward the gray-slate church building.

"Nor your lack of discomfort when you jumped out of the carriage," Bella replied. She chastised herself for speaking to him. Silence! That was the key to ridding herself of Taylor Manning. Somehow his words forced a rebuttal from her lips. If nothing else, surely all those years in the Shaker community had taught her restraint. She merely needed to put that teaching into practice.

Bella caught her breath as they entered the sanctuary of St. Anne's. The midmorning sun was glowing through huge stained-glass windows, casting a rainbow of colors across the rows of walnut pews. Midway down the aisle, Miss Addie stopped beside a pew. John unlatched a small door permitting them entrance to their seats.

"Why are there doors on the pews?" Bella whispered to Miss Addie.

"The sermons are boring, and the doors prevent our escape," Taylor said with a snicker.

Bella ignored his reply and waited for a response from Miss Addie. "In the winter, the church is difficult to heat. It's so large," she said, glancing toward the high ceiling, "and the heat all rises upward. In order to keep everyone a bit warmer, heating bricks or warming pans are placed on the floor inside each pew. The doors help keep the heat in," she explained. "However, I must add that there are probably others who share young Taylor's view," she said, giving him an agreeable smile. "Oh, here's Mintie," she exclaimed. "Do unlatch the door, Taylor."

"Good morning, all," Mintie greeted, squeezing herself into the seat alongside Taylor. Pushing against Taylor's chest with her parasol, she bent forward in an effort to gain her sister's attention. "Will you be attending the picnic, Adelaide?"

"Yes, we're all attending. And you?"

Mintie peered over the top of her glasses and pursed her lips. Before she could reply, her attention was drawn toward the girls entering the pew in front of them. Once again making use of her parasol, she tapped one of the girls on the shoulder. "You girls need to go to one of the pews near the rear of the church. That pew belongs to the Behren family."

Bella watched as the girls, their cheeks flushed with embarrassment, vacated the pew and hastened toward the rear of the church while the finely dressed citizens of Lowell strolled down the aisle, stopping to visit with one another as they moved toward their seats. Chattering and laughter had been evident in all the churches Bella had visited thus far. Worship in the churches of Lowell was unusual—so different from Canterbury, where the women and men formed separate rows and marched in through their individual doors of the Meeting House, with men on one side and women on the other, quietly taking their seats on opposing sides. What would Sister Mercy think if she could see Bella sitting beside a gentleman during church services? Well, perhaps not a gentleman, but a man, she decided.

Taylor leaned toward her. "You might want to take note of the fashions these women are wearing and give thought to wearing dresses that are a little more—" he hesitated a moment— "becoming?"

Bella held her tongue and remained silent. *How dare he comment on my apparel,* she thought. Obviously her Sunday Shaker dress didn't meet the standards of the world, but it was all she owned, and it was neat, clean, and freshly pressed.

"No need to clench up like that," he said. "Feel free to say whatever it is you're thinking."

Bella remained silent and kept her gaze turned forward, giving full attention to the services that had now begun. She wanted to impartially evaluate each church she attended. Otherwise, how could she decide where she belonged? Besides, it shouldn't be so difficult to find a church that followed the Bible's teachings. And yet, if that were true, why were there so many divergent beliefs? The Shakers had added Mother Ann's teachings to those of the Bible, and each of the Protestant churches appeared to have something that set it apart from the others, like the way they baptized or took communion. And the Catholics had their own way of interpreting things, too. It was, she decided, not such an easy matter to determine where one belonged.

"You're frowning," Taylor whispered an hour later as the benediction was given. "It doesn't become you."

"Shh!" Miss Mintie hissed with an index finger placed over her pursed lips.

"I was only—"

Before Taylor could complete his reply, Miss Mintie jabbed a sharp elbow into his side. "Quiet!" she commanded.

Bella arched her eyebrows and gave Taylor a warning look. Obviously Miss Mintie was a force to be reckoned with; she was not about to put up with Mr. Manning's tomfoolery.

Taylor waited until Reverend Edson left the pulpit and had walked to the rear of the church before asking, "Do I now have your permission to speak, Miss Beecher?"

"Don't be foolish, Mr. Manning. The church service is over; of course you can speak. You understood exactly what I meant when I told you to be quiet. I will not tolerate rude behavior." She lifted her closed parasol and tapped the pointed end into his chest. "And you, Mr. Manning, were being rude."

Bella leaned around Taylor and smiled demurely at Miss Mintie. "Will you be joining us for lunch, Miss Beecher?"

Mintie shook her head. "I didn't pack a lunch, but perhaps I'll return for some of the afternoon activities."

Taking her cue from Taylor's apparent look of relief, Bella sprung into action. "We would love to have you join us. Miss Addie has packed enough food to feed a small army. Haven't you, Miss Adelaide?" Bella inquired while tugging on Addie's sleeve.

"Haven't I what?" Addie asked, turning away from her conversation with John and several other parishioners.

"Prepared ample food—so Miss Beecher may join us."

Addie nodded. "Well, of course, sister. You are more than welcome. To be honest, I anticipated you would join us."

Mintie appeared to be giving the matter grave consideration before giving her reply. "Well, I suppose I might as well stay."

Addie nodded, Bella grinned, and Taylor's expression wilted. They gathered momentarily outside the church before the men rushed off to fetch the picnic basket. "Don't forget to limp," Bella cautioned Taylor as she walked off with Mintie and Addie to seek a shade-covered site for their blanket.

Bella managed to seat herself between Mintie and Addie until they'd finished their lunch, but soon thereafter John suggested he and Addie take a stroll. Immediately Taylor moved to Bella's side, a lopsided grin spread across his face as he made himself comfortable.

"Gather up those dishes and hand them here," Mintie ordered Taylor as she began packing the leftovers into the wicker basket. "You can lie around in the sunshine after we're done."

Taylor grimaced as he dutifully followed Miss Mintie's commands and helped pack, fold, and organize everything to the older woman's satisfaction. "Have we finished?"

"You do have a smart tongue, young man. It's obvious we're finished—there's nothing more to put in the basket, is there?"

Taylor gave her a sheepish grin. "No, ma'am."

Mintie brushed some imaginary crumbs from the folds of her skirt and then directed her attention toward Bella. "I'm pleased we have this time together, Bella. I've been wanting to ask you about those Shakers up in Canterbury," she began. "I've heard all kinds of stories about them."

"Really? Like what?" Bella inquired.

"That they dance and twirl around in church and sometimes even commence to shouting and running during worship. I also heard," she continued, "that the women and men can't even talk to each other. Is that true?"

"There's dancing during church, and occasionally someone becomes filled with the Spirit and whirls, but the dancing isn't like the world's dances. Our dancing is a form of worship offered to God. I don't know who told you the men and women can't speak to each other, but that isn't so. The men and women converse, but a man and woman are not permitted to go off alone and keep company," she explained.

Mintie nodded. "So how does that work?"

"Yes," Taylor chimed in. "How does that work?"

"We converse during Union Meetings about topics of interest. For instance, if I found a piece of literature particularly interesting and one of the gentlemen was also fascinated by the same writing, we would sit opposite each other in Union Meeting and discuss the merits of that piece of work."

"But didn't those conversations cause men and women with similar interests to become attracted to one another?" Taylor inquired.

"The conversations were never intimate, and if the elders

feared any impropriety might arise, they would have another person join you."

"And did that ever happen?" Taylor asked, moving closer.

"Yes, frequently," Bella replied honestly.

Taylor appeared taken aback. "To you?"

Bella laughed and then felt a blush begin to rise in her cheeks. "Only once."

Suddenly Miss Mintie became interested. "Aha! So that's why you left. You have a beau," she announced smugly.

"No, it wasn't like that," Bella defended. "Jesse is my friend—just like Daughtie. We had made plans to leave Canterbury because we didn't believe the teachings of Mother Ann—at least that's why I left. However, I fear Daughtie came along because of my influence rather than her own convictions."

"And this Jesse, why did he leave?" Mintie inquired.

Taylor drew closer, his gaze unwavering as she answered.

"I'm not certain he left," she quietly replied. "He didn't appear as planned, so Daughtie and I left on our own. You see, we were a little late arriving at the meeting place we'd decided upon, and I don't know if he decided to go on without us or if he arrived after us and left on his own. Or perhaps when we didn't arrive, he remained behind."

"Or never appeared at all! Just like a man—leaving you to fend for yourself," Mintie retorted.

Bella glanced up at Miss Mintie. The older woman's words echoed Bella's thoughts, but she hadn't wanted to give voice to them. Jesse had failed her, just as her father had in the past.

"Well, it's not as though he had pledged his love," Taylor replied, obviously feeling a need to defend the man.

"Yes he had. He said he loved me and wanted to be married," Bella blurted out without thinking. She wanted to snatch back the words the moment they were spoken. Miss Mintie was giving her a pitying look while Taylor appeared self-satisfied—pleased that he had successfully elicited such revealing information.

He reached over and patted Bella's hand. "Don't spend another minute concerning yourself with this Jesse fellow. I always have time for a beautiful woman," he said while running his fingers through the hair that had fallen across his forehead.

Bella felt herself become rigid at his words. He was going to use this to his advantage if she didn't soon turn things around. "Miss Beecher, did you know that the Shakers believe in the complete equality of men and women?" she inquired.

"You don't say! Now, that's a belief I could probably take hold of," she said. "Tell me more," she encouraged, giving Bella her rapt attention.

She quickly determined that she wouldn't explain the basis for the equality. Instead, Bella decided she would explain the benefits of equality. After all, Miss Mintie might look askance once she realized such equality was based upon the Shaker's belief that Mother Ann represented the second embodiment of Christ's spirit. The first, of course, had been Jesus, but this second embodiment in a woman now made both sexes equal—at least that's what Mother Ann proclaimed. It was only one of several proclamations Bella couldn't bring herself to accept. But just because she didn't accept Mother Ann's deity didn't mean Bella didn't believe in the equality of men and women.

"The men and women share equally in all things. There is nothing granted to a man over a woman—or a woman over a man. The Shakers have both male and female Elders; they share work equally. They are educated equally. If a woman is more skilled in caring for the ill or keeping ledgers, she is permitted to do so. Women may discuss matters of social concern on equal footing with men and are encouraged to make their views known. The men don't go off into a drawing room and discuss matters of import while the women are relegated to gossip and stitchery in the parlor."

"Now, that makes good common sense. Women are every bit as bright as men. Personally, I believe they fear we are more intelligent, and that is why they send us off to another room. Now the Judge, my deceased father," she explained, "tended to be more like your Shakers—at least in that respect. Well, only where I was concerned. He never included Adelaide in discussions regarding the business of the day because, quite frankly, she wasn't interested. But I was. The Judge and I would talk well into the evening hours. He coveted my thoughts and opinions regarding matters of substance. Men like the Judge are few and far between," Mintie soulfully replied. "My, how I miss that man," she added softly.

"I believe in equality for women," Taylor interjected.

Both women turned to stare at him, Bella giving him a look of disbelief. "Did you say you believe in equality?" she asked.

He puffed his chest. "Yes, absolutely."

"Why, that's marvelous news, Taylor. Then I assume you'll be permitting the young ladies of Lowell access to the Mechanics Association library and lectures. Isn't that wonderful, Miss Beecher?"

Taylor turned ashen while Bella smiled and reveled in the moment.

CHAPTER *10*

Liam Donohue planted his work-worn hands on his hips and gave a satisfied nod. He'd been working in the home of James Paul Green, known as J. P. to his close associates. And although Liam wasn't considered such an associate, Mr. Green had specifically sought him out to carve and lay the intricate stonework he desired around each of the five fireplaces in his fancy Boston home. Unfortunately, the work had been both tedious and worrisome. Liam had split, shaped, and sculpted the granite, fieldstone, limestone, flagstone, shale, and slate into a combination of sizes, shapes, and textures, all with an eye toward enhancing the imported Italian tiles that had been individually carved as the focal point of each fireplace. Liam had been handsomely paid for the work, but most of the funds had already been sent to Ireland to care for his aging parents as well as several brothers and sisters who still remained at home.

A satisfied smile graced Mr. Green's lips as he surveyed the fireplace in the library that doubled as his office. "You've done a fine job, Liam. I don't believe an Englishman could have performed better stonework."

Liam held his tongue, though it was difficult. Personally, he doubted whether Mr. Green could have found anyone to perform better stonework, much less an Englishman.

"If you're in need of a recommendation, please use my name," he said while extending his hand.

Liam gripped Mr. Green's soft, fleshy hand in a muscular handshake. "I'll be thankin' ya for yar kind offer. I'll not be in Boston long, 'owever. I've been offered a position in Lowell, and I'll be leavin' once I've finished cleanin' up here," he said in a thick Irish brogue.

Rubbing his jawline, J. P. leaned against the walnut mantel in a swaggering fashion. "So it's Lowell you're off to. I have many connections there, also. Nathan Appleton, one of the founders of the Boston Associates, is my partner in the shipping business. We export almost all of the textiles produced in Lowell," he said. "Surely you're not going to waste your talents building mills?"

"No. At least not for the present. Hugh Cummiskey contacted me regardin' the Catholic church bein' constructed in Lowell. He's hired me to complete the decorative stonework at the church. After that job's completed, I'm not sure what I'll be doin'. But certain I am the good Lord will provide."

Green gave him a derisive laugh. "After you've seen the living conditions of your fellow countrymen in Lowell, I'd wager you'll be looking to your own talents for provision. I don't think God's spending much time providing for the Irish," he callously remarked before continuing. "Appears you'll be finished before noon. I'm expected at a meeting in a few minutes. You can let yourself out."

Liam nodded, glancing over his shoulder as Green exited the house. He might need Mr. Green's recommendation one day. Otherwise he would have told Mr. J. P. Green what he thought of arrogant, uncaring men who grew fat and stodgy while others starved.

Leaning down to gather his tools, Liam began placing them in his case and then sat down in front of the fireplace to clean a small trowel. He scraped at the tool, his glance shifting toward the hearth. A bundle of papers was lying in the grate alongside several pieces of wood. Reaching in, he pulled out one of the pages and gave it a cursory glance. It had writing on only one side.

Did J. P. Green not realize that the other side of the paper could be used for writing letters, drawing plans, or compiling lists? He glanced toward the hallway, wishing Mr. Green hadn't left. If Liam took the paper, it would be put to good use and save him hard-earned coins. Surely Mr. Green wouldn't consider it stealing. After all, if he left it in the fireplace, the papers would be destroyed.

Folding the pages, Liam packed them into his satchel, left the house, and made his way to the Beacon House, where he would board a stagecoach for Lowell. He'd considered going by boat, using the canals that wound their way into Lowell, but he didn't want to wait until morning.

He pulled a thick-crusted chunk of bread from a loaf he'd purchased earlier that morning and sat in front of the hostelry.

Within half an hour, the coach came rumbling into town at breakneck speed. The driver yanked back on the reins, which caused the wide-eyed horses to dig their hooves into the dusty roadway and bring the coach to a jarring halt. The carriage continued to sway on its leather straps for several minutes, the driver appearing to take great pleasure in the jostling he'd caused his passengers.

Spitting a stream of tobacco juice, the driver jumped down from atop the carriage. "All out that's getting out," he hollered, pulling open the door.

Several frazzled, travel-worn passengers disembarked from the coach as the driver tossed their baggage onto the street. "You that's riding with me, get on in there. I ain't got time to waste. I'm on a schedule," the driver barked.

Liam and two other men boarded the coach, all of them seated along one end of the coach facing two women on the opposing side. He was grateful the center seat remained empty, permitting them a bit more space for their legs.

"Schedule? Not so as anybody would notice," one of the women called back. "The only time you hurry is to delight yourself in throwing us around inside this torture chamber."

The driver chortled and slapped his leg. "Surely you don't think I'd do such a thing as that, ma'am," he said, his coarse laughter continuing as he climbed up to his perch.

"That man is a maniac," the woman said to no one in particular as the driver flicked the reins and the coach lumbered out of town.

"He seems to have settled down a bit," one of the men commented as they made their way through the outskirts of Boston.

A wry smile crossed the woman's lips. "Just wait. He takes great delight in urging the horses into a full gallop when we're on a deep-rutted road or crossing a rickety bridge. And don't bother asking to get out and walk across the bridges—he ignores our pleas," she warned.

Regrettably, the woman's words proved accurate. By the time the stage rolled into Lowell, Liam had bounced off the side of the coach, as had everyone near him. His body was bruised, and his head ached. He'd lost count of how many times his head had thumped the top of the carriage. At least those huge leghorn hats provided the women's heads with a bit of protection.

He stepped down from the coach, thankful he had to travel no farther and sorry for those who would remain and go beyond Lowell. The woman was right—the driver was a maniac. He enjoyed every minute of discomfort the passengers had endured. Liam picked up his case of tools, which the driver had tossed to the ground. He'd kept his satchel with him in the coach and now slung it across his shoulder as he glanced in all directions.

"That way," the driver snapped as he pointed northwest.

Liam gave him a look of surprise.

"You're going to the Acre, ain't ya?"

Liam nodded.

"Well, it's thataway. You'll know when you've arrived," he declared before throwing the remaining luggage onto the ground.

"Thank you," Liam replied and headed off.

Lowell certainly wasn't as large as Boston, but it was a likeable town, he decided, passing the shops that lined Merrimack

Street. It appeared to be a place where a man could settle down and be happy. He walked onward, not sure how he was to know when he'd arrived at the Acre, but he was enjoying the sights while remaining mindful to watch for his destination. He passed the mills, impressed with the brick facades and grandeur of the buildings with their many windows and small flower gardens. Soon the well-kept street ended, and a few rods from the canals, Liam was confronted with a hodgepodge of shanties built of slabs and rough boards that varied in height from about six to nine feet high. Stacked flour barrels or lime casks sat on the roofs, obviously topping out the fireplaces inside the shacks. Chinked-out holes served as windows, while makeshift doors hung open, with pigs and chickens roaming freely from the muddy streets into the shanties. Liam shuddered at the sight. The Acre.

"I'm lookin' for Hugh Cummiskey," he told a raggedly clothed boy sitting outside one of the hovels.

"Over at the church," the boy replied, running his hand across the dirt smudge on his face and then pointing toward the church.

Liam nodded and thanked the boy before heading off to the church. Mercifully, the church was as Cummiskey had described, an edifice worthy of a skilled stonemason. At least something in this part of town wasn't an eyesore. Liam approached a group of men preparing to leave for the night. "Can ya be tellin' me where I might find Hugh Cummiskey?"

One of the men stopped directly in front of Liam. "Who wants to know?"

"Liam Donohue, stonemason from Boston."

The man nodded. "He's inside. Go on in."

Liam voiced his thanks and entered the building. No doubt it was going to be a beautiful church once completed. Nothing comparable to the great churches of Ireland, but a fine structure nonetheless.

"Are you looking for work?" a man asked, walking up behind Liam.

Liam turned. "I think I've found it," he replied. "I'm Liam

Donohue, stonemason from Boston, lookin' for Hugh Cummiskey," he once again explained.

"Well, you've found him," Hugh replied, holding out a beefy hand. "So you're Liam Donohue. I pictured you to be a bigger man," he said in a light, almost nonexistent brogue. Apparently the man had worked to rid himself of sounding too Irish.

"Go on with yarself. I'm big enough to get the job done, and besides, I'm not thinkin' ya've got much size on me," Liam retorted with a quick grin.

Hugh laughed and slapped him on the shoulder. "Well, then, I don't imagine your stature is of any consequence. What do you think of our church?"

Liam took another glance about the building. "It appears to be the only structure o' consequence in all of this part of town. I'm understandin' this is called the Acre?"

Hugh nodded. "That it is, or the Paddy camp, or New Dublin, or any number of derogatory names the Yanks could think of since we first arrived to build this place. We came to build the mills and canals—all of the heavy manual work. Some refer to us as lords of the spade. No matter—I suppose that's what we are. The Associates have continued their expansion in Lowell, which has been good for us. Their expansion provides us with jobs. 'Course, more and more of our countrymen have arrived from Ireland looking for work. But now the Yanks are beginning to raise a ruckus. They don't want any more Irish settling in Lowell."

"Aye. The good folks of Boston aren't overly welcomin', either, although I expected wee better living conditions here."

Hugh shook his head back and forth. "We're on the same small acre of land me and my men camped on when we first arrived here. The Yanks won't let us expand any farther if they can avoid it. Trouble is, we don't help matters much. There's still the fightin' among the clans, which the Yanks use against us. Fact is, the Corporation donated the land for this church in the hope it would bring the clans together. I'm hoping it will help."

"Seems that sometimes we hurt ourselves even more than the outsiders do," Liam noted.

"That's true. Come on now and let me show you what I've got in mind for this stonework. I'd be pleased if you could do some carving for us, but we'll have to see what that will cost. I fear your talent is beyond our purse."

Liam smiled. "We'll see. I'm sure we can work somethin' out. My dear old mother back in Ireland would never forgive me if I rejected work for the church."

The two men talked for several hours, well into the evening. Liam's excitement over the stone designs in the new church had surpassed the gnawing of his stomach, but now it would not be silenced. "It's getting late, Hugh. I've not found a place to live, nor have I eaten since I departed from Boston early today."

Hugh nodded. "I've kept you much too long. Come along with me. You can spend the night at my house, and tomorrow morning we'll find a sleeping space for you to rent."

Cummiskey's home far surpassed anything else in the Acre, yet it was little more than a hovel. The meal, however, was another matter. Not only was Hugh's wife cheerful, but she could cook a meal that would give his own mother strong competition. Both the meal and clean bed provided a welcome sanctuary for which Liam was thankful.

Early the next morning, Liam's safe haven disappeared like a mist. The pealing of the tower bell startled him awake hours before any of the roosters wandering the Acre had been given an opportunity to announce dawn's arrival.

"I'll take you to meet Noreen Gallagher," Hugh said as they finished their five o'clock breakfast. "My wife tells me Noreen may have a sleeping space for rent."

Liam glanced about the candlelit room. "Will she be awake at this time of the day?"

Hugh's laughter filled the small room. "She'll be up. The bells that wakened you this morning do the same for all the other residents of this town. It's not just those working inside the mills whose lives are governed by the sound of the bells. Noreen's no exception. The people living with her either work for the Corporation or are looking to get hired. Either way, she'll have them up and out of her house as soon as humanly possible."

Liam wasn't certain that calling upon someone at this time of day was entirely suitable, but he placed his reliance in Hugh. After profusely thanking Mrs. Cummiskey for her kindness, he gathered up his belongings and followed Hugh out the door and into the muddy street that fronted the hovel. They followed the crooked road until it became no more than a path winding its way among the maze of shacks. Hugh stopped short and pounded on the door of one of the shanties. A wiry woman with matted reddish-brown hair cracked open the dilapidated piece of wood that served as a front door She blinked against the darkness, obviously unable to make out the faces of her visitors.

"It's Hugh Cummiskey, Noreen. I've brought you a new tenant."

The woman stepped aside, permitting them entry. "Mr. Cummiskey! Come in, come in."

She bent from the waist while gesturing her arm in a sweeping motion that crossed her body, obviously pretending royalty had arrived on her doorstep. Liam smiled. Perhaps she wasn't pretending. Conceivably Mr. Cummiskey was viewed as royalty among the residents of the Paddy camp.

The smell of fetid bodies mingled with the odor of a mangy dog, two chickens, and an indistinguishable scent that curled upward from an iron pot hanging over the fire. The stench nearly caused Liam to retch. Filthy pallets lined the floor where the dirty bodies had lain only a short time earlier. The group now sat huddled near the fire, spooning the foul-smelling concoction that bubbled over the fire into makeshift bowls.

"Mr. Donohue's in need of a sleeping space, and my wife said you had one available. That true?" Hugh inquired.

The woman narrowed her eyes into thin slits and looked Liam up and down. She appeared to evaluate his every feature. "Have ya money to pay?" she asked, her gaze darting toward his bags.

Liam nodded. "Could I talk to you alone for a moment, Mr. Cummiskey?" Liam inquired.

Noreen gave Liam a disgruntled look but moved to the fire when Hugh waved her away. "Is there a problem, Liam?"

He didn't want to appear ungrateful—or offensive. He hesitated a moment and then cleared his throat. "Might there be another place, uh, a hotel, or . . ."

Cummiskey shook his head. "You've the luck of the Irish with you to find this," he replied. "As for a hotel—we've no such luxury in the Acre, and ya'd not be welcome at the Wareham. Yanks only, ya know." His brogue seemed a bit more pronounced.

"I see. Well, then, I suppose I'll stay here, but if you or your missus should 'ear of anything better, would ya keep me in mind?"

Hugh nodded his head. "That I'll do, my boy, that I'll do," he said before waving Noreen back to where they stood.

"I'll vouch for Mr. Donohue. He'll be working with me over at the church, so you've no need to worry about being paid regular. See that he gets a decent place to sleep—and you might try cooking something of substance for your tenants," he suggested with a glance toward the fireplace. "I'm sure you could find yourself a few potatoes to toss in with that water you boil every day."

Noreen dug the toe of her shoe into the dirt floor as a splash of red tinged her cheeks. Liam wasn't sure if the woman's embarrassment was due to the poor treatment of her tenants or the fact that Hugh Cummiskey had noted her neglect. Probably the latter, he surmised.

"We're heading off to work at the church, but Mr. Donohue will be back this evening. I trust he'll find enough food to fill his belly, Noreen."

"If 'e pays me before you leave, 'e will," Noreen countered.

The woman watched closely as Liam reached into his satchel and then handed her two dollars, which, from the gleam in her eyes, was more than she'd received in many a day.

"Where'd ya work before comin' to this place?" she asked while rubbing the coins in her hand.

"Boston."

Hugh gave Liam a reassuring pat on the back. "Mr. Donohue's a stonemason—very talented. God's blessed us yet again by sending him to work for us."

The woman kept her gaze fixed on Liam's satchel. "Indeed, a blessin'," she agreed, reaching out toward the shoulder strap of Liam's bag. "Ya can leave yar belongings here. I'll see to them while ya're at work."

Liam turned, stepping out of her grasp. "No, I'll keep my belongings with me," he replied before joining Hugh outside the shanty.

Hugh gave him a hearty laugh as they walked back down the muddy path. "I know Noreen's place isn't particularly appealing, but I doubt you'll spend much time there. Most of the single men spend their evenings at the pub."

Liam's thoughts wandered back to the boardinghouse where he'd roomed in the Irish part of Boston. It hadn't been palatial by any means, but the house had been neat and clean, and the food had been wholesome and plentiful. Liam wasn't one to spend his time sitting in pubs, but there was no doubt he would soon begin. A reasonable alternative to Noreen's shack would be a necessity.

"Once you've begun your work at the church, I'll head off for the canal. We're running a few days behind, and I need to push the blokes a bit," Hugh said as they moved toward the church.

"Perhaps you need to hire some extra help," Liam suggested.

Hugh gave a growling snort and pushed back his flat woolen cap. A mop of black curly hair fell across his forehead. "The Yanks are already up in arms about the number of Irish living and working in Lowell. There are about five hundred of us now. The Yanks want us to perform their labor and disappear like a vapor until we're needed for some other grueling manual labor. Instead, they must face the fact that the Irish are here to stay. They don't like that idea, and they surely want no more of us coming here."

"So that's why ya instructed me to say me work was temporary?"

"Exactly," Hugh replied. "But as I told you, I'm certain I can keep you busy should you decide you want to remain in Lowell.

Personally, I'm anxious to have skilled artisans stay among us."

"Ya don't think ya'd be happier somewhere else? A place where ya'd feel more welcome?" Liam inquired.

"Hah! And where would that be, Liam? Surely you don't think there's a city out there anxious to see the Irish arrive? Lowell's not a bad place for the Irish—better than most. I've made my place here and you can, too, if you like. Keep yourself clean, work hard, stay away from the liquor, and try to stay out of the Yanks' way."

Liam felt an overwhelming sadness envelop him. "What I'd be likin' is for all of us to 'ave the same advantages as the Yanks born in this country without anyone carin' for whether we were born in Ireland—or any other country, for that matter. I'd like a bit of equality for all of us."

"Well, I doubt you'll find that here or anywhere else, my friend. We're a step above the slaves down South, but the Yanks will make sure we don't move much higher. It seems as if we get one matter of dissension solved between us and another arises."

"Like what?" Liam inquired.

"As I told you earlier, the Yanks feel we're taking jobs away from them, even though a few years ago they wouldn't consider dirtying their hands with this kind of work. When there's a fire anywhere but the Acre, the fire company shows up to fight the blaze. But they don't come here—they'd prefer the whole Acre burn to the ground. I suppose the most recent agitation with the Yanks is due to the Irish girls that have come up missing. No one seems to care. We can't even get the police to talk to the families. I tried—even went and talked to the police myself—but they don't appear to care," Hugh explained.

Liam stopped outside the church and turned toward Hugh. "How long have these girls been missin'? Would they be knowin' each other? Were they all separate incidents?"

"Do you double as a policeman?" Hugh inquired with a chuckle.

"No, but this is a frightenin' matter."

"That it is. All the girls have been of marrying age, but none involved with a fellow; all of them were pretty. The girls knew each other—we all know each other in the Acre. Each one disappeared at a different time and from a different place," Hugh explained. "I fear the Yanks' lack of concern will soon cause some of our men to retaliate against them."

Liam shook his head. "Not against their womenfolk?"

"Let's hope not. I've been talkin' my heart out to them. Violence returned for violence serves none of us well," Hugh replied.

CHAPTER 11

Bella gathered with twelve other girls in the parlor of Miss Addie's boardinghouse, a stack of books on her lap. She gave the group a tentative smile, uncertain whether the others shared her passion for this idea.

"How long will we be?" Jennie asked. "Lucy and I are going to Mr. Whidden's store; a new shipment of lace arrived this morning," she added, already wiggling in her seat.

"I suppose it depends on how interested we are in expanding our minds," Bella replied more curtly than she'd intended.

Jennie appeared offended. "You needn't attempt to make me feel guilty because I want to purchase a piece of lace, Bella."

"I'm sorry, Jennie. You and Lucy, and any of the rest of you," she said as she looked about the room, "may leave whenever you choose. The purpose of this gathering was to determine if there's enough interest for us to form a literary circle. I have a few books Miss Addie has donated for our use until we can perhaps purchase some others."

Lucy straightened in her chair while furrowing her brow. "I thought you convinced Taylor Manning we should be admitted to the Mechanics Association library. I'd rather use their books."

"I'm not sure Mr. Manning was able to secure agreement from the membership. And even if he does, it would be laudable if we had some books and offered to donate them to their library, don't you think?" Bella asked.

"Perhaps," Lucy replied with little conviction in her voice.

"I don't have money to spend on books. My family needs every cent I can send," Hannah dolefully responded.

Bella smiled at the girl. "I realize that for you and several others who must send all of your money home, purchasing books is out of the question. But others of us, the ones who have additional funds to purchase a piece of jewelry or lace, might want to think about using the money for a book instead."

Hannah raised her hand, and Bella nodded toward her. "If we don't help purchase books, will we still be permitted to read them and join in with your group?"

"That would certainly be my desire, Hannah. There are many good things we could accomplish as a group—not just for ourselves but for others, as well."

Jennie gave her an apprehensive look. "Like what?"

"Tutoring lessons for the girls who have difficulty reading, and perhaps classes or topical discussions of foreign languages, literature, or current events. I even hoped we might secure enough funds to host our own speakers from time to time—a poet, perhaps. If we can elicit enough interest, we could charge an admission fee to help defray costs of the speaker, and if we could host the event at St. Anne's or one of the other churches, it might be successful," Bella enthusiastically offered. "We could start out with a lending library among the girls in all of the mills, not just the Appleton."

"I think it's a wonderful idea," Ruth agreed.

Addie pulled off her apron as she entered the room. "Yes, it is. And you girls should use every opportunity available to expand your education. After all, an education is something no one can ever take away from you."

Bella smiled as a murmur of excitement began filling the parlor. "Perhaps our first step would be to schedule a meeting inviting all of the girls."

Miss Addie nodded. "If you girls make invitations, I'll deliver them to each of the boardinghouses and ask the keepers to post them for their girls."

"That would be wonderful," Bella replied. "We could work on the invitations tomorrow evening. Oh, but where can we meet? Do you think St. Anne's would give us permission to meet there?" she asked, turning toward Addie.

"I'll go and talk with Reverend Edson tomorrow, and although I'm certain there will be no problem using the church, I think he'll want to know exactly what day and time you plan to meet. Perhaps you should give me several dates in case there's a conflict," Addie suggested.

"If there's nothing else," Jennie said, "Lucy and I want to leave for town."

"I told you earlier, you're free to leave whenever you want," Bella said, unable to hide her irritation. "No one is forcing you to expand your mind, Jennie."

"There's no need to scorn me," Jennie replied as a knock sounded at the front door. Turning on her heel, Jennie marched into the hallway and pulled open the front door.

Bella glanced toward the open door just as John Farnsworth and Taylor Manning entered. "Good evening, everyone," John greeted the group of ladies in the parlor. "I hope we're not disturbing anything," he said, giving Addie a questioning look.

Before Addie could answer, Jennie sidled up to Taylor. "I understand the Mechanics Association has refused permission for us to use their library. Rather selfish, I'd say."

"To be quite frank, I haven't made a proposal to the association regarding your use of the library just yet."

"You haven't?" Bella asked, walking closer.

Jennie gave Bella a triumphant grin. "Oh my, Bella! It appears as if Mr. Manning didn't take your request seriously." She turned toward Taylor. "Now you've gone and done it."

Taylor appeared totally confused. "Done what?" he asked.

"I believe you may have offended our literary organizer. I doubt whether Bella will want to keep company with the likes of you, Mr. Manning. However," she said resting a hand on his arm, "I wouldn't be affronted if you would care to call upon me." She gave him a beguiling smile before flashing Bella a fleeting glance of victory. "Would you care to accompany Lucy and me into town?"

John moved forward, breaking Jennie's grasp on Taylor's arm. "I'm afraid Taylor is with me this evening," he replied on behalf of his nephew.

"That's a shame," Jennie responded, fluttering her eyelashes.

"Or perhaps a blessing," John muttered as he and Miss Addie moved into the parlor. "I didn't realize you were otherwise occupied this evening," John apologetically remarked.

Bella followed behind Taylor as he made his way along with John and Miss Addie. She wanted to find out why he hadn't bothered to talk to the Mechanics Association on her behalf.

Addie patted his arm. "There's no need to concern yourself, John. After all, I knew you were coming to visit this evening. I think the girls have completed their business, and they'll be scattering into town or up to their rooms. We can go into the dining room if you prefer."

"No, no, I enjoy the young people."

Addie gave him a bright smile. "I'm pleased Taylor came along. Perhaps he and Bella will have time to visit about the association's library. The girls are planning a meeting to form a literary group." She glanced over her shoulder and smiled.

"Did I hear my name?" Taylor asked as he took the seat beside Miss Addie.

Addie nodded and beckoned him closer. "Indeed you did. I was just telling your uncle that some of the girls are hoping to form a literary group. Bella was under the assumption the men had voted against the girls using their library."

Taylor shook his head. "Well, it sounds as though Bella is taking my advice and starting her own little reading circle. Besides, I never told Bella any such thing."

Bella seethed. "No, but you made it clear you didn't like the idea. I knew you wouldn't promote the concept of nonmembers using your library, and I was correct. You didn't even present it for a vote, did you?" she challenged.

Taylor grew wide-eyed as Bella marched toward him and then stopped directly in front of his chair. She was on the attack, and it was obvious Taylor was surprised at the confrontation.

"Well, did you?" she reiterated, her voice rising a decibel.

Taylor stood up and faced off, toe-to-toe with Bella. She didn't retreat. Instead, she looked upward into his eyes and leveled an accusatory stare. He looked down, his hair falling forward over one eye, which gave him a mischievous appearance.

He winked the other eye, gave her a playful grin, and in a velvet-smooth voice replied, "No, dear Bella, I didn't. But if you'd care to have a seat here beside me, I'd be happy to explain my egregious behavior."

"You find this enjoyable, don't you, Mr. Manning? Withholding something of value to others obviously makes you feel powerful. It's rather sad that your insecurity causes you to stoop to such a level," she retaliated.

"Wh—wh—what?" he stammered. Clearly shaken by her comment, Taylor lowered himself into a nearby chair. "You think I'm insecure?"

"Among other things," Bella said, plopping down on the settee while enjoying his obvious bafflement. "Why else are you afraid to permit women in your library?"

"It's not my library," he countered.

"Exactly!" she retaliated, pointing her finger. "So why don't you permit the membership to make the decision rather than withholding it on your own? Why didn't you present our request?"

John leaned forward and gave his nephew a hard stare. "Yes, Taylor, I'd be interested in your response to her question, also."

Taylor shifted in his chair like a caged animal seeking escape. "Well, I thought it could wait until our next meeting. We had a full agenda and several other committee meetings afterward. I have every intention of bringing it before the membership next week."

John shook his head back and forth. "I don't think that was your decision to make. You should have brought the request before the group and let them determine whether to act upon it or wait until the following meeting, Taylor. The Mechanics Association grants all members equal rights in the decision-making process."

Addie pulled a lace handkerchief from her sleeve and dabbed at her brow as she glanced back and forth between John and Taylor. Clearly, John's stern lecture to his nephew was causing her discomfort. "Perhaps Bella and I should prepare some tea," she suggested.

"Tea would be nice," Taylor replied, a grateful smile crossing his lips.

John nodded. "Yes, that would be fine."

Addie rose from the settee and waited a moment. "Bella?"

"What?" Bella unwillingly turned her gaze away from the unfolding scene between John and Taylor and gave Addie a questioning look. "Oh, you want me to help in the kitchen?" She remained seated and turned back toward Taylor, hoping Miss Addie would permit her to remain behind.

"Bella!"

No further words were necessary. Bella stood up and dutifully followed Miss Addie out of the room. Truth be known, she longed to remain in the parlor and hear John Farnsworth continue lecturing his nephew. Perhaps if she lagged behind just a little, she could catch a few more words. But it was not to be. Her ability to overhear the conversation was snuffed out by the clattering of dishes in the kitchen.

"Eavesdropping is unbecoming, my dear, and I believe young Taylor has already suffered enough embarrassment," Addie chastened.

Bella whirled around. "He brought this upon himself, Miss Addie. Surely you don't condone his behavior," Bella challenged.

Addie busied herself arranging a plate of biscuits. "I think Taylor used poor judgment. Clearly he was wrong. However, his uncle is taking him to task for his actions. I take no pleasure in observing his comeuppance."

A blush stained Bella's cheeks. "Unfortunately, I do, Miss Addie—my imperfection revealing itself. Sister Eunice enjoyed telling me my flawed character rose up as regularly as cream floating to the top of the milk." She frowned and thought maybe there was no hope for her character. She tried to be of a more generous nature—tried to offer forgiveness, knowing there would certainly be times when she needed it.

Miss Addie lovingly hugged Bella. "Oh, dear me. It doesn't sound as though Sister Eunice was a very charitable woman. You're a sweet girl, Bella, with many, many fine attributes. Any parent would be proud to have a fine daughter such as you. Why, you're bright and industrious and generally very kindhearted," she said with a bright smile.

A tear trickled down Bella's face and fell upon her bodice, the wetness creating a black splotch on the gray fabric.

"What is it, Bella? Why are you crying?" Addie's voice was filled with distress as she pulled Bella into another embrace. "I truly believe Taylor acted improperly, too," she said, obviously searching for a clue to the girl's tears.

"It's not Taylor," Bella sniffed, searching for her handkerchief. "It's what you said about any parent being proud to have me as a daughter," she continued in a warbly voice. "My father didn't feel that way about me. He chose life among the Shakers rather than living with his wife and daughter." The pain of her thoughts caused Bella to realize the source of so much bitterness. Her father had walked away from her as though she were nothing more than a spare dog.

"Oh, Bella," Addie lamented as she pulled the girl into a tighter embrace. "Sometimes we're not meant to understand— at least not at the time a particular happenstance occurs. Perhaps one day you and your father can discuss his decision and you'll have a clearer understanding of his motives. I know it's painful to feel rejected by your father. But you must remember that our heavenly Father is the only one who is perfect. We humans are flawed. Unfortunately, we tend to hurt those people we love the most. Possibly because we think they'll continue to love us in spite of our behavior, though I'm not sure that's always true," she added.

Bella leaned back and stared into Miss Addie's clear blue eyes. "Did your father love you?"

A faraway look clouded the older woman's eyes. "The Judge? Yes, he loved me—in his own way."

"What does that mean, 'in his own way'?" Bella asked.

Miss Addie removed the boiling water from the fire before she spoke. "He loved Mintie and me differently, but he loved us both. Equally, I believe. Mintie and I have very different personalities, so beyond his affectionate peck on the cheek each evening, the Judge exhibited his love uniquely to each of us. He would sit and discuss business matters with Mintie. He realized that doing so exhibited the fact that he valued Mintie's opinions; it expressed his love for her. With me, he would comment on my pretty dresses or ask me to accompany him to social events. He knew I enjoyed being in the company of others. He expressed his love for me by acting as my escort. However, he didn't tell us he loved us, and I truly wish he had. I'm not even sure whether he enjoyed those discussions with Mintie or attending dinner parties with me. But the time he spent with each of us was an expression of his love. And whether you choose to believe it or not, Bella, I'm certain your father loves you in his own way."

"I find it hard to believe my father loves me, Miss Addie, but I thank you for your kind words. I suppose we'd best get this tea into the parlor or Taylor and Mr. Farnsworth will think we've deserted them," Bella said, tucking her linen handkerchief into the pocket of her dress. "Of course, Taylor is most likely hoping I won't return," she added with a nervous giggle.

Addie chuckled. "I doubt that. I think Taylor has taken an interest in you," Addie remarked as she bustled off with one of the trays. "Bring the other tray, please," she said, walking out of the kitchen.

Bella stood staring after her. Taylor interested in her? Preposterous! The only person Taylor Manning cared about was himself.

Long after his evening with Bella and Miss Addie had concluded, Taylor Manning continued to think of their gathering.

Bella saw nothing wrong in speaking her opinion. He liked that in some ways but in others he found it annoying. She was certainly unlike any other young woman he'd had a chance to know. Usually all he had to do was smile or throw a girl a wink and she was his. Bella was clearly not going to be that easily conquered. Perhaps that was why Taylor found her all the more intriguing.

All of his life he'd known he had the charm and looks to captivate the girls. He'd used it to his advantage over and over. His mother's warnings aside, Taylor simply didn't see that it caused that much harm. Of course, there was that whole matter back in England. What a jolly time that had been.

But even as Taylor considered the women of his past, it was Bella's face that came to mind. She wasn't going to be easily swayed. He smiled. *Maybe not,* he reasoned, *but the game will be only that much more challenging. Winning Bella—bringing her to a place where she's captive to my charm—will give me something to do.* He snuffed out the candle beside his bed and smiled again. "Ah, Miss Newberry, if you only knew the plans I have for you."

CHAPTER 12

Liam hunkered down in a corner of Noreen's shanty. He longed for the peace and privacy the quiet room in Boston had afforded him. Noreen's place was filled with a constant din that she seemed to enjoy. If the room began to grow quiet, she would break the silence with her yammering until she stirred the others into a frenzy of noise and activity. Worse yet, he didn't trust the woman. Her frizzy auburn hair spiraled upward in wiry coils while her green-eyed gaze flitted about the room like the beacon in a lighthouse searching for trouble. It was obvious nothing in the house escaped her scrutiny. Moreover, she'd been obsessed with his belongings since the day he arrived, constantly encouraging him to leave them behind when he left for work in the morning.

His eyelids were growing heavy and he'd just begun to doze off when Noreen edged to his side and dropped to the floor. The odor of her body mixed with the smell of the cheap liquor she'd obviously been drinking all afternoon. The smell was dreadful. Liam leaned aside, hoping to avoid the stench. "And what would ya be wantin', Noreen?" he muttered.

"Just lookin' for some friendly conversation, Liam. I get

lonely stayin' in the 'ouse all day with nothing but my cookin' and cleanin' to keep me occupied."

Liam emitted a loud guffaw. "For sure ya must be keepin' yourself occupied with something other than cookin' or cleanin', woman. This place is filthy, and the food isn't fit to slop hogs."

"Now ya've gone and insulted me again. Why is that? For sure I'm just wantin' a little company. Used to be I could go and visit with me sister, Kathryn. Did I tell ya she died?" The words were slurred yet laced with an edge of melancholy.

"Several times," Liam replied.

She ignored his comment. "I loved Kathryn and the wee babe—little Cullan. Kathryn let me name him, did I tell ya that?" She didn't wait for an answer before continuing with her recitation. "Cullan was a sweet one, always smilin' and cooin'. He'd just begun to talk when Kathryn died. How I wish I coulda kept him. But I promised Kathryn that if anythin' ever happened to 'er, I'd see the boy was protected," she said, her voice trailing off.

Liam knew he'd regret asking, but his curiosity got the best of him. "What of the boy's father? Couldn't he care for 'im?"

Noreen turned a hate-filled stare in his direction. "Cullan's father is a well-to-do Yank. The child was born out o' wedlock. You can be bettin' yar life that the Yank would prefer the child 'ad never been born. I took Cullan away from Lowell because I feared for him."

Liam straightened a bit. "Ya think the Yank would have done the child harm?"

Noreen shrugged. "Who knows? But certain I am 'e worried his wife would find out about Kathryn and the child. He didn't want his powerful friends to be findin' out, either. It woulda been an embarrassment for 'im, now, wouldn't it? I told Kathryn he was takin' advantage of her, but she wouldn't listen. Ha! Tweren't nothin' lovable about that man," she spat.

"So you knew 'im?" Liam asked.

"I wasn't never formally introduced, but Kathryn told me his name, and I know how 'e treated her. He never worried about her welfare or the child's, for that matter. All he worried about was a warm bed where 'e could be takin' his pleasures. I couldn't have kept the child safe here in the Acre if the Yank had decided to do 'im harm. And I'd rather go the rest of my life without seeing Cullan than have harm come to him at his father's hand."

"If I was in your shoes, I'd be watchin' me tongue. Those are mighty strong accusations to be makin' against a Yank," Liam warned.

"I ain't worried. The Yanks don't care what some Irish-woman has to be sayin' about them. Besides, I'm speakin' the truth. The Yanks take advantage at every turn, treat us worse than animals, they do. Them highfalutin' Boston Associates never give one thought to the livin' conditions in the Acre. The only time thar thinkin' about us is when there's some canal to be dug out or stone to be hauled. It's not fair," she said, her eyes bleary from the ale.

"You'd best be gettin' some sleep, Noreen," Liam said.

He watched as Noreen moved off to the area she referred to as her room, which was merely a small space cordoned off by a blanket hanging across a piece of rope. Most likely everything she'd said was true. Distaste for the Irish was prevalent every-where, not just in Lowell. Yet he wondered about Noreen and how she reconciled the mistreatment she doled out to her kins-men. Did she not believe it grievous to furnish only putrid gruel and lice-infested bedding to her fellow Irishmen in exchange for their hard-earned coins? She constantly derided the Yanks for their misbehavior while nosing about to steal from one of her Irish boarders. She wasn't, Liam decided, much different from the Yanks whom she abhorred. Her behavior only confirmed what he already knew: he must locate another place to live, but until then, he needed a place to store his belongings. Leaving his satchel unattended in Noreen's shack was an invitation to disas-ter.

The next morning Liam bypassed the gruel bubbling in Noreen's fireplace. He decided he'd rather pay for a decent meal at the pub.

"You can leave your satchel here while ya're at work,"

Noreen said while grabbing at the sleeve of his jacket. "I'll watch after it for ya." She gave him a crooked smile and held out her hand. She recited the same litany each time he prepared to leave.

Liam pulled away. "I'll be takin' it with me," he said without meeting her gaze. Noreen's actions only served to confirm what Liam already knew—given any opportunity, Noreen would steal him blind.

It was a short distance from Noreen's hovel to the church; that was the only positive thing Liam could say about boarding with her. As usual, he was the first of the small crew to arrive at the church, even after stopping at the pub for breakfast. After lighting one of the whale-oil lamps inside the front door, he found a candle, held it to the flame of the lamp, and then located an opening in the foundation permitting entry into a crawl space under the church. The space was higher than he could have hoped, which allowed him easy movement on his hands and knees. Pulling a chisel from his coat pocket, Liam began to carefully loosen the mortar surrounding an interior stone. He dug until his fingers could finally grasp a tight hold on the piece of granite that abutted the outer wall of the foundation. Methodically, he wiggled the stone back and forth until he felt it release and then slid it forward, finally placing it on the dirt floor.

He placed the candle close at hand, removed a few belongings from the satchel, and carefully counted the money. He placed enough for a few meals in his jacket pocket and returned the remainder of the money to the satchel, along with some letters from home and a few personal items from Ireland.

The sheaf of papers he'd retrieved from J. P. Green's fireplace lay scattered before him. Liam gathered the pages, glancing from time to time at the long rows of figures—some sort of business accounts, he decided. He ruffled through the papers, hoping to find at least one sheet that was clean on both sides. Two weeks had passed since he'd written home, and his parents would be concerned if they didn't hear from him soon. He knew his parents well. Each letter would be bandied about the village for all to know that the Donohues' dutiful son was writing home and thriving in America. Permitting his parents a scrap of prominence among their neighbors was the least he could do for them, but he dare not waste any more time. Grabbing several sheets, he shoved them into the box with his tools and then returned the remainder of the pages to his bag. Wedging the satchel into the existing hole, Liam pushed the piece of granite back into place. The stone didn't fit tightly, but at least his satchel was out of Noreen's grasp.

Several men were arriving to work as Liam made his way back to the entryway of the church. "Did ya fall on yar way in to work, Liam?" one of the men asked while looking at Liam's trousers.

Liam glanced down and brushed off the dirt. "No, for sure I was doin' a few chores before startin' work," he replied.

"Ain't ya the industrious one," Thomas O'Malley commented with a boisterous laugh before heading off with several other men to work on the roof.

Liam gave him a broad smile in return. "Will ya be goin' to the pub for dinner, Thomas?"

"Sure! I'll be needin' a glass of ale come noon. If ya want to join me and some o' the boys, just meet us out front when the noon bell sounds."

"Aye, I'll do that," Liam replied, waving a hand before walking into the sanctuary to begin carving on a large block of limestone.

The morning hours passed quickly for Liam. The creativity of stonemasonry excited him, especially when he was given a bit of freedom. Unlike J. P. Green, who had insisted there be no deviation from his prepared sketches, Hugh Cummiskey had given Liam free rein in designing the stonework. It was a level of trust that Liam had never before experienced, and he was determined to excel.

When the noonday bell sounded, Liam's stomach was growling with hunger. Removing the coins from his toolbox, he placed them in his jacket pocket before joining the group of men in front of the church.

They made their way to the bar and found Michael Neil standing behind his makeshift bar, obviously awaiting the crowd.

"Ales all around?" he asked as the group entered the doorway.

The men gave their hearty approval to his question and soon were downing their mugs. Mrs. Neil appeared with crockery bowls filled with fish chowder and placed a bowl in front of each man. A young boy followed behind carrying loaves of soda bread. Liam tore off a chunk of the bread, dipping it into the creamy chowder before stuffing it into his mouth. It was the best food he'd eaten since leaving Boston.

"So what do you think of our church, Liam?" one of the men called from the end of the table. Beckoning to Mrs. Neil, he pointed toward his empty bowl. She refilled it and moved on to the next man. Liam wiped the back of his hand across his mouth and swallowed hard. "It's goin' to be a beauty, and I'm goin' to do my best to make sure o' that," he shouted back as he held up his mug of ale in salute. "It's a well-built church of good outward design. Any town would be proud to 'ave it in their midst."

"For once I think the Yanks are doin' right by us," O'Malley agreed.

Liam nodded. "I've looked that buildin' over, and it's a fine piece of architecture. Looks a bit out o' place among all the shanties, but you can be sure it'll stand the test of time. It's good and tight—secure! You could hide a king's ransom in that buildin' and it would be safe and sound."

"Probably a lot safer than those banks the Yanks are sayin' we should use. I can tell you that the Yanks and their fancy banks won't ever see a coin outta my pocket," O'Malley replied.

A middle-aged Irishman sitting at the bar turned and lifted his glass in the air. "If any of us had the good sense God gave the Irish, we'd hide our money and maybe even some rifles in the church. With the help of the good Lord, we could come together and overtake the Yanks and their fancy banks. I'm not about to mix any o' my money with the Yanks'. They'd steal us blind for sure. And there ain't a man here who doesn't believe we could run those mills better than the Yanks, but they ain't never gonna give us the chance. Only way we'll ever get outta the Acre is to take the town by force," he said in a slurred voice that seemed to quell the anger flashing in his eyes.

All gazes were fixed on the man as the barkeep snapped his fingers. "Settle yarself, Robert," he warned while glancing nervously about the room.

"I know there's them that don't belong in this pub that sit around snooping," the man slurred, turning to look toward a table in the corner. "That fancy pants from Boston comes to the Acre and noses about our business. I wonder how it would set if some of us went to the bar in the Wareham House and hid out in a corner listenin' to them Associates discuss their business. And ya don't suppose they'd mind if we were to take up with their women, do ya? After all, we've got the likes of 'im and his friends doin' just that," he continued while pointing toward the well-dressed man.

Liam leaned toward O'Malley. "Who is that Yank over there, and why's 'e in this place?"

"His name is William Thurston, and Robert's speakin' the truth. Thurston is one of the Boston Associates and he spends far too much time in the Acre. He had him an Irishwoman for quite a while, but then she died. . . ."

"Not Noreen Gallagher's sister?" Liam asked.

"Yeah, that's exactly who she was—Noreen's sister, Kathryn. Some folks say she had a baby by Thurston, but I'm not certain. She was married to a fellow named O'Hanrahan, but I don't know what ever happened to 'im. Might have been his whelp. Who knows? Come to think of it, I don't know what happened to the child. Seems as though I recall it was only Kathryn that died."

Liam hunched forward and glanced over his shoulder. The fellow known as Thurston seemed oblivious to the comments circulating the room. He continued drinking his ale, acting as though his presence among the Irish was desired and welcome. "Noreen says the child is alive, but for some reason she feared for 'is life—thought perhaps the child would come to some harm at his father's hand. Anyway, she took him away."

"Did she now? Seems as though Noreen has taken you into her confidence, Liam. Best watch yarself, or she'll be settin' her cap for ya," O'Malley said with a loud guffaw.

Liam shook his head in disbelief. "Noreen's enough to make any man want to remain single. There's nothing comely about her, not her appearance or her words—and worst of all, she can't even cook."

O'Malley gave Liam a sly look. "So cooking's where your heart is? In that case, why don't you come to my place for supper? I've got a sister I'd like you to meet. She prepares a tasty pot of stew."

Liam slapped O'Malley on the shoulder. "What I'm truly looking for is a decent place to room and board. Nothing would please me more than to move out o' Noreen's place. Can you help me find a place to live?"

O'Malley shook his head. "Don't know of anything offhand, but if my sister took a likin' to ya and you two was to marry, you could live with her. She's got two rooms in the back of our place."

"I think I'll turn you down on that offer—at least for the time being. I'll be sure and let you know if I change my mind."

"Suit yourself, but she ain't half bad to look at neither," O'Malley urged as the group pushed away from the table.

Before Liam rose to leave he turned for one final glance over his shoulder. William Thurston met his stare, and a chill rushed down Liam's spine. Even at a distance the man emanated evil.

————

William Thurston stared after the group of men as they walked out of the pub and then lifted his empty mug into the air. "Another!" he shouted when the barkeep glanced in his direction. He pulled an engraved silver watch from his pocket, clicked open the case, and stared at the time.

"Here you are, Mr. Thurston," Mr. Neil said, placing a full mug of ale on the table. "Anythin' else? Something to eat, perhaps?"

"No, not now," he replied without looking up. His thoughts weren't on food. Instead, he was mulling over the ramblings of the drunken man the barkeep had referred to as Robert, wondering how much of what he'd said was fact and how much was fiction.

A short time later two shabby men approached William's table, interrupting his thoughts. "Sorry we're late. I thought you said we would meet at the Wareham. We been waiting outside of there for half an hour," Jake Wilson said.

"I told him you said we was meeting here at the pub, but he wouldn't listen," Rafe Walton rebutted.

Thurston gave them a look of disgust. "Why would I ever consider meeting you two at a place like the Wareham? Do you ever use your brain to think, Jake?" he sneered. "Sit down," he commanded. "Bring them each an ale," he shouted to the barkeep.

"Thanks, Mr. Thurston. I'm mighty thirsty," Jake said.

"Your thirst is the last thing I'm concerned with, Jake," William said as he turned his attention toward Rafe. "You heard anything about money or rifles being stockpiled in that Catholic church that's being built down the street?"

"Where'd you ever get such an idea?" Rafe fired back.

Thurston noted Rafe's startled countenance. "Why are you answering my question with one of your own?"

Rafe shrugged. "I was surprised, that's all. I don't know anything about rifles or money."

Thurston leveled a cold stare across the table. "You'd best not be lying to me, Rafe. If the Irish have a plan underway, I want to know about it, do you understand me?"

"Plan for what? I don't know what you're talkin' about, Mr. Thurston."

Thurston smirked and pointed his finger. "I'll remember we've had this conversation. If I find you're being less than honest with me, you'll have the devil to pay. I want to know if there's anything going on in the Acre. Do I make myself clear? And that goes for you, too, Jake," he added, turning toward the other man.

Rafe nodded. "I'm being straight with you, Mr. Thurston."

Jake took a long drink and then wiped the mustache of foam from his upper lip. "I ain't got no idea what's goin' on down here in the Acre. He's the one who spends his time with the Micks."

"Watch your mouth, Jake," Rafe scowled.

"Be quiet, both of you! I didn't come down here to listen to you two exchange barbs. Just find out what's going on."

CHAPTER 13

Matthew and Kirk disembarked the *Governor Sullivan,* one of the finest packet boats traversing the Middlesex Canal, at Charlestown, where a stage was waiting to transport them into Boston. "This was a pleasant journey, Matthew. Traveling the canal brought back fond memories. When we lived in Boston, Anne and I used to traverse the canal to Horn's Pond for picnics during the summer months. We should make time to do that again this summer," Kirk mused. "You and Lilly would enjoy a weekend at Horn's. They've made it into quite a tourist attraction."

Matthew smiled at the thought. "Perhaps I'll arrange a surprise for her. Lilly loves surprises—and picnics," he added.

Kirk glanced at his pocket watch. "Three o'clock. We made good time. I want to get settled at the hotel and rest my leg. The aching is constant."

"I'm sorry to hear that, Kirk. Fortunately, you'll have ample time to rest. We're not meeting Nathan and J. P. for dinner until seven o'clock."

Kirk slipped the engraved watch into his pocket. "We're dining at the hotel?"

Matthew shook his head. "No. J. P. wanted us to dine at his

home. He's just completed renovations . . ."

"And wants to show off," Kirk said, completing the sentence.

Matthew laughed as he seated himself beside Kirk in the stagecoach. "Exactly! He's quite proud."

"That's an understatement. The man borders on pompous, though I'm not certain why—he's not overly bright, not overly handsome, and is certainly far from being overly wealthy," Kirk remarked.

They rumbled off toward the hotel, the coach now filled with jostling passengers who, after a leisurely passage down the Middlesex Canal, were anxious to join the hustle and bustle of Boston's city life. The women were chattering among themselves, exchanging information about the location of shops and the best places to find the latest fashions. Kirk looked at Matthew, rolled his eyes heavenward, and tightened his lips into a thin line. Matthew grinned and settled back on the uncomfortable seat, glad they would have only a short ride in the coach.

After stops at two other hotels, the coach came to a jerking halt in front of the Brackman Hotel on Beacon Street. The driver was unfastening their luggage when Kirk stepped down. "Don't throw that case to the ground!" Kirk shouted at the driver, who was now holding Kirk's bag in midair above his head.

The driver obediently lowered the bag and handed it down to Kirk. "And don't toss that one, either," Kirk ordered while pointing toward Matthew's case.

"Yes, sir," the driver sheepishly replied.

Matthew laughed as they walked into the foyer of the hotel. "Apparently you carry a good deal of authority in Boston, too."

"No, I just surprised him," Kirk replied as he signed the register. "Is Nathan meeting us here this evening or going directly to J. P.'s?"

"He's going to bring his carriage to the hotel so that we can travel together," Matthew replied.

Kirk took his room key from the clerk and turned toward

Matthew. "Good. And we meet with Bishop Fenwick in the morning?"

"No, not until tomorrow afternoon at three o'clock—for tea," Matthew added.

Kirk flashed a sardonic grin. "Ah, yes, I forgot the bishop likes to sleep late."

Matthew wasn't privy to the bishop's sleeping habits but somehow felt as though he'd erred in scheduling the afternoon appointment. "I didn't think you'd mind. We'll be required to remain in Boston an extra day no matter what time we meet."

"I don't mind, Matthew. You're correct, it makes little difference what time we meet. We'll have the morning free in the event Nathan or J. P. needs additional time with us. I'll see you out here in the lobby a little before seven."

Matthew nodded and watched as Kirk moved down the hallway and began to climb the circular staircase. He was limping, favoring his right leg, which was a sure indication Kirk's pain was greater than he'd mentioned earlier. Matthew understood his necessity for rest. Besides, he could use this time to review some of the paper work for expansion of the shipping company. Several months had passed since Nathan originally proposed the matter, and the Associates were now ready to expand their overseas market.

The ledger of figures and calculations was mind-boggling. Matthew studied page after page, quickly becoming envious of Kirk's ability to decipher and then remember facts and figures after one presentation. Several times he dozed off, his head falling forward onto his chest and awakening him with a start. Finally he gave up and permitted himself the luxury of a short nap.

By the time Matthew left his room, he was refreshed and ready for the meeting. Nathan and Kirk were waiting in the foyer as he approached.

"Right on time," Kirk said. "You have all the paper work?"

Matthew patted the leather case. "Right here."

Nathan's carriage was much more comfortable than the stage, and Matthew relaxed on the leather-upholstered seat. "Is it quite a distance to Mr. Green's residence?"

"No, not far. His home is in the Beacon Hill district. It would be more to my liking if we met at the hotel, but J. P. is so anxious to entertain in his home, I couldn't dissuade him," Nathan explained.

"As I told Matthew earlier, the man's pride is unfounded; but I find that's generally the way of things. The man who has the least reason to boast usually crows the loudest."

Nathan nodded. "True, Kirk, but if this shipping venture grows as I believe it will, J. P. stands to become quite wealthy."

"But not as wealthy as you, Nathan," Kirk responded with a wide grin.

"Well, no. But formation of the shipping venture is my idea, and I began the company. With the help of the other Associates," he added quickly.

"And since J. P. doesn't have earnings from the mills—only the shipping company itself—he can't begin to compete with your wealth and stature," Kirk replied.

Nathan gave an embarrassed laugh. "What stature? I'm a businessman with humble beginnings."

"No need to be modest, Nathan. There's nothing wrong with wealth—you've accumulated yours honestly. And worked hard for it, I might add."

"Not nearly as hard as you've worked in Lowell, Kirk. I don't know what we'd have done without you to manage the business," Nathan responded. "Goodness knows, none of us wanted to live in Lowell. I believe that my wife would have deserted me had I even expressed the vaguest interest in leaving Boston."

"If the two of us continue bragging upon each other, perhaps J. P. will realize how he sounds and keep quiet," Kirk remarked as the coach rolled to a halt in front of the Green mansion.

"He's a bit pompous, but he means well," Nathan said. "Don't spend the entire evening taking him to task."

Kirk disembarked the carriage and gave Nathan a slap on the back. "Only as a personal favor to you, Nathan."

The house went beyond Matthew's idea of good taste. It was opulent—every nook and cranny was crowded with ornately carved furniture, the windows were draped in the most expensive velvets, and inlaid marble floors surrounded carpets of the finest weave. No cost had been spared in building the house, but it was such a mismatch of styles and designs that nothing looked quite right.

"It is a genuine pleasure to host such illustrious visitors in my humble home," J. P. said as he led the men into his library. "May I offer you something to drink? A glass of port or sherry?"

"Port is fine," Nathan replied, seating himself on the tapestry-covered couch in front of a huge fireplace. "Fine craftsmanship," he said, pointing toward the stonework.

J. P. nodded in agreement. "The best I've ever seen—an Irishman, if you can believe that! He came highly recommended, but I didn't let him take a chisel to any of the stones until I'd seen some of his work. Much of this stone is imported from Italy, and I didn't want it ruined by some Mick," he added. "You might look him up if you have need of some masonry, Kirk—said he was going to Lowell."

"Lowell? He'll not find folks willing to spend their hard-earned money on fancy work such as this," Kirk replied as he waved his arm toward the fireplace.

"He said he was going to do the stonework at some new Catholic church being built in Lowell. Surely you're knowledgeable about something as important as a new church, aren't you?"

Matthew looked toward Kirk, whose face had tightened, a slight twitch evident along his jawline. It was obvious J. P.'s remark had not endeared him to Kirk.

"I'm aware of everything of consequence that occurs in Lowell. And that includes the Catholic church. In fact, we're meeting with Bishop Fenwick tomorrow to finalize plans for the dedication," Kirk replied from between clenched teeth. "By the way, what's this stonemason's name?"

J. P.'s chest puffed out at the question. "Donohue. Liam Donohue. He's expensive but worth every cent, and you'll have your wife's undying devotion—believe me."

Kirk laughed. "I merely wanted his name; I'm not planning on hiring him," Kirk said as a servant approached, held a whispered conversation with J. P., and scurried back out of the room.

"I apologize for the interruption, gentlemen. Life has been in a bit of an upheaval of late. Someone entered the house and managed to break into my safe. I had hoped the matter would be resolved before our meeting, but it appears the police have had little success. It has been most trying."

"I can imagine, but thank goodness for banks. At least we no longer keep vast amounts of wealth in our homes," Nathan replied.

J. P. gave a feeble smile. "Yes, banks are a wonderful institution, but it is imperative I recover the contents of my safe. My future depends upon it. I kept important records in that safe."

Kirk shook his head. "No need to be dramatic, J. P. Life will go on even if you don't recover those few stolen belongings. I'm sure you can duplicate any lost documents."

"Of course, you're right," J. P. replied, although his nervous countenance belied his words. "Let's have supper," he said, leading the men into the dining room.

Kirk motioned Matthew to drop back a few paces. "When we return to Lowell, I want you to find out if Hugh has hired that Irishman—Donohue. If so, I want to know what he's paying him. I didn't authorize hiring any new employees, especially Irishmen. We've got enough problems brewing between the Yanks and Irish as it is."

Matthew nodded. "I'll see to it."

"J. P. has certainly worked himself into a frenzy over a small robbery, wouldn't you say? It makes no sense that a man who can afford to spend this kind of money," Kirk said as he looked about the house, "would be so upset over the contents of a small house safe."

"He did say there were important documents," Matthew whispered as they sat down at the table.

"What idiot would keep important papers in his personal safe unless he had duplicates stored elsewhere?"

Matthew shrugged. Having never been faced with such a problem, he hadn't given the matter much thought, although what Kirk said made sense. There should be duplicates of important papers. After all, the Corporation maintained duplicate signed copies of its important documents.

From the twenty-foot-high ceiling of the formal dining room, not one, but two crystal chandeliers offered candlelight on the elaborately decorated table. And the meal was much like the house—overindulgent, with their host remaining preoccupied throughout supper. Kirk and Nathan discussed politics, both of them excited over the possibilities of new tariff laws.

"The Tariff of Abominations will soon be a thing of the past," Kirk announced. "The legislators who so stupidly voted in those legal means by which to pick our pockets will soon have to reckon with President Jackson's ideas for improvement."

"I suppose Calhoun will be his biggest opponent," Nathan said, sipping his wine. "The man has been a thorn in his side since taking the vice-presidency."

"He was a thorn in his side prior to that," Kirk said, laughing, "as Adams' vice-president. The Tariff of 1828 was not pleasing to the poor man. I thought for certain he might very well have South Carolina seceding before the year was out."

"He still threatens it," Matthew threw in. "I heard of quite an incident over a birthday party for Thomas Jefferson. It seems President Jackson gave the toast, 'Our Federal Union—it must be preserved!' and Vice-President Calhoun came back with, 'The Union—next to our liberty, the most dear!' According to the report, the men are worse enemies now than when they began their administration."

"To be sure," Kirk said, nodding. "I share a rather casual acquaintance with Calhoun. It wouldn't surprise me to see the man resign his position and return to South Carolina."

"Resign the vice-presidency?" Nathan questioned. "That would be sheer lunacy."

Kirk smiled and pushed his plate away. "No, sheer lunacy is having those two under the same roof for any purpose—much less the running of the country." The men enjoyed a good laugh over this.

"So, Nathan, I understand the Corporation has given you the nod to expand into some new markets," Kirk commented as the men finished their meal and retired to the library. J. P.'s butler followed the men into the room, poured drinks for all, and offered cigars. Matthew had no interest in either refreshment and settled back into the plush wing-backed chair. The supple cushioning and upholstery seemed to embrace Matthew. He'd have to look into purchasing some of these chairs for his own home.

Nathan took a cigar from the humidor and clipped the end. "There's ample interest in the carpets being produced at the Lowell Mill, and we can't seem to keep up with the demand for Negro cloth. I'd like to expand markets for our calicos, finer linens, and cotton to the southern states. The demand is certainly strong in all of the larger cities of the South for those fabrics. I've also received several missives from a New Orleans businessman who wants to purchase carpets—probably more than we can produce in the next year."

J. P. came to attention. He waved his butler away and questioned, "New Orleans?"

"Yes. He wants to distribute carpets throughout the South as well as overseas. By my calculations, the Corporation would make more money shipping directly to him for further distribution. That may not always hold true, but for now we can make more money sending to only one destination."

"I like the idea of New Orleans. I'd be pleased to go and meet with the distributor you're considering," J. P. offered excitedly.

Nathan glanced at Kirk then back toward J. P. "I'll keep your offer in mind. A trip to New Orleans may be necessary to finalize the agreement," Nathan replied as he blew a puff of blue gray cigar smoke into the air.

Matthew glanced toward J. P. The man had appeared to be daydreaming as they had discussed shipping fabrics to the South—at least until Nathan mentioned New Orleans. It was at that point J. P. had come to life, his behavior becoming quite animated. It was obvious the mention of New Orleans and the overseas markets excited him more than anything else they'd discussed all evening. Matthew couldn't help but wonder why. After all, the profits from the other markets would be much greater than those for the carpets. It was, he decided, an interesting conundrum.

CHAPTER 14

Bella and Daughtie stood among the throng of girls gathered in the hallway. Miss Addie clapped her hands several times, resembling a schoolteacher summoning an unruly class to attention. "Now, remember that I expect each of you to be on your best behavior. This is an excellent opportunity to utilize the manners you're forced to push aside during weekday meals. I know that you can have a good time and still make me proud of your conduct."

Janet Stodemire was standing on the steps. "I've changed my mind. I'm not going," she called out.

"I sent a formal response on behalf of all those who signed up to attend Lilly's tea. Did you sign the sheet?"

"Yes, ma'am, but a friend who works over at the Lowell Mill saw me in church this morning. She invited me to spend the afternoon with her. We're going on a picnic with two boys," she proudly announced.

"No, Janet, you're not going on a picnic. You have a prior engagement, and you will attend with the rest of us. If there is time for your picnic after the tea, then you may go," Addie staunchly replied.

Janet's eyes flashed with anger. "You can't force me to go."

Bella gasped. "You ought not speak to an elder in such a fashion," she said without thinking.

"Stay out of this, Bella. We all know you and Daughtie are the perfect little Shakers or Quakers or whatever you call yourselves. This is none of your business."

Bella glanced at Janet and then toward Miss Addie. "You're right; it isn't. I apologize for interfering."

"Thank you for your apology, Bella," Miss Addie replied before tilting her gaze upward to meet Janet's stare. "Come along, Janet," she said firmly. "Otherwise, I'll be forced to write a letter to your supervisor that I'm requesting your removal from my house for failure to abide by the rules."

Janet clenched her fists and glared at Miss Addie. "Where does it say I must attend a tea at Lilly Cheever's home?"

"The contract you signed says that you will conduct yourself in a proper ladylike manner. The rules also say that I am the judge of acceptable behavior. Now please get your cape and let's be on our way. I don't intend to be late."

It was a beautiful early summer day as the girls walked down Jackson Street, two by two, with an excited buzz filling the air as they passed the row of boardinghouses. It wasn't often the mill girls were invited to visit one of the fine homes in Lowell. Several of Miss Addie's girls had known Lilly before she married Matthew Cheever, when she had been a resident of Miss Addie's boardinghouse while they all worked at the Appleton. Now they dreamed about the same fairy-tale marriage occurring in their own lives.

Bella thought them rather silly. It wasn't a matter of not wanting to ever marry; it was the way the girls seemed to put such stock in marrying someone well-to-do. Whatever happened to marrying for love? Marrying a man whom you love, no matter his station, made you glad to be alive. Bella wanted that kind of marriage.

She ignored the chatter of her friends and thought instead of Jesse. She wouldn't have had that kind of marriage with him. He was sweet and gentle-natured, but he would never be the kind of man Bella needed. Bella needed a man who could stand his ground with her—who wouldn't be overrun by her temper or opinionated manner.

Not that I don't need desperately to alter those areas, she thought. *I need a man who won't be afraid of my mind or the fact that I enjoy learning and expanding my knowledge. I don't need someone of high status or lofty ambitions, but I do need a man who can provide for his family.*

Bella's breath caught in her throat as they arrived at the Cheever home. It was a large frame house with a wide porch wrapping around the front and side, unlike anything Bella had previously seen. Willow chairs sat on the porch, beckoning visitors to sit awhile and smell the early summer blooms that lined the stone walkway and surrounded the outline of the covered porch. Rosebushes with their buds revealing a hint of pink were strategically planted in a small garden on the east side of the house, and the afternoon breeze was heavy with the smell of fragrant honeysuckle blossoms.

"It's difficult to imagine living in a place such as this," Bella whispered to Daughtie.

Daughtie nodded her head. "It's as big as the house all the Sisters and Brothers lived in. Don't you love the porch? It's a shame the Society thought porches too worldly."

Bella smiled. "It's not so much the porch, Daughtie, it's the ornamentation a porch provides that causes the Believers to fault them. The Brothers and Sisters would be aghast at the ornate carving on the front door," she said. "But I find it beautiful."

"Ohhh, and look at the columns. They look like the drawings from the Roman Empire in our history book. Don't you think?"

"Yes, that's probably where they got the idea. Sister Minerva said every generation copies from the preceding generations—that nothing is original," Bella replied.

"Well, I find that statement difficult to believe. There are new inventions every day. Aren't those monstrous machines we use at the mills a new idea? I don't think any of that machinery was in use several generations ago," Daughtie replied.

"Perhaps you're correct, Daughtie. It would be nice to think of Sister Minerva being wrong at least once in her lifetime, wouldn't it?"

Bella and Daughtie giggled in unison as they walked into the foyer, where Miss Addie stood alongside Lilly to introduce each guest as she passed by.

"And these are my two newest friends and boarders," Miss Addie told Lilly. "This," she said, patting Daughtie's shoulder, "is Miss Daughtie Winfield. And this," she continued while taking Bella's hand, "is Miss Arabella Newberry—we call her Bella. Both the girls have come from the Shaker community outside of Concord."

"Oh yes, I've heard tell of it. In Canterbury, isn't it?" Lilly inquired.

"Yes, that's correct," Bella answered.

Lilly gave them an inviting smile. "I'm eager to visit with you. Please be sure to save a few moments so that we may chat."

"Why does she want to talk to us?" Daughtie inquired as the girls worked their way into the parlor and then moved onward into the adjoining music room.

"She was merely being courteous, Daughtie. You needn't be so suspicious of everyone. Oh, look at this piano. Isn't it beautiful?"

Lilly approached and stood to one side. "Do you play?"

Bella nodded and turned. "My mother was quite accomplished. She taught me when I was very young, but I haven't played for years."

"You're welcome to entertain us," Lilly offered.

"No. It's been too long, and playing the piano reminds me of my mother. She died several years ago," Bella explained. Sometimes it seemed as if her mother had died only yesterday—the pain was so tangible.

Lilly took her hand. "I understand."

Daughtie drifted off with Miss Addie and the other girls as they took their places visiting in the various rooms. Because of this, Bella felt free to question Lilly Cheever. "Your mother is deceased, also?"

"Yes," Lilly replied. "Come sit down and let's visit. Miss Addie tells me you've become one of her favorite people, and she's an excellent judge of character."

Bella followed Lilly to one of the settees across the room and sat down. The cushioning made Bella feel as though she were sitting on a cloud. "Your home is beautiful," Bella complimented while gazing about the room. Gold-framed oil paintings decorated the wall opposite her. The paintings were of a variety of pastoral settings. The only exception was the large oil over the fireplace. This painting was a most becoming memorial to Lilly Cheever's wedding day. Bella couldn't imagine what it might be like to sit and pose for such a thing. Pulling her thoughts back to Lilly's questioning gaze, she added, "I particularly like the porch."

Lilly smiled and nodded. "Matthew said large porches belong in the South, but I envision lots of children playing out there, even on rainy days. Wouldn't that be delightful fun?"

Bella laughed. "Yes, I suppose it would. Miss Addie is quite proud that you once lived with her. She tells all of us how you saved her position with the Corporation by teaching her how to cook. I'm sure you know that you have her undying devotion."

Lilly blushed at the praise. "Miss Addie gives me far too much credit for her success. I am pleased, however, that her boardinghouse is considered one of the finest in Lowell. It's obvious she enjoys her work—perhaps too much."

"How can it be harmful to enjoy your work?"

"Sometimes she tends to put you girls ahead of her personal life," Lilly hedged.

Bella gave a knowing look. "You mean with Mr. Farnsworth, don't you?"

"He's a fine man. I think she should marry him, move into his home, and begin a joyous life with him. Unfortunately, she thinks if they marry, he should move into the boardinghouse, where she would continue with her boardinghouse duties. I doubt whether he'll come around to her way of thinking. But I fear she'll lose him to another if she doesn't change her mind," Lilly explained, shaking her head. "I'm not sure why I'm telling you this except I can tell you've come to care for Miss Addie, as I did. Perhaps we can conspire to convince her to reconsider."

"I would think Mr. Farnsworth would be delighted to move into the boardinghouse if for no other reason than to rid himself of his nephew," Bella confided. The memory of her encounters with Taylor Manning caused Bella to twist her hands together.

"Taylor Manning? You don't find him amusing?" Lilly inquired.

"Frankly, I find him rather pompous and lacking in manners."

Lilly didn't immediately respond. Instead, she gave Bella a curious smile. "You would agree that he's very handsome, wouldn't you?"

"I would agree that Taylor Manning believes himself very handsome. To me, however, his appearance is completely diminished by his boorish behavior," Bella countered. "Someone is attempting to gain your attention," she said, glancing toward the doorway.

"If you'll excuse me, I believe the servants are ready to serve tea. We'll visit again," Lilly said, rising from the settee.

Bella watched as Lilly swept away in a gown of amber and cream. The dress was most magnificent, with a scalloped flounce along the skirt's edge and ruching tucked with piping along the bodice. Bella looked down at her own gown of gray homespun. The simplicity was a sharp contrast to Lilly's gown. Bella glanced around the room and realized that her gown was quite plain compared to everyone else's, save Daughtie's. Taylor had chided her for not dressing more fashionably, and seeing the beautiful dresses of the other girls made Bella almost wish she could comply. *But if I make a new dress now,* she reasoned, *Taylor Manning will think I'm doing it merely to impress him*. She stiffened at the thought. There would be no new gown.

The time passed quickly as the servants poured tea and offered scrumptious egg and watercress sandwiches accompanied by fancy breads and jelly-filled pastries. Tea was followed by a tour of the house for those who were interested. Bella couldn't decide what she found the most intriguing, the beauty of the home or the fact that only two people lived alone in this large house.

The girls clustered together in small groups, one discussing the new millinery shop opened by a widow from Boston who was abreast of the latest fashion news from England, while another group discussed several men who had recently arrived in town. Bella and Daughtie stood on the fringes of one group, where one of the girls whispered that Lilly was expecting a baby. The remark was followed with oohs and aahs from around the circle.

"What ever happened to her brother's child?" someone asked.

"They never found him, but I understand Lilly hasn't given up hope. She believes the boy is still alive somewhere, but don't you think it's doubtful they would find him now? How long has it been?"

"A couple years, I think," another girl replied.

Bella was intrigued by the conversation and sat down beside Marmi, one of the girls who had known Lilly prior to her marriage. "What happened to Mrs. Cheever's brother?" Bella asked.

"He died in a fire at the mill. Some say he set the fire, while others say he was helping to put it out. Either way, he died shortly afterward. While on his deathbed, he supposedly told Lilly he had fathered a child. . . ."

"By an Irishwoman," another girl added in a hushed voice.

Marmi shook her head. "It doesn't matter to Lilly if the mother's Irish. She wants to find the boy. Some thought Lilly might never have a child of her own. I'm truly pleased to hear her news. Perhaps it will ease her pain in case they never find her nephew."

Several more girls joined them, and the talk soon shifted to clothing and jewelry, one of them mentioning the recent shipments of lace and gloves that had arrived in Lowell earlier in the week. Bored with their conversation, Bella excused herself and sauntered into the parlor. Finding an unoccupied chair near a large window overlooking the flower garden along the west side of the house, Bella seated herself. A stoop-shouldered man busied himself pruning bushes and packing fresh dirt around several plants, and as she watched him work, her thoughts drifted back to her earlier conversation with Lilly Cheever. It was clear Lilly had suffered her share of sadness. To lose her mother and brother was difficult enough, but then to know there was a child—one that couldn't be found—would be a tragedy. It was good, Bella decided, that Lilly had a fine husband and would soon have a child of her own to love. She stood to gain a better view of the gardener as he began planting a bush.

"I'd like to think you find me as intriguing as you find the gardener."

Bella whirled around and found herself face-to-face with Taylor Manning.

"What are you doing here?" She forced herself not to notice the sparkle of his sapphire blue eyes.

He gave her a wide grin. "I'd like to tell you that I knew you would be here and I couldn't stay away. But that wouldn't be the truth, and I know with all the religion that's surrounded your life, you might take a dim view of my lying to you. Actually, I've come to fetch Mr. Cheever. He told me I could wait in here while he informs Mrs. Cheever he must take his leave; there's a bit of difficulty that needs his attention. By the way, I'm pleased to see you've taken the time to fancy yourself up a bit."

Bella stared at him in disbelief. "Taken the time to fancy myself up?"

"That trim," he said, pointing his finger toward the lace that now surrounded the cuffs and neckline of her dress. "You fancied your dress a little. Of course, another color would be better. In fact, a whole new dress would be best, but at least you made an effort."

Her mouth dropped open and formed a small oval. "Do you spend all of your free time practicing rude behavior, or is your appalling conduct a natural happenstance, Mr. Manning?"

Taylor appeared completely baffled by her remark. "What do you mean? I paid you a compliment."

"No, you insulted me," she retaliated.

"Then I apologize. I was attempting to point out that those

Shaker dresses don't enhance your beauty." He crossed his arms and gave her a proud grin.

Bella glanced heavenward. "Shaker dresses, as you call them, are specifically designed to detract from a woman's . . ."

Taylor laughed. "Shape? Size? Form? Figure? Beauty?"

Bella could feel the heat rising in her cheeks. "All of those," she huffed, quickly turning to walk away.

Taylor stepped forward and blocked her path. "Don't rush off after pointing out that my manners need improvement. The least you can do is remain and lend your assistance."

"There isn't sufficient time in my day to correct your manners, sir."

A wide grin spread across Taylor's face. "Then perhaps we'll need to schedule several sessions. I'll make myself available at your convenience."

Had she not been so angry, the expectant look on his face would have caused her to laugh. "Either I have a problem speaking or you have a problem understanding. Your manners are reprehensible. I am not available to instruct you in proper etiquette."

"Well, then," he replied, obviously unruffled, "I suggest you accompany me to the lyceum. I understand there's to be a talk on phrenology. The speaker is personally acquainted and has studied with J. G. Spurzheim while in Europe."

Bella hesitated. The Brothers and Sisters at Canterbury had discussed the possible benefits of phrenology in Union Meeting on several occasions. The topic was controversial yet one that had captured the interest of the forward-thinking Shakers—one that Bella found unbelievable but intriguing.

Taylor shifted his weight to one foot and casually leaned against the thick oak woodwork surrounding the doorway. "You don't know what phrenology is and you don't want to ask me, do you?"

His smug tone annoyed Bella. "Do *you*?" she inquired.

"Well, no, but Uncle John said that J. G. Spurzheim is quite renowned in Scotland and England."

"Phrenologists teach that the human skull takes its shape

from the brain. Therefore, by reading the skull an individual can be evaluated for psychological aptitudes and tendencies," Bella articulated.

"What?"

Matthew and Lilly laughed at Taylor as they approached. "By all appearances, I would guess that Bella has completely confounded you, Taylor," Lilly observed.

"Perhaps just a bit," he admitted. "I invited her to attend the phrenology lecture with me."

"Oh yes, I can hardly wait. We're planning to attend. Perhaps we could all go together," Lilly suggested.

Taylor gave her a satisfied grin. "Why, that would be wonderful. Wouldn't it, Bella?"

She knew what Taylor was up to. But it wouldn't work. "Quite frankly, I would enjoy attending the lyceum. However, Mr. Manning has insulted me numerous times since his arrival this afternoon, and I find his company abhorrent."

Matthew's eyebrows arched. "Well, in that case . . ."

"I'm sure Taylor would be on his best behavior, Bella. And the lecture is sure to be a fine one. Why don't you rethink your decision?" Lilly interrupted. "In fact, if it will make your decision easier, you can pretend that Taylor isn't even along—except for the ticket, of course. I understand that the program is sold out," she added.

"He's already insulted my attire. I'm sure my dowdy appearance would prove an embarrassment," Bella explained.

Matthew cleared his throat and grinned at his wife. "I hate to interrupt before you've reached a resolution to this quandary. However, Taylor came here to fetch me. Seems there may be some difficulty brewing with the Irish, and neither Kirk nor Paul can be found."

Lilly gave Matthew a frown. "On a Sunday afternoon? What kind of difficulty, Matthew?"

"There are rumors spreading that the Irish have begun stockpiling weapons in the foundation of the new church. I want to put a stop to it before trouble begins," Matthew replied.

"That's preposterous. Why on earth would the Irish want to accumulate weapons?"

"I doubt that there's any truth to the rumors."

Lilly's mouth was agape. "But what if . . ."

Matthew patted her shoulder. "Nothing to concern yourself with, my dear. I'm certain that at most it's only a small group of troublemakers, but the Corporation does need to halt any rumors. I'll see what I can do," he said. "While I'm gone, why don't you ladies make a decision regarding attending the lyceum? Taylor and I will be pleased to accommodate your choice. Won't we, Taylor?" he asked while moving toward the front door.

Taylor didn't appear pleased with the pronouncement but he was obviously unwilling to argue Matthew's position. "Yes, sir," he replied. "Will you . . ."

"Whatever the decision, I promise I'll get word to you," Matthew said, while pushing Taylor onward.

Lilly giggled as they walked out the door. "That young man is enchanted with you, Bella. And I believe you're quite smitten with him, also," she said, linking arms with Bella. Before Bella could protest, Lilly pulled her toward a corner of the foyer. "Proper attire isn't a problem. I have several dresses that would fit you handsomely," Lilly offered. "I would be honored if you would permit me to give you one. I don't know if you've heard, but I'm going to be a mother. My waist has thickened, and most of my dresses no longer fit."

"But they'll fit you again—after the child," Bella replied.

"I promise I'll give you one that will soon be out of fashion. Would that make the gift more acceptable?"

"I didn't mean to imply that I find your offer unacceptable," Bella apologized. "However, it's a thorny issue, changing my attire to suit Taylor Manning's request—although I very much want to attend the lyceum," she confided in a whisper.

"Do you find wearing worldly clothing goes against your religious tenets, Bella? Because if you believe you must continue to wear your Shaker dresses, I would never encourage you to disobey your beliefs. But if it's merely that you don't want Taylor to win an argument . . ."

Bella blushed and turned away. "I've never believed that it was necessary to wear drab clothing in order to love God. As you can see, I've already added some lace to this dress," she replied, then hesitated. "And although Taylor is prideful, he's probably no worse than most men."

Lilly grasped Bella's hand, her face etched with concern. "What's hardened your heart toward men at such an early age, Bella?"

"In the case of Taylor Manning, I find him arrogant and entirely self-absorbed. He believes himself to be the finest thing in shoe leather. He has an attitude of pride regarding his looks, and I can tell by the way he acts that he's used to getting his own way with the ladies."

"But Taylor Manning isn't the one who started this feeling toward men, is he?"

Bella gave Lilly a wistful smile as her thoughts wandered down a dark path of memories. "There have been two men in my life. My father and Jesse Harwood—and even though they both avowed their love, neither chose me over life among the Shakers. I trusted both of them; they both disappointed me. I've finally concluded that the pain meted out by men is more than my heart can withstand."

Lilly pulled her close. "Sit down here," she said, leading her to a small divan. "Not all men are the same, Bella. I've experienced pain at the hands of men I've loved, but there are good men, men who will love and cherish you. As I labored with my own pain, my heart was quickened to pray for those who caused the pain. It was difficult, but there is a balm of healing that comes with prayer for wrongdoers. Perhaps if you could begin praying for your father and Jesse, it would help. Tell me about them—your father and Jesse."

Bella felt as though she'd met a kindred spirit. The chattering girls and tea party formed a hazy milieu while she poured out her heart to Lilly, first explaining the pain of rejection at her father's hand, then her mother's death, and then Jesse's unexplained nonappearance the night she and Daughtie left Canterbury.

"So you love Jesse and wanted to become his wife. Now I understand why you find Taylor's advances offensive," Lilly said.

"No, I don't want to marry anyone. I'm not sure what that kind of love is—between a man and woman, I mean. Jesse said he loved me, but I knew my love for him wasn't the same. He insisted we should be married, and I thought perhaps he was right, although I confess I was fearful of the arrangement. My mother loved my father, and he deserted her love for the Shakers. What if Jesse decided he wanted to return to Canterbury after we were married? I was frightened, but I wanted to leave the Family."

"But not because of Jesse?"

Bella shook her head back and forth. "I find fault with some of their important beliefs; they go against what the Bible says—at least I think they do," she replied.

"I see," Lilly replied. "Then you actually left the Shakers in order to exercise your religious freedom."

"Exactly," Bella replied, gracing her hostess with a grateful smile.

"Good! Then you can wear my dress and attend the lyceum without compromising your beliefs," Lilly triumphantly replied. "You remain behind with Miss Addie after the others leave this afternoon, and we'll decide upon a dress. In fact, it appears as if several of my guests are preparing to leave. I'd best resume my hostess duties. Promise you'll stay," Lilly urged.

Bella nodded her agreement. She hoped her decision would prove judicious.

———

Taylor mulled over the conversation he'd had with Bella and couldn't begin to imagine how he'd insulted her. Yes, he'd been forward and open with his statements, but he didn't believe it served him very well to veil his thoughts. Still, she had been upset with him. As if reading his thoughts, Matthew interrupted with a question.

"You didn't really insult that poor young woman, did you?"

Taylor shrugged. "I didn't think so, but apparently she found my words offensive. Bella is a true mystery to me."

"That's why you've come to like her so much more than the other girls, correct?"

"I never said I liked her more than anyone," Taylor replied defensively. "I've no need to choose one woman over another. I tend to spread myself among the ladies," he said, grinning.

Matthew frowned. "That's hardly the kind of attitude I would brag about. Your heart seems not to care at all for the misery you cause, yet you seem considerate enough with some. I suppose you find the attention rewarding at this stage of your life, but let me assure you, Taylor, the love of a good and godly woman cannot compare to the adoration of hundreds of addle-pated ninnies. Find a woman of character—godly character—and you'll have found something of great value."

The words stung Taylor's pride. Surely Matthew Cheever believed in more than inward beauty. After all, the man was married to a beautiful woman, had an opulent home, and dressed impeccably in the best of fashions. Taylor smiled to himself. Matthew was probably just speaking in such a manner because his wife had suggested it. He nodded to himself and felt the weight of his concern lift. That's all it was. Lilly Cheever had probably instructed her husband to chide Taylor for his brusque and open manner with Bella. It was surely nothing more than that.

CHAPTER 15

William Thurston relentlessly plodded down one of the mucky paths toward Michael Neil's pub in the Acre. It wasn't his need for liquor forcing his portly body into the rapid pace; rather, it was the overheard conversation from a nearby table the evening before while he had dined at the Wareham House. He'd briefly considered going to the Acre last night, but going after dark was risky for a Yank. He decided his visit could wait until today. If luck was on his side, several of his lackeys would be in the pub downing ale.

He pressed onward, keeping his head bowed against a warm breeze, the stench of the litter-filled streets assaulting his senses. Relief washed over him when he finally reached the pub and recognized the faces of two men sitting in a darkened corner. Weaving his way among several tables, Thurston motioned at the barkeep to deliver ale to the corner table and then seated himself.

He leaned across the table toward the two men in an intimate fashion. "I understand there was a bit of a ruckus down here yesterday."

One of the men nodded. "How'd you find out?"

"I keep telling you boys I've got eyes and ears everywhere. When something happens, I hear about it. Remember that." He wasn't about to tell them he'd been eavesdropping in the hotel restaurant. Besides, whether real or perceived, the veiled threats gave him a feeling of power. "Now, tell me what occurred. I'm anxious for all the details."

Rafe took a swig of his ale, set his tankard down with a thud, and leaned in toward Thurston. "I've been doing like you said, snooping about for any word of an uprising or hidden weapons," he reported.

"Or money," Thurston added.

"There've been a few stories circulating, but most of the talk seems to be among the Yanks. The tales appear to have died down, right, Jake?"

Jake nodded. "Word I'm hearing is there's a handful of Yanks convinced the Irish are planning an uprising. They believe there are guns and money hidden away in the church. There are plenty of Yanks wanting the Irish run outta town, saying they can't find work because of the Irish. Like Rafe said, there doesn't seem to be much talk in the Acre, and if there are any rifles or money stored in the church, it's the best-kept secret in the Paddy camp. But it don't take a whole lot up here," Jake said while pointing to his head, "to figure out the Irish ain't got enough money to live on, let alone use it to buy rifles to stash away in that church."

"As though you have a lot up here," Thurston sneered, pointing to his own head. "The Catholic Church has lots of money, you fool. Don't you think the church would finance a rebellion if it was in its best interest?"

"I think you're takin' this whole story out of proportion," Rafe said. "Things have already begun to quiet down; they always do. The Irish will stay down here in the Acre except for work, and the Yanks will stay in their part of town."

Thurston glared at Rafe. He sounded just like Kirk Boott, thinking the Irish belonged in Lowell. Well, he didn't want things to settle down. The Irish were a blight on this idyllic community, and Thurston had been prophesying problems to the Boston Associates for three years. The Associates wouldn't listen—none of them. They always sided with Kirk Boott, believing his rhetoric that the Irish were necessary—that locals didn't want to perform manual labor. Well, it appeared the good people of New England were changing their attitude about the interlopers, and he was going to do everything in his power to prove the Irish were the problem he'd predicted. He'd see this town free of the lowlifes if it was the last thing he did.

"The two of you listen to me. Rafe, I want you out here in the Acre talking to your Irish friends. You tell them you have it from a reliable source that the Yanks are preparing to expel them from the Acre. Tell them the Yanks want their jobs and are willing to fight for them." Turning his attention toward Jake, he said, "Spread word around Lowell that the Irish are storing up arms with an eye toward a takeover of the mills."

Both men stared at Thurston in disbelief. Rafe spoke first. "When I'm asked about my reliable source, whose name should I use? Yours?"

Jake appeared to draw courage from Rafe's question. "I don't care if there is some murmuring around town about money and guns in the church. Nobody is going to believe that the Irish are storing up weapons in an attempt to take over the mills. That's the craziest thing I ever heard. Nobody in their right mind would believe they'd try such a thing. How many Irishmen are there? Only three hundred—maybe five hundred if we count the women and children? And you want me to tell people they're gonna attempt a takeover?"

"The Yanks'll think he's daft," Rafe agreed.

"No they won't—they'll want to believe the story, and the gossip will feed upon itself as it spreads. I expect you both to do as you're told—why do you think I pay you? And if you want to chart your own course, there's always an alternative. If you no longer want to work for me, you say the word. I've had others leave my employ."

"I didn't say I wouldn't do what you asked, but I know I'll be questioned about my source," Rafe replied.

"Tell them you heard it from Hugh Cummiskey," Thurston responded.

Rafe's eyes grew wide at Thurston's response. "Cummiskey? I can't use his name, Mr. Thurston."

"Why? You fear him more than you fear me? If you don't want to use Cummiskey's name, you figure out whose name to use. Once word begins to spread, it shouldn't take long before the fires of hostility spread," Thurston said. He leaned back, took a long drink, and gave them a satisfied smile. "Yes, fear and whispered accusations should do the trick. You boys pass the word among your cronies; tell them to feel free to share the information," he emphasized. "And don't forget that I hear rumors the same as everyone else. If I haven't heard the gossip around town, I'll assume you're not doing your job."

Jake nervously pulled at the two-day stubble growing on his chin. "You said earlier you've had others leave your employ, Mr. Thurston. What if I decide that's what I wanna do?"

Thurston leveled a wicked smile in Jake's direction. "You might want to rethink that decision. No one who has quit working for me is alive."

"You mean . . . Are you saying . . . Did you . . ." Jake stammered.

An evil gleam shone in Thurston's eyes. "Draw your own conclusions," he replied.

"Well, I was merely asking—I plan to remain in your employ just as long as you want me," Jake replied, keeping his gaze focused on the tankard of ale before him.

"In that case, I'll leave you men to your work," Thurston said, hoisting his ample body from the chair. "I'll be in touch." He made his way to the door and donned his hat. Squaring his shoulders, he walked out the front door, knowing the two men were watching his every move, hating him. He smiled.

CHAPTER 16

Daughtie had openly expressed her dismay when Bella confided her plan to attend the phrenology lecture with Taylor. This evening it was obvious that Daughtie was even more apprehensive as Bella twirled about in Lilly Cheever's rose-colored silk gown.

"You look like a bird prepared to take flight," Daughtie said while flapping her arms up and down. "I think the dressmaker should have taken some of the fabric out of those enormous sleeves and used it in the bodice to give the gown a modicum of modesty."

Bella ran a finger along the folds and cords decorating the double collars that served to widen the shoulders of the dress. "You believe the dress immodest?"

Daughtie appeared taken aback by the question. "Perhaps just a bit."

An embroidered muslin overlay topped the double collars. Bella tugged at the muslin and bunched it over her neckline. "Is this better?" she asked with a giggle. "Look at the shoes Lilly gave me—and they fit ever so well," she added while holding up the shoes of thin woolen cloth with a pleated frill at the top. "They lace down the back. Isn't that clever?"

Daughtie sat on the bed watching Bella's every move. "The shoes are quite clever," she replied. She quietly cleared her throat and then hesitated a moment. "I . . . um . . . fear you're straying from your beliefs." A note of recrimination hung in the air.

Bella ceased tying one of the shoes and gave Daughtie a thoughtful look. "Which beliefs that were truly my own have I disavowed, Daughtie? Years ago, before my parents joined the Believers, I saw my mother and other godly, chaste women wear fashionable clothes; their religious convictions weren't compromised. And although the Shakers don't attend lyceums, they are quick to gather the world's latest intelligence and discuss it among themselves. I'm merely gaining my information first-hand," Bella replied. Somehow the words sounded defensive, which wasn't her intent. Still, she didn't want Daughtie thinking her wayward.

Daughtie glanced at the floor and then gave Bella a sheepish grin. "You're right, Bella. Perhaps I'm feeling a tinge of jealousy because I'll be sitting home while you attend the lecture. Please accept my apology for acting the spoiled child."

"There's no need to apologize. We'll attend the next lecture together—I'd much prefer your company to the pomposity of Taylor Manning. Had we known in advance, we could have purchased our own tickets like most of the other girls. Ruth told me this is the first lecture that has sold out so quickly," Bella replied. "I'll be careful to remember every word of the speech and share it with you the minute I get home."

Daughtie gave her a delighted smile. "Promise?"

"Promise!" Bella said, pulling her friend into a quick hug before picking up her hairbrush.

"Let me," Daughtie said as she reached for the brush. "I think I can fashion your hair in the looped braids that appear popular with the society ladies," she said, parting Bella's hair down the center.

A short time later, Bella gazed into the oval mirror. "It looks lovely, Daughtie," Bella said, touching the tightly formed braids her friend had woven with ivory ribbon and looped on each side. She turned and gave Daughtie a hug. "Thank you, dear friend."

"You look quite beautiful," Daughtie said. "Keeping Taylor Manning at a distance may prove difficult this evening."

Bella shook her head. "I'll stay close to Mrs. Cheever," she said, hastening toward the door as one of the girls called up the stairs that her escort had arrived.

Taylor stood at the bottom of the stairway, tugging at the sable-brown claw-hammer jacket that topped a frilled white shirt and silk vest. Giving Bella a smile, he leaned down in a courtly bow, causing his hair to fall forward over one eye. "You look lovely, Miss Newberry," he said, his voice barely a whisper as he straightened.

"Thank you, Mr. Manning. I trust that Mr. and Mrs. Cheever are in the carriage?"

He appeared momentarily confused by her question. "Oh yes," he finally replied. "My uncle and Miss Addie left a short time ago. They've promised to save us seats should the lecture hall become overly crowded before our arrival," he added as they walked out the door.

Bella took his extended hand and stepped up into the carriage. Scooting into the far corner, she gathered the fullness of her dress across the seat. There was barely enough space for Taylor to squeeze in and be seated near the opposite door.

Lilly Cheever turned and looked over her shoulder. "I can hardly contain my excitement. Matthew was unusually late coming home, and I feared we would be late," Lilly said, grasping her husband's arm in an affectionate squeeze.

"We have more than sufficient time, my dear. You fret overly."

She gave him a winsome smile before turning back toward Bella and Taylor. "You two make quite a handsome couple," she complimented.

"Thank you, Mrs. Cheever. I was thinking much the same thing," Taylor replied.

Bella gave him a sidelong glance. "We're not really a couple, but I thank you for the kind words."

Taylor leaned his head back and chuckled. "I don't think she wants to be associated with me, Mrs. Cheever. I believe Bella finds me crass and arrogant; the only reason she's willing to be seen in my company is because of her interest in the lecture."

Bella wasn't certain if what she was feeling was embarrassment or anger—perhaps a combination of both, she decided. "As I recall, my acceptance of your invitation was forthright, Mr. Manning. You're aware I'm not interested in your companionship."

"There you have it, Mrs. Cheever. If there was ever any doubt of Bella's undying devotion, we know that it's not directed at me," Taylor said as the carriage came to a halt in front of the lecture hall.

Bella carefully positioned herself beside Lilly as they entered the lyceum. "There's Miss Addie and Mr. Farnsworth. They're waving us forward to join them. It appears Miss Mintie is with them," Bella added as she and Lilly made their way down the aisle with Taylor and Matthew following behind.

"We've saved you chairs," John said, stepping into the aisle.

When the group finally juggled into their seats, Mintie was seated to Bella's left and Addie to her right. Taylor was sandwiched between John and Matthew. Bella gave a self-satisfied grin as Taylor leaned forward to verify her whereabouts.

Mintie glanced over the top of her spectacles and clucked her tongue. "You'll have a spasm in your neck if you remain in that position much longer, Mr. Manning. Sit up!" the older woman commanded, straightening her own spine as she gave the order. She nodded in obvious satisfaction as Taylor wedged himself back between the two other men. "I'm pleased you're sitting beside me," Mintie said, patting Bella's hand. "Tell me, do you Shakers practice any of these skull readings?"

Bella smiled, trying to repress a giggle. She tried to imagine Sister Evangeline or one of the Brothers trying to read the bumps on one of the other Believers' heads. "No, at least not in Canterbury, although we've read about it—and discussed it at length. It's very interesting, don't you think?"

Mintie's eyebrows curved into two half moons. "Yes,

although I find it a bit disconcerting to think someone can evaluate you through touching your head."

"It's my understanding that there are employers in England and Scotland who demand a character reference from a phrenologist before they hire a prospective employee," Bella said.

Mintie lifted a hand to her head as if to ward off any stranger's hand that might be moving in her direction. "What ever would make them do such a thing?" she asked with a note of incredulity in her voice.

"Supposedly, they want to ensure a person is honest and hardworking," Bella replied.

"Well, I certainly hope the Corporation doesn't take up those strange practices," she said. "Did you hear that, Adelaide? The next thing you know, we'll have someone running his fingers through our hair before he'll hire us," she said as she reached across Bella and clutched at her sister's arm.

"Rest easy, Miss Mintie. I doubt the Corporation will agree to pay a phrenologist any time in the near future," John Farnsworth commented.

Had Bella not recognized the genuine concern etched upon Miss Mintie's face, she would have giggled at the older woman's shocked appearance. "They're ready to begin," Bella whispered as two men walked onto the stage at the front of the room.

After an impressive introduction, Lucius Applebaum stepped to the podium and began his oration. It was only after he'd talked for ninety minutes that he scanned the audience and said, "May I have a volunteer who is willing to have a skull reading join me on the stage?"

Taylor immediately stood up and began waving toward the speaker.

"Wonderful! We have a willing participant," Mr. Applebaum told the audience as Taylor made his way toward the front of the room.

Bella was surprised yet privately pleased Taylor had volunteered. She was curious to see exactly how the reading was performed. In fact, she would have gone forward herself had she not been certain a female volunteer would be considered inappropriate.

She watched and listened carefully as Mr. Applebaum explained that the bumps on Taylor's skull told of his honesty, veneration of God, and intelligence—completely confounding Bella. After diligently listening to the presentation, Bella had been growing convinced the readings might be quite scientific. Now, however, her convictions were dashed. To hear Mr. Applebaum assign such noble characteristics to Taylor Manning was preposterous. Taylor didn't revere or worship God! And he wasn't brimming with intellect—of that she was certain!

The lecture concluded and Taylor made his way back toward them as his companions began making their way into the aisle.

"So," Taylor said, meeting Bella's gaze, "wasn't that marvelous? It was as if he knew me through and through. Like he'd reached inside my soul and pulled out all the wonderful bits for the world to see."

"It was very much like he pulled something out, but I wouldn't call it wonderful bits," Bella muttered.

Taylor took hold of her elbow as several people jostled past them. Leaning over he whispered, "The entire lecture hall knows how wonderful I am. Why do you continue to deny it?"

Bella stopped in midstep and looked into Taylor's blue eyes. "You may be the most intelligent, marvelous specimen of humankind," Bella said. "But if you are, no one knows it better than you do, and that, Mr. Manning, I find most unattractive."

She made her way out without giving Taylor a second glance. Would that she could put him from her mind as easily as she put him from her sight.

"Do tell us what it was like, having Mr. Applebaum perform the reading," Lilly insisted as they began the carriage ride home.

"The procedure was extremely enlightening. I expected it might be rather painful—that he would push and prod without consideration," Taylor began. "However, he was quite gentle, merely circulating his fingers upon the skull in a relaxing manner. I fairly enjoyed the whole thing. Would you like me to demonstrate, Bella?" he inquired, giving her a grin.

Bella scooted farther into the corner. "Absolutely not!" she exclaimed.

"I'm sure she'd give me permission were it not for her fancy hairdo," Taylor said, causing Matthew and Lilly to laugh.

"I'm not certain I agree with your analysis of her decision, Taylor, but I must say that I admired your willingness to go up on that stage this evening. Did you ever consider the possibility that Mr. Applebaum might have given the audience a report that would have embarrassed you?" Matthew inquired.

Taylor shook his head and laughed. "How could that ever happen when he had such an excellent subject?"

Lilly and Matthew joined in the laughter, but Bella merely gave him a thoughtful glance. It was obvious Taylor held himself in high esteem—a quality she didn't find endearing.

"Shall we wait for you?" Matthew asked Taylor when they arrived at the boardinghouse.

"No need," Taylor quickly replied. "I don't want to detain you. Thank you for permitting us to accompany you this evening."

With a sweet smile, Bella expressed her genuine thanks before descending the carriage.

"I hope to see you again very soon, Bella," Lilly replied. "And don't be too harsh with Taylor," she added in a whisper. "I think he means well."

Bella nodded and gave Lilly a faint smile as she walked alongside Taylor to the front door. Once inside, she turned toward the parlor and began to unfasten her cape. Yet her hand remained suspended in midair, her mouth agape as she stared at Jesse Harwood sitting beside Daughtie on the velvet-covered settee.

"Jesse." His name spilled from Bella's lips with an ease that belied the wave of nausea sweeping over her. Her knees began to tremble and dizziness washed over her in waves. Jesse, dressed in his dark blue Shaker surtout and straw hat, moved toward her.

"Bella," he greeted warmly, taking long strides across the room. Lightly grasping her shoulders, he held her at arm's length, his gaze traveling up and down the length of her body before finally looking into her eyes. "You are even more beautiful than I remember. And the color of that dress is perfect on you," he said, pulling her into an embrace.

The rasping sound of Taylor clearing his throat startled Bella. Pushing away from Jesse, she moved to his side and glanced toward Taylor. "Jesse, I would like to introduce you to Taylor Manning. He furnished me with a ticket to the phrenology lecture at the lyceum this evening."

"And escorted her," Taylor added, giving Bella a sidelong glance before extending his hand toward Jesse. "Bella has mentioned you," he said while pumping Jesse's hand up and down.

Jesse beamed a smile in Bella's direction. "That's good to hear."

"You're the one who pledged your love and then left her in the woods to fend for herself, aren't you?" Taylor inquired.

Bella wanted to stomp on Taylor's foot. How dare he interfere? Poor Jesse looked as though he'd taken a strong fist in his midsection.

"You told him that I left you to fend for yourself?" Jesse gave her a baffled look.

"You didn't appear. Daughtie and I finally left Canterbury, certain you weren't coming. Isn't that right, Daughtie?" Bella asked, hoping Daughtie would affirm her reply. However, Daughtie had apparently fled the room unnoticed, as the settee was now unoccupied.

Jesse's forehead creased into deep lines. "You believe I would willingly abandon you?"

"What else was I to believe? Daughtie and I waited. You didn't arrive. Now you suddenly appear and rebuke me for saying you broke your promise."

"It wasn't intentional. I couldn't leave that night without . . ." He hesitated and glanced at Taylor and then back at Bella. "Could we possibly have this conversation alone—without him?" Jesse asked as he pointed a thumb in Taylor's direction.

Bella moved toward the door. "Taylor, I'll see you out," she said, turning the doorknob.

"I'm not anxious to leave. It's still early," he said, remaining in place.

"It would please me if you would exhibit your fine English manners and leave Jesse and me to discuss this matter in private.

Thank you for permitting me the opportunity to attend the lecture," she said while holding the door ajar.

Taylor turned to face her, leaned down close to her ear, and said, "I'll bid you good-night if you promise to see me again in the very near future, dear Bella."

"I won't bargain with you, Mr. Manning," she whispered firmly.

Taylor smiled. "That's fine. I'll be happy to remain here with the two of you," he said, beginning to push the door closed.

Bella seethed inwardly as she pulled back on the door. "Very well. I'll agree—just leave."

Taylor nodded. "Good! I feared we were going to ruin Miss Addie's door by shoving it back and forth," he said, emitting a chuckle. "Nice to meet you, Jesse," he said, tossing a mock salute in Jesse's direction. "And you," he said, turning back toward Bella, "I'll be calling on you soon," he said loudly enough for Jesse to hear.

He was out the door before Bella could object to his boorish behavior. Had Jesse not been watching and waiting, she would have chased him down the street and insisted upon an apology! Instead, she took a deep breath, exhaled slowly, and closed the door with a resounding thud before smiling at Jesse.

"Shall we sit in the parlor?" she inquired in what she hoped was her calmest voice.

Jesse followed close at her heels and seated himself beside her. Bella folded her hands, placed them in her lap, and gave him her full attention. "Well? I'm awaiting your explanation."

"I was prepared to meet you. My belongings were packed; I was certain the other Brothers were asleep. But I was wrong. I rose from my bed and went down the stairs. However, when I went to the barn where I had stored my belongings and some food, I couldn't find them. I searched for what seemed an eternity, knowing I was late to meet you. When I finally realized someone must have found my satchel, I hurried from the barn and ran headlong into Brother Ernest. He grabbed me by the ear and pulled me back into the barn, demanding I explain my conduct. I told him I was leaving, that I could no longer adhere to the beliefs of the Society. He asked why I was sneaking off like a thief in the night when I could have gone before the Elders and told them of my decision. He wondered why I would choose to leave the Society without at least a modicum of dignity and enough money for a few meals and a room. I fumbled for words, knowing anything I said would make no sense to them."

Bella sat transfixed as she listened to Jesse's words. "So what did you tell him?"

"I decided I could either tell him I was planning to run off with you, which would have immediately explained why I didn't go before the Elders, or tell him I decided to sneak off because I lacked the courage to face the Elders. However, I knew I would be caught in my lie if they discovered you missing the next morning. So I told him the truth."

"That we were leaving together?"

Jesse nodded his head.

"Well, then, I'm even more pleased I didn't remain behind. Just think what might have happened if I had returned to my room—the wrath of the Elders would have poured down upon us," Bella observed.

He gave her a tentative smile. "It did pour down—upon me. Until I finally took a firm stand and told them I was leaving."

Bella ran a finger down a deep fold in the rose-colored dress, her gaze fixed upon the painting of the New England country-side hanging on the far wall. "My father—" she haltingly began—"did he appear concerned or distraught that I was gone?"

"He said he would be praying for your swift return to the Society, adding that you'd surely lost control of your senses. He was angry that you'd broken your vows," Jesse replied in a plain-tive tone. "Of course, his words of recrimination were directed toward me. He said it was my behavior that rekindled your desire to live in the world and gave you the courage to make such a foolhardy decision."

Bella shook her head in anger. "How can he call himself a good Shaker when he speaks falsely? He knows that I never adjusted to life among the Shakers and my desire to leave the

Society always remained firm. Had you been the catalyst for my departure, I wouldn't have left without you. I think it should have been obvious to all of them that you were not to blame."

"I'm not sure who or what they believe. I departed two days after you and Daughtie, before their meetings and discussions had ended. I'm sure they knew I was coming to find you. Sister Mercy requested I give you her love and best wishes. I agreed to do so, not realizing so much time would pass before we would reunite. Most likely, they all believe we are married by now," he said, taking her hand.

Bella lifted her hand from his and wriggled into the far corner of the settee. "Where have you been for all this time, Jesse?"

He appeared taken aback by her question. "In Concord. That's what we planned," he replied. "I attempted to locate your relatives, but I didn't know where to begin looking."

Bella nodded. "I should have given you the address," she agreed.

"Or at least a last name. All you ever told me was that your Aunt Ida and Uncle Arthur lived in Concord. Of course, I thought we would be traveling together, so I never asked. When I arrived in Concord, I wasn't sure what to do. Thinking you might still be there, I didn't want to leave, yet I worried you might not be there. My decision was difficult. However, the innkeeper mentioned a local cooper was in need of an assistant. When the cooper hired me, I decided it was providence that I remain and look for you. What if I had headed off for Lowell while you were waiting for me in Concord? Besides, I didn't think you and Daughtie would venture to Lowell on your own. I wanted to believe you were anxiously awaiting me, ready to become my wife."

She intentionally ignored his statement regarding marriage. "Then what made you finally come looking for me in Lowell?"

"As the days passed, I began asking customers if they knew anyone named Arthur or Ida. Each time someone gave me a name, I would search for the person. Eventually, a man who knew your uncle came into the shop. He gave me the address of your aunt and uncle. Your aunt told me you and Daughtie had been there but that you had left for Lowell the day after you arrived in Concord. I can't tell you how devastated I was when I heard that piece of news," he said in a saddened tone.

"You found my aunt in good health?" she inquired, wanting to keep the conversation neutral.

"Yes, she's fine. In fact, she told me she had recently received letters from you and that you were doing well. I asked her if she would give me your address. At first she was reluctant, but your uncle convinced her I meant no harm. I've rented a small place for us to live—not far from my work. Your aunt is delighted we'll be living in Concord. She asked that we wait and marry in Concord so she and your uncle may attend the wedding."

It was difficult to ignore the hopefulness that punctuated his words. "I'm sorry, Jesse, but I won't be moving to Concord. I don't plan to marry you," she replied in a soft yet firm voice.

Jesse wiped beads of perspiration from his forehead. "My late arrival has permitted you to pledge your love to that other fellow, hasn't it? The minute Daughtie told me you had gone to the lyceum with another man, I knew my fate was sealed—that I had lost you to another. He's pledged his love, hasn't he?"

Bella stifled a giggle. The very thought of Taylor Manning pledging his love to anyone other than himself was wishful thinking. "You're overreacting, Jesse. First of all, you can't lose something you never possessed. I never promised to marry you. We agreed only to leave Canterbury together. You mistakenly assumed my decision to leave was based upon a betrothal pledge. And secondly, I am not planning to marry anyone," she staunchly replied.

"You need not attempt to protect my feelings, Bella. I saw the way he was looking at you. And whether you wish to admit to your feelings or not, I saw you return his look of affection," Jesse said with his tone growing louder and more accusatory.

Bella stiffened her back, her chin jutting forward ever so slightly. "Jesse Harwood! How dare you sit in my presence making false allegations! You're treating me no better than a tribunal of Shakers would. My decision to remain in Lowell has nothing to do with you or Taylor Manning. It has to do with me! I want an opportunity to make decisions for myself, to seek the truth of God's Word for my life, to heal from wounds, both old and new. Ultimately I hope to discover where I belong."

"And am I the cause of some of those wounds you speak of?" he asked.

She nodded her head. "Yes. Although after listening to your explanation, it does appear I judged you too harshly."

Jesse's face brightened. "Then if I remain in Lowell and find work, would you give me permission to call upon you? I know we are destined to marry, Bella."

His voice was filled with excitement, making Bella's reply even more difficult. "I cannot tell you where to live, Jesse; that is your decision. But I don't believe we are destined to marry. Since I've never experienced the kind of love I believe God intends between marriage partners, I don't even know that marriage will be a part of my future," Bella said. "You have been a dear friend, but I only agreed to leave the village with you because I was desperate to go."

He stood and gave her a waning smile. "It's obvious you have no desire for me to make my home in Lowell," he said mournfully. "Perhaps it's best I return to Concord. At least I have a job and there are a few people who have befriended me. May I at least write to you?"

"Of course. I would be pleased to correspond with you," she replied.

Jesse nodded. "It's getting late. I had best bid you goodnight. I'll leave for Concord in the morning. I'm staying at the Wareham Hotel—in case you should change your mind."

She escorted him to the door and watched as he dejectedly walked down the darkened street. He stopped and glanced over his shoulder for a brief moment before continuing onward.

"I pray I've made the right decision," Bella murmured into the quietude of the night.

Later that night, after the other girls in the room were sleeping soundly, Bella lit a single candle and took up her Bible. Sleep would not come, and she felt as though the weight of the world were on her shoulders. *Maybe I've done the wrong thing. Maybe I should have gone with Jesse. I don't love him, but maybe that isn't a part of the plan God has for me.*

She opened the book to the forty-first chapter of Isaiah. *Oh, Lord,* she prayed, *just show me the truth of what I need to know. I so desire to have answers to my questions. I'm afraid that maybe I'm making all the wrong choices. I'm afraid that I've done myself more harm than good.*

She looked down at the page and her gaze fell upon the tenth verse. *"Fear thou not; for I am with thee: be not dismayed; for I am thy God: I will strengthen thee; yea, I will help thee; yea, I will uphold thee with the right hand of my righteousness."*

Peace slipped in past the barricades she'd erected around her heart. "I don't want to be afraid," she whispered, her breath touching the flame of the candle and blowing it out. The darkness engulfed her at once. Bella thought of lighting the candle again, but instead she eased back against the pillow, still clutching her Bible close.

"Lord, I won't fear. I'll trust you, and you will strengthen me as you've promised."

CHAPTER 17

A steady stream of girls filed into St. Anne's Episcopal Church. Bella was surprised how their numbers steadily increased each time they gathered. "It's going to be our best turnout ever," Bella whispered to Ruth, who had become her strongest ally in forming the study groups and classes. Even Daughtie had worked alongside the others, distributing notices, encouraging the attendance of the mill girls, and quietly lending her support wherever needed.

Today Daughtie was seated in the front row, and Bella beamed a smile in her friend's direction. She truly hoped Daughtie would remain in Lowell, yet somewhere deep within she feared her friend's heart still remained in Canterbury. But for now, she knew Daughtie was doing what she had promised—she was giving this new life a chance before making her final decision.

Bella stepped to the platform and gave the crowd a welcoming smile. "I am pleased to see so many of you in attendance. It gladdens my heart to know that women are willing to come together and search for ways to educate and better themselves. I applaud your commitment," she said. "Together we are making great strides, and I want to report to you what has been accomplished thus far."

A smattering of applause began and then erupted into a loud ovation. When the room had sufficiently quieted, Bella thanked the group and continued. "We have successfully begun four study groups and have retained qualified teachers for each of them. Mr. Hazen, who has traveled extensively in France and Italy, even making his home in France for a period of time, is teaching two French classes. A waiting list is being compiled for the next sessions, so if you are interested, I suggest you give your name to Ruth Wilson. Ruth, why don't you stand so everyone knows who you are," she said, turning and motioning her friend to rise to her feet.

The group's attention was quickly divided between Ruth and the rear doorway, where a group of men had entered the room and were now seating themselves in the back rows. Bella ignored the intrusion and calmly continued with her speech.

"Ruth will take your name after the meeting today if you are interested in any classes. Thank you, Ruth," she said as Ruth took her seat. "We also have a group studying literature. I understand that each girl enrolled in that class will write an essay dealing with the literary work being studied. We have explored the possibility of printing those essays for all to read, as I feel certain they will be enlightening compositions. Mr. Leatherman has agreed to print them, charging only his cost to us. And for those of you who may not know it, Mr. Leatherman has printed all of our pamphlets at cost, and our fliers have been free. I would ask that if you have any printing needs, you support his business. He has been most benevolent to our cause.

"Now, back to our class schedule. Our final class is for those girls who, for various reasons, did not receive the basic level of schooling before moving away from home. This class teaches reading, penmanship, biology, arithmetic—I won't enumerate further, but the class offers all of these studies. It is tailored to each student's needs. So if you should find yourself lacking in only one or two areas, you could study only those particular topics. As I said earlier, all of these classes are full, but because you have shown there is a need and desire for education among women, we are seeking additional teachers in order to expand. We also welcome your ideas for new classes."

Ruth stepped forward and whispered in Bella's ear. "Oh, yes. Ruth has reminded me that next Tuesday evening Mr. Clark will begin violin lessons for interested pupils. There are three openings available in that class."

A girl near the front raised her hand, and Bella nodded in her direction. "Is the cost for all of the classes the same?"

"No, some are less than others. However, if the teacher requires specific study materials, you must agree to purchase those before the class begins. Some of the girls who have already purchased books for the current classes have agreed to loan those to the next group of students."

A round of applause and murmuring among the audience followed this remark.

"The sharing of class books caused me to wonder how many of you own books that you might be willing to loan for other girls to read. In fact, even more than educational classes, it was the sharing of reading materials that originated the formation of this group. As some of you know, I had hoped—"

A shuffling of feet and scraping of chairs near the back of the room caused Bella, along with most of the audience, to shift her gaze toward the commotion. The men who had earlier entered the auditorium now stood, one of them with his hand high in the air.

"Yes, what is it?" Bella inquired of the man and at the same time noticed that Taylor Manning was standing next to him.

"We're members of the Mechanics Association, and as you may know, our organization has a library."

Bella nodded. "I'm aware of your library, sir. In fact, I sought permission for women to use your library some time ago."

"So I understand. Well, it appears we men don't move with the same swiftness as the good women of Lowell. However, we have finally discussed your request at length, and upon Mr. Taylor Manning's recommendation, we have agreed to extend library privileges to your membership, Miss Newberry."

A roar of applause filled the auditorium while Bella met Taylor's gaze. He seemed rather proud of himself, smiling in his self-confident manner. What was he up to? she wondered. Why hadn't Taylor made the offer? And was there some reason they had come before the group rather than notifying her beforehand? Perhaps Taylor thought the girls would be overwhelmed with gratitude and accept the proposal without question. And from the enthusiastic response of the crowd, it appeared as if they would do so. She, however, wanted more information.

Bella patiently waited until the clapping subsided. "Thank you for your generous offer, sir. Are you prepared to discuss this matter at greater length for our group? If so, why don't you join me on the platform," she invited.

"Come on, Taylor," the man who had first spoken directed, pulling Taylor along by the arm until they were beside Bella on the stage.

"Why don't you introduce yourselves," Bella encouraged.

Taylor gave her a sheepish look. "This here's Taylor Manning," the other man said while pointing a thumb in Taylor's direction, "and I'm Oliver Franks. We're officers of the Mechanics Association," he proudly announced.

"Thank you, Mr. Franks. Will there be any cost for the use of your library materials?" Bella inquired with a sweet smile.

Mr. Franks shifted his position on the stage, moving behind Taylor. "Mr. Manning can share the details with you," he said as he bobbed his head around Taylor's shoulder.

Taylor cleared his throat. "Mr. Franks is correct that we have agreed to permit use of the library. However, because there is an expense connected with the operation of the library, we would expect you to pay the same yearly dues as the men. Of course, the dues need not be paid in one sum; they can be paid in a weekly or monthly sum—whatever best suits the particular needs of each patron."

Taylor's answer was followed by shuffling feet and murmurs as the women turned to discuss the matter with each other.

"Ladies! Ladies!" Bella called out. "May I have your attention, please. If there are questions, please raise your hand and Mr.

Manning or Mr. Franks," she said, looking first at one man and then the other, "will answer. I would like to begin by asking if these dues will afford us all of the same privileges granted to the men."

Taylor appeared momentarily puzzled by the question, glancing first at Oliver Franks and then back at Bella. "Exactly what privileges are you referring to, Miss Newberry?"

"Well," she began, "I was thinking we should have some-body on the committee that makes book selections as well as a representative on the committee that makes selections for the lyceum speakers—if those are different groups," she said, gracing him with a bright smile.

Her request brought excited agreement from the ladies in the audience.

Taylor pulled at his collar. "Those decisions are made by the officers and then reported to the members for their discussion and vote, which has been more of a formality as the men have never requested any changes," he replied. "With these rules in place, I don't see how a woman could become a part of that decision-making group, do you?"

His tone made it obvious he thought his question was rhe-torical, but Bella met the inquiry head on. "I think we could overcome that obstacle with little difficulty," she countered.

"Wh-wh-what?" he stammered. "A woman can't be an offi-cer of the Mechanics Association."

"No, but you could form committees to make these choices instead of using your board. That way, some of the committee members could be women," she suggested.

His mouth dropped open in surprise. "Some? You want more than one representative on the committees if they're estab-lished?"

"Naturally," she calmly replied. "If we pay equal dues, we should have equal representation."

"She has a point," Mr. Franks quietly remarked.

Taylor gave Oliver a stunned look. "Whose side are you on?" he whispered back.

Bella listened to the exchange with satisfaction. "He's

173

right—I do have a valid argument. And I'm sure you wouldn't disagree that women should have equality. Additionally, there are some of your members who might be pleased to turn over the duty of selecting books and speakers. It would free their time for other more important work of the Association," she submitted.

Together with the women in the audience, most of the men were murmuring and nodding their agreement. Taylor appeared surprised at their immediate willingness to succumb to Bella's persuasive words and sweet smile. She had won them over with little effort.

"But the men pay the rent, and they've paid for the books that are already in the library," he argued. "They must maintain primary control of this Association they've established. It is rightfully theirs."

Bella acknowledged a young woman in the audience who had raised her hand. "I think Mr. Manning is correct. The men should maintain control of their Association, but I believe the concept of creating committees with one or two representatives from our group would be acceptable. Perhaps we should vote on such a proposal."

Taylor quickly stepped forward. "If you want to vote on a proposal, I can't stop you, but I don't have the authority to accept or reject your suggestion. I'll agree to take your request before the Association and report back."

A show of hands verified the girls were in agreement. They requested Taylor take their proposal before the Association and report back the following week. Bella would have preferred to push for additional women on the committees, but this was a start. They could move toward further representation in the future. All things considered, she was pleased Taylor and his group of men had attended this evening, although she wasn't so sure Taylor himself was pleased with the outcome. The meeting concluded, and Bella began to gather the pamphlets and fliers, tucking them into a small case. The sound of approaching foot-steps caused her to look up.

"I was hoping to escort you home. There's a personal matter I'd like to discuss with you," Taylor said.

Bella hesitated, not sure she wanted to spend time alone with Taylor. She wasn't certain he truly believed women should be involved in the Association's decision-making process, and she didn't want to argue the matter with him privately. After all, he had agreed to take the proposal before the Association.

"I walked over with Daughtie and Ruth," she replied.

"I know. I told them I was going to escort you home. They've already departed," he replied. "And before you become angry, let me assure you that this isn't a ploy. Miss Addie is going to need your support over the next few weeks, perhaps longer."

His words captured Bella's attention. She reached out and grasped his arm with a sense of urgency. "Has something happened to Miss Addie? She was fine when I left the house this evening."

Taylor enveloped her hand in his own. "I didn't mean to alarm you; Miss Addie is in good health. This is more—" he hesitated, obviously searching for an explanation—"a matter of the heart. Yes, I think that would best describe the situation."

Bella was intrigued. Accepting Taylor's proffered arm, she accompanied him through the arched doors of the gray-slate church. Why would Miss Addie suffer from a matter of the heart? She and John Farnsworth were deeply committed to each other. Thoughts of their relationship caused her to stop midstep.

"Has John Farnsworth taken up with another woman?" Her words sliced through the air.

Taylor's mouth dropped open; he gaped at her in obvious disbelief. "What a terrible accusation! Do you think all men are unable to honor their word?"

Bella thought for a moment before answering. "My limited observation has shown me that it depends on the commitment and the person to whom it is made. I find men fall short in keeping their word when it is given to a woman."

"Really? Well, my uncle John is not one of those men. He's not a cad or philanderer. He cares very much for Miss Addie. He would never intentionally hurt her," Taylor defended as they moved onward.

"If this has nothing to do with your Uncle John, why would she be troubled?"

"You're twisting my words, Bella. You do that all the time— you win people to your point of view by manipulating words."

Once again Bella tugged him to a halt. "I do not manipulate words, but I'm not afraid to speak the truth. Why don't you just tell me about the situation with Miss Addie and then we won't be required to argue about my choice of words," she fumed.

"I didn't tell you outright because I wanted to spend some time alone with you. I knew you wouldn't permit me to escort you home if I merely blurted out what I had to say."

She glanced up and gave him an embarrassed grin. "You're right. I would have refused your invitation."

He gave a quick nod of his head. "My uncle must leave in the morning. He was called to Kirk Boott's office and told he is needed to journey to the southern United States for the Corporation."

Bella's eyebrows furrowed at his reply. "Why would the Corporation send your uncle John?"

"Mr. Boott was to make the journey, but his health has failed him during the past week and he's unable to travel. He requested Mr. Cheever take his place. However, Mr. Cheever didn't want to make the trip unless he could wait until after the birth of his child. When Mr. Boott said the journey must be made as soon as possible, Mr. Cheever suggested Uncle John."

"Surely a short journey to the South won't be overly upsetting to Miss Addie," Bella determined.

"I didn't say short journey. He may be there for some period of time."

"But why?"

"Uncle John didn't tell me the details, but he did remark upon the fact that his skills of diplomacy would be needed. He'll be meeting with plantation owners regarding cotton production and prices. Mr. Boott has been consulting with him for hours."

"Wouldn't you think there's someone equally as qualified as your uncle?" she questioned. For Miss Addie's sake, Bella didn't want the Corporation sending Mr. Farnsworth.

"I'm certain there are more qualified men, but apparently none of them will agree to make the trip. Uncle John doesn't have much choice in the matter. In fact, Mr. Boott is now convinced Uncle John will perform magnificently. Those are Mr. Boott's words, not mine."

"Poor Miss Addie. She will miss him ever so much."

Taylor nodded his agreement. "Miss Addie won't have much time to become accustomed to the thought of Uncle John's departure; he leaves in the morning."

"I'll do all I can to help Miss Addie while Mr. Farnsworth is away. Perhaps she would like to become involved as a representative on one of the committees."

Taylor chuckled. "Your mind never stops working, does it? You're always looking for an advantage."

"I was merely suggesting one way to keep Miss Addie busy," she demurely replied.

"Well, just keep in mind that the membership must approve this plan of yours before anyone's time will be filled choosing reading material," he jibed.

"And speakers," she quickly added.

"Yes, Bella," he said as they neared the boardinghouse, "speakers, too. That's Uncle John's carriage."

"At least they've had some time alone with all of the girls attending the meeting this evening," Bella commented as the front window revealed the silhouette of John and Addie.

The older couple had walked to the carriage by the time Bella and Taylor approached the front door.

"Ah, Taylor, you can drive me home," John said, affectionately slapping his nephew on the back.

The tear stains on Miss Addie's face were evident as she embraced John one last time. "Please take care of yourself. I want you to come home safe and sound," she cautioned in a choked voice.

"I'll be safe and sound and back here before you even know I've gone. Promise you'll give serious thought to our discussion."

Addie nodded her head. "You know I will," she said as the men drove away.

Bella gently touched Miss Addie's shoulder and drew near. "It's obvious he cares deeply for you, Miss Addie. Mr. Farnsworth seems a fine man. There's no doubt he'll be back as quickly as his business will permit."

Addie nodded and then gave Bella a look of surprise. "How did you know John was going away?"

"Taylor. He was concerned about you. I hope you don't feel he betrayed a confidence by telling me."

"No, it's quite all right. Everyone will know by this time tomorrow. Word travels fast in this small community. I had best tell Mintie first thing in the morning. If she hears from someone else, there will be no end to her bruised feelings."

Bella nodded. "Let's just take care of today, Miss Addie. Tomorrow will take care of itself—that's what Sister Mercy used to tell me. She said there were enough worries in one day without borrowing from the next."

Addie chuckled. "Perhaps Sister Mercy was right."

"Why don't we have a nice cup of tea?" Bella suggested while leading Miss Addie toward the kitchen. "I'm positive Mr. Farnsworth will make every effort to return quickly."

Addie made a valiant effort to smile. "I certainly hope so, my dear. I fear I'm going to miss him dreadfully."

———

Taylor stoked the fire in the stove and sat down to consider his evening. With John now gone to bed in order to accommodate his early morning travel, Taylor felt rather alone and found the memories of his past rushing in like a cold December wind. He remembered his home in London, the scent of rain in the air, the sounds of the merchants and their customers. He thought from time to time of the pleasures he'd stolen—a kiss here or there, a quiet moment under the stars. He'd thought such diversions were all he'd ever want, but listening to his uncle speak of Miss Addie Beecher tonight, Taylor was no longer all that certain of his choices. John had stirred something deep inside Taylor that he had thought dead and buried.

"There's something to be said for a good woman," John had

told him on the way home. "A woman who will faithfully await your return, no matter where you go or how long it will take. Just the idea of knowing someone is home, anticipating your arrival, well . . . it makes living worthwhile."

Taylor knew his mother and father had shared that kind of love. When his mother died it had nearly destroyed his father. He mourned her to his dying day—never quite being whole again. Never quite enjoying life as he had before her death. For that very reason, Taylor had difficulty in taking any kind of commitment seriously. He never wanted to duplicate the pain his father felt. It was easier to toy with women, to play the games they initiated. Games of pursuit—games to land a husband who would take care of them.

Taylor had played the game better than most. Maybe too well. Now he wasn't at all sure where the amusements left off and real life stepped in. A woman like Bella wasn't interested in playing the coquette, and because of this Taylor didn't know quite how to handle her. She wasn't easily swayed by his appearance or manners. Enticements that had worked on other girls simply eluded Bella Newberry. Taylor told himself it didn't matter, but deep down inside, it did.

He'd relied upon his good looks and quick wit all his life. They were his bargaining tools—even with men. He had a boyish charm and roguish nature that he could use at will, no matter the situation. Of course, it hadn't helped him with the matter of his last affair of the heart. That girl's father had not been interested in being charmed out of his anger. But that was all behind Taylor now.

"I've spent my adult life—short though it may be—avoiding the possible pain found in the commitment of genuine affection. And now John makes me remember the love of my parents, and I find myself confused. Have I only deluded myself?" he murmured. What more was there? Where was he to find solace and happiness?

"Taylor, my darling boy," his mother had once said, *"God did not put you on this earth with a fine face and solid mind in order to see you do the devil's work. He put you here for His will and glory. Find*

out what His will is and you will bring Him glory. And neither, I assure you, will have anything at all to do with your outward appearance. It will have everything to do with the quality of your heart."

Taylor felt more haunted by his mother's words here in America than he'd ever been in England. She'd been worried about him even as she slipped from this world. Burying his face in his hands, Taylor longed for peace of mind and heart.

My inability to deal openly with others has also hindered my ability to deal with God. The phrenologist said I was a man who respected God, but I seldom give Him the time of day, Taylor admitted to himself. *I've turned into that horrible man my mother warned me about, and I have no idea how to turn back.*

Looking up with a sigh, Taylor knew he'd find no answers that night. No, the things that troubled him deep in his soul would take time and effort . . . and most likely more commitment than he'd ever invested. Taylor, however, wasn't at all sure he had it in himself to give.

CHAPTER 18

"I've been offered a position as a drawing-in girl," Bella told Daughtie as the two of them hastened off toward the mill, the early morning still shrouded in darkness.

The tower bell clanged, warning them the gate would soon be closing. Several girls rushed past, while another group was clustered close behind. "That would mean more money, wouldn't it? Are you going to accept the position?"

Bella detected a hint of fear in Daughtie's question. "If you'll be happier if I remain nearby, I won't accept. The money isn't that important to me, Daughtie."

Daughtie shook her head back and forth. "No. Asking you to remain a weaver wouldn't be fair. You should accept the position. I hear that it's much quieter," she said, a note of longing in her voice.

"Would you be interested in the position?" Bella asked.

"It wasn't offered to me. I'm sure they feel you're better qualified."

"But we both know that I'm not. You would do a much better job; you have more patience, and you don't mind working independently. When I decline the position, I could recommend you."

They hurried through the mill yard and began their ascent up the spiraling stairwell. "I don't want you to refuse on my account. But if you should decide you're not interested, you could mention my name," Daughtie added quickly.

Bella gave her a smile. "It will be my pleasure, although I will miss you. But I fear that your Bible memorization will far surpass mine if you take the drawing-in position."

Daughtie giggled. "Then perhaps I will be forced to tutor you each evening."

"You go on to your looms. I'll stop and talk to Mr. Kingman," Bella said as they walked through the door of the weaving room.

Bella breathed a sigh of relief. Mr. Kingman wasn't occupied repairing one of the looms or busy with his paper work. He was a stern man, and the girls quickly learned he hated interruptions. "Mr. Kingman? May I speak with you?"

He turned and nodded. "Have you made a decision about the drawing-in position?" he curtly inquired.

Bella nodded. "I realize it pays more money, but I'd prefer to stay here in the weaving room—at least for now. But if I may be so bold, I would suggest you offer the position to Daughtie. I mentioned there was an opening, and I know she's interested. To be honest, Mr. Kingman, she would be much better at the position. She's much more patient and prefers more solitary work. You know how quickly she's learned her looms. She can even—"

"Bella," Mr. Kingman interrupted, "I'm aware of Daughtie's workmanship. I agree she would be a good choice. If you're not interested, she may have the position. Tell her to report to me. She can begin today. Now get to your looms."

"Thank you, Mr. Kingman," Bella enthusiastically said as she clasped her hands together. She rushed down the aisle, careful to keep her skirts away from the machines that had already clattered into motion. When she finally gained Daughtie's attention, Bella motioned her friend toward Mr. Kingman.

Daughtie nodded, slapped her looms to a halt, and hurried off. Bella was going to miss seeing her friend smile from across the aisle, but perhaps this new position would help Daughtie determine whether she should remain in Lowell or return to the Society. Already Daughtie had agreed that a portion of the Shaker beliefs were inconsistent with the Bible, yet Bella knew her friend was still drawn to the familiar environment in Canterbury. Perhaps God would speak to Daughtie's heart.

Daughtie had been gone for only a short time when Mr. Kingman appeared. He had a young girl with long chestnut hair and a rather sallow complexion in tow. He motioned for Bella to shut down her looms and pulled the girl forward. "Bella, this is Virginia Dane. You'll train her on the looms; she's been on the spinning floor working for Thaddeus Arnold. He recommended her for this position."

The girl appeared frightened. Bella offered a broad smile and took Virginia's hand. "Come stand by me at my looms and watch. I won't start you on your own loom until—"

"She can begin on her own looms this afternoon. You can move back and forth across the aisle and help," Mr. Kingman interrupted. "I don't want both of Daughtie's looms sitting idle any longer than necessary. Idle looms don't make money."

Bella didn't argue. She disagreed with Mr. Kingman, but she disagreed with many decisions regarding the operation of the Appleton. Nobody cared what she thought; after all, she was only an operative, easily replaced by another girl looking for work. Besides, the men who owned these mills touted themselves as forward-thinking simply because they employed women, when such an avowal was simply untrue. Bella had quickly realized the Associates hired women merely to benefit themselves and their profits. However, she believed these jobs would ultimately lead to a measure of equality for women. There was no doubt the Shakers were far advanced on the issue of equality.

When the breakfast bell finally rang, Bella pointed to the loom handle and motioned Virginia to stop the machine. "When we return from breakfast, I'll have you try your hand at the loom," Bella said, pulling the handle of the other machine.

Virginia's eyes grew large, and the smidgen of color in her sallow complexion drained from sight. The girl scurried along in Bella's footsteps until they reached the bottom of the stairs. Virginia's hands were shaking in spite of the warm morning sun.

"I don't think I can ever learn that," she said as she pointed up the stairwell.

"Of course you can, Virginia. If the rest of us can learn to manage those beastly machines, you can, too," Bella said, forcing a note of cheer into her voice. "You're going to do just fine, and in a couple of weeks, you'll wonder why you were ever concerned."

Virginia wagged her head back and forth. "I don't think so. I wish I could go back to spinning," she lamented.

Bella gazed into the girl's frightened eyes. "Why did you move to weaving, Virginia? The money?"

The girl continued to walk alongside Bella. "My family can certainly use the money, but Mr. Arnold gave me no choice. He said Mr. Kingman had requested a recommendation to fill a vacant position."

"Then you must have been a very good spinner; otherwise, Mr. Arnold wouldn't have recommended you. It appears as if Mr. Arnold believes you're bright enough to learn a new job, and he's giving you the opportunity to make additional money," Bella encouraged.

Virginia gave her a feeble smile. "No, that's not why. He wanted to hire another girl for the spinning room. She's quite lovely—long flaxen hair and sparkling blue eyes. Mr. Arnold likes pretty girls, and I'm not pretty," she said in a flat voice.

Bella startled at Virginia's comment. She had heard rumors about Mr. Arnold and his behavior—stories of abusive behavior toward his wife and aggressive behavior toward the operatives. But that had been a couple of years ago. The Arnolds now had a baby girl. Surely Mr. Arnold wasn't returning to his former way of life. Perhaps Virginia misunderstood his intentions.

Unsure how she should react, Bella gave Virginia an encouraging hug. "You'll be fine, Virginia. All you need is a little practice and a dose of confidence. I'll do my best to help you gain both."

Virginia tilted her head to the side as though it would help her digest the information. "Then I'll try very hard, and perhaps I will learn," she agreed.

They had reached the edge of the mill yard when Daughtie raced up behind them. "Well, did you miss me?" she asked with a grin.

"Of course I missed you," Bella replied. "This is Virginia Dane," she said, turning toward the new girl. "She's going to work your looms."

"Hello, Virginia," Daughtie said.

"Hello," Virginia replied. "I go in this direction," she said, pointing toward a distant row of boardinghouses.

"I'll see you after breakfast," Bella said, watching as Virginia departed.

"She's a frightened little mouse," Daughtie commented.

"Yes, very frightened," Bella agreed. "Come on—the bells will be ringing us back to work before we've had our breakfast," she said, urging Daughtie into the house.

After gobbling down her breakfast, Bella darted into the kitchen to check on Miss Addie before returning to work. Spying the older woman coming in the back door, Bella rushed toward her. "How are you today, Miss Addie?"

The older woman patted Bella's shoulder. "You need not fret about me, dear. I'm doing fine. Come visit with me tonight."

"There's the bell—I'll talk to you this evening," Bella promised as she rushed back into the dining room, through the parlor, into the hallway, and out the door. She quickly moved alongside Daughtie. "Did the morning go well for you, Daughtie?"

Daughtie nodded as they walked down the street at a brisk pace. "I think I'm going to be much happier, but it will take time to become proficient. It is quieter, and for that I am grateful. I'll give you all the details tonight," she promised.

Bella was pleased by Daughtie's enthusiasm. Perhaps they could visit with Miss Addie together this evening. Daughtie's new position could prove an interesting topic to keep Miss

Addie's thoughts on something other than John Farnsworth's absence, Bella decided.

Virginia, appearing even more fraught than she had a half hour earlier, stood beside Bella's looms, awaiting her instructions. "Did you have a good breakfast?" Bella inquired, hoping to relieve the girl's anxiety.

"It was fine. I promise I'll do my best, but I don't remember anything you showed me, and I've been gone only a half hour." The words tumbled from her lips as though she might forget them if she spoke slowly.

Patiently, Bella once again instructed Virginia, methodically moving her through the weaving process, step by step, until the girl appeared to gain confidence. Two hours later, Bella motioned to Virginia to take charge of one loom. Standing close at hand, Bella supervised the girl's every move. Her first attempt at threading the shuttle proved difficult, but she persevered, finally succeeding. Bella applauded her success, hoping the praise would bolster Virginia's confidence. Unfortunately, she appeared to grow more distraught each time a thread broke or a snag appeared in the cloth, her forehead lined with deep creases.

"You're performing as well as any of the new hires," Bella shouted.

"I find that difficult to believe," Virginia shouted in return.

Bella hadn't expected Virginia would believe her appraisal. The girl lacked self-confidence, and Bella wouldn't change the girl's level of assurance by speaking a few kind words. By mid-afternoon Mr. Kingman insisted on moving Virginia across the aisle. Bella didn't argue, but for the remainder of the day she moved back and forth across the walkway, assisting Virginia while continuing to monitor her own machines, thankful it would soon be quitting time.

Bella was tending her own looms when Virginia stopped her machine to insert a full bobbin. Bella watched as Virginia sucked a bobbin thread through her shuttle and placed it in the race box before pulling the handle of her machine, sending it into action. Without warning, the shuttle jumped out of the race and flew through the air.

A piercing scream sliced through the humid atmosphere of the room. Bella turned in the direction of the deafening cry. Irene Duncan was on her knees as rivulets of blood cascaded down the side of her head and face. Virginia's shuttle lay beside Irene.

"You! Bring some clean rags for her head," Mr. Kingman hollered as he rushed to Irene's side. "The rest of you get back to work. You're serving no good purpose standing around gawking." He grabbed the shuttle from the floor. "Whom does this belong to?" he called out while holding the piece of wood and brass aloft.

"It's mine," Virginia replied, her voice cracking with emotion. She retrieved the shuttle and dashed back down the row, her face as white as hoarfrost on a November morn. Not one of the other girls moved toward their looms.

Instead, Bella walked to where Virginia stood and drew her close. She wanted to ease the girl's obvious horror. "I'm sure Irene's going to be fine. This isn't the first time a flying shuttle has hit an operative, and I'm sure it won't be the last."

"That's for certain," another girl said as the other operatives murmured their agreement.

"Until they let us operate these machines at a safe speed, one where we can ensure quality and safety, there are going to be injuries," Bella replied, raising her voice in order to be heard above the clanging tower bell. "It seems the owners care little about anything but a quick profit."

"That's likely true, Bella, but we're here because we need the money, and I don't think the Boston Associates are much interested in what a bunch of girls think," another operative responded as they made their way out the door and began descending the winding staircase.

Bella nodded. She knew that come tomorrow morning, the machines would run at the same rapid pace as they had today. Yet the Associates' unwillingness to make changes didn't mean the men were right. In fact, Bella was certain they were wrong— dead wrong.

Daughtie rushed to meet Bella at the bottom of the steps.

"Who was that Mr. Kingman carried down the stairs?"

"Irene Duncan," Virginia lamented. "She's my first victim."

Daughtie grinned at Bella. "I think you're overstating just a bit. I mean, it's not as though you set out to intentionally harm her, Virginia. Accidents occur frequently in the Appleton—I'm sure you've had your share on the spinning floor, haven't you?"

"Well, yes, but I didn't cause any of those."

"Had Irene's shuttle jumped out of the race and hit you, would you think she had planned to harm you?" Bella asked.

"Of course not," Virginia replied.

"Well, then, why would you decide Irene, or anyone else, would consider you some sort of villain? Stop condemning yourself for the accident. Instead, offer your apologies and then do something to show your concern for Irene's welfare. If she's unable to immediately return to work, seek out girls who are willing to operate her looms so that she doesn't lose her pay, offer to perform her errands, or offer to wash the clothing she was wearing at the time of the accident. She'll be grateful, and it will ease your feelings of guilt and helplessness," Bella suggested.

Virginia stared at her wide-eyed. "You're very wise, Bella. I'll go to her boardinghouse right now."

"Perhaps you ought to eat supper first and then go visiting," Bella offered.

"I'll do that, and I'll see you tomorrow morning at first bell," she added, rushing off toward her own boardinghouse.

Daughtie linked arms with Bella. "You *are* very wise, Bella. You gave her good counsel. The Sisters would be proud."

"It's the Lord I'm trying to please, Daughtie, not the Sisters at Canterbury."

"I know, I know, and I'm sure He's pleased, also," Daughtie said. "Come along. I'm hungry and I can't wait to tell you about my day."

When supper was over and the dishes washed, Miss Addie made her way back into the dining room, where Bella and Daughtie sat visiting. She carried a tray with a teapot and three cups. "I thought we could have a cup of tea while we visit," she suggested. "Would you like to join me in my sitting room?"

"Yes," the girls agreed in unison.

Miss Addie poured and served each of the girls, then stirred a bit of cream and sugar into her own cup before leaning back in her chair. "I hear you have a new position in the dressing room, Daughtie. I would enjoy hearing what you do. I've visited the mill on only one occasion and only got as far as the counting room. It's difficult for me to imagine what your workday must be like."

"My workday has gotten much better, thanks to Bella. She was offered the position first but turned it down. I think she would have accepted had it not been for me," Daughtie said to Miss Addie in a conspiratorial tone.

Addie winked at Daughtie and then gave Bella a warm smile. "I'm sure Bella would be willing to give up almost anything to make certain you're happy, Daughtie."

"Enough! Enough!" Bella protested. "Tell us about your day."

"As you're well aware, Bella, where I now work is much quieter than the weaving or spinning floors, and it's airier, too. Of course, there are fewer girls on the floor, which helps, also. Today was Nancy Everhardt's last day. They told her she was to train me for the full day. Can you imagine? She was very patient and kind."

"And I'm sure you were an exceptional student," Miss Addie interjected.

Daughtie smiled at the compliment. "The dressers with their frames are on one side of the room to ensure the yarn is properly sized and dried before being wound onto the take-up beam, which is a job I don't think I would enjoy. But once they have the warp threads on the beam, the beam is moved to the drawing-in girl. One by one, the warp threads are drawn through the harness and reed with a long metal hook before the beam is delivered to the girls in the weaving room."

Addie appeared surprised. "You pull each thread by hand? I thought everything was done by machine."

Daughtie's face shone with a bright smile. "Praise be, they've not yet developed a machine to perform this task, Miss Addie."

Bella considered Daughtie's explanation. "So if I understand correctly, you sit on a stool or chair all day long, using a metal hook to pull the individual threads through the weaver's beam?"

"That's right," Daughtie said in a pleased voice.

"Then I'm glad you have the job. I think after one day, my back would ache from leaning and reaching through to pull the threads," Bella said.

"No, Bella. It's much better than standing at those noisy, monstrous looms that threaten injury at every turn. The drawing room has no flying shuttles such as you experienced on your floor today."

"What's this? Another accident? Was anyone injured?" Miss Addie inquired, her eyes filled with concern.

"Irene Duncan. I don't think you know her," Bella replied. "This morning I was training Daughtie's replacement, Virginia Dane." Bella continued with the story, explaining the unfolding events to Miss Addie.

"These injuries concern me. Some time ago I discussed them with John, but he says they are a common occurrence when man and machine join forces. And what of Irene? Were her injuries serious?"

"She was terribly stunned by the blow, and her head was bleeding. Mr. Kingman took her to the doctor. I'm not certain if she'll be well enough to return tomorrow, but I don't expect to see her. But what of your day, Miss Addie? I hope it was peaceful."

Addie poured another cup of tea. "Yes, it was a good day. I accomplished a great deal. I went into town—oh yes, and that reminds me, I saw a notice posted by Reverend Edson concerning the graded school system he's proposing. There's to be a meeting of the residents of Lowell concerning the proposal. Word about town is that Kirk Boott is strongly opposed to Reverend Edson's plan and will be at the meeting to argue against the concept."

Bella's eyes sparkled with excitement. "We need to discuss

this at our next meeting with the literary group. Having most of the girls attend the meeting could give the proposal a boost. I, for one, hope Kirk Boott doesn't win this argument. Education is one of the necessities of a civilized society, and as citizens of Lowell, we need to support the best possible form of schooling—for both the boys and girls."

Miss Addie listened attentively while nodding her agreement. "You make valid arguments, Bella, and I'm sure your comments would sway those who attend the meeting. Your eloquence is a testament to your excellent education."

Bella gave her hostess a sheepish grin. "I've been pontificating again, haven't I?"

Daughtie giggled. "That was Sister Phoebe's favorite way to end a debate; she'd accuse Bella of pontificating and call a halt to further discussion," Daughtie explained. "But the Society did provide us with superior schooling, didn't it, Bella?"

"Yes, I'll give you no argument on that issue. Fortunately for us, they value education for both men and women. They know it is through education a person can live a better life."

Miss Addie gave her a thoughtful glance. "I'm sure I didn't appreciate the education that was offered to me nearly as much as you girls do. And I certainly didn't learn as much! But I believe the true path to a better life is achieved through drawing closer to God."

Bella pondered the remark a moment before responding. "Let's see," she began, her index finger pushing a dimple into her chin. "Is education or the pursuit of God the true path to a better life? That would be quite a topic for debate," she concluded.

"I'm not so sure. Perhaps the topic is better suited for personal reflection and prayer than public debate," Addie responded.

"I believe you're right, Miss Addie," Bella replied, glancing toward the mantel clock above the fireplace. "The hour is growing late—it's almost ten o'clock. I suppose we'd best go upstairs and prepare for bed," Bella said as she stifled a yawn.

"Oh, I've nearly forgotten to tell you about Clara," Daughtie said, suddenly sounding very excited.

"The little doffer whose fingers were broken in the machinery?" Addie questioned.

"Yes. Her mother works just down the aisle from me. She said that Clara has recovered nicely. She may have a crooked index finger, but she seems to be able to use her hand without any trouble."

"That's wonderful news!" Bella declared. "I've wondered what became of her. No one ever likes to mention the accidents or even the recoveries."

"Well, hopefully there will be no more accidents for a while," Addie said as she gathered the teacups, placing them back on the tray. "I've enjoyed our time together," she added, picking up the tea tray and following the girls toward the door.

Bella stopped and glanced over her shoulder. "Have you seen Mrs. Arnold lately, Miss Addie?"

Addie beamed. "Why, yes, I saw her just this morning. She was outdoors with the baby, and what a darling child she is—smiles at everything and has lots of wispy dark hair."

"Did Mrs. Arnold appear content?"

"She appeared quite happy. Why do you ask?"

"Oh, nothing . . . just curious," Bella replied. "Sleep well, Miss Addie," she said with a wave of her hand.

"And you girls do the same," she replied.

The bed that evening seemed lumpy and the gentle snores of the sleeping girls louder than usual. The stale air hung heavy with an insufferable dampness, and Bella could not sleep. She tossed and turned, but sleep would not come. Miss Addie's words flitted through her mind. Were her good works not considered a means of drawing closer to God? Did she place too little emphasis on her relationship with Him? But wasn't helping others meet their full potential a godly thing to do? After all, relationships required hard work and commitment, and she had tried that with her father. She had longed for him to love her, but her efforts had been met with his rejection. If her flesh-and-blood father wasn't interested in her presence, how could Almighty God desire a relationship with her?

Her eyes fluttered closed. She lay silent, drifting to sleep when a still voice whispered to her heart, *If you will but seek me, I will be your constant companion. I loved you enough to die for you—I will not turn away.*

CHAPTER 19

Hugh Cummiskey hailed greetings to several Irishmen, his bass voice resonating throughout the interior walls that now formed the outer shell of the Catholic church. The boisterous sound caused Liam to turn from his work and sit back on his haunches. He squinted against the filtering sunlight in an effort to identify the man at Hugh's side.

"There you are, my boy," Hugh shouted. "I've brought someone to meet you. This here's Mr. Matthew Cheever, Kirk Boott's second-in-command," he continued while pointing a thumb toward Matthew. "Seems Mr. Cheever and Mr. Boott saw a bit of your handiwork when they last visited Boston."

Liam turned his gaze toward Matthew and swiped one hand on his jacket before reaching out to shake Matthew's extended hand. "For sure? And where was that?"

Matthew grasped Liam's hand in a firm shake. "At the home of J. P. Green. He spoke highly of you," Matthew replied. "But had he not said a word, your craftsmanship would have spoken for itself. In fact, I'm amazed that someone with your talent was willing to leave Boston. I'm sure there's more than enough work to keep you busy among the wealthy Beacon Hill residents."

Liam wiped off his trowel and gave the men his full attention. "Ya're probably correct, but who could be turnin' down the likes of Hugh Cummiskey and the opportunity to live in the Acre?" he asked, giving Hugh a wink.

"Ah, so you've noticed the Acre isn't languishing in luxury, have you?" Matthew asked with a chuckle.

Liam gave an appreciative grin. "I like a man who can meet a barb head-on, Mr. Cheever."

"Then I'd say we ought to get along famously. And if all it took was Hugh's coaxing to bring you to Lowell, I think we've underestimated his abilities."

"In that case, I'll be glad to see your appreciation when I go through the pay line on Friday," Hugh replied. "To be honest, I don't think it was me that brought Liam to Lowell; I think it was the church."

"So you're a man of faith. I'd say this is a perfect place to use your talents for the Lord. I applaud your willingness to make such a sacrifice," Matthew replied.

Liam shook his head back and forth. "My intentions are not so lofty as servin' the Lord. Truth is, I don't consider meself a man of God. I've never quite figured out the whole concept o' religion. For as long as I can remember, my mother filled our house with shrines that were a confusing mixture of elves, fairies, and saints. Each morning she'd scurry off to church as if the devil himself was sweepin' her out the door, but when problems arose, she expected no more from God than she did from the elves and fairies. I found it all very bewilderin'—still do. Trouble is, I wrote a letter home tellin' me mother about this church and Hugh's offer. She immediately wrote back sayin' she'd had a divine word from either God or an elf—I'm not sure which— that her life was in danger unless I came to Lowell."

Hugh clapped a beefy hand against his thigh. "Good for your ma. We'll be counting it as God's intervention since we're erecting this church for His glory and not the elves'," he said.

"Ah, she's not foolin' me. It wasn't intervention by God or the elves; it was because she wanted to do a bit of motherly braggin'. She'll be goin' about the village tellin' everyone that I'm buildin' a church for the Irish immigrants in America, and the women will all be in awe until someone else has somethin' better to make a fuss about," Liam replied.

"But that's what mothers are for, my boy," Hugh put in. "They keep us on the straight and narrow one way or another. I'll use any advantage offered if it means I get a skilled craftsman like you working on this church building."

Matthew glanced back and forth between the two men, a look of confusion etched upon his face. "Who is paying your wages, Liam? The Corporation donated the land, but Hugh agreed to provide the necessary labor from among the Irishmen living in the Acre."

Puzzled, Liam didn't know how to respond. Certainly he had discussed his wages with Hugh prior to accepting the job, agreeing to an hourly wage that was somewhat lower than the sum he normally charged. Inquiring where the money would come from had never entered his mind. He looked toward Hugh for an answer.

Hugh flipped his broad hand as though he were shooing a fly. "Don't worry yourself over Liam's pay. It's taken care of," he said, quickly turning his attention toward Liam. "I've a bit of good news for you, Liam. I've found you a new place to live. You'll soon be able to bid Noreen a fond farewell," Hugh said, smoothly turning the conversation away from Liam's pay.

Liam gave Hugh a broad smile. "You've made me a happy man, Hugh Cummiskey! When can I be movin' in?"

"You're not even going to ask the location or cost?"

"No! I trust that whatever ya've found will be an improvement."

"You can move in tomorrow. I think you'll find your new home and the food a bit more to your liking. But remember that nothing in the Acre will compare to your room in Boston."

"All I want is edible food and a bed that's free of lice. As I told ya, my accommodations in Boston were meager but clean."

Hugh nodded. "Then I think you should be happy."

Matthew ran an appreciative hand over a portion of the intricate stonework. "This design is truly outstanding, Liam," he complimented before turning back toward Hugh. "Could we return to our earlier discussion, Hugh? I need to report to the Associates within the week regarding the progress on the church. We're attempting to schedule the dedication service. Mr. Boott and I visited with Bishop Fenwick when we traveled to Boston, and the three of us began making preparations for the dedication. Bishop Fenwick is available the first week in September. Does that seem a good date for you, Hugh? And what about you, Liam? Will your work be completed by then?"

"I'll be meetin' my finish date—never missed one yet," Liam replied.

Hugh nodded. "September sounds fine to me. The building should be completed by then."

"Good! And since I know the diocese is furnishing funds for any of the materials you haven't been able to wangle out of Mr. Boott, I'm going to go ahead and report that they're also paying Liam's wages. We both know that J. P. will make Liam's craftsmanship a topic of discussion; the subject of wages is bound to arise. I want to answer truthfully, Hugh, but if you'll not give me a direct answer I'll take your silence as an affirmative reply."

Hugh gave a hearty laugh. "I thought we left the matter of Liam's wages in the dust, but it appears as if Mr. Boott has trained you well, Matthew. You may report that Liam's wages are being paid by the diocese—but please do so only should the topic arise. I'm certain that if some of those tightfisted Associates find out the diocese agreed to pay Liam's wages, they'll think the church should have paid for the land instead of asking the Corporation to donate it."

Matthew smiled and nodded. "I'd say you're likely correct about that assumption. You have my word. I won't volunteer the information unless asked—except to Mr. Boott, of course."

Hugh grinned. "Of course. And if you'd like to complete your inspection, we can move along and Liam can get back to his work."

Matthew offered his hand to Liam. "A pleasure meeting you. I hope we'll have an opportunity to visit in the future. Especially about those religious issues you mentioned."

"We'll see, Mr. Cheever—I'm not one to get into discussions dealin' with religion. Seems that even those folks who are usually even-tempered get themselves all heated up when they start talkin' religion."

Matthew nodded. "You're right about that, Liam. Perhaps I should have phrased my invitation a little differently. Instead of talking about religion or religious issues, why don't we get together and talk about God—not how folks choose to worship or what church they attend, but how a man goes about seeking and building a bond with his Maker."

Liam hesitated, mulling over Matthew's suggestion—a bizarre concept, indeed. Yet his pulse quickened at the notion of mankind being drawn into some sort of personal connection with Almighty God. "Ya've captured my interest with yar words, Mr. Cheever, but I doubt we'll be frequentin' many of the same places," Liam replied, giving Matthew a broad grin.

"Who knows? Some barriers are more easily overcome than we think," Matthew replied as he turned and began following Hugh.

Liam filled his trowel with mortar and began spreading it between two smooth pieces of Italian stone. A wry smile creased his face. The thought of Matthew Cheever wanting to discuss God with him was reason for more than a grin—it was a laugh-out-loud event. Why would a Yank, especially an important one, want to talk to a lowly Irishman about anything except his ability to lay stone? It made no sense. Why, if they were ever seen together, the good people of Lowell would certainly wonder about such a liaison. The barriers between Irish and Yanks in Lowell would not be so easily overcome. Certainly Liam and Matthew could meet in the Acre and discuss God, but barriers would remain intact. The Yanks would stay in their part of town, and the Irish would stay in the Acre.

Carefully smoothing the mortar, Liam continued filling the crevices between each stone. Attempting to push Matthew Cheever's words from his mind, he studied the stones piled before him and concentrated on his choices before picking up a beautifully formed stone. He rubbed his thumb across the intricate pattern of the rock, mesmerized by the beauty created in a simple stone that had been pulled from the ground. Why was he thinking about the creation of a rock? He'd never had such thoughts before. And then another question came to mind—when Matthew spoke of a barrier, was he talking about the difficulty between the Irish and the Yanks or the break between man and God? And who had caused this break by declaring God unapproachable? Was it man or God? Surely it must have been God, because the concept of God desiring to associate himself with a lowly Irishman was almost as improbable as Matthew Cheever ever reappearing to discuss the multitude of questions exploding in Liam's mind.

The bell tower clanged in the distance, hushing Liam's thoughts as the workday came to an end. Packing up his tools, he placed them in the wooden box and then headed off, stopping to visit with several fellow workers. Turning at a fork in the narrow, dusty path, Liam remembered Hugh's news of another living arrangement. Anxious though he was to depart from Noreen's squalid house, he dreaded telling her of his plan to move. He decided her degree of sobriety would control the level of tongue-lashing hurled in his direction. Dinner at the pub seemed a better option, he decided as he turned back in the direction from which he'd come. If he waited long enough, Noreen would be passed out in a drunken stupor when he returned home, and if he arose early enough the next morning, he could avoid her entirely. His rent was paid for three more days; he wasn't about to ask for a refund. Instead, he would leave her a note stating he had terminated his tenancy. Liam was seeking the path of least resistance, and a simple letter of explanation prudently placed on Noreen's kitchen table appeared to be his answer.

The pub was nearing a capacity crowd when Liam arrived. Several men who regularly worked at the church called out to him. Waiting until his eyes adjusted to the semidarkness of the room, he wove his way through the groups of drinking, joking workmen who were enjoying a tankard along with the company of one another before returning home for the night. Squeezing between two men who worked at the church, he seated himself and soon joined in the laughter and conversation, now certain that he'd made the correct decision. The camaraderie in the pub far surpassed being harangued by Noreen Gallagher.

The men surrounding the table were prodding each other to buy another ale when shouts at the rear of the pub captured their attention. Liam and several others leaned back from the table and looked toward the back of the room, where the talk continued to grow louder and more heated.

"You mark my words—if you don't go after those uppity townsfolk first, they'll be storming and ransacking that church you're building," a man yelled.

Liam squinted his eyes until an obviously drunk William Thurston came into focus. The Yank was spouting his opinion for all to hear.

"I know you think I don't know what I'm talking about, but the Yanks aren't going to tolerate losing jobs to the likes of you," Thurston yelled, waving an arm about the room. "They know you're planning to take over the town and steal their mills, thinking you'll have a ready-made place to bring in more and more of your kinfolk from Ireland. Do you really think they're so stupid they don't know what you're up to? They'll be down here in the Acre stealing both your money and rifles out of that church building before you have a chance to finish building up your arsenal of weapons. If you're smart, you'll take what weapons you've got and make the first move. Take them by surprise!" he yelled, the words a slurred, shrieking command. He was obviously hoping to provoke the crowd into action. Instead, he passed out and fell to the floor.

The men turned back to their conversation, ignoring the Yank in his fancy suit except to occasionally step over him as they made their way back and forth to the bar.

"You think there's anythin' to what he was saying about the Yanks stormin' the church?" Liam asked.

One of the men took a long swig of ale and then leaned across the table, his dark eyes sparkling in the candlelight. "Why? Are you scared of gettin' a bit o' blood on yar hands?" he asked before emitting a rancorous guffaw.

Liam met his stare. "I never fight when a disagreement can be settled another way," Liam replied. "Just wonderin' if and when you thought this battle might occur."

"Don' know if it ever will. Then again, might happen before mornin'. Can't tell what them Yanks is thinkin'. And that one," he said, nodding his head toward Thurston, "nothin' he says or does can be trusted. I wish he'd stay outta the Acre and mingle with 'is own kind."

"I ain't heard nothin' about the Yanks comin' this direction to take over the church, and I sure ain't heard nothin' about the Irish taking over the town. Not that it wouldn't be a pleasant enough thing to see 'appen. Right, McGruder?" another asked, poking an elbow into his friend's side.

"Right ya are on that one," McGruder replied. "But I ain't got time for this all-important conversation ya're having—got to get home to my missus afore she throws my stew to the dogs," he said, rising from the table.

"I best be getting home, too," another man agreed until soon all of the men except Liam had risen and left the tavern.

It was much too early to head back to Noreen's—she'd still be awake. He moved to a corner and sat by himself, thinking about William Thurston's remarks. The man had been drunk when he'd begun his ranting, but given Noreen's comments about William Thurston, perhaps the only time he spoke the truth was when he'd had one too many. What if the Yanks were planning to storm the church? His belongings were stored there. As soon as he left Noreen's in the morning, he'd go to the church and remove his satchel. He couldn't take a chance on losing the money he'd worked so hard to save. If he was going to bring his parents from Ireland, he needed those coins. Perhaps he could leave his satchel at his new lodging without concern of theft. He would make that determination once he moved into the house.

Remaining in the corner for the balance of the evening, Liam ate a bowl of fish chowder and then borrowed pen and ink from the barkeep, who was willing to oblige. He penned a short note to Noreen, choosing his words carefully, thanking her for making space available when he desperately needed a place to live. Asking her to please keep the balance of his rent as well as the extra dollar beside his note, he went on to explain he'd been successful in finding a private room to rent. The Acre, after all, was small; he didn't want to make enemies.

Before the bell pealed the next morning, Liam left the shanty, his money and handwritten note awaiting either Noreen's delight or wrath, depending upon her mood when she awakened. A dog barked in the distance as he tripped on some unknown object and then stepped on something that squished underfoot. The cloudy moonless night withheld its light and caused Liam to slow his step. It seemed he'd taken forever to walk the short distance to the church. He found the stub of candle and a short time later, satchel in hand, sat down to await Hugh Cummiskey's arrival.

Liam spotted Hugh's outline in the semidarkness as the sturdily built Irishman approached, his arm extended in a wave. "Appears you're anxious to go and meet Mrs. Flynn," he said. "How long have you been waiting?"

"An hour or so," Liam replied.

Hugh gave a loud guffaw, breaking the quietness of the morning. "Noreen send ya packing when she found out you were moving?"

"No. I didn't get home until after she was asleep last night. I left a note on the table this mornin'. She was still asleep when I left," he added.

Hugh slapped him on the back as he continued to laugh. "You're scared of that feisty little Irishwoman, aren't ya?"

Liam gave Hugh a sheepish grin. "For sure, I didn't see any need to be upsettin' her and everyone else last night. Figured the letter and an extra coin or two would be the easiest—"

"Escape?" Hugh interrupted. "It's all right, my boy. I understand. Noreen's a handful and that's a fact. 'Course, she can't read," he said, once again bursting into boisterous laughter.

Liam stopped in his tracks, staring at Hugh. "She can't read?"

"I doubt it—but rest assured she'll find someone who can decipher your note before day's end."

They walked a bit farther before Hugh pointed toward a small shanty.

Liam's hopes plummeted as he looked at the shack. "This one?" he asked, unable to hide his despair.

Hugh gave Liam a grin as he knocked on the door. "Trust me, Liam."

A cheerful dumpling of a woman greeted them at the door. "Good mornin', Mr. Cummiskey. And you must be Mr. Donohue," she said, giving Liam a wide smile that plumped her cheeks into two rosy orbs. "Come in, come in," she offered, stepping aside to clear the entrance.

They stepped inside the hovel and then followed Mrs. Flynn into a large room that obviously served as the main living area in the house. "Liam, this is Mrs. Flynn," Hugh said.

Liam nodded, his gaze flashing about the room. "Pleased to meet you. Mr. Cummiskey tells me ya've an opening for a boarder."

"Is that what he told ya, now?" she questioned, turning a merry smile in Hugh's direction. "He stretched the truth just a wee bit, Mr. Donohue. Truth is, I've never rented space in my house to anyone, but after a pitcher of ale, Hugh convinced the mister he was missing out on a good opportunity."

Liam's cheeks heated with embarrassment. The woman didn't appear upset over his arrival, yet it sounded as though Hugh and her husband had forced her into taking him in as a boarder. He didn't want to be an intruder in this kind woman's home, but once inside, he knew he couldn't return to Noreen's. Mrs. Flynn's home was neat and clean; this was a place where he could be comfortable.

"Now look what you've done. You've gone and embarrassed him," Hugh said, returning Mrs. Flynn's smile. "You'd best be tellin' him the whole truth, or he'll be headin' back to Noreen's."

Mrs. Flynn folded her chunky arms beneath an ample

bosom. "Go on with ya! We both know better than that! Given the choice, nobody in his right mind would live with Noreen Gallagher. Ya're more than welcome in our home, Mr. Donohue. The mister asked me if I'd be interested in makin' a bit of extra change for meself by taking in a boarder. Ya'd best know from the outset that you won't have much space. I hung a curtain to give you a bit o' privacy," she said, showing him where he would sleep. "You can use this chest for yar belongings. 'Course ya can spend as much time as ya like out here with the mister and me of an evenin'," she continued. "Ya can be payin' me the same amount as ya were payin' Noreen," she added.

A sense of relief washed over Liam. "Ya have a new boarder, Mrs. Flynn—a happy one, I might be addin'."

"Good. I do washin' on Mondays. Ya can leave yar dirty clothes on the floor by yar bed."

Liam looked at her in stunned silence. "Ya'll be doin' my washin'?"

"Of course. Ya get three meals a day, laundry, and cleaning," she replied. "Don't want ya smellin' up the house," she said with a chuckle.

He could barely contain himself as he thanked her. Reaching into his pocket, he pulled out enough money to pay her twice what he'd given Noreen. "Here's for my first week," he said, shoving the coins into her hand.

She looked down at the money and then shook her head back and forth. "That's enough for more than two weeks. Mr. Cummiskey told me what Noreen charges," she said, taking several coins and holding them out to him.

"I want to pay ya more, Mrs. Flynn. Noreen provided me only one meal a day, her house was filthy, and she didn't wash my laundry. Ya're offerin' much more."

Liam watched as she glanced toward Hugh. He nodded for her to accept. "Thank you, Mr. Donohue, but if ya find yarself fallin' on hard times, ya let me know and we'll go back to the lower amount."

"Now that we've got things settled, we'd best be gettin' to work," Hugh said.

"Ya can put yar belongings on the bed and unpack them this evenin'," Mrs. Flynn offered.

Liam nodded. He was certain his money and belongings would be safe in this woman's care.

"Thank ya for yar efforts," Liam said as he and Hugh walked toward the church.

"You're welcome, my boy. I didn't want you rushin' off to some fancy job in Boston because you were forced to live at a place like Noreen's. Just remember—you owe me now. You can't be leavin' until your work at the church is completed."

"I'll be around at least that long. Ya've got my word," Liam said as he stopped in front of the church and momentarily watched as Hugh strode off.

Both the noonday and evening meals exceeded Liam's expectations. The food was hearty, well prepared, and served with a dose of pleasant conversation. Mrs. Flynn and her husband proved to be a good match. Both had a cheerful attitude and enjoyed good discussion, and they were quick to involve him in their repartee.

Liam rose from one of the wooden chairs that formed the sitting area of the large room. "If ya'll excuse me, I'd best unpack my belongings before bedtime."

"Ya don't need to ask our permission to move about the place," Mr. Flynn replied as he tapped his pipe on the hearth. "This is yar home, too."

"Thank you, Mr. Flynn," Liam replied before moving off to the cordoned area that was now his room.

Everything was exactly as he'd left it. The satchel, his small trunk of clothing—nothing had been touched. He ruffled through the trunk, moving his clothes, except for his heavy winter clothing, into the small chest the Flynns had provided.

Sitting on the edge of the bed, Liam opened the satchel that had remained hidden in the church until this morning. Digging into the bag, he pulled out the sheaf of papers he'd retrieved from J. P. Green's fireplace and tossed them behind him on the bed as he dug deeper, his fingers tightening around a small leather bag and pulling it into sight. Untying the cord, he carefully counted the money and then returned it to the sack, refastened the tie, and with a satisfied smile, tucked it into the bottom of his trunk.

Gathering the loose papers, he began stacking them together. Seeing row after row of figures penned on the sheets of paper, Liam ceased stacking the sheets and spread them out on the bed, reviewing the entries and becoming more and more fascinated as he looked at the numbers. He was no mathematician, but he'd had his share of education both in school and under the tutelage of a stonemason in Ireland. The old man had insisted a business could be successful only if you maintained proper ledgers.

For the next two hours Liam sat on the bed, matching the pages of the export business of J. P. Green and Nathan Appleton, unable to understand exactly what lay before him. He juggled a few more pages and then stared intently at the papers, suddenly realizing he was looking at a system of bookkeeping that revealed thousands of dollars being siphoned out of the company owned by Appleton and Green. It appeared J. P. Green was systematically transferring funds into his own company and falsifying the books of Appleton & Green Exports. Liam's hands trembled as he stacked the sheets. No wonder Green had thrown the papers in the fireplace. He folded all of the papers except a small stack of pages that still were unclear. Dates were listed in each row, followed by a last name, first initial, and amount of money. The entries made no sense, but he didn't want to uncover any more surprises. No doubt his knowledge of the siphoned funds could put his life in jeopardy; discovering further incriminating information would only serve to tighten the noose around his neck.

CHAPTER 20

William Thurston selected a small table in a far corner of the Brackman Hotel on Beacon Street. He'd arrived in Boston last evening and hoped to be on the *Governor Sullivan* early the next morning, heading back to Lowell. This journey to Boston did not need to be lengthy, and he was pleased there was no need to linger. The social circle to which his wife and her wealthy parents belonged had already departed Boston for the summer. Of course, he'd have to make at least one appearance at The Haven this summer; after all, they must keep up appearances. His wife's family name provided him with access to Boston's high-powered elite, and he saved her from being called an old maid. The arrangement was unspoken but understood. It suited both of them.

He took a sip of coffee while perusing an old copy of the newspaper he'd picked up in the lobby and waited. He glanced at his pocket watch a short time later, neatly folded the paper, and kept his gaze fixed on the entrance, hoping to conclude his business as early as possible.

"More coffee, sir?" a waiter inquired.

"What? Oh, yes," he replied.

"I'd like one also," J. P. Green said as he walked up behind the waiter.

Thurston breathed a sigh of relief. He was beginning to wonder if Green had forgotten their engagement.

"Sorry for the delay, William. Hope I haven't kept you waiting too long," Green said as he seated himself opposite William. "Did you have a pleasant trip? Lovely weather for making the journey by boat."

Thurston stirred a dollop of cream into his coffee. "Pleasant enough. I found several gentlemen willing to rid themselves of their money at the gaming table."

Green laughed at the remark and then downed his coffee. He set the cup down hard before bending forward and placing his folded arms atop the table. "We've got a bit of a problem, William, and you're the one who will need to correct it," he said.

A knot formed in William's belly. Green hadn't mentioned any problem in his letter—he'd merely written to say that they needed to meet and go over future plans. "You know me, J. P., I'm always willing to work with you. I didn't know I'd done anything that required altering. How can I help?" he asked, feigning cheerfulness.

"I hope I didn't give the wrong impression by my remark. It's not so much that you've done anything wrong, William. I suppose it's more a matter of change . . . yes, that's it. Things are changing, and I need your help if we're to be successful."

The tension in William's face relaxed slightly. "What kind of changes?" he inquired tentatively.

"Good ones—at least financially good. For both of us," he added, wagging his finger to and fro. He moved closer and cupped his hand along one side of his mouth. "We've opened several new markets. One, in particular, excites me. The expansion is going to be greater than either of us ever imagined. So much so that I doubt we'll be able to meet the demand," he said, now leaning back with a look of defeat replacing his earlier excitement.

"Wait—don't give up before you've even told me the

details," Thurston said, his excitement building. "Where are these new markets?"

"Some additional overseas markets, particularly India, have captured Nathan's interest, but we've begun additional shipments to the South, specifically New Orleans, and that is the market that most interests me," J. P. answered.

Thurston's eyes grew wide. "New Orleans?" He rubbed his fingers along his jaw. "Oh, how I love that city—the decadence is a joy to behold. I've not found a better place to wallow in sin," he said, thinking of his last visit to the city and the mulatto girl who'd been his constant companion for five satisfying days.

"I agree. And that's what makes it such a wide-open market for us—but only if we can provide quality merchandise." He leaned in close once again. "If we're going to succeed and corner the market, I need the highest obtainable quality. Better than what you've provided in the past."

Thurston was shocked at his comment. "Higher quality? Surely you jest. I've given you nothing but the best. I can't believe there's any better to be had in New Orleans—or any-where else for that matter."

"Don't play games with me, William, or I'll find someone else who's willing to supply what I want. It's not as though you don't have access. But if you're averse to the risk that might be involved . . ."

"Might be involved? You don't realize what you're asking, J. P.," he replied.

Green pushed away from the table and began to stand up.

"Sit down! I didn't say it was impossible or that I wasn't interested. I said there's a great risk involved. Sit down," Thurston repeated. "Please," he added, waiting until J. P. was once again seated before continuing. "You understand that what you're asking for is going to create an uproar in Lowell—this will go beyond Kirk Boott—and the citizens will expect a higher level of participation from the Corporation. They'll expect involvement by at least some of the Associates."

J. P. nodded. "You act as though you're not one of the Asso-ciates, William. That's the beauty of this whole thing. You spend more time in Lowell than all the rest of the Associates combined. You can volunteer to lend your assistance on behalf of the Associates, permitting them the freedom to continue their lives without interruption, yet giving an appearance of concern and support. What better way to remain operational while thwarting the investigative process? It's a beautiful concept," he gleefully determined.

William was silent for a moment. "And the funds? This plan increases my risk dramatically. I'm certain you've already considered that I will need additional money."

"Ah, William, there are some matters where I know I can always depend upon you . . . and the desire for more money is one of them."

"That's entirely unfair, J. P.! I'll need men that I can trust implicitly, and such men don't come cheap. I don't want to have someone turn on me for a few dollars. Besides, your level of involvement doesn't change at all while mine increases substantially. The only people who know you're involved in this scheme are the man you've hired to negotiate with the ships' captains and me. Otherwise, you're in the clear."

"And who's told you that I don't negotiate with the ships' captains myself?" Green inquired with a curious grin.

William met J. P.'s gaze. "I don't need anyone to tell me. I know you're too smart to involve yourself with talkative seamen."

J. P. nodded. "I'll take that as a compliment, William. And I know you're too smart to take a greater risk without additional payment. I'll pay you half again what you've been receiving on each delivery. Do we have an agreement?"

Thurston nodded. "How soon will you want to begin shipping the higher quality?"

J. P. gave him a cunning smile. "We can begin immediately, but I'll bow to your expertise as to the amount of time needed to make arrangements in Lowell. And if you foresee a problem with storage in Lowell, I have ample space available in Boston.

Send word of the time and mode of transportation, and I'll have men available to assist with the transfer."

"I'll begin making arrangements upon my return to Lowell," William replied.

CHAPTER 21

Bella paced back and forth between the parlor and hallway, her shoes clicking on the wooden floor with each step.

"Do sit down, Bella," Daughtie urged.

"You're going to wear out your shoes with all that pacing," Ruth added.

Bella ignored the request and moved into the hallway. "I do wish Miss Addie would hurry. I'm sure the meeting will be crowded, and I want to get a good seat."

"She can't see you out here, so continuing to clomp back and forth is not going to hurry her along. I'm sure she's moving as quickly as possible. After all, she did have to clean up after supper," Daughtie retorted.

Bella stalked into the parlor and plopped down beside Ruth, her eyes flashing with anger. "Are you happy?" She folded her arms and leveled a steely gaze in Daughtie's direction.

Daughtie tilted her head and gave Bella a playful smile. "You needn't attempt to intimidate me, Arabella Newberry. I've known you far too long for such antics. Save it for the meeting."

Bella bit her lower lip. She didn't want to smile; instead she needed to gather courage from her anger in order to speak eloquently should the need arise this evening. And she was certain a strong argument would be needed for education to blossom in Lowell. Yet the issue wasn't so much education as it was money—and reforming the present school system would take money—something near and dear to the hearts of those in opposition.

Miss Addie's door burst open, and she bustled into the room while still tying her bonnet. "I'm sorry to keep you waiting, girls. Shall we go?"

"I just hope we can find a seat," Bella mumbled as they moved off toward St. Anne's Episcopal Church.

Addie gave Bella a reassuring pat on the arm. "I asked Mintie to save our pew for us. We'll be close to the front."

"Your pew was probably taken by the time Miss Mintie arrived. She had dinner chores to perform after supper, didn't she?" Bella countered.

Addie nodded. "Yes, but she's employed Lucy's younger sister to help out now and again. She paid her to do the dishes tonight."

"Still . . ." Bella permitted the word to hang in the air as a silent accusation.

"Besides, if there's anyone sitting in our pew, you know Mintie will shoo them out—with her parasol, if necessary."

"I suppose you're right on that account! She's quite adept with a parasol," Bella agreed, remembering how the older woman had wielded her umbrella against Taylor Manning in that very church pew.

They hurried along, arriving at the church doors only minutes before the meeting was to begin. Mintie was standing guard over the pew, waving them forward with a dark green parasol as they entered the rear of the church.

Addie shook her head back and forth and motioned for Mintie to sit down. "I suppose she thinks I've forgotten where we sit every Sunday. For someone who's worried about what other people think, she's certainly making a spectacle of herself waving that parasol in the air," Addie said to nobody in particular.

"That's true, but you'll notice nobody is going anywhere near her with that pointed instrument flailing in all directions."

Nodding in agreement, Addie worked her way down the aisle, clearing a path for the three girls.

"Finally!" Mintie greeted. "I thought you would never arrive. Saving these seats was no small task. Everybody wants to be near the front," she announced in an explosive burst.

"I was certain you'd be up to the feat," Addie replied as she seated herself. "Come on, girls, sit down," she instructed, patting the space beside her.

The three girls plunked down as instructed, Bella taking the seat closest to the aisle. After all, she might need immediate access to the aisle if she wanted to step forward and voice her opinion. Of course, if the discussion went well, she might not speak at all. That concept seemed improbable, yet she acknowledged the possibility.

Bella quickly surveyed the church. Matthew and Lilly Cheever were two rows in front of them, along with several other prominent-looking men with their fashionable wives in tow. The pews were full, and an overflow crowd was gathering at the rear of the church when a shadow fell across the pew and Bella looked upward.

"May I?" Taylor Manning inquired, looking over her head toward Miss Addie.

"Taylor! Do join us," she invited. "Scoot down, girls—we've plenty of room for one more."

Bella held fast to her position as the other girls began sliding down the pew. She wasn't relinquishing her aisle seat to anyone. "Why don't you sit next to Miss Addie? I'm sure she'd enjoy your company," Bella said loudly enough for the older woman to hear.

"Oh yes, do sit here," Addie said as she pushed closer to Ruth, making a space between Mintie and herself.

Taylor arched his eyebrows and then gave Bella a defiant grin. "Perhaps it would be easier if I went around to the other side. Or, better yet, since the meeting is about to begin, why don't you move down, Bella, and I'll take the aisle. That way I won't disturb quite as many people."

"How thoughtful! You are a dear boy," Addie replied, giving him a winsome smile.

"Bella?"

Taking great effort to move her legs and tuck her skirt closer around her body, Bella looked toward the empty space to her left. "I prefer to remain near the aisle," she said. "You can sit there." She nodded toward the vacant seat. "Or you can go around and sit by Miss Addie, whichever you prefer."

"You win," he said while wedging himself between Daughtie and Bella. "At least this time," he added with a grin.

Bella frowned before placing a finger in front of her pursed lips. "Shhh! The meeting is about to begin."

"If we could come to order, I'd like to present the recommendation of the school board," Reverend Edson said. "Once I've finished, I'll open the floor for discussion, but I would request you wait until you've been acknowledged before speaking. Otherwise, we'll have chaos and nothing will be accomplished.

"The board members have spent countless hours studying the problems of our current district school system and the possible resolutions in order to provide a better education for—"

"The children of Lowell are already receiving a decent education," a booming voice declared. All eyes shifted to the rear of the sanctuary, where an impeccably dressed Kirk Boott was making his way down the aisle. "I'm sorry to interrupt your little speech, Theodore. Oh, excuse me. I should be addressing you more formally since this is a public meeting. Do you prefer reverend or doctor, Theodore?"

"I really don't have a preference. In fact, Theodore will be fine. As soon as you've been seated, I'll continue."

"That's Kirk Boott?" Bella whispered to Taylor.

"Yes. Making quite an entrance, isn't he?"

Bella nodded and watched while Mr. Boott casually sauntered down the aisle, obviously enjoying the attention his entrance was eliciting. When he finally took a seat beside Matthew and Lilly Cheever, Reverend Edson continued.

"As I was saying, the board has considered the present school system, and we are of the opinion that the district system served the residents well prior to the expansion and incorporation of Lowell. Now, however, we believe our children would be best educated if we changed to a graded system. There are certainly more than enough children in the community right now to sustain the graded system, and with each passing year we'll have additional students to educate. The board believes two new schools would adequately provide for a transfer to the new educational system."

There was an eruption of applause throughout the room.

Boott rose to his feet. He didn't request permission to speak. Rather, he immediately took control, motioning the crowd to silence. "You can applaud the recommendation, but new schools are not going to be erected in Lowell. Everyone in this room is expecting the Corporation to pay for these schools. Well, the Corporation has paid for everything else in this town, and it is not going to pay for two more schools. Our investment in this community is going to be conducted in an economically sound manner. In order to accomplish financial stability, debts must be paid rather than incurred. I know that concept may be difficult for some of you to understand, but trust me when I say that you'll need to find some other method to finance these schools."

"The Corporation got our land dirt cheap, thanks to you. It won't hurt them to make up the difference by building a couple of schools," someone called out from the back of the room.

A man sitting several rows behind Bella shouted, "If the cost of the schools is paid by taxes, the Corporation will have no choice but to pay its fair share."

Reverend Edson rapped a wooden gavel on the podium and began calling for order. "Please—stand and be recognized before speaking. We need to conduct this meeting in an orderly fashion."

Once again Kirk Boott stood and turned toward the crowd without being recognized. "It would behoove all of you to vote against this measure," he said. "You're all in line for your pay every week. Remember where your loyalty belongs. If the

Corporation fails, you'll all be without jobs. It would be folly to impose further burdens upon the Corporation."

Bella rose to her feet and waved an arm in the air, waiting to speak until recognized by the moderator. "You," Reverend Edson said, pointing in Bella's direction.

Bella cleared her throat and met Mr. Boott's indifferent gaze. "Fear and intimidation are a poor substitute for a worthwhile defense, sir. The children of this community deserve an education that will one day help them achieve their full potential. It is education that will aid them in contributing to the future growth and expansion of Lowell. Surely your Corporation is willing to invest in the further development of what it has already begun."

By the time she finished speaking, Mr. Boott's apathetic stare had evolved into a condescending sneer. "I realize this will be difficult for your female mind to understand, Miss. . . ?" He waited.

"Newberry. Arabella Newberry," she replied through clenched teeth.

"Yes. Well, Miss Newberry, let me explain a thing or two. This community is an experiment. Never before has such a concept been attempted, and we have yet to determine the success or failure of Lowell. Quite frankly, in only a few years a traveler may find nothing but a heap of ruins where Lowell now stands," Kirk solemnly stated.

"And if a traveler should examine the relics of this town in a few years and find no trace of a schoolhouse," Bella responded, "he would immediately know what led to its demise. Education is the backbone of a solid society. Educate the children and your town will stand firm, your Corporation will be strong, and your coffers will be filled with the gold you so earnestly seek."

Applause and hoots of laughter filled the room as Kirk leaned down and talked to Matthew Cheever and then whispered something to Theodore Edson. Moments later Matthew stood alongside Mr. Boott.

"Unfortunately, I have a previous engagement I must attend. In my absence, Matthew Cheever will speak on behalf of the

Corporation. I trust that before this matter comes to a vote, you will all give considerable weight to my words." That said, Boott stalked down the aisle and out of the building.

The crowd quickly turned its attention back to Reverend Edson. "Thank you for your fine remarks, Miss Newberry. And for waiting to be recognized before speaking," he added. "Other comments?" he asked, looking about the assembly and then pointing to a woman on the other side of the aisle.

"I appreciate what Miss Newberry said. It's clear from hearing her talk that she's had good schooling. I'd like to be sure the girls here in Lowell receive as much education as the boys. It appears that the schoolmaster spends more time and effort with the boys and discounts the need for education for our girls. I'm told that lately he's discouraged the girls' attendance by telling them they don't need schooling once they're able to read a bit and sign their names."

A man jumped up two rows behind her. "That's because the Corporation is counting the number of pupils. They've begun keeping records in an attempt to prove there's no need for more schools."

Matthew raised his hand and waited to be acknowledged before replying. "That, sir, is a false statement. It is true that the Corporation has recently taken a head count at the schools. However, we have performed such a count every year in order to track growth, not for the reasons that you allege. We also track the number of residents living in the community. There's nothing secret about our actions."

Bella rose from her seat. "But it's those very numbers that identify the needs of a community. A town of three hundred has fewer children than a town of ten thousand, hence the need for fewer schools, particularly schools of the graded system. However, a town with only ten Catholic residents does not need a Catholic church in which to worship. A town with a growing Irish population that is primarily Catholic needs a church. The same holds true for fire and police protection—the larger the community, the greater the need. So whether it be directly or indirectly, I believe your figures do contribute to the decisions made for the citizens of this community, Mr. Cheever."

Matthew hesitated. "What you've said is partially true. However, the Corporation did not coerce the schoolmaster into making such statements. I'm a staunch advocate of education, but the Corporation does not believe Lowell needs two more schools."

"Of course not. The Lowell school system doesn't affect the lives of the wealthy. You send your children off to fancy private schools without regard to what's available for ours."

"Now, just a minute. I grew up and attended a district school in East Chelmsford, and my education served me well. I consider my fundamental education to be as fine as that of any of the others attending Harvard University," Matthew replied.

"We were a small farm community back then," Lilly Cheever rebutted.

Bella glanced first toward Matthew and then toward Lilly, unable to believe her ears. Lilly had contradicted her husband's opinion in a public forum. Surely she would apologize and shrink quietly into the background.

Instead, Lilly continued with her lecture. "I have no intention of sending my children off to boarding school to ensure that they receive a quality education. We have an obligation to provide our children with a superior education right here in their own community."

Matthew didn't respond to his wife's remarks. Instead, Reverend Edson, with wisdom and kindness, came to Matthew's rescue. "It's getting rather late. Perhaps we should put the matter to a vote."

"Are you certain you wouldn't prefer to wait? Perhaps hold another meeting?" Matthew suggested.

The crowd immediately began murmuring, voicing their disagreement. "We want to vote now," several men hollered.

Matthew Cheever and Reverend Edson exchanged a look and then spoke privately for a moment. Bella leaned forward, listening.

"I think these folks prefer to vote now," Reverend Edson replied.

Matthew shrugged his shoulders. "I fear you're taking quite a risk, Reverend."

Reverend Edson nodded. "Perhaps. But it's the proper thing to do."

CHAPTER 22

Matthew insisted Lilly remain seated in the pew until the crowd dispersed. He said he wanted to visit further with Reverend Edson, but she suspected he didn't want to subject himself to any further questioning by the townsfolk. She sat quietly while the two talked and the sanctuary emptied.

Finally, Lilly rose. "Matthew, there is absolutely nobody left in this church except Reverend Edson and the two of us," she said, moving toward where the men stood. "I'm exhausted. May we please leave?"

"Yes, of course, my dear," he said. "Thank you for your time, Reverend Edson."

"Of course, Matthew. Anytime you want to visit further, please stop by," Reverend Edson replied, escorting them to the front door of the church. "Good night," he called out from the doorway when they finally reached their carriage.

"After the way you acted tonight, I'm surprised that Reverend Edson is still speaking to you," Lilly commented as Matthew assisted her into their carriage.

"He's a man of the cloth: he's supposed to forgive. Besides, he knows I wasn't attacking him personally. I was merely doing my job."

Matthew walked around the carriage, hoisted himself up, and dropped onto the seat. He flicked the reins and set the horses into motion as a refreshing breeze began to stir the air. Shimmering stars illuminated the distant sky, and a hazy full moon hung overhead. Although it was a beautiful evening for a carriage ride, Lilly found it impossible to savor their surroundings.

"I find it repugnant that you're taking sides with the Corporation on this issue. Surely you don't truly believe what Mr. Boott said this evening."

"Lilly, I think the new schools and the graded system would be best for Lowell, but I will not go against the Corporation on this. I would lose my job, and we can't afford for that to happen, especially with a baby on the way."

"How can you believe one thing and argue for another? Don't you find such behavior immoral?"

"Immoral? We're not talking about depraved conduct, Lilly. I'm doing my job."

"You're living a lie," she replied.

"What would you have me do, Lilly?"

Lilly leveled a look of exasperation in his direction. "What I want is for you to admit you've acted improperly. The fact is, Matthew, making me feel better is not the issue. You're the one compromising your standards and beliefs. You've shown Mr. Boott that you're willing to do whatever is necessary to protect your job and the Corporation."

Matthew's eyes blazed with anger. "That's completely unfair, Lilly. The people at that meeting knew I was speaking on behalf of the Corporation. Kirk told them I was doing just that prior to his departure. I'm not living a lie, but you are speaking in anger. I suggest we move on to another topic. I don't want to argue with you, Lilly."

"What did you and Reverend Edson discuss?" she asked.

"His future at St. Anne's," Matthew answered simply.

Stunned by Matthew's reply, Lilly remained silent, waiting to revisit the subject until they were preparing for bed.

"What did you mean earlier when you mentioned Reverend Edson's future at St. Anne's?"

"It seems that Kirk told him that if he went against the Corporation and continued fighting for the graded system and new schools, there would be no further monetary assistance for the church."

"From the Corporation, you mean?" Lilly inquired.

"From the Corporation or from Kirk personally. He's threatened to leave the church and withdraw his substantial weekly gifts as well as donations by the Corporation. It could prove devastating to the future of the church."

Lilly stared at Matthew, a look of skepticism etched on her face. "Reverend Edson was Mr. Boott's personal selection as rector of St. Anne's. He brought Reverend Edson to Lowell," she argued. "Why, the church is named after Anne Boott," Lilly continued weakly.

"I know, I know," Matthew replied. "None of it makes any sense, but Kirk is determined to prove his power will withstand this school movement. I think he almost views it as a personal affront that the town would oppose his point of view."

Lilly unfastened her hair, letting it fall around her shoulders. "We can't afford for him to win, Matthew. I want our children living at home with us—not off in some boarding school growing up without our love and the comfort of their own home. And what of Lewis's son? When we find him, he's going to need all the love and comfort of a family, too. Sending him off would be devastating. You've got to find some way to convince Mr. Boott he's wrong on this issue."

"I think the vote this evening has already proven that he's wrong—at least in the eyes of the community. I doubt whether he'll find any way he can stave off the new schools now that the vote has passed, and I don't intend to take up the banner of convincing him he should gracefully accept the decision."

Lilly turned and faced Matthew. "You could assist in making this matter go more smoothly if you truly embraced the idea."

"Don't start . . ."

Lilly's eyes widened as loud knocking sounded at the front

door. "Who can that be at this hour?"

Matthew quickly donned his trousers and rushed down the steps while Lilly stood in the bedroom doorway. She heard Matthew open the door and then heard another man's voice. Sitting on the edge of the bed, she repetitively pulled a silver hairbrush through her long, thick mane until she finally grew weary and slipped under the bedcovers.

"I almost fell asleep," she said when Matthew finally returned. "Who was that?"

"Mr. Cummiskey," he replied, removing his trousers. "Problems in the Paddy camp. Another girl has disappeared, and the Irish are up in arms."

Lilly bolted upright in the bed. "Not another one," she said in a choked whisper.

"How stupid of me! I shouldn't have said anything. I don't want you upsetting yourself, Lilly."

"Then tell me what has been occurring," she insisted.

He sat down on the bed and took her hand. "At first we thought perhaps the girls had run off with their beaux or just run away from home. However, it appears that's not the case. At least the families say none of the girls had reason to run off and none of them had a steady fellow. Hugh has given the police a great deal of information regarding each of the girls, but it seems that the police aren't doing much. Folks in the Paddy camp think the police don't care because the girls are Irish."

"Do you think that's true?" Lilly asked.

"Possibly. If the girls were Yankees, I imagine the matter would receive more attention. Most townsfolk haven't given the disappearances much thought, although the mill girls appear concerned. I think they worry such a thing could happen to one of them."

"Oh, Matthew. How terrible!" She clutched the coverlet into her fist and drew the knotted fabric to her chest. "I know how my heart aches with longing to be united with Lewis's son. The girls' parents must be suffering intolerable anguish. Surely there's some way to help them," she pleaded.

He pulled her into an embrace, stroking her hair. "I've

promised Hugh that I'll do all in my power to help. I'm going to talk to the police tomorrow, but I want you to promise that you'll not overly worry yourself."

She tilted her head back and looked into his eyes. "I promise, Matthew. And while you're with the police, would you talk to them about Lewis's boy again? See if there's anything to report?"

"Yes, dear, I'll inquire. Now I want you to get some sleep."

Slumber came, followed by dreams—visions of a little boy, a miniature Lewis, lost in a dark abyss, stretching a tiny hand toward hers. She grasped her hand around the pudgy fist, pulling, pulling, until she awakened—exhausted and aching. Aching for Lewis's child but beginning to lose hope that he would be found.

CHAPTER 23

A sharp rapping sounded at the front door, interrupting Addie and Bella's conversation.

"Sit still, Miss Addie, I'll go. It's probably another suitor come to call on one of the girls," Bella said, rising from the settee. "I think Daughtie should be joining us soon. She wanted to finish her laundry first," Bella continued, glancing over her shoulder as she moved toward the front door. There were several girls gathered around the dining room table, and four more were entertaining young men in the parlor. The quietude of Miss Addie's rooms was a pleasant reprieve from the deafening noise of the weaving room and the chattering of the girls and their beaux.

Bella's smile disappeared when she opened the door. "Taylor! Were you expected this evening?"

"No, but I thought perhaps I'd find you at home," he said, still standing on the step. "May I come in?"

Bella hesitated for a moment, then moved aside. "I suppose, but I can't be long. I'm visiting with Miss Addie in her parlor."

"Oh, good. I was hoping to see Miss Addie. Shall I join the two of you?" He didn't wait for an answer. Instead he moved toward Miss Addie's living quarters.

Bella stood staring after him as he waited just inside the parlor door.

"Taylor, do come in. What a pleasant surprise," Addie greeted. "What brings you calling this evening—and what's happened to Bella?"

Bella walked to the doorway. "I'm right here, Miss Addie."

Miss Addie patted the settee cushion. "Come sit down. I thought you'd deserted me."

Taylor was leaning against the mantel, oozing charm as he smiled down at Miss Addie.

"Why don't I leave the two of you to visit? I'm sure you'd both enjoy an opportunity for some private conversation," Bella suggested.

Taylor immediately moved away from the fireplace. "I think our conversation would be much livelier if you remained. Don't you agree, Miss Addie?"

"Of course. We have nothing to say that you can't hear. Now come sit down," Addie insisted.

"Have you heard from Uncle John?" Taylor inquired as Bella seated herself.

"I received a short letter yesterday. He said the journey was tiring and he had hoped for a few days' rest before beginning his meetings, but that wasn't the case. He fears his meetings thus far haven't gone as well as he had hoped. I got the impression he's very tired and hasn't had much time to himself. I'm concerned about his health," Addie replied.

Bella moved closer and took Miss Addie's hand in her own. "Perhaps the best thing we could do right now is pray for Mr. Farnsworth."

Taylor jumped up from his chair as though he'd been jabbed by Miss Mintie's pointed parasol. "I'm not much on praying. I'll wait in the other room until you've finished," he said, attempting to make a hasty retreat.

"Sit down, Taylor," Miss Addie instructed. "Bella and I will pray after we've concluded our visit." The words were spoken in a chiding tone, followed by an unmistakable frown leveled in Bella's direction.

Why was Miss Addie upset with her? After all, she was offering to help. Taylor was the one ready to flee from the room without praying for his own uncle. Dismayed, Bella watched Taylor seat himself on the brocade-covered chair close to the door—obviously preparing to bolt and run should Bella once again mention prayer or God. She now wished she had insisted upon leaving when Taylor first arrived. Instead, she was trapped in this room, feeling very much the fool.

Bella's gaze was fixed upon her folded hands, half listening as Miss Addie and Taylor discussed Mr. Farnsworth's whereabouts and the contents of his recent letter.

"I was wondering if you'd be interested in a carriage ride tomorrow."

"Bella?"

Miss Addie's voice drifted through her hazy thoughts, drawing her gaze upward. "Yes, ma'am?"

Miss Addie's forehead was creased into thin ridges, her eyebrows arched in an upsurge of expectation. "Were you going to answer Taylor?"

Befuddled, she glanced back and forth between Taylor and Miss Addie. "I'm sorry. Answer what? Apparently I wasn't listening," she apologized.

"Perhaps you should repeat your question, Taylor," Miss Addie prompted.

"I was wondering if you would like to accompany me on a carriage ride tomorrow," he said.

"After church?" She glanced toward Miss Addie. "I suppose if Miss Addie would like me to accompany her on an outing with you, I'd be willing to come along," she replied.

Now they were both giving her a dumbfounded look. "I believe Taylor was inviting you, Bella," Miss Addie replied.

"Oh! I don't think . . ." she stammered. "Unless you'd care to join us, Miss Addie, I don't believe it would be appropriate for me to accompany Mr. Manning on a carriage ride without a chaperone."

Addie gave her a look of surprise. "All of the girls go on unaccompanied outings—especially during the daytime hours. And it's not as though Taylor were a stranger."

"Exactly right, Miss Addie. Why, in the near future, Miss Addie and I will likely be related. At least I'm sure that's Uncle John's desire," he said, giving her a charming smile.

Miss Addie's cheeks immediately tinged pink at the comment. "I think a carriage ride would be a wonderful escape from your daily routine, Bella."

Bella didn't want to encourage Taylor Manning's attention. In fact, she preferred to avoid his company completely, but from all appearances, Miss Addie was of a different mindset—and Bella didn't want to argue.

"We can leave immediately after church services. That way I can be home in ample time to complete some unfinished tasks," Bella replied as she glanced toward Miss Addie for a sign of approval.

Bella sighed in relief as the older woman nodded and smiled her affirmation.

"I was thinking later in the day would be more suitable. I have some business for the Mechanics Association and had already made plans to meet with several other members tomorrow afternoon," Taylor replied.

"I have an idea," Miss Addie said, her face glowing with excitement. "Why don't you pack a light picnic supper, Bella. A picnic near the falls, or some other lovely spot you locate while on your ride, would be restful, and it will be much cooler in the evening."

Taylor appeared to be delighted with the idea, his head bobbing up and down in agreement. "Yes, and that would permit you time to complete your tasks before we leave for our carriage ride."

"Right!" Miss Addie agreed. "It's much more relaxing to have your work completed beforehand."

Bella felt as though she were being sucked into a swirling black whirlpool. She could barely breathe, and there was no doubt she had lost control of this conversation.

"I'll be here at five thirty," Taylor said without waiting for further discussion. "Now, if you ladies will excuse me, I must be on my way as it's getting rather late."

Bella remained in her chair while Miss Addie rose to escort Taylor to the door. The older woman's words floated back into the room as she reminded Taylor to speak to Matthew Cheever and told him she looked forward to seeing him in church the next morning. Before bidding him good-night, Miss Addie promised to find some delightful morsels to place in their picnic basket the next day.

Miss Addie returned to the room, giving Bella a comforting pat on the shoulder as she walked by. "You and Taylor will have a fine time tomorrow. You do need a bit of relaxation, you know." The words hung in midair—expectantly, longingly, anxiously—awaiting Bella's confirmation.

But Bella wasn't interested in discussing her need for relaxation. She wanted an explanation of Miss Addie's earlier behavior and she wanted it now. Pushing any doubts aside, she charged forward with her interrogation. "Why did you appear offended when I offered to pray for Mr. Farnsworth?" she quizzed, more anger in her tone than she'd intended.

Miss Addie appeared to shrink back at her words. "It's obvious I've hurt your feelings. I'm sorry," she apologized. "Truth is, I've been earnestly praying for Taylor and his relationship—"

"Then why wouldn't you allow me to pray?" Bella interrupted.

"Permit me to finish, dear," Miss Addie calmly replied. "I truly appreciated your offer to pray for John. When we've finished talking, I want to do just that—and I hope you'll join me," she said with a sweet smile. "However, it appeared Taylor was extremely uncomfortable with your suggestion. I've found that forced participation in almost anything can have an adverse effect. Taylor struggles against God—at least that's what John has told me. Had we continued, I fear we would have appeared sanctimonious. Now, I may be wrong," she concluded.

"No. You're absolutely correct, Miss Addie," Bella replied. "In all honesty, I wanted him to feel uncomfortable. I'm terribly ashamed of myself," she admitted.

"It wasn't my intent to cause you discomfort, Bella, but since you've broached the topic, remember that if Taylor is to be won to the Lord, we need to set an example. Once he sees how wonderful life can be when you have a close relationship with God, he'll begin asking questions. But if you won't spend time with Taylor, it's going to be difficult for you to guide him in the proper direction," Miss Addie instructed.

"Me?" Bella wasn't sure she wanted to guide Taylor Manning anywhere, but Miss Addie's plea was heartfelt. "Even though I don't want to go with him tomorrow, I'll do my best," she told the older woman, not wanting to disappoint her.

"Thank you, dear. I think Taylor will be much more apt to listen and learn from someone closer to his own age," Miss Addie said, leaning back in her chair with a sigh. "You know, Taylor is a very lonely young man. The past troubles him. He lost his mother when he was only seventeen. John tells me that he suffered greatly, eventually turning to John for encouragement when his father became more and more lost in his grief."

Bella thought of her mother's grief when her father forced the lifestyle of the Shakers upon them. Her mother's sorrow at being separated from her husband had killed her as sure as anything. As if reading her mind, Miss Addie continued.

"Losing his father was equally difficult. But Taylor felt his father really died the day he lost his wife."

"I saw my mother's own will to live diminish as my father became more and more devoted to the Shakers," Bella admitted.

"Taylor may come across as rather . . . ." Miss Addie paused, as if thinking for a word.

"Crass, rude, bossy?" Bella offered.

Addie smiled. "I was thinking more along the lines of independent. He tries very hard not to need anyone, John says. I think the loss of John during these days, however, has impacted Taylor more than he'd like to admit. Since coming to America over a year ago, Taylor has had John to keep him company. I hope you'll do whatever you can to ease his loneliness—for my sake. He seems to genuinely like you, and I think that if you'd allow yourself the luxury, you might very well find him plea-surable company."

"But I'm not looking for pleasurable company, Miss Addie. I've no interest in acting like those girls who are only here to seek out a husband."

"Then what are you seeking, my dear?"

Addie's question pierced Bella's heart. *What am I seeking?* She gave the question some thought for several minutes. The ticking of the clock reminded her that the hour was growing late. "I don't know," she finally whispered. "I suppose I desire to know God better—to better understand His word. I would like to make a comfortable life for myself, and I know for sure it won't always include working at the mill." She met Addie's concerned expression. Feeling the weight of the topic, Bella shrugged it off and gave a light laugh. "I'll accompany Taylor if it makes you happy, Miss Addie."

"I think it would be a very charitable thing—a good thing to do. Just don't tell Taylor you've set him up as a charity case. He would be most grieved. Besides, as I said, I think you very well may be able to reach Taylor for God in a way that might have eluded the rest of us."

"And it will give me an opportunity to further persuade him he needs women on the selection committee of the Mechanics Association," Bella said, giving the older woman a satisfied grin.

That night, Bella took up her Bible. The last thing in the world she wanted to do was join Taylor for an outing and bear him a Christian witness in her kindness and gentle spirit.

"I feel neither kind nor gentle," she murmured, hoping Daughtie, who also was reading her Bible, wouldn't be dis-turbed.

She glanced up momentarily, seeing the other girls in the room content to chatter about their day. Ruth was draping still-damp stockings over the end of their bed while one of the newer girls, Elaine, shared an animated tale of her life in New York City.

Bella tried to ignore them all and put her mind to reading the Bible. The seventh chapter of Romans led her to a most convicting verse. *"For I know that in me (that is, in my flesh,) dwelleth no good thing: for to will is present with me; but how to perform that which is good I find not. For the good that I would I do not: but the evil which I would not, that I do."*

The good that I should do would be to extend kindness to Taylor, she told herself. *But he's so very smug and self-serving. He irritates me with his manner—or rather his lack of good manners. He isn't very nice, and he speaks whatever he pleases without giving thought to how the other person might feel.*

A voice spoke to her heart. *But you do the same thing.*

The painful truth settled over her. Bella had used her quick wit and ability to speak eloquently to hold many people at arm's length—but surely no one suffered from this as much as Taylor Manning. She swallowed hard. Her own pride was an equal match to his.

She snapped the Bible shut with such vehemence that Daughtie and Ruth immediately looked to her as if to question the problem. Bella smiled. "I didn't realize it was getting so late."

She put the Bible aside and quickly scooted down into the bed and pulled the covers high.

"Good night, ladies," she called out as cheerily as possible while tears trickled down her cheeks and dampened her pillow.

CHAPTER 24

Bella, Ruth, and Daughtie walked in the front door of number 5 after returning from church on Sunday. Miss Addie crooked her finger and beckoned Bella into her parlor. "Come see me for a minute, Bella," she requested.

The older woman was carefully removing a decorative pearl stickpin from her hat. "Taylor was quite disappointed because you weren't at the Episcopal church this morning," she reported.

"Was he? I'm surprised to hear he was in attendance." Bella tilted her head slightly to the side and gave Miss Addie a thoughtful look. "I was just thinking—this would be the first Sunday he's been in church since Mr. Farnsworth's departure, wouldn't it?"

Miss Addie appeared amused by the question. "I'm not certain. It appears you've been maintaining a closer watch on his attendance than I. In any event, I would have enjoyed your company this morning."

"Had Daughtie and I not promised Ruth we would attend the Methodist services, you know I would have gone with you, Miss Addie."

"I know, my dear. Now don't let me hold you back from

your chores. I want you to be ready for an enjoyable carriage ride, and you needn't worry about the food. Since I suggested the picnic, I'll pack a nice basket for the two of you." She beamed.

Bella returned the smile. "That's kind of you, Miss Addie, but I don't want you to go to any bother. In fact, some bread and a bit of cheese will be plenty."

Miss Addie pursed her lips and made a soft clucking sound. "On with you. Take care of your mending or letter writing or whatever it is you must accomplish this afternoon," she said, shooing Bella from the room. "I'll tend to the food."

Bella slowly climbed the stairs. As the temperature grew warmer with each step, she became thankful that she wasn't on the top floor of the house any longer, where the rooms remained intolerably warm all night during the summer months.

Daughtie was busy writing a letter while Ruth was mending the hem of her skirt when Bella entered the bedroom. "Another letter to Sister Mercy?" Bella asked.

Daughtie glanced over her shoulder and gave Bella an apologetic look as she nodded her head. "I miss her so much."

Her friend's words rekindled Bella's guilt. She doubted that Daughtie was any more comfortable in Lowell than she'd been the week they arrived. "You need not apologize," Bella replied, giving her friend a hug. "I miss her, too. And the children— how I miss each of them."

"Do you remember when we found the bird's nest and little Minnette stuffed tiny pieces of strawberries down the fledglings' throats until they were so full they nearly burst?" Daughtie asked with a giggle.

"And how Eldress Phoebe reduced the poor child to tears by telling her she'd most likely killed the baby birds?" Bella continued.

Daughtie nodded. "Had it not been for Sister Mercy taking Minnette out to see those birds were still alive the next day, I don't think Minnette would have recovered from Eldress Phoebe's tart words. What would she have said had she known of the days we pulled off our shoes and stockings and waded in the creek?"

"I doubt she could have withstood the shock," Bella replied.

"I wonder if anyone else has left the Society since our departure. I do wish I could see some of them again," Daughtie reflected aloud. "Minnette was such a sweet little girl. And the two tiny boys who were always clamoring for you, Bella, toddling about in their oversized butternut breeches and little shirts."

A pang of sadness stabbed at her heart. "Yes. How they missed their mothers. I'm sure they still do." She paused, then wanting to forget the little boys who cried for their mothers, said, "I'd best get busy or I'll not be done with my laundry by the time Taylor arrives."

"So you're going?" Daughtie asked.

"Yes. Miss Addie would be very upset if I backed out now," she explained.

Daughtie gave her a sidelong glance. "I think you want to go. You're beginning to have feelings for him, aren't you?"

Bella attempted to squelch her rising sense of exasperation. "I've already explained this to you, Daughtie. Miss Addie is hopeful Taylor will open his heart to God. She's hoping I can help point him in the right direction."

"The only thing open in Taylor Manning's heart is fulfillment of his own desire," Ruth said with a blush.

"Amen to that," Daughtie replied. "Bella, I fear you're leaving yourself at risk to his scheming ways."

"I'm not afraid of Taylor. Besides, this will be a good opportunity to further plead our case for representation on the selection committee. I plan to find out just how much he's accomplished in scheduling a vote by the Association."

"As you wish, but I doubt he'll remain on that subject for long," Ruth countered.

"I believe I'll go downstairs and begin my laundry. Please don't follow me—I can see you two are in agreement on this issue and I'm rushing off to escape your scolding," she said, giving them a giggle as she walked out the door.

By the time Bella had completed her laundry and mending and had written a letter to Aunt Ida in Concord, there was little time to prepare for her outing with Taylor. Dashing upstairs, she quickly rearranged her hair, slipped out of her gray-striped Shaker work dress, and donned a yellow organdy with embroidered crewel work, one of the gowns Lilly Cheever had given her. A quick glance in the mirror caused her to stop and straighten the lace at one sleeve before rushing downstairs and off toward the kitchen.

Miss Addie gave her a bright smile while tucking a linen cloth atop a basket that appeared to contain more than ample supplies for two people. "I hope the size of that basket indicates that you plan to join us," Bella said with a grin.

"Young men have large appetites. Mintie tells me that no matter how much food she prepares for the men in her boardinghouse, they empty the bowls and ask for more. Besides, I'm sure Taylor hasn't been eating well since John's departure," Addie replied. "Their housekeeper has been ill and still hasn't returned to her duties."

Bella shook her head back and forth. "I doubt whether Taylor Manning will starve. Although I don't think he'd attempt any cooking on his own, I'm certain he'd solicit dinner invitations in order to keep his stomach filled."

"Now, now," Miss Addie clucked.

Bella had just opened her mouth to answer when a knock sounded at the front door. Miss Addie bustled past her, obviously excited to welcome Taylor. Bella lifted the hefty basket, the wooden handle cutting into the fleshy padding of her fingers. She edged down the hallway with the cumbersome container shifting at her side.

Taylor moved toward her and in one fluid motion took the basket from her hand. "Let me help you. You must be anxious to be off," he said, giving her a broad smile.

Bella decided his smile bordered on a smirk. Most likely he truly believed she was fervently anticipating his company. "I'm in no hurry. Did you want to come into the parlor and visit with Miss Addie for a while?" she inquired in her sweetest voice.

He fidgeted for a moment, obviously uncertain how to answer without offending Miss Addie. Bella, on the other hand, was enjoying his discomfort.

"You children be on your way," Miss Addie said, shooing them toward the door and saving Taylor from further uneasiness.

Moving with unusual celerity, Taylor whisked Bella to the carriage, loaded the picnic basket, and climbed up beside her. "My! Suddenly it appears you're in a hurry—or is that my imagination?" Bella inquired with a demure smile as he flicked the reins.

"You did that on purpose!" he accused.

She swallowed hard and sucked in on her cheeks to keep from laughing. "Did what?" she innocently asked.

"You know exactly what I'm talking about," he countered.

Her eyes grew wide as she gave him a questioning look and feigned innocence.

"You intentionally suggested we visit with Miss Addie in the parlor before leaving the house in order to make me uncomfortable," he alleged.

"And you, sir, did the same to me. I returned no more than you gave," she said, giving him a winsome smile.

"I suppose you're right about that," he said, giving her a hearty laugh. "I'm not accustomed to ladies who . . ." He hesitated for a moment, appearing befuddled.

"Ladies who don't care if they keep company with you?"

His eyes darkened as he met her gaze. "You care—you just won't admit it," he replied.

Bella shook her head. "I'll not argue with you. It's obvious you need to feed your ego with such nonsense. Where are we going for our picnic?" she asked, abruptly changing topics.

"I had planned on stopping near Pawtucket Falls, but then Matthew Cheever mentioned a spot that's a bit farther away. He says the view is worth the extra time it takes to get there. Of course, I can't think of a lovelier view than the one I'm gazing upon at this moment."

Bella turned in the opposite direction, her gaze fixed upon the passing countryside. Her cheeks surely resembled two bright red apples. He would enjoy knowing that he'd caused her embarrassment.

"You have no response to my compliment?" he asked.

"No. We both know such talk is inappropriate."

"I spoke the truth. Surely that's not improper."

"What was the topic of Reverend Edson's sermon this morning?" she inquired.

"Let's see—how do I summarize an hour of preaching in one sentence? It is best to perform acts that are in the best interest of the body of Christ, even though such acts may be detrimental to you as an individual. God will honor your obedience. That was two sentences, wasn't it? See there? It took him an hour to say what I told you in less than a minute."

Bella turned in her seat and faced him. "It sounds as though Reverend Edson's sermon was directed at the people who oppose the school issue," she replied. "Was Mr. Boott present?"

"Indeed he was—at least for a portion of the sermon. However, after the topic became evident, he and his wife got up and walked out of the church."

"No! Surely they wouldn't act in such an offensive manner. Miss Addie didn't say a word about this. Are you making up this story to entertain me?"

Taylor laughed as he pulled the horses to a stop. "This is beyond my storytelling ability. Obviously Kirk Boott doesn't care what other people think. On the other hand, his wife doesn't appear to share his views; she appeared extremely uncomfortable as they left the church," he said as he assisted her out of the buggy.

Bella spread one of Miss Addie's quilts on the nearby bed of grass, then gazed about her. "Mr. Cheever is right. This is a beautiful spot."

"I'll tell him you approve," Taylor replied as he placed the basket between them. "Are you hungry, or would you prefer to take a short stroll?"

"Perhaps we should eat first and take our walk afterward," she suggested as she began unpacking the basket of food. "And you enjoyed the sermon?" she asked.

Taylor gave her a look of confusion. "You do change issues rapidly. I'm going to have to stay on my toes if I'm going to keep up with you," he said with a grin. "I suppose the sermon was as interesting as most. Personally, I don't see the need to talk so long in order to say something people already know."

"Obviously the words bear repeating since people don't live by them," she replied. "And I'm certain Reverend Edson used the additional time to detail his thoughts and point the congregation toward the Scripture he used as the basis for his sermon."

"That's exactly what he did, but please don't ask me to quote the Scripture. I listened to enough of that when I was growing up," he replied absently.

Bella placed a piece of Miss Addie's baked chicken on a plate and handed it to Taylor. "You learned to quote Scripture as a little boy?"

"Um," he said, nodding his head affirmatively as he stuffed a piece of chicken into his mouth and licked a finger. "That's right."

She was amazed at the revelation. A young Taylor Manning committing Scripture to memory was quite difficult to envision. "How did you make the transition from a child reared in a godly home to someone who, who . . ."

"Are you at a loss for words, Bella? Let me help you. Perhaps you were going to say someone who enjoys life? Or someone who enjoys the company of ladies?"

"Or someone who enjoys life by keeping company with nearly married ladies," she snapped. She slapped a hand across her mouth the moment the words slipped off her tongue.

"You seem to know a great deal about my past. I find it charming that you know of my past indiscretions yet you permitted me to call upon you and agreed to accompany me on a picnic to this secluded place," he said while moving closer.

"Stop right there, Mr. Manning," she commanded. "I don't find your actions humorous."

He leaned back against a large maple tree and gave her a wide grin. "Anything else you've been told about me that you'd like to share?"

"No, but I wondered when the Mechanics Association was going to vote on our request to have representatives on the selection committee."

His forehead furrowed in deep creases. "There you go changing subjects again," he said. "But because I'm such a gentleman, I'll answer your question anyway. We'll be voting on that issue soon."

"It seems as if it's taking quite a while for the matter to come to a vote," she said, slicing a piece of cheese.

He picked up an apple and tossed it into the air, caught it, and then pitched it upward again. "These things take time. We presented the proposal at our last meeting, but because of machinery problems at the Merrimack, there were very few members in attendance. It seemed unwise to move forward."

"Until you had enough men there to vote it down?" she asked.

He raised a brow. "That's not what I said. In fact, I've decided having additional representatives would be a good idea, and I think many of the men are in agreement," he replied in a gentle tone before giving her a tender smile.

His words surprised her and she returned his smile. "Thank you, Taylor." She thought of her convictions from the night before. Here she had such grand plans to be all gentleness and kindness, and she'd really done nothing but antagonize Taylor since they'd come out together. Her thoughts were quickly shattered, however.

Before she realized what was happening, Taylor had gathered her into his arms, his lips capturing her mouth. She momentarily struggled against him and then succumbed to the warmth of his embrace.

Moving back ever so slightly, he waited until her eyes fluttered open and then gave a soft chuckle as he cupped her face in his hand. "I knew you'd fall prey to my charms. Even a straight-laced little Shaker girl can't resist me."

His words and actions ignited her anger. Without further thought, Bella drew back her arm and, with all the force she could muster, slapped his face. She gave a self-satisfied nod as red welts began to form along his cheek. Attempting to jump to her feet, Bella dropped back to her knees as Taylor's fingers grasped her wrist.

"Turn me loose," she commanded, wresting her arm from his hold and moving out of his reach.

"Bella! Come back! It'll be dark before long," he called out.

She hurried, relieved to find the narrow road before darkness began to fall. Rushing off had been foolish, yet she wasn't going to abide Taylor's boorish behavior. Gray clouds were moving in overhead, bringing darkness sooner than usual. Without benefit of illumination, she tripped along the rutted path. Twice she twisted her ankle before deciding the grassy area alongside the road might provide more stability.

Soon she could hear Taylor's slowly approaching carriage. Obviously he was looking for her, hoping to rectify the situation he had so callously created. He certainly wouldn't want Miss Addie to find out he hadn't changed a jot since moving to Lowell. Secreting herself among a stand of trees, she pulled her skirts close and peeked around the trunk of a towering elm, watching for his approach. Let him worry. He needed to suffer the consequences of his ill-mannered behavior, she decided.

"Bella!" he called out.

Permitting herself only the shallowest of breaths, Bella flattened herself against the tree and waited until the buggy passed. She remained sculpted in place until the clopping sound of the horses grew faint to her ear. Suddenly she realized how very alone she was.

"You're being silly, Bella," she told herself. "You spent the whole night in the woods before traveling from the Shaker's village to Concord. You are no more at peril here than you were there." The words bolstered her courage. "And look what you've done. You've put that pompous ninny in his place once and for all. God would surely never have expected you to compromise yourself all in hope of sharing the Gospel."

She took only a moment to bask in the delight of having outwitted Taylor before departing her hiding place. The hoot of an owl startled her into movement. Perhaps she should have kept the buggy in sight, she thought as she attempted to remain close to the path. The bushes up the road appeared to rustle. Was it the wind? Her palms grew wet, her breath coming in short, shallow spurts. Her instincts told her to run, yet her feet remained firmly planted. She couldn't make them take flight. There was a sticky dryness in her mouth, a tackiness akin to a sturdily woven spider's web. And in the midst of this fear, why was she remembering the stirrings of Taylor's embrace, the warmth of his kiss? She pushed the unseemly thoughts from her mind, feeling cheap. She'd been nothing more than one of his conquests.

Finally able to force one foot forward, she slowly moved along the path, though she was still unable to allay her increasing terror. *If there is anyone out there, it's Taylor attempting to assure himself I'm going to make it back to town,* she decided. *He's probably still hoping to convince me to remain silent about his behavior. Or possibly he thinks he can frighten me and I'll rush to his carriage. He would certainly enjoy playing the hero!*

Shadowy branches stretched in eerie patterns across the road as a breeze once again whispered through the trees. "I know you're out there, Taylor," she uttered in a trembling voice, realizing her newfound courage had already deserted her.

She was making a futile attempt to pray when her thoughts went careening off in another direction. What about those Irish girls who'd been reported missing? Only last week she'd heard of another one. Most likely those girls had been out alone—just like her. The thought sent a chill coursing down her spine, and her heart began pounding.

Bolting as though she'd been shot from a cannon, Bella heeded her innermost warning. She ran as though the devil himself were on her heels, hysteria nearly overtaking her as she arrived at the edge of town and finally the boardinghouse. She stood on the front step, grasping the door handle while hoping she could avoid prying eyes.

"Thank you, Lord, for getting me home safely," she whispered, trying hard to bring her breathing under control. "Help me now so that I don't have to answer any of Miss Addie's questions."

She opened the door, looking hesitantly into the house. No one was nearby. If she hurried, she might enter and be up the steps before anyone noticed. Drawing a deep breath, she gathered her skirts in one hand and widened the door's opening with the other. *I won't let them see me as the fool,* she told herself. *Let Taylor Manning explain this one.*

CHAPTER 25

Taylor knew he would have to find out if Bella had made it back to the boardinghouse safely, but he didn't want to arouse unnecessary suspicion. It had been too late to go the night before. Besides, he knew if he showed up without Bella and she was still out there somewhere on foot, he'd never hear the end of it from Miss Addie.

Why had Bella become so annoyed? Surely she could see how giving in to her feelings for him was better than living a lie. His hope had been to push her into accepting that she felt something for him other than disdain. He'd hoped to convince her . . . convince her of what? He wasn't at all sure. He had to admit there was that prideful side of him that was more than a little bit delighted to have felt her grow yielding in his arms. But there were other feelings that he didn't understand. He felt guilty for having pushed himself on her—guilty for toying with her emotions. But why? Why did he suddenly feel so vulnerable? Taylor decided he would return Miss Addie's picnic basket and see what Bella had told her, since he had a bit of time on his hands before the mills would let out for the day. If Bella had told Miss Addie all that had happened, he was certain to get an earful, but at least the girls wouldn't be around to hear it, as well. And if she had said nothing, then he might get out of this situation without much more than a slap to the face.

With basket in hand, he knocked on the boardinghouse door. Miss Addie opened the door and for a moment looked at him as though he'd grown wings. "Taylor! What brings you here? You haven't had bad news from John, have you?"

He breathed a sigh of relief and held up the picnic basket. "I brought this back. We forgot to return it last night."

"Oh, do come in and have a cup of tea. I have a bit of time, and you can tell me all about your outing with Bella. I'm afraid she must have been very tired when she came home for she went right to bed without a word."

Taylor followed, after allowing her to take the basket. "Now, you sit here in the parlor," she told Taylor. "I'll just take this to the kitchen and bring back some tea and cookies."

Within a few minutes she was as good as her word. Taylor sat uncomfortably on the edge of the settee, still uncertain as to what he might say about the night before. He certainly couldn't lie to Miss Addie.

She smiled and handed him a cup of tea. "Would you care for sugar or lemon? Cream?"

He shook his head. "This is just fine."

"I'm glad you came by. I haven't had any word from John and sometimes I miss him so much. Seeing you is almost as good as having him here."

Taylor took a long drink and tried to think how he might voice his concern about Bella without arousing her suspicions. "So was . . . ah . . . Bella overly tired today?"

Miss Addie laughed. "She didn't appear so. She came home for breakfast and dinner with the other girls but said very little. Did you have a pleasant time together?"

"Not exactly," he said, refusing to tell her the truth. "You know things have never been right between us. She's hated me since she first laid eyes on me." *She especially hates me now,* he thought.

"I don't believe she hates you, Taylor, so much as she dislikes your pride and self-assured nature. You must understand—you two are very much alike. You pride yourselves in needing no one . . . God included."

"Now, Miss Addie, that might be true for me, but Bella is a very godly young woman. She's always praying and talking of her faith and of what God wants for mankind."

"Yes, but she has trouble, just as you do, in believing God can be relied upon and truly trusted. You both need to come to an understanding that there is something more than religious notions when it comes to putting your faith in God."

In the silence that followed, Taylor grew most uncomfortable. He finished his tea and got to his feet. "I should go. I know you'll need to see to supper soon."

Addie followed him to the door but never tried to stop him. "Taylor, your Uncle John and I care a great deal about what happens to you. Please understand that you might put the topic of God off for a good long time, but you'll never be able to put off God himself. He'll always find a way to reach you."

Taylor nodded, saying nothing more. He took up his hat and hurried down the street. What he'd hoped would be a journey to ease his mind and comfort him had only made matters worse.

———

Ruth rushed in the front door, her face flushed with excitement as she skidded to a halt in the parlor. "Good news, Bella," she announced. "I saw one of the men who attended our meeting at the church. He said the Mechanics Association voted last night, and the vote was in favor of female representation on the selection committee!" she screeched while jumping up and down.

"Are we forgetting how proper young ladies behave?" Miss Mintie inquired as she poked her head out from Miss Addie's private parlor.

"I'm sorry," Ruth apologized. "It won't happen again."

Miss Mintie gave a satisfied nod and disappeared.

"Where did she come from?" Ruth whispered with a giggle. Daughtie pointed toward Miss Addie's parlor. "She's been visiting with Miss Addie for the last hour."

"Poor Miss Addie," Ruth lamented before quickly changing back to her news. "Are you surprised? Or had Taylor already told you?" she excitedly inquired while dropping onto the chair across from Bella.

"I'm very surprised, Ruth. I knew the men were meeting, but I hadn't heard the results," Bella replied. She forced herself to smile. "This is going to provide the girls with an excellent opportunity."

"The girls? You make it sound as though you're not one of us," Ruth said, giving her a quizzical look.

"Of course I'm one of you. I just don't plan to serve on the committee."

Ruth nodded, seemingly unconvinced. "I see."

"We'll need to arrange a meeting for our own election. I'm sure many of the girls would like to participate," Bella said.

Ruth appeared to contemplate her words before speaking. "I'm surprised Taylor didn't come to the house immediately after the voting was concluded."

"I'm sure he was aware someone would get word to me," Bella hedged.

Ruth leaned forward, propped one elbow on her knee, and rested her chin on her palm. "Yes, but you two are . . ."

"Are what?" Bella snapped.

"Friends?" Ruth ventured.

"Taylor Manning doesn't know the meaning of the word *friend.*"

"I see," Ruth replied, standing up. "I'm not certain how many of the girls have heard anything. I'm going to Mrs. Desmond's boardinghouse to visit Sally and the other girls. I promised I'd let them know if I heard the results. When do you think we'll have our meeting, Bella? I'm sure I'll be asked."

"Next Tuesday evening?"

Ruth nodded. "That should give us plenty of time to get word to all of the girls," she said, tying on her bonnet. "Maybe Sally or one of the girls will want to go with me to some of the other boardinghouses. We could stop just long enough to tell one of the girls in each house the outcome of the vote and that we'll be meeting next Tuesday. She could then tell the others in her house."

"That's an excellent idea, Ruth," Bella replied.

Obviously pleased with the compliment, Ruth graced them with a broad smile and waved good-bye.

"I believe I'll go upstairs, Daughtie. I've a letter to write," she said.

"To Jesse?"

Bella nodded. She'd received Jesse's letter five days ago; he deserved a reply.

"You never did tell me what he wrote. Is he happy in Concord? Does he still want to marry you? Or has he decided to return to the Society?"

Detecting the wistful longing in her last question, Bella took Daughtie's hand. "You still want to return, don't you?"

"Not so much as before. I'm beginning to adjust. But if you tell me you're going off to Concord to marry Jesse, then I'll return to Canterbury," she said. "I wouldn't want to live in Lowell if you weren't here."

"Well, you need not worry. I'll not be going off to marry Jesse. It seems he's quite happy in Concord. In fact, he's going to become a partner in the cooperage where he's working."

Daughtie folded her hands and stared wide-eyed at Bella. "My! He's done quite well for himself. Of course, the Brothers always said Jesse was an excellent craftsman, and it appears he's put his woodworking skills to good use."

"He's marrying the cooper's granddaughter," Bella replied flatly.

"What? You're jesting, right?"

"No, it's true. He said that after receiving my last letter, he determined he should move forward with his life—without me."

Daughtie gave her a frown. "What did you say in your last letter?"

"The same thing I told him when he was in Lowell: that I didn't see any more than friendship in our future. And I told him that if he was in love with the cooper's granddaughter, he should ask for her hand."

Daughtie appeared aghast. "Bella! You didn't."

"Yes, that's exactly what I told him. I have no hold on Jesse's future. If he's found love with another, he should marry her," Bella replied.

"Then why must you write? What remains to be said?" Daughtie inquired.

"He told me he would wait to propose until he had my final word on the matter. I must not keep him waiting any longer. It's unfair."

Daughtie was wringing her hands. "Are you certain you want to completely dismiss him from your life?"

Bella glanced toward Daughtie's hands. "I thought you'd broken that habit," she said, touching Daughtie's hands. "I can either dismiss Jesse from my life or marry him. Those are my choices. I certainly can't marry him, so I'll write and tell him I wish him happiness in his marriage to the cooper's granddaughter." Bella stood and walked toward the stairs. "Are you staying down here for a while?"

Daughtie nodded. "Miss Addie's asked me to assist her in making some needle cases once Miss Mintie leaves."

"Needle cases?"

"Yes, Miss Addie saw mine and thought it quite lovely. I told her the needle cases were one of the items that the Sisters made and sold in Canterbury. She thought they would make nice gifts for the ladies in her sewing circle."

"Yes, they will. How very thoughtful of you to help her, Daughtie. I believe I may retire after I finish my letter, so I'll bid you good-night."

"Good night, Bella," Daughtie replied.

Bella climbed the stairs slowly, weighed down by her thoughts of Jesse and Taylor and all that had happened to her since leaving the Shakers. She went to her room, grateful to find it empty. Sitting on the edge of the bed, she reached for her writing paper.

"I don't love Jesse as a wife should love a husband," she whispered. "This is the right thing to do. If I had feelings for him like I have for . . ."

She pushed the thought aside. "No!" She jumped up from the bed. "I won't have feelings for Taylor. I won't give in and be just one more of his conquered ninnies. The man I give my heart to will love me in return. Just me. He won't be given to toying and teasing women. He won't be heartless and rude."

She straightened her shoulders and drew on all of her reserved strength. "He won't be Taylor Manning."

———

Bella found it impossible to discern whether she was awake or dreaming, certain she'd heard a woman's screams followed by thumping and slapping noises. She scooted up into a sitting position. Leaning against the wall, Bella strained to listen for further unfamiliar sounds. All was quiet.

Then there it was again, a thump against the wall and the sound of a woman crying. The muffled words of a man's angry voice seeped through the walls. He was commanding the woman's silence. Was Mr. Arnold abusing his wife? Bella could think of no other explanation. After all, the Arnolds' place and Miss Addie's boardinghouse shared a common wall. Bella shuddered as she remembered Virginia's comment the day she'd arrived in the weaving room—Mr. Arnold likes pretty girls, she'd said. And then there were the stories from a year or two ago, allegations that Mr. Arnold had abused his wife. Although unconfirmed, rumor was that Lilly Cheever had played a part in rectifying the situation. Bella decided she wasn't going to wait until Mrs. Arnold suffered an irreparable injury before bringing the matter to someone's attention. Besides, if Mr. Arnold was returning to his abusive behavior, he might injure their little daughter. Perhaps Lilly Cheever would be willing to intervene once again.

Too anxious to sleep, Bella hoped Daughtie and Ruth would forgive her for awakening them. She reached down to arouse the girls but found only Daughtie in the bed.

"Ruth's probably gone out back to the privy," Bella murmured. Quickly deciding she would meet Ruth downstairs, Bella quietly padded across the room and down the steps.

A short time later Bella returned to the bedroom, the earlier concern for Mrs. Arnold swept from her mind.

Bella grasped Daughtie's arm and jostled the limp appendage. "Daughtie, wake up!" Bella whispered as loudly as she dared. Daughtie's deep breathing continued. Leaning closer to Daughtie's ear, she again whispered her friend's name.

"What?" Daughtie croaked, attempting to turn away. "I didn't hear the bell."

"The bell didn't ring," Bella whispered. "Ruth isn't in bed." She faltered momentarily. "Did she return home before you came upstairs this evening?"

Daughtie rubbed at her eyes while scooting her body upward. "I don't remember seeing her. She's probably gone out back to relieve herself."

"No!" Bella replied while wagging her head back and forth. "That's why I'm awake. I was just now outside; she's not downstairs and she's not in bed."

"Do you think we should awaken Miss Addie? I don't want to get Ruth in trouble for staying out beyond curfew, but she's never been late before. If she's in trouble . . ." Daughtie's whispered words trailed off into the darkened room.

"She's beyond merely being late, Daughtie. It's probably near time to get up, and you know Ruth isn't one to break the rules. Besides, there's no earthly reason for her to remain out all night."

"Perhaps she has a secret gentleman friend," Daughtie offered.

"I seriously doubt Ruth could keep from telling us if she had a beau. And even if she did, Ruth wouldn't likely break the rules. Besides, her plan was to visit the boardinghouses and advise the girls we'd be having an election, but she couldn't go to any of the houses after ten o'clock."

Daughtie pulled her knees to her chest and wrapped her arms around them. "I know! Maybe she realized she wouldn't make it home before curfew and stayed at one of the other houses."

"Maybe, but I think Ruth would just come home, explain the circumstances to Miss Addie, and take her punishment," Bella replied in a hushed voice.

"You're probably right, but I don't know what else could have happened to her."

"I fear something terrible."

"What could happen?" Daughtie asked in a raspy whisper.

"She could have disappeared—like those Irish girls we've heard about."

"Oh, Bella, don't be histrionic. Those girls disappeared from the Acre. There's never been a problem anywhere else in Lowell. Besides, I heard the girls disappeared in order to hide the fact that they had shamed their parents."

"Daughtie! What a vicious story. Who told you such a thing?"

Daughtie shrugged her shoulders. "Some of the girls in the folding room. I don't know their names, but they said all the Irish girls have loose morals."

"That's as preposterous a statement as saying all the Yankee girls have perfect morals."

"There's no need to become angry, Bella. I'm merely telling you what I've heard. She's probably fast asleep somewhere while you're keeping me awake," Daughtie replied as she plumped her pillow and then lay down.

"Go back to sleep. I'm going downstairs," Bella replied. "I think I hear Miss Addie. It must be near time for first bell."

"Oh no," Daughtie moaned as Bella exited the room and bounded down the steps at breakneck speed. She skidded to a stop only inches before colliding with Miss Addie, who, properly ensconced in a lightweight green-striped wrapper, was making her way toward the kitchen.

Miss Addie gave her a wide-eyed stare, her hand tightly clasped over her heart. "You nearly frightened the life out of me!" the older woman scolded. "I'm on my way out back," she explained. "And you?"

"What time is it?" Bella quizzed.

"Too early to be up scampering about. I think it's close to three o'clock."

"May I wait until you come back inside? I need to talk to you."

"If it can't wait until morning," Miss Addie replied in a tone that suggested she, too, would prefer sleep rather than conversation.

"No, it can't wait," Bella replied, following Miss Addie through the kitchen. When she reached the back door Miss Addie turned to face Bella. "You need not follow me to the privy, Bella. I promise I'll return."

"I'll light a fire," Bella remarked.

Miss Addie's face sagged at the offer. "So this is going to be a long conversation?"

"I'm not certain," Bella replied tentatively. "I thought you might like a cup of tea."

"Not nearly as much as I'd like another hour of sleep," the older woman replied with a feeble smile. She patted Bella's cheek. "Don't look so forlorn. I'll be right back."

Bella nodded. She didn't know if she should start a fire or not but finally decided she'd wait. Perhaps Miss Addie would go directly back to bed after hearing her concerns. If so, there certainly wouldn't be time to lay a fire, much less heat water for tea.

The back door opened and Miss Addie bustled back into the kitchen, obviously more awake than when she'd left moments earlier. "Now, then, what did you need to talk about?" she inquired, pulling a chair away from the small worktable and seating herself.

"Ruth," Bella replied. "She's not in bed."

Miss Addie gave her a look of concern. "She didn't come home tonight?"

"I don't know. I went to bed before the others. Daughtie said she didn't see her come home this evening. I noticed she wasn't in bed when I got up a little while ago. Now I'm worried. She was making stops at boardinghouses last evening to tell them we'd soon be having a meeting to elect delegates for the

Mechanics Association committee. I fear some harm may have come to her."

Miss Addie patted her hand. "Let's not panic just yet. She may be sleeping in one of the other rooms. She may have even decided to remain at Mrs. Desmond's for the night. I know you girls do that from time to time," she said with a grin.

"That's true," Bella acquiesced. "I suppose it would be best to wait until morning and see if she appears."

Miss Addie nodded. "There's only an hour until first bell, and we won't resolve much in that short time," she said, giving Bella a comforting smile. "I'm going to return to my room and rest until then. I suggest that you do the same. You're going to be weary." Miss Addie walked her to the foot of the stairs. "Off with you now. Try to get a little sleep," she instructed.

"I will," Bella hesitantly replied, though she would have preferred to remain in Miss Addie's company. Instead, she trod up the stairs and walked to the bedroom, though her steps were heavy and halting. For a moment she remained in the doorway of the bedroom, her gaze lingering on Ruth's unoccupied section of the bed.

CHAPTER 26

One look at Miss Addie's face dashed Bella's expectations. "Nothing?"

"No," Miss Addie woefully reported. "I enlisted Mintie and Mrs. Desmond, and we spent the entire afternoon going to all the boardinghouses. Many of the keepers reported Ruth visited at their houses last night, but she didn't remain very long at any one place. Mrs. Desmond told me that Sally Nelson went along with her but grew weary after an hour and returned home. Sally reported that Ruth appeared determined to continue calling at the boardinghouses until curfew."

"Did Sally say what direction Ruth was headed when they parted company?"

"It seems Ruth called upon the houses on the east side of the street on her way to Mrs. Desmond's house and was calling upon houses on the west side of the street on her return. Of course, she may have gone off onto the side streets along the way. I doubt whether there's any way to track exactly where she was at a specific time. Folks don't tend to remember those little details," Addie replied. "I think we should report Ruth's disappearance to the police. I do wish John were here. He'd know what to do.

Did you speak to Ruth's supervisor regarding her absence?"

"He was more angry than concerned, saying his production was already off this week. He said Ruth's absence would only make matters worse for him and unless she had a very good excuse, he'd make certain that she would never be hired again. I told him Ruth was responsible and needed her job, but he wouldn't listen. He thinks she's run off with a man," Bella replied.

Janet Stodemire glanced toward the ceiling and arched her eyebrows. "You're the only one who thinks she's met with foul play, Bella. The rest of us are more realistic. She was very interested in that salesman, but I'm sure you didn't notice," Janet remarked.

Bella's jaw tightened as Janet spoke. "And you don't even know if the salesman was in Lowell yesterday," she argued from between clenched teeth. "I'm willing to appear foolish in order to learn what's happened to Ruth."

"Now, girls, bickering won't solve anything. We need to be unified if we're going to help Ruth," Addie cautioned.

"You're right; I'm sorry," Bella replied.

"It's still early. Why don't we go and pay a visit at the Cheever home? I'm certain Lilly would be pleased to see us, and if Matthew isn't home, she can relate our concerns to him. I think someone from the Corporation should be informed of our apprehension."

Bella jumped up from her chair. "I'll get my cape." She moved swiftly and retrieved her wrap from one of the pegs near the door. Tossing the shawl around her shoulders, she then turned back toward the parlor. "Aren't you coming?"

Miss Addie nodded. "Yes, but I'm not planning on running a foot race," she replied with a grin. "We should be back by nine o'clock," she told the girls who were gathered in the parlor visiting.

Although it was difficult, Bella was forced to slow her stride in order to accommodate Miss Addie. She wanted to run at full tilt rather than promenade down Merrimack Street at a snail's pace. Somehow she needed to expend some physical energy in order to feel as if she were actually doing something to help Ruth. But she knew Miss Addie could walk no faster, and she couldn't rush off, leaving the older woman behind. It seemed an eternity had passed by the time they reached the front door of the Cheever home.

"Miss Addie—and Bella! What a wonderful surprise," Lilly greeted as she opened the front door. "Do come in," she offered, stepping aside to permit them entry. "Let me take your capes," she said. "Matthew, come see who's here to pay a visit," she called out.

Matthew strode into the foyer with a smile curving his lips. "This is an unexpected pleasure," he said, leading them into the parlor.

Addie gave him a bright smile as she followed along. "I hope we're not taking you away from anything important."

"Not at all. I had just completed plans for the dedication ceremony for the Catholic church. I'm hoping it will be a momentous occasion for the Irish folks."

"With you in charge, I'm sure it will be grand. I didn't realize work on the church had been finished," Addie said.

"Sit down, sit down," Matthew offered. "Construction of the church is still in progress, but the only date the bishop is available is the first Sunday in September. So completed or not, we'll have it dedicated on that date."

Lilly placed a hand on her husband's shoulder. "Now, Matthew, no more talk of work. Ladies, make yourselves comfortable, and I'll get us some tea."

"No, we don't need tea, Lilly. Please sit down and relax."

Lilly gave Matthew a winsome smile. "You sound like my husband. He says I'm not happy unless I'm fluttering about."

"She doesn't listen well," he answered, returning her smile before turning toward Addie. "To what do we owe this unexpected visit?"

Addie wriggled forward just a bit. "Actually, it concerns one of my girls, Ruth Wilson. She attended the tea you hosted. Ruth is fair skinned, her hair a rather mousy brown, and she has—what color are her eyes, Bella?" Addie asked.

Bella furrowed her brow, anxious to give an accurate description. "Gray—yes, cloudy gray. She's rather thin, not very big at all, and her teeth protrude just a bit," Bella explained, looking at Lilly rather than Matthew.

"I remember her. She was quite taken with my garden."

Bella straightened in her chair and bobbed her head up and down. "Yes! That's her. She loved your flowers."

"Well, what about her?" Matthew was obviously ready for the discussion to move forward.

"She's disappeared," Bella proclaimed. "Without a trace."

"What? One of the mill girls has truly disappeared?" he questioned loudly as he stood and began pacing.

"We *think* she's disappeared," Miss Addie said, her voice calm and steady as she revealed the facts of Ruth's departure the evening before and their subsequent efforts to find her.

"So she did have a gentleman caller?" Matthew asked.

"Not last night," Bella quickly replied. "I don't believe he was in Lowell yesterday. At least nobody remembers having seen him since last week. He wasn't due back until the end of the month."

Matthew glanced toward Lilly and then at Bella. "I doubt she would have confided her plans to run away, and I'm sure her suitor would keep himself secreted in order to keep from arousing suspicion."

"I know Ruth, and she didn't run off with a man. Something terrible has happened to her. Why won't anyone help?" Bella lashed out in frustration. "Now I understand how the Irish people must feel when no one will help find their missing girls."

Matthew came to attention at her words. "You think your friend has been kidnapped?" He appeared to think the idea incredible.

"Yes, I do," Bella replied. "She vanished, just like the other girls. She visited a number of boardinghouses last night. Why would she have even bothered to do such a thing if she planned to run off?"

"You have a point," Matthew agreed. "Have you gone to the police, Miss Addie?"

Addie tugged at the lace border of her handkerchief. "No. I wasn't sure what I should do," she said. "Do you want me to go and talk to them?"

"No, I'll go and talk to them. If they want further information, they can stop by the house and talk to you. Bella, did you happen to notice if any of her belongings are missing?"

"All of her belongings are in the room. Nothing has been disturbed," she replied with certainty. "If she'd been running off to marry some salesman, she surely would have taken her clothes and other belongings. Why, she just bought a new pair of gloves," Bella added as though that should sum up the speculation and assure them Ruth had been taken against her will.

"I don't want to be an alarmist, Matthew, but if Ruth has actually been kidnapped, it's not safe for any of us to be out and about at night," Lilly said.

"If you can manage to encourage the girls to travel in groups without causing undue alarm, it would be wise," Matthew said to Miss Addie. "You might want to pass that instruction on to the other keepers, as well."

Bella wasn't certain if Mr. Cheever's words brought a sense of satisfaction or dread. Perhaps it was a strange mixture of both, for a tight knot had now formed in her stomach, and her mouth was curiously dry as she attempted to speak. "So you do think Ruth was abducted."

Matthew gave a one-shouldered shrug and raised his eyebrows. "I'm not certain. But it makes sense to take simple precautions, don't you think?"

"Yes," the three women replied in unison.

"I do believe we should return home," Addie said, obviously taking her cue from Matthew, who was fidgeting with his pocket watch.

"I was just planning to leave, myself. Permit me to take you in the carriage," Matthew insisted as he leaned down to place a kiss on his wife's cheek.

They journeyed in silence, each of them wrapped in disquieting thoughts, until the carriage drew to a halt in front of the boardinghouse. "I plan to stop by the police station on my way home," Matthew assured Miss Addie as he held out a hand to assist her.

"Thank you, Matthew."

"Should any news of Ruth surface, please let me know. I'll do the same," Matthew said before bidding them good-night.

"Any news?" Daughtie inquired as they stepped inside the house.

"No, I'm afraid not. Mr. Cheever is going to talk with the police, though. Perhaps they'll agree to help," Miss Addie replied. "Bella, I'd like to visit with you a moment in my parlor before you retire for the night."

Bella followed Miss Addie and seated herself. "What is it, Miss Addie?"

"I'm probably acting like a foolish old woman, but all this talk of the missing girls has caused me additional worry about John. He said he wasn't feeling well in his last missive, and it's been longer than I expected between letters. I know he's probably fine and my concerns are likely unnecessary," she confided.

Bella took Miss Addie's hand. She wanted to comfort her, yet she respected the older woman too much to spout platitudes. "How may I help?"

"I'm going to pen a note to Taylor and ask if he's heard from John. I was hoping you would deliver it for me," she said. "Of course, you mustn't go alone—but I want your companions to be discreet."

Bella swallowed hard before answering. "I'm sure there are any number of girls who would be pleased to deliver your note to Taylor. Why don't I ask one of them?"

Miss Addie wagged her head back and forth. "No. I don't want all the girls chattering about my personal business. I know you wouldn't breach my confidence. I can't be sure about the other girls. I'm worried, Bella. Won't you do this small thing for me?"

Bella's lips formed a tight line. "You know I would do almost anything for you, Miss Addie. However, I must refuse this request. I can't deliver your note." Her shoulders drooped. She couldn't meet Miss Addie's gaze.

"Something has happened between the two of you, hasn't it?" Miss Addie asked, placing the palm of her hand under Bella's chin and lifting her head until their eyes met.

"Yes." Her voice was a hoarse whisper.

"Tell me, child."

"You remember we went on a picnic?"

"Yes, of course," Miss Addie replied, her eyes filled with concern.

"Taylor's behavior was less than gentlemanly. He kissed me and then laughed, saying I'd fallen prey to his charms. I was so angered by his behavior that I ran from him and walked home alone, and I haven't seen him since. If I go and deliver your note, he's sure to think it's merely a ploy so that I can see him."

Miss Addie's face had gone ashen. She appeared horror-struck by the revelation. "I do believe that young man needs to be taken down a peg or two. Don't you give the delivery of my note another thought! I believe I'll pay our young Mr. Manning a visit tomorrow evening."

CHAPTER 27

William Thurston hunkered down in a rickety chair near the rear of Neil's Pub. His gaze remained fixed on the door as he hoisted a tankard aloft. The barkeep nodded and sent a buxom waitress in his direction. The woman leaned forward in order to reveal a bit more of her bosom and gave Thurston an exaggerated wink. She shoved a full tankard in front of him. "See anything else you'd like?"

"No. Get out of the way. I can't see the door."

She leveled a steely glare at him before walking away. He knew she was intentionally obstructing his view of the entrance as she undulated her hips in suggestive movements and sauntered back to the bar. William Thurston knew her type. She wanted him to lose his temper and create a scene, some sort of confrontation that would make her the center of attention. But he wouldn't give her the satisfaction. Instead, he took a drink of his ale and silently seethed.

Jake Wilson and Rafe Walton walked into the pub a few minutes later. They stopped and picked up their drinks before joining William at his table. Jake had already downed half of the dark, stout ale before seating himself.

Rafe pulled a chair away from the table and seated himself. "Your message sounded urgent."

Thurston kept his gaze fixed on Rafe as he leaned forward and rested his arms on the pockmarked wooden table. "Is everything arranged?"

Rafe nodded. "Just as you instructed. Is there a problem?"

"No. I merely wanted affirmation. Let's go over the plan one last time," Thurston insisted. "I worry about him," he continued while pointing his extended thumb toward Jake.

"No need. He'll do as he's told. Come this evening, the Yanks'll be storming the church, all of 'em hoping to walk away with gold lining their pockets or at the very least enough dead Irishmen to assure themselves jobs."

Thurston rubbed his hands together. "This is going to be delightful. If this ruckus doesn't make the Associates take a long, hard look at Kirk Boott and his inability to manage the Irish, nothing will," he said before emitting a malicious laugh. He glanced to his left, where an old Irishman sat staring out the dingy window and nursing a half-empty mug of ale. "Lowell will be better off without the likes of him," Thurston said as he pointed to the old man.

Pushing away from the table, Rafe looked at William. "Are we through?"

"As far as I'm concerned, we're through," Thurston replied. He stood up and edged his way between the tables, the other two men following close behind. Thurston turned toward the two men once they were outside the pub. "I expect you to be merciless. Destroy that church if you must! Do you understand me?"

"Yeah. Now quit your worrying. Everything will go as planned," Rafe replied.

Thurston nodded, turned, and walked off. "It better," he muttered when he was out of earshot.

Liam cleaned and packed his tools into his old wooden toolbox. He'd worked later than usual, but there was no reason to hurry. The Flynns were in Boston for a funeral and wouldn't return until tomorrow. He decided to eat supper at the pub, drink a mug of ale or two, and have a quiet evening at home. He examined the stones he'd laid in the form of a cross only a short time ago and gave a quick nod of satisfaction. The pattern had turned out better than he'd expected.

Ominous-appearing clouds were rolling in, darkening the early evening sky as Liam walked out of the church. For a moment he thought his eyes were deceiving him. An old man was perched atop a pile of granite stacked alongside the church. Liam lifted his arm and hollered, "Good evenin' to ya. How are ya on this fine night?"

The old man hoisted a gnarly walking stick into the air and brandished it about. "Good as can be expected, better'n most," he replied, giving Liam a toothless grin. "Best be gettin' away from that church," he warned.

"And why would that be?" Liam inquired, walking toward the hunched-over figure.

"It's not gonna be safe in there much longer," he replied simply.

Liam flashed him a smile. "I think it's probably safer inside the church than atop that pile o' stone."

The old man shook his head back and forth, wisps of white hair forming a billowy cloud above his head. "There's gonna be a battle happenin' any time now."

No doubt the old man was feebleminded. Yet something forced Liam to continue talking. "What kind of battle?"

" 'Tween the Yanks and us," he replied. "Irish are better at fightin', so it shouldn't take long to finish them off," he cackled in a gleeful voice. "And I'm gonna have the best view."

Liam drew closer. "How'd you come by this piece of information?"

"Some fancy-pants Yank and a couple of his lackeys talking down at the tavern earlier today. Said the Yanks was gonna storm the church and steal the rifles and gold this evenin'."

A shockwave coursed down Liam's spine. He bounded up the pile of rocks and stood towering over the ancient Irishman.

"Have you told anyone else about this?"

The old man cowered at Liam's approach. "I told the barkeep once the Yanks left the pub. He spread the word among the rest of his customers. Did I do wrong?"

"No, ya did just fine. Did the men talk as though they were comin' to defend the church?"

"They talked like they was gonna defend the church with every man and boy who could hold a weapon—said they'd be here afore the Yanks arrived. They're gonna hide and surprise 'em," he said in a hushed voice. "Fer all I know, some of 'em may already be hiding in there," he said, pointing his stick toward the church. "I told the barkeep those Yanks might just be talkin' big—might not even show up, but he said we should be prepared."

Liam feared the story was true. After all, it hadn't been so long ago that he'd heard similar talk in the tavern. He glanced over his shoulder at the impressive stone edifice. Only yesterday he'd helped mortar two stained-glass windows into place—gorgeous works of art from a Boston benefactor. The thought of those windows being pelted by stones or bullets struck horror in Liam's creative soul.

He would not stand by and do nothing. "A battle will not serve the Irish well. 'Tis our church and homes that will be pummeled. I'm going to find someone with a voice of reason. Perhaps we can halt this madness before anyone is injured. It would be best to keep the fight away from the church. Tell our men to stand firm at the old stone bridge. They must stop the Yanks before they come into the Acre. With a bit o' luck, I'll be back before the Yanks," Liam told the old man.

"Ya'll need more than the luck of the Irish, me boy. I'll say a quick prayer for ya," the old man replied. He shoved a thin, knobbed hand into the depths of his pants pocket and pulled out a string of wooden beads. The strand dangled from his finger momentarily before the old man took hold of one bead and automatically began his rhythmic litany.

Liam quickly descended the heap of rocks and hurried off toward town. By the time he reached the edge of the Acre, he had only one thought in mind: he must locate Matthew Cheever. Although it was well past the last bell, he would go to the mill first. He hoped Matthew was working late, for it would take five additional minutes to reach Matthew's home. As he neared Jackson Street, he glanced in both directions. There were small clusters of men gathering, moving toward each other as if to join forces. Liam's breath was coming hard; he gasped, inhaling as much fresh air as his strained lungs would permit without slowing his pace.

The iron gate to the Appleton was tightly closed. Liam reached up and pulled the dangling rope hanging from the gate bell. He clanged it hard and waited, his face pressed against the cool metal gate, willing Matthew to appear. Again he clanged the bell, long and hard. He continued yanking the rope, determined to stir Matthew to attention if he was nearby.

"What's going on?" Matthew shouted as he rounded the corner of the countinghouse and hurried toward the gate. "Liam?"

"Aye. There's a problem, Mr. Cheever! Hurry!" Matthew shoved a key into the gate and pulled open the cumbersome barrier. "Ya've got to come with me," Liam commanded, grasping Matthew's arm. "There's an uprisin' between the Yanks and Irish. I fear it will already have begun by the time we reach the Acre."

Matthew's forehead furrowed into deep creases, causing his eyebrows to settle into parallel strips of concern. "Settle yourself, Liam, and tell me exactly what has happened."

"I'll explain while we walk," Liam insisted. "There's no time to waste." Unwilling to stand idle, he continued tugging on Matthew's arm, pulling him along as he explained the old man's warning. "Should Mr. Boott be informed?"

Matthew shook his head back and forth. "He's in Boston," he explained. "And you think the battle is imminent?"

"I've never seen groups of men gatherin' together with their weapons in Lowell until today," Liam replied. "I fear they'll destroy the church, or worse yet, there will be deaths and injury on both sides."

"You believe your people are ready to fight?"

"I don't know. I'm hopeful Hugh is aware of what's happenin' and has called for level-headedness among the Irish. I left word that if the Irish arrived first, they should attempt to hold the Yanks at the bridge."

Before Matthew could respond, a volley of shots rang out. The men glanced at each other and immediately increased their pace, the street dust billowing from under their pounding feet. They rushed onward until the church was finally in sight. Yanks armed with weapons stood at each corner of the building. One of them yelled out a warning and leveled his rifle as Matthew and Liam approached.

Liam's face was lined with concern. "It appears the Yanks crossed the bridge and took siege of the church before the Irish even arrived."

Matthew nodded. "It would appear that way," he said as they neared the church. "Thomas Lambert, you'd best aim that weapon somewhere besides my belly," Matthew shouted.

"Don't you get in the middle of this, Matthew!" the man hollered back.

Liam and Matthew slowed their pace but continued moving closer to the church. "What's going on here?" Matthew asked.

"Nothin' that we can't handle without interference by the Corporation," Lambert replied.

In front of the church, men's voices mingled with the sound of breaking stone. "I'm going in there," Matthew defiantly announced. "And you'd best not attempt to stop me, Thomas."

Immediately Thomas moved to block the door. "I wouldn't . . ."

Matthew pushed him aside. "Quit acting like a fool, Thomas," he growled. "Come with me, Liam."

Liam followed, his shoulders squared and head high. He wondered if Thomas Lambert would shoot him in the back. "What are we doin'?" Liam whispered.

"Getting these men out of the Acre before there's a bloody battle," Matthew replied.

It took a silver tongue, along with several threats, to finally convince the men to leave. Liam wasn't certain whether it was

Matthew's words or the realization there was nothing of value hidden in the church that dislodged the men, but at last they began filing out of the building. Unfortunately, at that same time the inhabitants of the Acre began to descend upon the church with picks, shovels, rocks, and rifles in hand.

"Matthew!" Liam shouted. He pointed in the direction of the crowd.

"Do you see Hugh among them?"

"Not yet, but I'll try and stop them," Liam replied. He rushed toward the crowd, waving his arms above his head. "Hold up! I need to talk to ya!" he shouted as he drew closer.

"Out of the way or we'll trample ya," a voice in the crowd cried out.

"Hugh! Hugh Cummiskey! Are you among these men?" Liam shouted.

"Right here," Hugh replied, waving a rifle in the air.

Liam rushed alongside Hugh, explaining Matthew was with the Yanks. "It appears everything is under control," Liam said. "Ya need to stop the men before they confront the Yanks, or there may be bloodshed. I know ya don't want that to happen, Hugh."

Hugh held up his arm and halted the men not far from the church. "If they've damaged our church, and I suspect they have, the Yanks had best get busy with repairs," Hugh told Liam. "What's your stake in this matter? You sidin' with the Yanks?"

Liam held his anger in check. "Ya'd be knowin' better than that, Hugh. I'd rather see this resolved peaceably. Surely ya feel the same."

Hugh nodded. "I do, but the Yanks started this fight, and they need to pay for their actions."

"You're the voice of reason for the Irish, Hugh. Tell them to settle themselves and listen to what Matthew has to say. Matthew knows it's not the Irish that have caused this upheaval, and he'll not be speakin' ill of them."

Hugh hesitated for a moment, then spoke to the men. There were a few murmurs of dissent, but the majority of the men appeared relieved they'd not have to do battle this night. They moved forward with Hugh and Liam in the lead until they stood opposite the Yankees.

Matthew stood on the top step of the church, looking down upon the segregated groups and then turned his attention to his fellow Yankees. "You men have embarrassed yourselves this night with your irrational behavior. I don't know who or what convinced you to act in such a manner, but I'd appreciate some insight."

The men glanced back and forth among themselves until finally one of them confessed that they had expected to find gold and weapons hidden in the church.

"And why on earth would you believe such nonsense? Why would these people be amassing weapons?" Matthew questioned.

"We heard talk that the Irish were storin' up weapons and money in order to attack Lowell and take over the mills," one of the men reported.

"Does that really seem plausible? Knowing that almost all of these men send money back to Ireland to help support their extended families, just how much gold do you think they could accumulate? Someone planted an evil seed among you, and you embraced it. In fact, you watered it and watched it take root. There's no denying the differences between our people, but attacking one another, destroying property, and believing the worst of each other is not God's design for us."

"You don't know what they're capable of," one of the men called out from the Yank side of the group. "They perform sacrifices and all manner of evil. That's probably what happened to their missing girls."

This created an angry surge of comments from the Irish.

"Ya don't know what ya're talkin' about, Yank."

"Ya're daft in the head. That's the kind of talk that gets men killed."

Matthew raised his hands to calm the crowd. "You know, you fellows remind me of a story. Once there was a farmer who had a jack mule and a gelding bay. He found it necessary, for the sake of plowing his field, to yoke the two animals together. Each morning he took the animals to the field, where they steadily pulled the plow, until one day he started experiencing problems. The mule wanted to pull left and the gelding wanted to pull right. Try as he might the farmer couldn't get them to work together. With his field unplowed, the farmer had no choice but to quit for the night and hope he might have better luck the next morning.

"In the meanwhile, the mule and the gelding had their own conversation. The mule told the gelding that he was a horse and horses were notoriously uppity and full of self-regard. The mule said he wasn't about to work with anyone who lived in a fancy barn and ate from a fancy trough.

"The horse was equally offended. 'You're just a lazy mule. You lay about the field all day, eating here and there, never making yourself useful at all until the master actually puts a yoke on you and forces you into work. You're dirty and smelly and totally useless.'

"The next day, the farmer tried again to put the mule and horse together, but neither one would have any part of it. They bucked and brayed, whinnied and kicked. Finally the farmer had no choice but to take the jack mule back to the barn and then proceed to plow the field with the gelding alone. The horse labored under the strain, and by noon he was spent and the farmer exchanged him for the mule. By night the mule, too, was exhausted."

Liam saw that Matthew had the attention of every man in the audience. "When the mule and horse came together, they realized that their stubbornness had caused them to bear the entire burden of responsibility on their own. There was no one else to share the load, so they pulled the plow alone. And all because they refused to work as a team."

"Are you saying the Irish are mules?" a man called out.

Liam couldn't tell if it had been an Irishman or a Yank who'd asked the question. Matthew chuckled. "Not at all. My father used to tell this story to my brother and me whenever we fought. The whole point I want to make here is that we need not let our cultures and backgrounds separate us. Neither should our religious beliefs and worship practices. If we allow issues to separate us, we'll be just like the mule and the horse—pulling the full weight of responsibility all alone. We aren't perfect and neither is religion. God alone is perfect, and He calls us to be at peace with one another. To love our neighbor as ourselves."

Liam saw the men around him relax a bit, their expressions conveying a certain understanding. Matthew was smart—Liam had to give him that. He approached these people by bringing something bigger than themselves to the table. Matthew Cheever didn't bother with threats of the supervisors or the Boston Associates, however. He went straight to the heart of it. He went to God.

"God would see His people work together—to encourage and lift each other up. The Bible says that we should esteem others as better than ourselves. Would you men deny the Word of God—reject its truth?"

The audience remained completely silent. Matthew nodded. "I thought not. Now I'd like for all of you to return to your homes. There's no cache of guns or gold. There are no plans to ruin the church. Go home and sleep off your anger."

One by one the crowd dispersed until only Liam, Matthew, and Hugh remained.

"I didn't think you'd manage to keep the peace here, but I'm glad you did," Hugh commented. "I'll bid you good-night and see to it the rabble-rousers get to bed instead of the pub."

Liam waited until Hugh had gone before he turned to Matthew. "It seems that you hold great stock in this issue of God and what He wants for His people."

Matthew smiled. "I do indeed."

"And ya're believin' that God truly cares about the people on earth—that He'd be listenin' to our prayers?"

"I do."

Liam shook his head. "Why? What has God ever done to prove this to ya?"

"He's answered my prayers," Matthew replied. "He's not always said yes when I'd have liked Him to, but He's blessed me in many ways, and I honestly believe this is the result of His love and concern for me as an individual."

"But why would God be givin' us any more consideration than He gives the beasties in the field?"

Matthew smiled. "I believe the Bible when it says we're made in God's image. I believe He did that because He desired fellowship with us, Liam. I believe God desires our love and adoration, our worship and praise. I believe we're here on this earth to serve Him first and foremost, and the best way we can do that is by serving each other."

The words made more sense to Liam than his mother's superstitions and his church's threats. "I'd like to be thinkin' on this for a time. Do you suppose we might be discussin' it again?" Liam questioned.

Matthew grinned. "I'd like that very much."

CHAPTER 28

Addie's cheeks were flushed bright pink as she tucked a damp wisp of graying hair behind her ear and hurried from her warm kitchen to the front door. The pounding at the front door was continuous.

"Patience! I'm coming!" she called, unable to hide her irritation as she pulled open the door. "Yes?"

A small woman with doelike eyes stood clinging to the arm of a stout, dour-appearing man. "We're Mr. and Mrs. Wilson—Ruth's parents," the man said.

"Adelaide Beecher. Pleased to make your acquaintance," Addie replied. "Please excuse my appearance; I've been busy in the kitchen." She stepped aside and gestured them into the foyer. "We can visit in the parlor," she said, leading the way.

The couple perched side by side on the larger of the two overstuffed settees and stared at Miss Addie. Then Mr. Wilson cleared his throat and leaned forward, his forearms resting upon his bulky thighs. "What time will our daughter return from the mill?" he asked.

Addie's mouth involuntarily dropped open, and it took a moment for her to regain her deportment. "The girls will be home in less than an hour. I was busy preparing supper when you arrived," she replied. "Did someone from the mill contact you?" Addie haltingly inquired.

"From the mill? No. Why should someone from the mill contact us? We're here to fetch Ruth home," Mr. Wilson explained.

Addie stared at them, suddenly unsure how to proceed. Truth was always best, but it was obvious Mr. and Mrs. Wilson were ill prepared for the news she would soon give them. "Did Ruth write that she wanted to come home?" Addie hedged.

"No. Her letters were always quite happy—content, you might say," Mrs. Wilson answered. "But I need her at home right now. I wrote and told her we'd be coming so she could give her proper notice at work."

"I see," Addie replied. She prayed God would give her words to ease the pain these unsuspecting parents would soon feel. "There is no easy way to tell you this . . ." she began.

Like a guard dog hearing an intruder, Mrs. Wilson perked to attention. "Has something happened to our daughter?"

"Ruth has disappeared," Addie replied in a hoarse whisper. "We thought, rather, we wanted to believe that Ruth had returned home. Obviously we were wrong. Ruth has disappeared."

Mrs. Wilson's eyes grew wide. She pounced across the room and grasped Addie's hand in a death grip. "What do you mean? How could she disappear?" she quizzed, her voice abruptly warbling into a high-pitched squeal. But before Addie could answer, the harried woman bounded back across the room to her husband's side. "I told you something was wrong." Her accusatory words permeated the room. Mr. Wilson's stern expression faded in the wake of his wife's indictment.

"Perhaps you could give us more particulars," Mr. Wilson suggested. He encircled his wife's shoulder and shushed her as though she were a small child.

Addie nodded. Her gaze remained fixed on Mrs. Wilson as she recounted the few details surrounding Ruth's disappearance. It seemed a paltry bit of information to give two devastated parents who had come seeking a reunion with their oldest daughter, yet there was nothing more she could add. She said it all in a few brief sentences.

Mr. Wilson's cold, hard exterior appeared shattered by the details, or lack of them—Addie wasn't certain which. Mrs. Wilson sat coiled beneath her husband's protective arm, her eyes glazed with grief.

"Has anyone contacted the police or sheriff?" Mr. Wilson questioned.

Addie glanced at Mrs. Wilson. The woman appeared fragile, as though one more gloomy report would shatter her delicate exterior. "They talked to us, but it is their opinion Ruth ran off with a gentleman friend," Addie replied hesitantly.

Mrs. Wilson slid from under her husband's protective wing. "Ruth has a beau? She never mentioned a man in any of her letters."

"Well, I didn't think it was anything serious. He's a young salesman who called on her when he was in Lowell on business. I believe they went to dinner on a couple of occasions and he visited with her here in the parlor. They may have attended a few church functions, though I'm not altogether certain. I've questioned all of the girls who live here. Ruth hadn't mentioned that she had any plans to elope or that she was even interested in marrying the young man. I told the police I didn't believe Ruth had run off with him. She's a bright girl with a good head on her shoulders. Besides, I don't think she would intentionally worry you."

"Nor do I," said Mrs. Wilson. "Perhaps we need to go and talk to the police," she suggested to her husband.

"I think you should stay here and rest. I'll go," Mr. Wilson replied. "I'm sure Miss Beecher wouldn't mind if you rested in the parlor until I return."

"Of course," agreed Addie. "You're more than welcome."

"No," Mrs. Wilson adamantly replied. The feather decorating her outdated hat danced overhead as she shook her head back and forth. "I'll be overly anxious if you insist I remain behind."

"As you wish," her husband replied. "Thank you for your kindness, Miss Beecher."

"Will you return after talking with the police? I'd appreciate knowing of any progress."

"Yes, we'll be certain to return," Mrs. Wilson agreed.

Addie fidgeted with her handkerchief as she walked Mr. and Mrs. Wilson to the front door. "Would you like me to pack Ruth's belongings so that you may take them home with you?" She couldn't bear to look at Mrs. Wilson while awaiting an answer. "I hope you'll forgive me. I realize my question appears insensitive, but the Corporation has advised me they'll be sending Ruth's replacement to board with me. The new girl will need space for her belongings."

Mr. Wilson glanced toward his wife. "Thank you for your offer, but we don't want to impose. We can pack her things," he said.

"Tell you what—if there's time before you return, I'll do my best to have things prepared. If not, I'll help you when you return."

"Fair enough," Mr. Wilson replied.

Mrs. Wilson's dark brown eyes were wet with tears. "Taking her belongings makes it seem like we're never going to see her again."

"I don't think that's true," Addie quickly replied. "I'm sure Ruth will be in touch with us soon."

"I pray she will," Mrs. Wilson whispered.

Addie watched the Wilsons walk down the street, her gaze turning heavenward when they turned the corner and were out of sight. The clouds were hanging low and gray, hiding any patch of blue from sight. It might rain after all, she decided, closing the front door and then scuttling off to the kitchen. She'd best hurry or supper wouldn't be on the table when the girls arrived home.

Working with diligence, Addie carved generous pieces of ham and arranged them on a platter. Fortuitously, she'd placed the kettle of potatoes to boil over a low fire before the Wilsons' arrival and had set the table after the noonday dishes had been washed and dried, a timesaving trick Lilly Cheever had taught her years ago. It wouldn't take long to cream the potatoes with some nice fresh peas she'd shelled early this morning, and she'd open several jars of her canned apples. The girls liked them sprinkled with a dash of cinnamon and nutmeg.

Addie finished slicing loaves of freshly baked bread and was carrying large serving platters of ham to the table as she heard the familiar sound of the girls coming in the front door.

"I'm a bit off my schedule. Just give me a minute," she said before rushing back to the kitchen.

"Did Miss Mintie come visiting this afternoon?" one of the girls inquired with a chuckle as Addie carefully carried a large platter of ham into the dining room.

"No, but I did have visitors. Ruth's parents arrived in Lowell this afternoon," she told the girls.

Silence. For just a moment it was as though all of them had stopped breathing, but an endless barrage of questions immediately followed the short-lived quietude. They wanted details of Ruth and her parents. Addie wished there were more she could tell them, wished she could say that Ruth had merely gone home for an unexpected visit and was now back, safely in the fold. But she couldn't.

"There's nothing much to report. Ruth's parents haven't heard from her, either, and they've gone to talk to the police. They promised to stop back after supper. Perhaps they'll have something more to tell us upon their return," Addie replied before returning to the kitchen to retrieve two brimming bowls of creamed potatoes and peas.

The girls moved on to other topics as the meal progressed, and it wasn't until the Wilsons arrived later in the evening that the subject of Ruth once again became fresh. The girls surrounded the Wilsons, all of them interested to hear any shred of news. Addie feared the sight of Ruth's housemates would overwhelm Mrs. Wilson. It appeared, however, she found some sense of comfort seeing their youthful faces filled with anticipation.

"I expected to be back earlier, Miss Beecher," Mr. Wilson said as he took the steaming cup of coffee Miss Addie offered.

"Our visit with the police was of little assistance. They were dismissive, telling us they didn't believe there was any foul play surrounding Ruth's disappearance. I confronted them with the fact that we knew some Irish girls were missing. He suggested that perhaps Ruth had gotten into trouble—in a family way—and didn't want us to know."

Mrs. Wilson nodded in agreement as her husband spoke. "I was disquieted by their lack of interest in Ruth's disappearance, but the police are even less concerned about the Irish girls. The policeman said the Irish girls were never officially reported missing. He even went so far as to say the girls were probably just hiding from a heavy-handed father and now they're even more afraid to return home. I find their attitude appalling," she added.

"Yes, it's pitiable," Addie agreed. "And so you are no further along than when we parted earlier today?"

"It appears the police have done nothing to find Ruth. However, just as we were preparing to leave our meeting with the police, a lady came in and reported a missing boarder. It seems this girl worked at the Hamilton Mill. She had gone out alone last evening and was seen purchasing some ribbon in town. Later in the evening she was seen by some girls who said they'd observed her walking toward home, but the keeper said she never arrived."

"Dear me!" Miss Addie exclaimed. "I'm going to want to keep my girls under lock and key. Did the police appear alarmed by this latest report?"

"They said they would look into it, but somehow I didn't believe them, so I asked if they had talked with anyone from the mills regarding Ruth. One of the policemen mentioned a man named Matthew Cheever. I located his address and took the liberty of calling upon him at his home," Mr. Wilson explained.

The idea of Mr. and Mrs. Wilson calling at the Cheever home, uninvited, took Addie by surprise. "Were you kindly received by Mr. Cheever?" she inquired.

Mrs. Wilson nodded her head up and down. "Oh yes, and he has a lovely wife. She was most sympathetic to our plight."

"When I mentioned the new report of a girl missing from

the Hamilton, Mr. Cheever appeared quite alarmed. He was on his way to the police station when we departed his home. I told him that we couldn't remain in Lowell."

"We have other children at home and the farm to look after," Mrs. Wilson quickly interjected.

"He's promised to keep us informed and said that if the police are reluctant to investigate further, he will hire a private investigator. He's going to go talk with a man named Hugh Cummiskey in the Irish part of town and see if any of the Irish girls have reappeared. I believe he will keep his word," Mr. Wilson added.

"Mr. Cheever is a good man," Addie concurred. "I'm glad he's agreed to move forward with the investigation. Will you folks be leaving soon?"

"Early tomorrow morning. We're staying at the Wareham Hotel tonight," Mr. Wilson said.

"Two of Ruth's friends helped me gather her belongings. I've put them in my parlor. If you'd rather wait until morning . . ."

"No, we'll take her things tonight," Mr. Wilson replied. "I left our address with Mr. Cheever. He's promised to contact us the moment there's any word, although he didn't expect any immediate results."

Addie led them across the hallway to the parlor and then, for the second time in one day, bid Mr. and Mrs. Wilson farewell.

Addie remembered only after they'd gone she had unfinished business with Taylor Manning. The very thought of him stepping out of line with one of her girls was enough to fuel her with newfound energy.

"I'll return shortly," she told Margaret.

"Aren't you afraid of going out alone? Maybe one of us should go with you," Margaret suggested.

"No," Addie replied, putting on her bonnet. "I'm not worried that someone will attack an old woman like me." After all, she was forty-eight. With that she picked up her shawl and exited the house. The less said the better—for Bella's sake and for her own.

John's house wasn't all that far, only a matter of blocks. The walk in the night air gave Addie strength for the words she had to say. She had thought Taylor might stop by the boardinghouse as he'd done the day he'd returned the picnic basket. *Oh, if only I'd known his actions then,* she fumed, *I would have set that young man straight then and there.*

She approached the house, and seeing that a light shone from the parlor window, she knocked. *Lord, help me to deal with this boy in a reasonable but firm manner. Let him see the error of his ways.*

The door opened and a rather ragged-looking Taylor Manning stared back at her. "Miss Addie?"

"Taylor, we need to talk. There is the none-too-small matter of the liberties you took with Miss Newberry."

Taylor paled. "Come in. I figured that sooner or later Bella would tell someone."

Addie stepped into the house. "Taylor, how could you? Your uncle told me of your philandering ways, but how could you take liberties with a girl such as Bella? She's made her opinions of you very clear."

Taylor shrugged. "I suppose that was part of the attraction, but believe me, Miss Addie, I've been wracked with guilt. I know what I did was wrong, and for once I really care about it—but I don't know what to do."

Addie softened, feeling sorry for the young man. "Taylor, women and their feelings are not to be trifled with. You know better than most, having grown up in England, where the women have few choices but to take a husband or labor as someone's slave. Here young women are encouraged to make a living for themselves, and the girls who work for the mills are the lucky few who enjoy such freedom.

"Still," she continued, "you knew that Bella had no interest in hunting a husband and yet you pursued her."

"I know," Taylor said, pushing back his blond hair. "But there's something about her."

"Forbidden fruit?"

"No, it's more than that. Bella has a spirit to her that seems more open and honest than other women. Perhaps it's because she's the first woman I've ever met who didn't play games with me and fall at my feet when I offered her a soft word and appreciative glance."

"But relationships are built on far more than that," Addie answered. "Bella has been deeply wounded by the men in her life, and you've done nothing but perpetuate that problem."

"I honestly didn't mean to, Miss Addie. I kissed her and would have done nothing more. Please believe me. I wouldn't have pressed her for anything."

Addie nodded. "I suppose I do believe you. Still, you hurt her, and you need to make amends."

"But how? She won't see me."

"I think you'd better start with a reckoning of your soul. Taylor, you wouldn't even begin to act in such a manner if God were guiding your heart. I'd rather not have to be so bold on this issue, but Taylor, every man and woman is called to account before God. Without an acceptance of Jesus Christ as Savior, they will make that accounting alone." Taylor said nothing, so Addie pressed home her point. "Jesus died for your sins long before you were even born, Taylor Manning. He longs for you to come to Him and to seek forgiveness and rightness before Him. You're the only one who can make that choice. John can't do it for you, although he would in a heartbeat if only he could. I can't choose that way for you and neither can Bella. But, Taylor, mark my words: by rejecting what I'm saying—by rejecting Christ—you're making your choice. And that choice will only lead to certain destruction."

CHAPTER 29

Matthew had seen the look Lilly leveled in his direction as the Wilsons detailed the plight of their missing daughter and then began telling of an additional missing girl who worked at the Hamilton Mill. Instantly, he knew there would be no peace in his household without another visit to the police station. Truth be told, he believed Ruth Wilson would return to Lowell on the arm of her salesman with a wedding ring on her finger. And the same could likely be said about the recently reported missing girl from the Hamilton. However, he wasn't about to further upset the Wilsons—or Lilly. Knowing there could be no delay, Matthew abandoned the rest of his leisurely evening for the company of policemen who likely would become offended when he began questioning their inability to solve the puzzle of Ruth's disappearance.

He entered the small brick building that sported two small iron-barred cells, an unpleasant reminder of the consequences associated with the town's growth. Martin Hensley waved him forward. "I sincerely hope you've not come to discuss missing girls," he warned. "I've had enough of that nonsense for one evening."

"I'm afraid that's exactly why I'm here, Martin. What makes you believe it's all nonsense?" he asked, hoping Martin would give him something tangible to support his argument.

"Aw, come on, Matthew. These girls take a fancy to some fellow, and next thing you know they skedaddle out of town, get married, and have themselves a passel of babies. What's so different about these girls? We know the Wilson girl had a beau. I'm checking on the gal from the Hamilton, but it'll probably be the same thing."

"What's her name—the one that works at the Hamilton?"

"Hilda Beckley. Don't know much else. Figure I'll go over there come morning. With a little luck maybe she'll have returned."

"Don't get your hopes up, Martin. I understand there are several Irish girls missing. What information do you have on them?"

"None. Nobody ever came in and talked to me. Far as I'm concerned, there aren't any girls missing from the Acre."

"But you know there are—and people are beginning to get a little apprehensive with all this talk of disappearing girls. I think you'd best make some effort so folks settle a bit. It will affect the local businesses if the girls are afraid to leave the boardinghouses. I'd like to have your word you'll treat these disappearances as abductions rather than runaways."

Martin grunted. "I'll see what I can do," he said and immediately went back to cleaning his gun.

Obviously Matthew had been dismissed. He clicked open his pocket watch and then walked out of the building, deciding he'd pay a visit to the Acre before heading home. Perhaps Hugh would be at the pub. If not, their visit would wait until morning. It was certainly too late to go calling at Cummiskey's home.

Wending his way through the mucky streets of the Acre, Matthew arrived at the pub shortly after nine o'clock. The shouts and laughter of drinking men overflowed into the street long before he arrived at the door. But surprisingly, there were few patrons at the bar. Instead, they appeared to be congregated toward the back of the room, most of them circling one table and hollering out instructions.

"Appears you've got some entertainment going on back there," Matthew commented to the barkeep.

The man nodded. "Arm wrestlin'. What's your pleasure?"

"I'm looking for Hugh Cummiskey. Does he happen to be here?"

The barkeep eyed him critically. "Who wants to know?"

"I'm Matthew Cheever—a friend."

The barkeep emitted a grunt before pointing toward the table. "He's back there with the rest of 'em."

Matthew thanked him and moved toward the crowd. Circling the outer perimeter of men, Matthew edged a bit closer. Two men were battling each other in a fierce arm-wrestling match. A pile of gold coins lay on the table awaiting the victor. Matthew ceased searching the crowd as his gaze fell on one of the participants. Before him sat a shirtless, sweating, seemingly drunk William Thurston fighting to take down the arm of another man.

Astonished by the sight, Matthew found it impossible to look away. Thurston was hurling insult upon insult while attempting to push his opponent's arm to the table. Matthew felt himself being shoved toward the action as the crowd tightened. He was now standing to one side of Thurston, the man's beefy arm in full view. Matthew's breath caught in his throat as he stared at a prominent mushroom-shaped birthmark on William Thurston's right arm.

Without warning, someone grabbed his shoulder. "Now, what would you be doing in the Acre at this time of night?"

"Hugh," he said, relief flooding his being. "I came to talk to you. The barkeep said you were amongst the crowd," he explained.

"Come on over here," Hugh said, pushing several men aside to make a path. "There's plenty of tables available with everyone crowded over there to watch William Thurston make a fool of himself."

"Seems William's in the Acre every time I make a visit,"

Matthew commented, looking back toward the table. "Is that J. P. Green over there? I wonder what in the world he would be doing here."

"I don't know. Mr. Green has begun coming down here occasionally. Mostly when Thurston is sniffin' about. They appear to be on friendly terms. Now, Thurston is another story. He spends a great deal of time in and about the Acre. For a man who hates the Irish, he certainly seems to find something that pulls him back here all the time. What problem is it that brings you here?" he asked.

"Why do you think there's a problem?"

"Come now, Matthew. You wouldn't be in the Acre at this time of night unless there was some kind of problem brewin'."

Matthew nodded. "You're right, of course. I was hoping you could fill me in on any information you might have regarding some missing girls—missing Irish girls. The police tell me no one has filed a complaint with them, but it seems to be common knowledge around town."

Hugh nodded. "I went and talked to the police after the first ones disappeared. They said the girls probably ran off to get married or were hiding out somewhere in the Acre because they feared their drunken fathers. I've finally accepted the fact that they're not going to do anything, and so I haven't reported any disappearances beyond the first three. Personally, I think they're pleased to hear when our numbers decrease."

Matthew's eyes grew wide. "First three? How many have disappeared?"

"Seven so far—at least seven that I know about. There may be more."

His stomach lurched. "Seven! And none of these girls' parents can explain why their daughters are missing?"

"No, although they were all comely lasses—at least that's my opinion. I don't know that the police would agree with that view."

Matthew remained silent. Now that he was armed with more information, he wasn't sure what to do. He could feel Hugh's gaze upon him. Finally he looked up and met the Irishman's stare. "I'll do something, Hugh. I don't know how or what, but we've got to get to the bottom of this and find these girls. Bring me a list of the girls' names, along with the names of their parents, tomorrow morning."

"Thank you, Matthew. I appreciate your willingness to help. I'll get the list to you first thing in the morning."

Matthew pushed back from the table, stood, and shook Hugh's hand.

"Not interested in watching the remainder of the wrestling match? It's best out of five," Hugh said with a lopsided grin.

"I think I'll pass on that offer. To be honest, I find William's behavior rather disgusting."

Hugh gave a resounding laugh. "So do I. However, I enjoy watching him lose his money," Hugh said as he walked with Matthew to the door. "I'll stop by your office with a list of names in the morning."

Matthew nodded his agreement and stepped out into the street. An angry-sounding dog barked in the distance as he hurried out of the Acre. Slowing his pace, Matthew considered what Hugh had told him. Seven girls. What could have happened to them? It couldn't possibly be a coincidence. And now Yankee girls were disappearing. Certainly there was a greater risk attached to these latest abductions. Since the Irish girls had been kidnapped without causing any stir from the police, it was little wonder the abductions had continued. He needed to devise a plan, and it was obvious the police weren't going to be helpful.

His thoughts shifted to William Thurston sitting at the marred wooden table with his sweating hefty arm exposed—and that birthmark, an exact replica of the birthmark Lewis, Lilly's brother, had described to Lilly as he lay dying. Why, Matthew wondered, did William Thurston spend so much time in the Acre? It made no sense that a man who constantly denigrated the Irish would languish in their company. Unless he had a mistress . . . and not just any mistress, but an Irish mistress. And if he had a mistress, might he have a child? And if he had a child, might that child have a mushroom-shaped birthmark? Could the child whom Lewis spoke of be William Thurston's child rather than Lewis's progeny?

Matthew attempted to remember exactly what Lewis had related to Lilly. He'd said there was a baby boy and that he was alive. He'd said the words *Paddy camp* and that the child had a mushroom birthmark on his arm. Lewis had been a handsome man who'd always had women falling at his feet—American women. Why would he have gone to the Acre to find companionship with a woman? William Thurston, however, was another story. Thurston would want to hide any illicit relationship from his wife. What better place than in the Acre? And yet, would William Thurston, a man who held an innate hatred for the Irish, take an Irishwoman as his mistress?

Matthew wondered what Lilly would say to his thoughts. She desperately wanted to find the mysterious child. But would she want to continue the search if there was a possibility the boy was not her nephew? Knowing Lilly, it would be difficult to convince her the child could possibly belong to another man. Even confronted with evidence of Thurston's matching birthmark, it was doubtful whether Lilly would concede that she had misunderstood Lewis's deathbed confession.

He sprinted up the steps leading to his front door. "Lilly, I'm home!" he called out, greeting her with a smile as she rounded the corner of the parlor and walked toward him.

He quickly weighed his options. Lilly would want to take immediate action; likely she'd expect to march into the Acre, inspect William's arm, and confront him regarding the mysterious child. But at this time he couldn't be sure the child's birthmark and Thurston's were alike. *I must find the child,* he decided. *There's no other way to be certain.*

CHAPTER 30

September was a fine month for dedicating the new Catholic church. Matthew and Lilly were pleased to see the large turnout, and the bishop appeared surprised at the sizeable congregation that gathered. After the official blessing, he commented to Matthew that he'd underestimated the growing Catholic community. Lilly knew Matthew would have liked to have believed the man's interest was because of the souls who would need guidance and direction. Instead, he'd already told her that the man saw a large congregation as a means of milking money out of those who were already dirt poor.

To Lilly's surprise, Miss Addie and Taylor Manning had also decided to attend the celebration. Other than the four of them, there were no other non-Irish to be seen. Addie appeared astonished by the conditions of the Acre and the people around her, but she said nothing. Lilly, too, eyed the surroundings with disdain. Here was an expensive church, yet another monument to God . . . and all around the area children went to bed hungry, unclothed, and without so much as a pillow to lay their heads upon.

"What are you considering?" Matthew asked softly. "You're scowling."

Lilly shook her head. "Sorry. I was just concerned with the conditions. I've seen so many little children who have no shoes and who are caked in dirt. Does the Corporation care nothing for them?"

"They care," Matthew replied. "They care that they're here—instead of in Ireland. The Corporation would just as soon sweep them under the rug. They were never intended to be here. The Associates wanted only those big strapping men who could dig from dawn till dusk. Children and women were never part of the arrangement."

"But now that they're here, surely Kirk Boott and the others see the need of helping them to live in a proper manner."

"Lilly, you're positively radiant," Addie said, coming to embrace her friend.

Matthew smiled at Taylor and extended his hand. "Well, there were times when I wondered if this church would get built, but here it is."

"Looks as though it's built to stay," Taylor replied. "I suppose you're surprised to see us here, but we promised John we'd attend and tell him all the details."

"I didn't know John was all that interested in the Irish or their church," Matthew stated.

"He's made friends among the men and I think he sees it as a duty of friendship to see to the matter. But that aside, Mr. Cheever, I wondered if we might talk of other business—briefly. I realize it's the Sabbath, but I want to ask you about some designs we're having trouble with."

Matthew looked to his wife. "Would you spare me for a moment?"

Lilly nodded. "Of course. Addie and I will visit. Why don't you walk us back to the carriage and we can wait for you there. Afterward we can give them a ride home." She turned to Addie. "Unless you drove also?"

"No, we walked. A ride home would be lovely," Addie said as Matthew guided Lilly toward the carriage.

Once they'd been secured in the carriage and the men had stepped away several feet, Lilly turned to Addie. "What have you heard from John?"

"I'm afraid not very much. I so long for a letter from him, but he's much too busy to write," Addie explained.

"I suppose he is. I'm sure he's pining for you just as much as you're pining for him," Lilly said, patting Addie's hand.

Addie smiled and motioned toward the church. "Such opulence in the midst of poverty. Can you believe the conditions here? I had heard stories—some I didn't believe—but now I'm beginning to wonder. Taylor says there isn't much to be done about it because most of the Yanks would just as soon see the Irish perish. He told me of one man who commented that he didn't care if the children starved or froze to death this winter, so long as it eliminated more Irish from the face of the earth."

"How awful," Lilly said, shaking her head. "Surely there is something we might do to help them. Perhaps we could start some sort of aid society."

"I doubt you'd find too many who feel as we do," Addie declared. "I've heard negative comments even among my girls. Prejudice is such an ugly thing."

Lilly considered this a moment. "You know, Matthew has mentioned scraps, even bolts, of cloth—flawed cloth. . . . Do you suppose we might get the Association to let us have those?"

"Not if they know they're for the Irish."

Lilly smiled and raised a brow. "Well, what if they're for the Lowell Ladies Society, a collection of like-minded women who desire to make quilts for the poor?"

Addie grinned. "We just won't mention who the poor are."

"Exactly."

Addie, Daughtie, Bella, and Lilly Cheever were gathered in Lilly's parlor, each diligently stitching on a square that would eventually be quilted and fashioned into a coverlet of embroidered lambs and daisies for Lilly's expected child.

"I'm so pleased you invited us to spend the evening with

you," Addie commented as she knotted a piece of pale blue thread.

"I thought it would be prudent to put some structure to our organization," Lilly explained. "I know you've spoken to Daughtie and Bella about the society. Are you girls in agreement that it doesn't matter who will receive our finished quilts?"

Bella nodded. "I think it's a marvelous idea. I'd like to mention it at the regular meeting of our mill girls' organization. I believe there might be many there who would lend their skills to helping to make quilts."

"So long as they don't question where the articles we make actually go. We can't risk having Kirk Boott refuse to give us seconds and scraps just because the items are going to bless the Irish."

"Did Matthew believe that would be Mr. Boott's response?" Addie questioned.

"Matthew said that Kirk would see this as yet another issue the community would fight about. However, if we give quilts, clothes, and whatever else we choose to make to more than just the Irish, then the community as a whole will benefit. My heart is in seeing that the poor have something warm to get them through the winter."

"Maybe next year we could plant a vegetable garden and raise food for the poor, as well!" Daughtie exclaimed.

"I like that idea very much," Lilly replied. "Matthew's parents have a great portion of land that wasn't sold to the Boston Associates. I wouldn't be surprised if they would allow us a nice plot of land. If the girls agreed to help with the work, we might plant several acres in vegetables."

"This ladies' aid society is getting off to quite a start," Addie said with a smile. "Who knows what we might accomplish."

They had worked for nearly an hour when Lilly stretched and put her sewing aside. "Would you like to see the baby's room?"

"Indeed we would," Miss Addie replied.

Bella was enchanted as Lilly led them up the wide staircase and into a small bedroom adjoining the one she and Matthew shared. The baby's room was equipped with a beautifully carved maple cradle and matching chest. A rocking chair had been strategically placed near the lace-curtained window that overlooked Lilly's small flower garden.

"It's a lovely room," Bella said as she peeked out the window. "And what a lovely view. The children's dormitory in Canterbury overlooked a flower garden. I always found great joy watching the flowers bloom each spring."

"Did you spend a great deal of time with the little children?" She inquired, seating herself in the rocking chair.

Bella nodded her head. "We rotated our duties, but Daughtie and I always looked forward to our time with the children, didn't we, Daughtie?"

"Oh yes," Daughtie agreed. "It was such fun teaching them. Bella and I would take the little ones into the garden and read and sing. The children always lifted my spirits."

Lilly's eyebrows furrowed. "The Shaker community does require celibacy, doesn't it? So how do they have young children?" she inquired, a slight blush tingeing her cheeks.

"Most belong to families who join the Society. Others are left because a mother or father can no longer care for them and the parents believe the child will be safe among the Shakers. Sometimes they return for their children, but most of the time they don't," Bella explained.

"How devastating it must be for those parents to leave a child with complete strangers," Lilly commented.

Bella watched as Lilly's eyes clouded. "I'm sorry. It wasn't my intention to upset you with such talk," Bella said. "You'll never be in a position where you must even think of such a thing."

"Perhaps not that particular situation, but I know what it's like to lose family, and I've almost lost hope of ever finding my brother's child," Lilly replied.

"Now, dear, you mustn't upset yourself," Addie said, taking Lilly's hand in her own. "Your husband won't want you inviting us back to visit if he sees our conversation has given you cause for concern."

"Matthew knows there isn't a day that goes by that I don't

think about Lewis's son. I fear he's given up on the search. He doesn't appear to share my longing to find the boy."

"Now, Lilly, I'm sure he has overturned every stone. I think it's likely he doesn't want you to build false hope. Finding one small child when you have no idea what he looks like or where he might be is a daunting task," Addie replied.

Bella observed the exchange between the two women, intrigued by the topic of the missing little boy. She'd overheard a snippet of conversation between Miss Addie and Lilly during the tea at Lilly's several months ago, but she had soon forgotten the conversation. It now appeared this would be the perfect opportunity to hear more.

"So your nephew has disappeared?" Bella ventured.

"Yes. However, I didn't even know of the child's existence until my brother was on his deathbed. Lewis was in dreadful pain and gave only sketchy information about the child. I've never seen him and have no idea where he is, although Lewis mentioned the Acre. Matthew and I agree that the boy's mother is probably Irish."

"With the Acre nearby, it seems you'd be able to easily locate the boy," Bella commented, then instantly wished she could snatch back the words as she watched sadness etch itself upon Lilly's face.

"You would think so, wouldn't you? However, my husband says he's expended great effort with no success. I'm not sure he's been completely forthright," she replied.

Addie wagged her head back and forth. "Surely you don't believe Matthew would lie to you, dear. You must keep in mind that the Irish folks keep to themselves. I'm certain the mother wouldn't want to give up her child, and if she's gotten wind that someone is looking for him, she's probably doing her best to keep the boy hidden."

"You forget that Lewis said the mother was dead. I have no idea how she might have died, but I believe Lewis told me about the boy so that I could provide him with a better life. I wouldn't attempt to take him away from his mother's family, if that's indeed who is caring for him now. But what if they don't want him now that Lewis is dead?"

"You can't spend your life worrying about 'what ifs,'" Addie admonished. "You're unduly upsetting yourself, and the child is probably doing remarkably well."

"Perhaps," Lilly halfheartedly agreed.

"Did your brother give you any other information?" Bella inquired.

Addie leveled a look of disapproval at her. "I think we should change the subject. Why don't we go back downstairs and resume our sewing?"

"Bella isn't upsetting me, Miss Addie. I want to discuss the boy. It's Matthew who attempts to squelch any conversation about the child." Lilly turned her gaze toward Bella. "The boy would be close to four years old now. I have no idea about his appearance except that he has a birthmark in the shape of a mushroom."

Bella's gaze immediately shifted to Daughtie. Her friend was staring back at her, eyes wide and mouth agape.

"Could it possibly be?" Daughtie croaked.

Lilly looked back and forth between the girls. "What? Could what possibly be?" Lilly asked in a frantic voice. "Tell me! Do you know something?"

Bella glanced toward Miss Addie, who was obviously upset over the turn of events. Bella raised her eyebrows and gave the woman a questioning look.

"It appears you'd best finish what you've begun, but I do hope that whatever you have to say won't cause Lilly pain," Addie chided.

Bella certainly didn't want to upset Lilly, yet her heart fluttered with excitement at the prospect of offering any valuable information. "During one of my assignments to work in the office at Canterbury a few years ago, I remember an Irishwoman bringing a little boy and signing him over to the Shakers. She avowed the child was not hers. She related to Eldress Phoebe that the boy had been born out of wedlock to her sister and the sister had met with an untimely death. When Eldress Phoebe asked about the father, the woman said he was a Yank who had no interest in the boy."

Lilly gasped and placed her handkerchief over her mouth. "You don't suppose?"

"Don't get yourself overly excited, Lilly. Those few facts don't mean that much," Addie replied.

The older woman stared at Bella, her lips set in a tight line and her eyes creased into narrow slits as she waggled her head back and forth.

Bella chose to ignore the warning. This was a matter of enormous importance, she decided. And so she forged ahead. "The little boy had a birthmark on his arm. I saw Eldress Phoebe examine the mark, and she had me write the information in the boy's paper work. She told me to write that the boy had a mushroom-shaped birthmark on his arm, the color of an under-ripe plum."

"It must be Lewis's child!" Lilly proclaimed. "Is he still in Canterbury?"

CHAPTER 31

In the privacy of the parlor, Bella eyed Taylor with apprehension, not certain whether she should believe his words. She wanted to accept his apology and trust that Miss Addie's talk had given him pause to consider his unseemly behavior.

"What more can I say that will cause you to give me another chance?" Taylor asked in a pleading voice. "Surely Miss Addie told you of her lecture regarding my behavior," he submitted with a lopsided grin. "We had a long conversation once she completed her reprimand. She made me see that the behaviors I've been exhibiting will not serve me well if I am truly interested in pursing a relationship with a young lady named Bella Newberry."

Bella felt the blood rush to her cheeks. Such talk made her more than a little uncomfortable, and she wasn't certain how to respond.

"Doesn't the church teach forgiveness?" Taylor asked.

Bella felt a twinge of indignation. "Why is it that people who have no use for God or the church attempt to use them as a weapon against those of us who do?"

"I never said I didn't have any use for God or the church,"

Taylor argued. "I believe in God. It's just that . . . well, it embarrasses me to say this, but I enjoyed the life I was living. And I certainly didn't want to attend church and be confronted with biblical teachings that wouldn't permit me to continue making those same choices. It wasn't until Miss Addie explained that if I ever hoped to call upon you again—and if I ever hoped to be right before God—I would have to change my ways."

Bella folded her arms across her chest and gave him a sidelong glance. "And after all these years of enjoying your carousing lifestyle, it took merely a word or two from Miss Addie to cause this dramatic change?"

"No, Bella. It took meeting you and realizing what I was missing," he replied. "Miss Addie simply pointed out the reasons why it would be impossible for me to win your love until I made significant changes in my life."

Once again she was unsure of herself. "I'm not certain I can believe you," she simply stated. And even if she did believe him, did she want the relationship he was suggesting? She looked at him standing there, hat in hand, his expression so full of hope.

"I understand," he replied, "but will you at least give me an opportunity to prove that I'm speaking the truth? That's all I'm asking for—just a chance. Surely you wouldn't deny me that."

Taylor's hair had fallen forward across his forehead. If she could look directly into his eyes, it would be much easier to evaluate the truthfulness of his words. Bella longed to reach across the distance between them and push the errant strands away from his face. Of course, she would never presume to do such a thing. Instead, she'd be forced to give him an answer without the benefit of seeing what his eyes might tell her.

"I will give you another chance, but should you do anything to make me regret my decision, I will be loath to forgive you again. Please don't disappoint me." Her final words were but a whisper—more a supplication than a request.

"Thank you, Bella. I won't disappoint you," he promised. "And now I want to share some news I think you will find most pleasing."

Bella sighed with relief. She had feared the remainder of the evening would be filled with idle chatter to fill the awkward silences that were certain to follow their earlier discussion. "What is it?"

"It has become evident that having women on the selection committee has already proved extremely beneficial. Last night the men voted to have female representatives assist with the lecture series—but only if they decide they'd like to be involved," he hastened to add.

"Of course they'll want to," she replied. "How wonderful! And did you play a role in this decision?"

"I'd like to say it was all my idea, but it wasn't. I did speak in favor of the proposal, but that's as much credit as I can take in the matter."

"I'm sure your influence helped sway the vote. This is wonderful news. I can hardly wait to tell the other girls," she said, giving him a winsome smile.

"Don't rush me out the door just yet. I have more to tell you."

She could barely contain her enthusiasm. "I can't imagine there's anything else that will excite me any more than what you've already shared."

"Perhaps not, but I know how interested you've been in the new schools. It seems that in spite of the fact that Mr. Boott has withdrawn himself from membership at St. Anne's, construction will soon begin on the first of the new graded schools."

"So Reverend Edson refuses to give in to Mr. Boott's threats? I admire the good man's tenacity. It's truly sad that Mr. Boott would use his position in the church in an attempt to force Reverend Edson to change his stance on the school issue. Let's hope his actions haven't created a cause for his termination."

"Since Mr. Boott has left the church, I doubt there will be a problem. The majority of the membership appeared to be in favor of the new schools."

Bella knew what Taylor said was true, but she also knew that people could become fickle when matters took an unexpected turn—especially when that unexpected turn wasn't advantageous to them.

"Yes, but since Mr. Boott has promised to withhold all of the money both he and the Corporation had been contributing to the church, some of those church members may change their minds," she rebutted.

Leaning back into the cushioned settee, Taylor gave her a grin. "And what good does all this worrying accomplish?"

"You're right. I'll stop," she agreed.

Several loud knocks sounded at the front door. Miss Addie bustled from the kitchen at full tilt, calling out, "I'll answer the door."

Bella heard the scraping of wood and then listened to Miss Addie warmly greet Matthew Cheever. She looked toward Taylor. "I wonder why Mr. Cheever has come calling," she said as Addie and Matthew walked into the room.

"Mr. Cheever would have a word with you, Bella," Miss Addie said. "Why don't you accompany me to the kitchen, Taylor? You can help me prepare some tea. If we're extremely fortunate, I may find some apple cake to serve you."

Miss Addie led the way, and Bella momentarily watched Taylor follow along behind the older woman. She then turned her attention to Mr. Cheever.

"Your wife is doing well?" Bella inquired as Matthew seated himself in a chair opposite the settee.

"Yes, quite well, thank you. In fact, we're preparing for a short journey. That's why I'm here."

Bella's eyes widened at the remark. "Oh?" She didn't know how to respond to his statement.

"It seems you know of a child in the Shaker village that bears a birthmark similar to the one described by Mrs. Cheever's late brother."

"Yes," Bella tentatively agreed. "I did mention such a child to your wife. Are you angry?" she hastened to ask.

"No, not angry—concerned. Lilly is insisting upon journeying to Canterbury to find the little boy. I have concern about Lilly traveling. The doctor says she's in good health but he'd rather not see her travel this late into her pregnancy. Added to that, I'm apprehensive about the outcome of the visit. Even if the boy is the one we're seeking, there's no way of being certain he is Lewis Armbruster's child."

"Perhaps you'll find there's a family resemblance," Bella suggested.

"Perhaps, but I think making the journey is folly. Lilly believes she's going to locate the boy and bring him home. She's already decided the boy is Lewis's child. I'm not as convinced of that fact. However, she is determined to go to New Hampshire, and that is what brings me here. We plan to leave for Canterbury the day after tomorrow, and quite frankly, we need you to accompany us. I doubt we'd be able to secure any information without you."

"No! I don't want to go," she blurted without thinking how her words would sound. Mr. Cheever appeared stunned by her pronouncement.

"I've already made arrangements for your absence from work, and I'll reimburse you for your lost wages. It is imperative that you make the journey, Miss Newberry. You're the one who told Lilly about the child. I implore you to reconsider your answer."

How could she face Eldress Phoebe and the other Sisters? Mr. Cheever didn't realize she had run away from the Society under the darkness of night and that she would be less than welcome.

"Let me explain, Mr. Cheever," she said.

When she had at last revealed the circumstances of her departure, Bella gave him a beseeching look. "And so you can now understand why I can't return."

He nodded. "I understand that returning to the Shakers will be uncomfortable for you. However, I beseech you to join us—for Lilly's sake."

Matthew's earnest plea on behalf of his wife touched Bella's heart, and she knew she could not reject his request. Like it or not, the time had come to face her fears. Her stomach churned as she met his gaze and whispered, "If you believe my presence is absolutely necessary, then I'll go."

"Thank you, Bella."

She closed her eyes momentarily and gave a faint nod. There was no taking back her words. She soon would be returning to Canterbury.

CHAPTER 32

Liam settled himself in a chair by the fireplace in the Flynns' tidy home and picked up a newspaper. "I see Mrs. Byrne's been here to visit," he said, picking up one of the outdated newspapers from the stack placed on a wooden footstool.

Mrs. Flynn's cheeks were pink from the heat of the fire. Her plump figure jiggled as she laughed at Liam's remark. "Mrs. Byrne believes she's doin' her good deed by sharin' the papers, Liam, and stale though the news may be, 'tis better than none at all."

"And for sure you speak the truth," he replied, turning the page of last week's paper and reading announcements of newly arrived dry goods that most likely had already been sold out. "Now, here's something interesting," he said. "There's a big advertisement askin' for any information regardin' the girls who have been listed as missing from Lowell."

"Is that a fact?" Mrs. Flynn inquired, taking up a position behind his chair and reading over his shoulder. "Well, would ya look at that," she said, reaching in front of Liam. "They've even listed the lasses who are missin' from the Acre. Now, that's a real surprise, isn't it?"

"That it is," Liam replied as he scanned down the list. There was something familiar about the names—not the names of the Yankee girls, but certainly those of the Irish lasses. Where had he seen them before?

Mrs. Flynn clucked her tongue and shook her head back and forth. " 'Tis a sad day when a mother sees her daughter disappear without a trace. I knew every last one of those Irish lasses, and there wasn't a bad one among them. Sweet girls—pretty, too," she added. "And now some Yankee girls are missin', too. Soon it won't be safe to go out of the house after sunset," she lamented.

Liam continued staring at the list, irritated that he was unable to jog his memory. "It appears the Corporation is beginnin' to take the disappearances seriously."

"One has to wonder if they would have ever taken the matter seriously if the Yankee girls hadn't started vanishin'," Mrs. Flynn commented as she peeled and quartered another potato and placed it in the pot.

"I'd like to think so, but either way, perhaps someone will come forward. It seems they're offerin' a reward," Liam said as he continued reading.

"If the promise of a few gold coins doesn't spawn some interest, I don't know what will. Folks will be scurryin' into that police station like mice after a piece of cheese," she said with a hearty laugh. "I don't suppose ya saw Mr. Flynn on your way home this evenin'?" she ventured.

Liam shook his head. "No, can't be sayin' that I did."

"I'm sure he's busy conductin' business down at the pub," she retorted. "If he isn't home soon, he'll be eatin' his supper cold."

"Ya say that every night, Mrs. Flynn, and every night Mr. Flynn walks in the door just as ya're setting his supper on the table."

"Rather amazin', isn't it?" she asked, her lips curving into a bright smile.

"Indeed," he said, continuing with his reading.

Just as Liam had prophesied, Thomas Flynn walked through

the front door while his wife was placing supper on the table. Liam and Mrs. Flynn exchanged a look and laughed aloud.

Mr. Flynn glanced back and forth between them. "I'm pleased to see I've been the cause of a bit of cheer for the two of ya," he announced, sitting down at the table.

Mrs. Flynn gave her husband a loving pat. "Ya've given me a bit o' cheer every day since I married ya," she replied, giving him a quick peck on the cheek.

Supper with the Flynns reminded Liam of his parents' home in Ireland. His parents had always enjoyed a special relationship, one that he hoped to emulate with a wife of his own someday. Not that he was apt to soon find a wife. Liam wanted a wife, all right. He just didn't want to spend time finding her, which was a matter that hadn't gone unnoticed by Mrs. Flynn from the first day of his arrival. She had now taken it upon herself to invite a different young lady for a cup of tea several evenings during the week. When a knock sounded at the door, Mr. Flynn and Liam would exchange a wink as they awaited a view of Mrs. Flynn's latest candidate.

"Do tell Thomas about that piece in the paper, Liam," Mrs. Flynn urged.

"Seems the Corporation is finally concerned about those missing girls. They've run an ad listin' their names and asked for anyone with information to talk to the police. They're even offerin' a reward."

"Well, I'm pleased to hear someone's finally takin' this seriously," Thomas replied. "I hope the reward will loosen a few tongues. Doesn't seem possible that all these girls could disappear without somebody seeing or hearing somethin'," he said, pushing away from the table and picking up his pipe.

Liam joined Mr. Flynn in front of the fire, retrieving the paper and once again reading over the names of the girls. Leaning his head back against the chair, he closed his eyes and gave thought to where he might have read those names before. Without warning, he jumped up from his chair.

"What's the matter, boy? Ya 'bout scared the life out of me," Mr. Flynn exclaimed.

"I'm sorry. I happened to think of somethin'. Excuse me, would ya?"

Liam didn't wait for an answer before taking the few steps to the cordoned-off area where he slept. He opened the small trunk and pulled out the sheaf of papers he'd salvaged from J. P. Green's fireplace months ago, the ones containing names he'd been unable to make sense of. Slowly, he ran his finger down the column of names, comparing them to the list in the newspaper. They matched—at least the names of the girls who'd been missing since before he'd snatched the papers from the fireplace. Beside each name was a column listing an amount of money. What could it mean? He sat on the edge of the bed, staring at the page and permitting his memory to carry him back to the home of J. P. Green.

Liam remembered the opulent house with its serpentine-shaped tables of mahogany, intricately carved mirrors, elaborate tapestries, and highly wrought wool carpets. And then he remembered something else. He'd been working late one evening while Mr. Green's family was away visiting relatives. There had been a noisy upheaval in the foyer when two coarse-sounding men had come seeking Mr. Green. Before Green finally got them out of the house, there'd been a terrible commotion.

Immediately after hearing the front door close, Mr. Green had come into the library where Liam was working and questioned him, asking if the ruckus had disturbed him. Liam lied and said he'd disregarded the matter and assumed it was some of Green's associates who were in their cups. Green appeared satisfied by Liam's response and said nothing further. But Liam had heard a portion of the argument. He'd heard Green threaten to horsewhip the men if they ever brought another girl to his home. And he'd heard one of the men repeating over and over that he was afraid they'd been followed. Green had finally screamed at the man to shut up, and when the men were finally quiet, he'd instructed them to take the girl down to the warehouse at the wharf.

The conversation Liam had overheard was now taking on a

frightening new meaning. In spite of the chill in the house, beads of sweat formed across Liam's forehead and upper lip. Could J. P. Green possibly be involved in abducting young women and selling them? Surely not! And yet, like a complex puzzle, the pieces were now coming together to form a picture, a horrifying mosaic of unspeakable crimes.

He must talk to someone, Liam decided—someone he could trust. Perhaps Hugh Cummiskey. But what could Cummiskey do about the likes of J. P. Green? This matter needed the attention of someone who wielded power in the community. Kirk Boott or . . . perhaps Matthew Cheever. Yes, that was it! He'd talk to Matthew Cheever—after all, he had talked to him several times since that day at the bridge. Each time had given him more reason to believe that Matthew was sincere and honest when he said that all men were equal in the eyes of God and that because of this, Matthew worked to make sure they were equal in his sight, as well. Perhaps Matthew had even been responsible for the advertisement in the paper. Yes, Liam felt he could trust Matthew with this information. He didn't seem the type to hide the details of a crime simply because one of his own social class was responsible.

Liam gathered the remainder of the papers from his trunk and grabbed his coat from the peg near his chest. "I'll be goin' out for a while," he announced to the Flynns as he shoved the papers inside his jacket.

"Tomorrow's a workday—don't tip too many or ya'll be havin' a big head come mornin'," Mr. Flynn replied with a laugh.

"Right you are," Liam called over his shoulder as he hurried out of the house with purpose in his step, his collar pulled high around his neck to ward off the damp chill in the fall evening air. He approached the Cheever house with uncertainty. What would Matthew Cheever think of a lowly Irish stonemason calling at his home?

"I'll soon find out," he murmured, running up the front steps and knocking on the door.

Matthew Cheever answered the door, a smile on his face as

he greeted Liam. "What a surprise. Come in, Liam," he offered, leading the way into the parlor. "Let me take your coat."

Liam reached inside his jacket and pulled out the folded papers before removing his coat. "I hope I'm not interruptin' ya."

"Not at all. In fact, my wife has gone to visit my mother this evening, and I had planned to do a bit of reading. The opportunity to visit with you will be much more enjoyable, I'm sure."

Liam gave him a tired smile. "I'm not certain it will be enjoyable, but I didn't know who else to come to."

"This sounds intriguing. I thought you'd come to discuss religious beliefs. Am I wrong?"

Liam unfolded the sheaf of papers and pressed them flat with his hand. "I'm afraid so. I've come to talk to you about these."

"Perhaps we should sit at the table. It may be easier if we can spread out your papers," Matthew suggested.

Liam separated and stacked the papers on the ornately carved mahogany table. "What I've got here are papers that I retrieved from J. P. Green's fireplace when I was workin' at his home," Liam stated. "Coming from a people who can't afford to waste anythin', I noticed only one side of the paper had been used. I decided I could use the other side for writin' letters home, so I removed the papers and put them in me satchel."

Matthew's eyebrows knit together in obvious confusion.

"I'm tellin' you this only so ya'll understand that I didn't steal the papers—they were in the fireplace, obviously discarded."

"Go on," Matthew encouraged.

"I never looked at the papers until the day I moved in with the Flynns—ya may recall that's the day after you visited the church with Hugh Cummiskey."

"Yes, I remember," Matthew replied.

"In goin' over the papers and the figures listed there, I discovered that Mr. Green has been keeping two sets of books. This set," he said, pointing to one stack of papers, "that shows the actual amount of money received by Appleton & Green and this one," he continued, while pointing to another stack of papers, "that shows the company makin' much less money. The difference between the two is what he's deposited in this account, which appears to be in his name only. It appears as if he's falsifyin' the records and stealin' money from the shippin' business."

Liam glanced at Matthew, hoping to gauge his reaction to the revelation. He didn't want to proceed if Mr. Cheever appeared in any way affronted by the information. Matthew didn't appear upset. In fact, he was carefully studying the papers and nodding his head.

Finally he looked at Liam. "Several months ago Nathan Appleton talked to Kirk and me when we were in Boston. He expressed some concern that J. P. might be stealing from the company. He was certain it had to be making more money than J. P. was depositing into the business account. I fear his suspicions are not only correct but that the thievery has been going on much longer than even he suspected. Having these papers gives me pause to wonder about something else, however," Matthew said, a thoughtful look etched upon his face.

"What's that?" Liam inquired.

"J. P. told us about a robbery at his home. He appeared unduly upset and spoke of missing papers of great importance. He went so far as to say it would be disastrous for him if the papers fell into the wrong hands. I'd wager these are the papers that concerned him."

Liam felt as though he'd taken a strong blow to the stomach. "Ya think I robbed Mr. Green? Is that what ya're sayin'?"

Matthew appeared startled by Liam's words. "No, of course not. If you had stolen from Mr. Green, you wouldn't have come here tonight. Besides, Liam, I think too highly of you to immediately assume you would ever consider doing such a thing. I'd guess that the thief pulled the valuables from the safe, considered the papers of no value, and tossed them in the fireplace. You went to work the next morning and, seeing the papers, assumed Mr. Green had discarded them and placed them in your satchel."

"What ya've said makes sense. However, I'm guessin' that Mr. Green is even more concerned about these papers than the ones I've already shown you," Liam said, picking up the remaining sheets. "I happened upon an old newspaper this evenin' and noticed an ad for the missing girls. I was pleased to see someone was finally taking their disappearance seriously."

Matthew nodded. "The Corporation agreed to pay for the ad. I had hoped it would yield some information. Unfortunately, it's done us no good thus far."

"Until now," Liam replied, handing the papers to Matthew. He watched while Matthew read one column and then another until at last he finished.

Matthew gave Liam a steely gaze. "So much for my trip to New Hampshire. Who else have you told about this?" he demanded.

CHAPTER 33

"Have you decided?" Bella asked as she plopped down on the bed beside Daughtie. "We leave in the morning, and you'll need to pack if you're going to return."

"I've decided I'm going to remain in Lowell," Daughtie triumphantly announced.

Bella reached around her friend's shoulder, pulling her into a warm hug. "I'm so glad. I hope it's because you truly want to stay and not because you fear Eldress Phoebe."

"I must admit that the thought of a confrontation with some of the Sisters was a bit of a deterrent," Daughtie said, giving a nervous giggle. "I've prayed very hard about my decision, Bella, and I believe I'm supposed to stay here. Not that I received a startling revelation like some members of the Society, but I've felt a kind of tugging in my heart as I've prayed. I don't seem to receive as much clarity as some of the Sisters, but then, I never did."

"That doesn't mean God isn't leading you or answering your prayers, Daughtie. I believe He speaks to each of us in different ways."

Daughtie gave her a halfhearted smile. "Do you think the

Sisters will treat you awfully?" Her voice was a mixture of sadness and fear.

"I doubt they'll be pleased to see me, but I've prayed God will give me the strength to face them so that I may overcome my fears. Besides, Mrs. Cheever needs me, and I can't bring myself to tell her I won't help by going with her."

Daughtie nodded. "Will you tell Sister Mercy I send my love to her?"

"You know I will. She's the only one I want to see."

"What about your father? Will you not make an effort to talk to him?"

Bella simply shook her head. "Let's go downstairs. I promised Miss Addie I'd visit her before I went to bed."

The two girls bounded down the stairs, and Bella tapped on the door as they walked into her parlor. The older lady sat at her desk staring intently at a sheet of paper lying before her. She glanced up as Bella and Daughtie entered the room and clapped her hands in obvious delight.

"Oh, good," she exclaimed. "You've saved me from writing a letter. Come sit down," she said, beckoning them farther into the room. "Are you prepared for your journey? I do wish I were going along."

"I wish I could stay here and you could accompany the Cheevers. I dread going back to Canterbury."

"You'll do just fine. Daughtie and I will be praying for you the whole time. You'll be back in no time at all. It will be a pleasant diversion, especially since Taylor is going along."

"What? Why would you ever think such a thing? Taylor has no interest in any of this," Bella replied.

"You haven't talked to Lilly, have you?"

Bella shook her head back and forth. "No."

"I called on her today. I wanted to wish her well on the journey," Addie explained. "While we were having tea, Lilly told me that Matthew has decided to remain in Lowell. It seems he's had an unexpected problem arise within the Corporation and he can't leave Lowell at this time. He suggested they wait until after the baby is born and then make the trip, but Lilly wouldn't hear of it. Finally he agreed to find someone who would drive the carriage and escort you and Lilly to Canterbury."

Bella sank back in her chair. She had forgiven Taylor for his improprieties, but she didn't want him as her escort on the trip to Canterbury. The choice of a young single man accompanying them would certainly create a flurry among the Shakers and give them yet another reason to find fault with her. She found it impossible to concentrate on Miss Addie's chattering and finally asked to be excused, saying she must get a good night's sleep.

Sleep, however, did not come easily. When the first bell sounded the next morning, she forced herself out of bed and began preparations for the day. The other girls were already working at the mill when a knock sounded at the front door. Bella's breath caught in her throat as she walked to the hallway to answer the knock. Perhaps Mr. Cheever's problem had been solved and when she opened the door he would be standing there to greet her . . . but he wasn't.

———

The journey was long and tiring for Lilly, with her condition necessitating frequent stops as they traversed the wending, bumpy roads to Canterbury, yet Taylor remained patient and thoughtful. Even when Lilly insisted they seek lodging for the night by midafternoon, Taylor had pleasantly acquiesced. Throughout the journey, Bella had critically observed his behavior, expecting to see him revert to his caddish manners. At the very least, she had anticipated he would attempt to kiss or embrace her when they were alone, but surprisingly, he had done neither. Instead, he had exhibited the epitome of gentlemanly behavior. Perhaps Taylor's declaration that he had changed his ways was true. But then again, she decided, perhaps he was merely using this trip to his advantage and would return to his old habits when she least expected it.

The inn they chose was small but clean. Lilly gave Taylor money and had him arrange for two rooms. When he returned to help with the luggage, Lilly told them both she intended to lie down for an hour or two. Taylor agreed it was a good idea, but Bella thought otherwise. She would be sharing a room with Lilly and she wasn't in the leastwise prepared to nap. That meant that other than sitting quietly in the room, Bella would have to find some other diversion for herself while Lilly slept.

Deciding a walk might be in order, Bella saw to Lilly but then decided this might be an excellent opportunity to broach the subject of Thaddeus Arnold.

"If it wouldn't overly tax you, Mrs. Cheever, I was wondering if I might discuss a matter with you. I promise to be brief," Bella quickly added.

Lilly lowered herself onto the bed. "If you don't mind if I lie down while you talk; my back is aching," she said while massaging her lower back in small circular motions.

Bella plumped one of the pillows. "Of course not. Please make yourself comfortable."

Lilly leaned back. "Ah, this feels much better." She closed her eyes. "I won't fall asleep until you finish talking. Sit down here on the side of the bed and tell me what concerns you."

Bella found it a bit discomfiting to talk to someone whose eyes were closed but decided she'd best seize this chance. It might be a long time before another opportunity would present itself. "Well, you may recall my friend Ruth, the one who is missing?"

"Mm-hmm," Lilly murmured. "I'm hoping she'll be safe and sound by the time we get home."

"As am I," Bella replied. "Anyway, the night Ruth disappeared I awakened. I thought I was having a nightmare, and although I couldn't remember what occurred in the dream, I remembered hearing noises. As it turned out, it was those noises and not my dreams that awakened me. The noises were coming from next door—at the Arnolds'."

Lilly's eyes opened wide. "What kind of noises?" she inquired, her full attention now riveted upon Bella.

"Thumping, slapping, and the sounds of a woman crying. Then I heard the muffled sounds of a man's voice telling the woman to be quiet. I'm quite sure it was Mr. Arnold. However, Ruth's disappearance drew my attention away from the happenings next door. But I felt I had to do something to help Mrs. Arnold before she or the little girl suffered injury."

Lilly nodded in agreement. "I'm glad you've told me. I thought this matter was resolved a couple of years ago. It appears that Mr. Arnold may have returned to his old habits."

"Do you think there's some other possibility? Perhaps I've jumped to conclusions because of Virginia's comment, but I certainly would never forgive myself if something happened to Mrs. Arnold or that sweet little girl," Bella said, her words tumbling forth in a flurry.

Lilly took Bella's hand and patted it. "Don't give this matter another thought, Bella. You've done the proper thing by telling me. I'll take care of it, and Mr. Arnold will be none the wiser as to how I've once again unearthed his despicable behavior." She gave Bella a sleepy-eyed gaze. "Even after hearing this unsavory news, I can't seem to keep my eyes open. I'm sorry, Bella, but I fear I must take a nap."

Bella nodded her head and rose from the side of the bed, hoping she'd done the proper thing. She then headed for the door. "I think I'll take a walk while you sleep," she offered. "I won't go far, so don't worry."

Lilly yawned and nodded. "I'm too tired to worry."

Bella slipped from the room and headed for the stairs just as Taylor came from his room.

"Running away, Bella?" he asked with a smile.

"I wasn't tired—at least not tired in the sense of wanting a nap. I'm a bit sore and road weary, so I thought a walk would do me good."

"May I join you?"

This was a different side of Taylor Manning. Asking instead of demanding. Bella shrugged. "If you must." Besides, having Taylor's company would keep her from dwelling on her conversation with Lilly Cheever.

He laughed and followed her down the stairs. "We haven't really had a chance to talk since coming on this journey. I suppose you were surprised to see me in Mr. Cheever's stead."

"Yes, I suppose I was."

"I was secretly glad Mr. Cheever couldn't accompany you," Taylor said, taking hold of her elbow as they exited the inn. "I'm glad for any extra time I can have to convince you of my sincerity."

Bella considered his words for a moment, then paused under a large chestnut tree. "Taylor, you mentioned not having much to do with God because He would get in the way of your lifestyle. Has that changed?"

Taylor let go of his hold on her and paced back and forth alongside her. With his hands clasped behind his back, Bella thought he looked more like a great orator about to speak than a young man making confessions of faith.

"I have to say that certain things Miss Addie shared have profoundly affected my soul. She told me every man and woman would be called to reckon for his actions. I remember my mother saying the same thing when I was a boy. I didn't take it very seriously," he said, pausing to meet her gaze, "but now I do."

"Because of what Miss Addie said?" Bella questioned softly. She was suddenly humbled by his declaration. Miss Addie had shared the Gospel with Taylor and had called him to account. Bella had only argued with Taylor. She hadn't concerned herself at all with the condition of his soul.

"Partly because of Miss Addie, but also because of you."

"Me? Why me?"

Taylor straightened and unclasped his hands. "You are unlike other girls. You didn't pursue me—you would scarcely even talk to me." He grinned. "I saw in you a gentle spirit yet a bold and courageous one. Miss Addie told me of your deep religious convictions shortly after I first met you. She told me about the Shakers and their strict beliefs."

"But I don't believe as they believe," Bella replied. "That's part of the reason I wish I weren't making this journey." She was astounded by the open manner in which she'd just spoken. Even so, it felt so very right.

"Are you afraid they'll hurt you—demand you return? I won't let anyone harm you—you must believe that."

"They can't hurt me physically," Bella replied, "but there are worse pains than those delivered by physical blows."

Taylor came to her and took hold of her gloved hands. "Bella, I promise you, they won't harm you. I won't let them."

Bella smiled at his sincerity. Maybe God *had* begun a good work in Taylor's heart. Yet it was so hard to trust—to believe. Not only that, but Taylor had no idea of the manner in which the Shakers could heap on guilt and punishment without ever raising a hand. This trip was going to test everything she'd come to understand. There was no hope that Taylor could comprehend that. "Thank you," she finally said, pulling her hands away from his. "I'm sure you'll do your best."

————

By the time they reached Concord, Bella's stomach was churning. She gave a fleeting thought of a brief stop at her Aunt Ida's, but Lilly was anxious to reach their destination, so she withheld the suggestion. Besides, Aunt Ida would most likely be embarrassed to entertain unknown guests in the dilapidated rented rooms on Franklin Street.

"The closer we get, the more excited I become. I hope there will be no problems and we can bring the boy home with us. You said the Shakers named him David?"

Bella nodded.

"I wonder what his mother and Lewis named him," Lilly commented.

"I don't remember, but it is common practice for names to be changed when children are left at the Village. The Sisters pick a name they think more suitable."

Lilly's brows furrowed. "Really? It seems that would be confusing to children, especially when they've already been placed in unfamiliar surroundings without their parents. Was your name changed, Bella?"

"No, but both my parents remained at the Village with me. My mother wouldn't permit a name change."

Bella gave Taylor directions as the coach rolled onto the road leading to the Trustees' Building. "We'll stop at the large stone

327

building on your right, Taylor," she said, the words tumbling out as her stomach continued churning. She wondered if she might faint.

Taylor held out his hand to assist her down from the coach. She stared at him, willing herself to move, yet she could not. Her body remained frozen in the seat.

"Bella?"

She heard him say her name. His voice seemed to echo in the distance; then she felt his arms lifting her out of the carriage and her feet touching the ground—ground that belonged to the Believers. She shivered and heard Taylor's voice asking if she was ill. She looked up into his sapphire blue eyes and saw his apprehension.

"I'll be fine. It's just this place—seeing the people, knowing they'll be judging me, and knowing I must listen to their recriminating words. I can't explain how difficult it is for me to be here," she whispered. "I told Mr. Cheever I didn't want to come back, but he wouldn't listen," she said, her voice cracking with emotion.

Taylor lifted her chin with one finger, forcing her to look into his eyes. "Remember what I said. I'll not let anything happen to you, Bella. If they speak ill of you, they'll suffer my wrath. You've done nothing wrong, and you have nothing to fear. We'll go in there, make our inquiries, hopefully gain control of the little boy, and be on our way home. Do you believe me?"

She nodded her head. "Yes," she whispered.

Taylor left her side momentarily and assisted Lilly down from the carriage. Bella held her breath as the three of them walked through the front door of the Trustees' Building. Brother Justice was situated behind the curved wooden counter where business was conducted and visitors received.

He glanced up from his paper work. "Sister Bella? Is that really you, or do my eyes deceive me?" he inquired as he rose to his feet.

Returning his smile, Bella approached the counter. "It's me, Brother Justice. It's good to see you." The tall, broad-shouldered Brother leaned on the counter, his shock of white hair neatly combed and his familiar smile a welcome sight. "I'm guessing Brother Jesse is not with you," he said, his pale blue eyes gazing expectantly toward the door.

"No," she softly replied. "I've come with two friends, Brother Justice. Mr. Taylor Manning and Mrs. Matthew Cheever. Mrs. Cheever has reason to believe the little boy known as David is her brother's child. She wishes to see him."

The smile on Brother Justice's face was now erased. "I can't assist you with that request, Sister Bella. You must talk to one of the elders. Eldress Phoebe is in the upstairs office. I'll fetch her."

Bella's heart dropped. Seeing Brother Justice had been one matter. But Eldress Phoebe was quite another. Bella quickly explained to Lilly and Taylor that a meeting with the Elders would be required. Neither appeared concerned or intimidated at such a proposal. She, on the other hand, was once again feeling light-headed at the prospect of such a confrontation.

The muted sound of voices could be heard from upstairs, and soon Brother Justice descended the staircase. "Eldress Phoebe will meet with you. I know I shouldn't ask, but is Jesse well?"

"I haven't seen him in some time, Brother Justice, but I'm sure he's fine. He's living in Concord, working for a cooper. The last I heard he was to be married to the granddaughter of his employer," she told him.

Brother Justice nodded. "He was the most talented young man that ever apprenticed with me in the woodworking shop. It broke my heart when he left. We all thought the two of you . . ." He looked at her with a questioning look in his eyes.

"Marriage was not my reason for leaving this place," Bella replied.

"And how is Sister Daughtie?"

"Daughtie is fine. She's living in Lowell with me—at a boardinghouse. We work at one of the mills," she hastily replied.

"It's good to know you are both well. I'm sure Brother Franklin is going to be pleased to see you."

"I have no plans to see him, Brother Justice. We'd best go upstairs. I don't want to keep Eldress Phoebe waiting."

"Yes, of course. You remember where the office is?"

She smiled and nodded. "I haven't been gone so long that I would forget."

"No, I suppose you haven't. It just seems a long time since I've had Jesse working alongside me in the shop."

There was a pang of sorrow in his voice that saddened Bella, but she realized there was nothing she could say to ease his pain. Jesse's absence created a void in the life of Brother Justice that only his return would fill. Regretfully, she doubted whether her own father missed her nearly so much.

She turned to Lilly and said, "This way," and then led them up the wide staircase to Eldress Phoebe's formidable office.

She hesitantly knocked on the closed door and waited until Eldress Phoebe's familiar voice bid them come in. After casting a worried look in Taylor's direction, she turned the knob and entered the room with Taylor and Lilly following close behind. The Eldress turned her attention away from the papers on the birch fall-front desk and peered over her spectacles. She gazed at them as though they were some form of foreign creature that had inadvertently entered her domain.

"I believe my eyes must be playing tricks on me," she said, her dark eyes riveted on Bella. "Could this girl in her shameful clothing and unadorned head be Shakeress Arabella Newberry? Surely she would not dress herself in the gaiety of Babylon and come back among her former people. Such blasphemy!" she proclaimed, rising from the low-backed birch chair.

Already things were going worse than even Bella had imagined. She silently censured herself for not wearing her Shaker gown but quickly changed her thoughts. To have done so would have been hypocrisy, she decided. Eldress Phoebe's disapproving eyes seared her very soul, and now she was glaring at Lilly and Taylor, obviously prepared to vilify them, too.

"And who are these invaders of my sanctuary?"

Taylor stepped forward. "We've not invaded you nor your office. The gentleman downstairs announced our presence and informed us we were to come to this room."

"Taylor, please," Bella whispered. "Let me talk."

He gave her a feeble smile and stepped back. "Mr. Manning

is our escort, and this," she said, pulling Lilly forward, "is Mrs. Matthew Cheever."

Eldress Phoebe leveled a look of disdain in Lilly's direction. "Brother Justice tells me you've come asking questions on Mrs. Cheever's behalf—about David."

"Yes. Mrs. Cheever believes David may be her nephew. The son of her deceased brother," Bella explained.

"Lewis Armbruster," Lilly added.

Eldress Phoebe ignored Lilly and kept her eyes focused on Bella. "And what did you expect? That I was going to summon David here and permit you to take him off to the world, where he will be condemned to hell?"

"We came because Mrs. Cheever wanted to examine the ledgers to see if the child's mother or father were listed."

Without a word, Eldress Phoebe returned to the desk, pulled open the upper drawer, and removed a ledger. She opened the book and began tracing her bony finger down the pages. "Here it is," she said, tapping her finger on the page. "Cullan O'Hanrahan—an obviously unacceptable name for the child," she mused before turning her attention to Lilly. "You don't look or sound Irish, and your name certainly is not O'Hanrahan," she accused.

"No. I believe the mother was Irish, but my brother—the father—was not. My brother is now deceased," she replied. Lilly was obviously no longer able to remain silent. She moved a few steps closer, eyed a chair, and asked, "May I sit down?"

"Yes, sit down," Eldress Phoebe replied. "All of you," she begrudgingly offered.

Lilly seated herself and immediately besieged Eldress Phoebe with the story of Lewis's untimely death and his dying declaration regarding the little boy. "The combination of facts—the birthmark, the Irish heritage, and the age of the child—makes me believe this boy is my nephew."

"The father is listed as unknown, the mother is listed as deceased, and I have a signed contract waiving all rights to the child," Eldress Phoebe proudly announced.

"Who signed the contract?" Lilly inquired. "May I see the paper?"

Eldress Phoebe appeared either offended or angry—Bella wasn't sure which. But she pulled the contract from a wooden file drawer and handed it to Lilly.

"Noreen Gallagher. She lists her address as Lowell, Massachusetts. This is the child's aunt?"

"That's what she told me. There was no reason to doubt her word, and we will not consider releasing the child to your custody," Eldress Phoebe responded forcefully. She placed the paper back in the drawer, pulled a set of keys from her pocket, and locked both the file drawer and her desk. "If there's nothing else, our meeting is concluded," she announced.

"May I at least see the boy?"

"Absolutely not!"

"But Eldress Phoebe, if she sees the child and there's no resemblance to her family, it could mean the end of this matter. Otherwise, I'm sure Mrs. Cheever will return with a lawyer or papers from a judge to support her request to inspect the child."

"It's obvious you've quickly become one of them—quick to use threats and the law to win your way," Eldress Phoebe charged. She pointed a bony finger at Taylor. "Go downstairs and tell Brother Justice I wish to see him."

A short time later, an uncomfortable silence filled the room. Brother Justice had been ordered off to retrieve the child while the three of them sat waiting in the office.

"What's become of Daughtie and Jesse?" Eldress Phoebe asked, breaking the silence.

"Daughtie is in Lowell. We work at the mills and live in a boardinghouse. Jesse is living in Concord, and I believe he has now married the granddaughter of the cooper he works for."

Her lips curled in disdain and she shook her finger at Bella. "You were always a willful girl. I told your father years ago you'd come to no good end."

"Don't you talk to her like that," Taylor warned.

Bella turned and gave him a feeble smile. "Don't bother, Taylor. This is her world, and she is speaking her opinion. However, it counts for nothing anymore."

"Well, I never! Brother Franklin is going to be devastated to see what a turn you've taken."

"Brother Franklin? My father? Why would he be devastated? He didn't care about me when I lived among you. Why would he care now that I'm gone? Talk of my father will not cause me to turn back to the Shaker ways, Eldress Phoebe, nor will your caustic words."

"Sister Bella!" David cried as he raced across the room and flung himself into her arms.

"Hello, David. You've grown," she said, giving him a bright smile. "I've brought some people to meet you. This is Mr. Manning and this is Mrs. Cheever," she said, turning him to face Lilly.

"Hello, David," Lilly said. "You're quite a fine young man."

David nodded his head in agreement.

"I'll wager you have big muscles. Could you roll up your sleeve and show me?" Taylor asked.

David nodded in agreement as Bella helped him roll up his shirtsleeves. Lilly gave a small gasp as the birthmark came into view. David turned and smiled at her. "You're surprised my muscles are so big, aren't you?"

"Exactly," Lilly replied. "I don't know if I've ever seen such fine muscles on a little boy. You must work very hard."

"I do, don't I, Brother Justice?"

"Indeed you do. Will that be all, Eldress Phoebe?" Brother Justice inquired.

"Yes, you may take him back."

"But I want to stay with Sister Bella," David whined.

"David!"

Eldress Phoebe's one-word command said all that was necessary. The child bid them good-day, grasped Brother Justice's extended hand, and quietly walked out of the room.

"Well?" Eldress Phoebe said, her gaze fixed upon Lilly.

"He doesn't look anything like my brother—or any other member of our family as far as I could tell. But the birthmark and his age together with the fact that an Irishwoman brought him here from Lowell all lead me to believe David must be Lewis's child."

"So you'll not let the matter rest?"

Lilly stood. "I'll discuss the boy with my husband and seek his counsel."

"If you plan to return here, I suggest you send a letter prior to your arrival. Otherwise, we'll not meet with you." Eldress Phoebe's words held an unmistakable note of finality.

"And you, Arabella, should not heap difficulties upon us. Unless you should decide to repent of your ways and return to the Society, please don't return."

Bella nodded. "As you wish, but I'll be stopping at my mother's grave before we leave the grounds."

Eldress Phoebe wagged her head back and forth. "You still insist on grieving over Sister Polly when she's gone to a better place. You never did successfully break your ties from her."

"I never believed it was a part of God's plan to split families or for children to look upon their parents with no higher degree of love and concern than for the other members of this sect. You'll have to count me as one of your failures, Eldress Phoebe. I always loved my mother much more than anyone else in this community." She paused. "Some of you I didn't love at all. Farewell," she added, feeling as though a terrible burden had suddenly been lifted.

When they reached the top of the stairs, Bella turned to face Taylor. Something about his defense of her had endeared him a bit. "Thank you for attempting to come to my rescue with Eldress Phoebe. It's been a long time since I've had anybody willing to fight for my cause."

"You're welcome, Bella. I only wish I could have done more," Taylor replied softly.

There was something surprising in the way he made that pronouncement—his words weren't filled with the old cockiness she'd come to expect from him in the past. Instead, she heard a new sincerity. It pleased her.

Brother Justice met them at the bottom of the stairs. "I told Brother Franklin you were here," he whispered to Bella. "He asked that I tell you he is praying that you will return and keep your covenant with the Believers."

"I think not," Bella replied. "This world is his choice, not mine."

CHAPTER 34

The sound of the front door opening caused Matthew to jump to his feet. "Lilly, I'm so glad you're home safe and sound. How are you feeling?" he questioned, pulling her into a warm embrace.

"I feel fine, just tired."

Matthew released her, studying her face momentarily. "Are you certain? I've been very worried about you." He spied Taylor bringing up Lilly's bag. "Here, I'll take that," he said, reaching for Lilly's satchel. "Did you have a good journey?"

"I'm afraid not. We must talk immediately," Lilly said, moving toward the parlor.

Taylor stood in the hallway, anxiously moving toward the door. "I'm going to take Bella back to the boardinghouse, and then I'll deliver your horse and carriage to the livery, Mr. Cheever."

Matthew grasped Taylor's hand in a firm handshake. "Yes, that would be of great assistance, and thank you for making the journey in my stead, Taylor."

"My pleasure. Good day, Mrs. Cheever."

"Good-bye, Taylor, and thank you again," Lilly called out from the parlor.

Matthew hastened back to his wife's side and took her hand in his own. "Now, then, what is it that requires immediate attention?"

Lilly sat down, wiggling a bit in an obvious effort to make herself more comfortable, her brow furrowed in a look of concern. "Before I begin recounting the problems in Canterbury, there is another matter we must discuss," she said. Cutting straight to the heart of the matter, Lilly related the information Bella had shared at the inn. "Thaddeus Arnold must be dismissed from the Corporation, Matthew. He was given his opportunity to change. He'll end up either killing or permanently injuring his wife or their child."

Matthew stared at his wife, stunned by the revelation. "I'll talk to him, Lilly. However, I can't fire him without first giving the man opportunity to defend himself against these allegations."

"Really, Matthew! You know he's up to his ghastly behavior once again. However, if you insist on talking to him, you must promise you won't mention Bella's name. I gave my word I wouldn't divulge where I received the information."

Matthew gave his wife a faint smile. "Of course. I wouldn't want to place Bella in harm's way, either. Now, tell me about your trip to New Hampshire," he urged.

Lilly sank back into the overstuffed settee and began recounting their misadventure in Canterbury.

"I can certainly understand why Bella and Daughtie were anxious to leave the place," Matthew replied. "Eldress Phoebe sounds like a bit of a fusspot."

"She's more than that, Matthew. She's a scheming fanatic, and she adamantly refuses to release the child to me."

"You must calm yourself, Lilly. All of this upset can't be good for you or the baby."

"I'll calm myself once we have Lewis's child here in Lowell with us. It's imperative we return for him, Matthew. Had you been with me, I know the boy would be with us now. You wouldn't have let that controlling Eldress Phoebe turn us away empty-handed. I think we should plan to leave by the week's end."

"Lilly, there's someone you must talk to. I believe you may change your mind about returning to Canterbury."

"I can't imagine what would cause me to change my mind," she replied before giving her husband a look of surprise. "And why are you home at this time of day, Matthew?"

"I arranged to meet Liam Donohue here at the house. In fact, it's Liam I want you to talk to regarding the little boy."

Moving to find a more comfortable position, Lilly leveled a look of confusion in Matthew's direction. "Why are you holding business meetings at the house? And what information would Liam Donohue have regarding Lewis's son?"

Before Matthew could answer, there was a knock at the front door. "That must be Liam now," he said.

Only moments later, Matthew escorted Liam into the parlor. Although Matthew had spoken of Liam from time to time, Lilly had never been properly introduced to the stonemason. With as little ceremony as possible, Matthew made the perfunctory introductions. "I was just telling Lilly I wanted her to speak to you about the child you mentioned."

Liam hesitated a moment and gave Matthew a questioning look. "Noreen's sister's child? Ya want me to tell her now?"

Matthew nodded his assent, and Lilly turned her attention to the Irishman.

"Well, Mrs. Cheever, yar husband was tellin' me about the child ya'd gone seekin' in New Hampshire," he began. "For sure, he mentioned the fact that the lad you were seekin' had a mushroom-shaped birthmark on his arm."

"Yes," Lilly interjected, now obviously anxious to hear what this man had to say.

"When I first arrived in Lowell I boarded with a woman named Noreen Gallagher for a short time. Noreen had the gift of gab, especially when she'd had too much to drink," he explained. "There were several occasions when Noreen spoke about a young lad, her nephew, who bore such a birthmark."

Lilly's hands were shaking. "Yes, yes. Noreen Gallagher is the woman who signed the papers Eldress Phoebe presented to us when we were in Canterbury." She turned to look at her husband, excitement etched upon her face. "You see, Matthew, it's all coming together. We must leave tomorrow."

"Wait, Lilly. Liam's not finished."

She gave Liam a nervous smile. "I'm sorry. Go on, Mr. Donohue," she said.

"Noreen told me the child's father was one of the Boston Associates. I later heard from several men in the pub that William Thurston and Kathryn O'Hanrahan had been involved in a . . . umm . . ." Liam stammered and looked to Matthew.

"Liaison," Matthew said.

"Yes. And these men mentioned that Kathryn had a child by this William Thurston."

"No! He's Lewis's child," Lilly objected.

Matthew moved to Lilly's side. "Lilly, William Thurston has a birthmark exactly like the one on the child."

"Why would Lewis mention a child on his deathbed if it wasn't his?"

Liam cleared his throat. "For sure I'm not knowin' anything about yar brother, ma'am, but I did ask Noreen why she hadn't kept the lad with her—not that he'd have been well cared for under that woman's wing. Anyway, she told me she feared for the lad's life and was sure he would come to some harm by his father's hand. She decided it would be best to give him up to the Shakers rather than have him suffer possible harm. Perhaps your brother possessed that same knowledge and was merely issuin' a warnin' to protect the wee lad."

Matthew pulled Lilly close. "I know you want to believe the boy is related to you, Lilly, but this evidence proves otherwise. You know that Lewis was involved with William Thurston to some extent. Thurston could have told him about the woman and boy. Remember, also, that Mrs. Gallagher says the father was one of the Boston Associates. That information further implicates William as the father, not Lewis. We must think this through. I wouldn't be able to live with myself if we brought that child to Lowell and he came to some harm."

Pulling a lace-edged handkerchief from her pocket, Lilly dabbed one eye and then the other. "I think I must rest, Matthew. This is all too much for me right now. If you'll excuse me, I believe I'll go upstairs and lie down."

"Of course, my dear. I think that's wise. You're tired from your journey and there's much information to consider. I'll come up once Liam and I have concluded our business."

Matthew escorted his wife to the bottom of the wide oak stairway. "Try to get some sleep, Lilly," he said, brushing her cheek with an affectionate kiss. He waited until she had ascended the stairs before returning to the parlor.

"I'm sorry me words caused yar wife such grief," Liam apologized.

Matthew placed his hand in a reassuring manner on Liam's shoulder. "You spoke only the truth. There's nothing to apologize for, Liam. I appreciate your willingness to help me sort out this whole issue of the boy. I don't know if Lilly will want to talk to Noreen Gallagher—I pray not. But should she insist, would you be willing to arrange for them to meet?"

"For sure I would, although I'd avoid such a meetin' if at all possible. Noreen's not the type ya'd want to have come callin'. And she might try to put the touch on ya for some money, too."

Matthew smiled and nodded. "I'm hopeful Noreen's presence won't be necessary. Now, have you been able to scrape up any more information regarding J. P. or the missing girls?"

Liam nodded and leaned forward, resting his forearms on his muscular thighs. A shock of dark hair fell forward across his brow, and he absently ran his fingers through the mass of thick black waves in an attempt to shove it back into place. "I've taken into my confidence an old Irishman who spends most of his time in the pub. Haven't told him why I want information, of course, but told him I'd stand good for some ale if he'd keep a listenin' ear directed toward J. P. and his cronies any time they're in the pub."

"Do you think you can trust him?"

Liam nodded. "I do. He dislikes havin' Yanks come into the pub—says they should keep to their own part of town since they expect the Irish to stay in the Acre. He spends most of his time at the pub. His son brought him over from Ireland, and he lives with his son's family in the Acre. Probably spends his time in the pub to stay out of the way at home. He says he's old but his hearin' is sharp," Liam explained with a hearty laugh.

"But has he come by any information that's helpful? I believe we've got to produce something even more substantial than those papers of J. P.'s before we go to the police. I'm afraid he'll refute the ledgers, insisting they were altered after being stolen from his safe."

"Seems the old man heard a conversation a few days back. Green and a couple scalawags were talking about needin' more high-quality merchandise right away."

"But that doesn't really tell us much," Matthew cut in.

"For sure, but as they continued talkin', one of the men said something about not likin' the idea of going after the Yankee girls. He said it was drawin' too much attention and mentioned the ad in the paper. J. P. told him he didn't care whether he liked it or not—he was bein' paid to do a job, and they needed at least three beauties to take down the canal very soon."

"Down the canal? They must travel by canal to Boston and then ship the girls out of the harbor," Matthew said, running a hand across his forehead. "The fact that this bartering in human flesh is taking place right here in Lowell sickens me. The families of the mill girls give approval for their daughters to come here and work because they believe they'll be safe. It won't take long until we'll have frightened girls rushing back home and disastrous results as we attempt to find their replacements."

"I'm supposin' that's true enough. If we've a bit o' luck on our side, perhaps they'll discuss when they plan to be takin' the girls to Boston."

Matthew looked up and met Liam's gaze. "I doubt we'll be that fortunate. Most likely their schedule revolves around whenever they're able to abduct the girls rather than a set timetable. Let's hope we're able to bring this whole ugly business to a stop before they're able to seize another girl."

Taylor slowed the horse a bit as the boardinghouse came into view. "I'm sure you're weary from all this traveling."

"Not really, although I must admit it seems odd to be riding about Lowell at midafternoon on a workday," Bella responded. "I do hope Miss Addie is home. I'm anxious to visit with her about our journey."

"I trust you plan to tell her that you've a growing admiration for me," he said, giving a somewhat embarrassed laugh. "I'd hate to bring on another of her lectures."

Bella graced him with a bright smile. "I plan to tell her that I believe your behavior was praiseworthy and that I was most pleasantly surprised with the changes I saw."

"Do those changes merit enough admiration that you'll grant me permission to call on you?"

A slight blush colored her cheeks. "Perhaps. It would depend on your intentions."

"My intentions are completely honorable, I assure you. However, I fear if I said more you'd consider me forward. So for now, I'll settle for the privilege of escorting you to your meeting at the Mechanics Association this evening."

Bella decided she best not question him further about his intentions unless she wanted to be completely embarrassed. "I'd completely forgotten we had a meeting this evening."

"Then I may call for you?"

"Yes, that would be fine," she replied. "Look! Isn't that Mr. Farnsworth's carriage in front of the boardinghouse?"

"Uncle John must have concluded his business down South ahead of schedule. I wasn't expecting him until next week." Taylor pulled the horses to a halt behind John's carriage and then assisted Bella down.

"Bella! You're home," Miss Addie greeted from her parlor. "Come in and visit with us. You, too, Taylor—and look who's here! Aren't you surprised?"

Miss Addie was beaming, obviously unable to contain her excitement over Mr. Farnsworth's return to Lowell.

"Indeed I am. Welcome home, Uncle John. I wasn't expecting you until next week."

John grasped Taylor's hand in a firm handshake. "Fortunately our negotiations went more smoothly than anticipated, permitting my early return. It is good to be home among family and friends. I hear from Addie that you've been on a journey of your own."

"Yes, although I don't believe we were as successful on our mission."

Miss Addie gave Taylor an encouraging smile. "Sit down and tell us all about it."

Taylor shook his head back and forth. "I'll leave the telling to Bella. I've got to take Mr. Cheever's horses and carriage to the livery. Glad you're home, Uncle John."

"Thank you, my boy. I'll be home shortly."

Taylor turned his gaze to Bella before leaving. "And I'll see you this evening, Bella." Bella smiled and nodded in agreement. Once Taylor had closed the front door, she took her cue from Miss Addie and began to relate the events of their journey.

"My, my," Miss Addie lamented as she wagged her head back and forth when Bella had finally recounted the tale. "Tell me, dear, did you have an opportunity to see your father or Sister Mercy?"

"I didn't see my father. He elected to send word to me that he was praying I would return to the Society and honor my covenant. However, I did have an opportunity to see Sister Mercy. We stopped at the cemetery as we were leaving, and there she was, waiting by my dear mother's small tombstone. I think Brother Justice told her of my arrival, and she knew I wouldn't leave without visiting my mother's grave."

"It sounds as though Brother Justice is a very kind man. I'm delighted you were able to visit with Sister Mercy. I know Daughtie is anxious to hear your report. She's been in a dither anticipating your return."

"I only wish we could have brought the little boy back with us. Mrs. Cheever was quite upset over the situation and even talked of returning with Mr. Cheever and a lawyer."

"There is no end to the measures Lilly will take if she believes that child is her blood relative," Addie replied.

"Well, if you'll excuse me, I believe I'll go upstairs and unpack and prepare for this evening. I'm to talk to members of the Mechanics Association regarding the prospect of teaching an English literature class."

"You go right ahead, my dear. I'm sure you've lots to accomplish," Addie replied.

Bella picked up her satchel and walked up the stairs to her room while silently enumerating the many changes in her life since she'd left Canterbury. Most of them were good, yet she'd given thanks for very few of them. In fact, she hadn't been diligent in her prayer time or Bible study of late, always putting God off until later, and still she'd been abundantly blessed. Instead of pulling out her notes on the literature class, Bella opened her Bible and began to read. God's Word spoke to her of His relentless love and everlasting grace, which were two topics that had not been included in her lessons among the Shakers.

She'd chided Taylor in the past for ignoring God, but she now found herself just as guilty. "I don't mean to be so fickle or unfaithful," she murmured in prayer. "I know I'm sorely lacking when it comes to doing things as I should." She glanced to the ceiling. "But I want to do right in your eyes. I want to yield the hardness of my heart and put aside the past.

"At the village, I felt so angry and bitter for the things they'd done—for the things my father had done. Lord, it's hard to just let go and put it aside. Sister Mercy said we were to look forward in our walk, not even glancing behind. Now I read in your Word that we are to actually forget what is behind us and press on toward the goal. But, Father . . . I don't seem to have any goals."

Love me. Serve me. Trust me. Let these be your goals.

The words were stirred from somewhere deep in her heart. Was God truly speaking to her heart? Was this what He'd been trying to tell her all along?

CHAPTER 35

Although he dreaded a confrontation with Thaddeus Arnold, Matthew decided it was best to address the situation without further delay. Arriving at the mill, he sent a message requesting Arnold's presence in his office.

A short time later a knock sounded at Matthew's door. "Come in," he called.

Thaddeus Arnold entered the office, closing the door behind him. "You wanted to see me?" he asked. In spite of the cool temperature, beads of perspiration had formed on Arnold's forehead and damp half-moons now circled his underarms.

Matthew pointed toward a chair. "Sit down, Mr. Arnold," he offered and then waited until Thaddeus seated himself. "I've received some distressing information regarding your behavior. From the accounts I've heard, it appears that you've returned to your past behaviors—behaviors, as you well know, the Corporation will not tolerate."

Thaddeus pulled a checkered handkerchief from his pocket and wiped his brow. "I suppose I need not attempt to defend myself—I'm certain you'll never believe me over those who have made these accusations."

Matthew leaned forward and rested his arms atop his desk. "On the contrary. I'm hopeful you can shed light on this matter. If you have a defense, by all means, let me hear it."

Thaddeus shook his head back and forth. "No. I'll not honor such vicious lies with a defense. But remember, Mr. Cheever, if you terminate my employment, my wife will suffer more from your actions than she has from my hand."

Matthew stared across the expanse between them in disbelief. Too late, Thaddeus realized the full weight of his words. "You've condemned yourself, Mr. Arnold. I'll escort you back to your living quarters so that you may pack your belongings. As for your wife and child, I'll not see them punished for your behavior. Mrs. Arnold will be given opportunity to remain in the house and take in boarders to support herself, should she desire."

Thaddeus's complexion turned a shade of purplish red. "Why is it that men such as you can't seem to understand women need to be kept in their place? Give them too much freedom and they consider themselves our equals. I'll not tolerate such behavior from my wife or any of those uppity girls you hire to work in the spinning room," he spat.

Standing up and walking around his desk, Matthew opened the office door. "Then it appears I've done you a service, Mr. Arnold. You'll no longer have to contend with either the mill girls or your wife. Shall we go?"

Bella stood in the foyer awaiting Taylor's arrival. She had prepared a few notes after supper and then decided she would extract additional information from the attendees. Surely some of them had specific titles or authors they hoped to study. Perhaps she would take a vote and they would make their choice based upon the majority decision. Yes, she decided, the class would benefit from assisting her with the selection.

Deciding upon what she would wear to the meeting had taken a bit of thought, even though she had few choices. After considering her options, Bella had chosen her plaid dress of myrtle green and black. She'd purchased the fabric quite reasonably and fashioned the style after one of the gowns Lilly Cheever had given her. With a few minor alterations to the pattern, the dress had taken on a unique appearance.

Taylor arrived in his uncle's wagon and immediately upon greeting her at the door complimented her on the gown. A good choice, she decided, giving him a warm smile.

"I thought perhaps Daughtie would be going with us."

"So did I, but she decided to walk with the other girls instead."

"I'm sorry to have the buckboard. I had hoped to have Uncle John's carriage this evening. Unfortunately, he's using it himself. He has a meeting with Mr. Boott and Mr. Cheever and then plans to visit Miss Addie again this evening."

Taylor held her books and papers as Bella donned her gray woolen cape. "She's so delighted to have him back in Lowell. She tells me your uncle John had a letter waiting for him from his father in England when he arrived home, stating he'd moved to London," she said as he assisted her up into the wagon.

"Yes, and the move appears to have been an excellent decision. Apparently Grandpa Henry—that's Uncle John's father—found a doctor in London who can better treat his medical condition."

"Miss Addie said the doctor required Mr. Farnsworth's father move to London so he would be close at hand for the treatments."

"Exactly. As luck would have it, Grandpa Henry was able to lease his house in Lancashire to a distant cousin. So it appears to have worked out well for all concerned. I know Uncle John holds out hope that his father's health will one day improve enough to bring him to Massachusetts. In fact, he tells me Miss Addie has been very supportive of his desire to bring Grandpa Henry to the United States."

Bella glanced into a shop window as they passed by. "That doesn't surprise me. Miss Addie is such a generous, loving person. They do complement each other, don't you think?"

"Indeed. I wouldn't be surprised to see them marry soon— if Miss Addie's willing to give up the boardinghouse."

"It would be difficult if she were to leave the house—nobody could take her place. And yet I would very much like to see her snatch this opportunity for happiness."

"I'm certain it would please Uncle John," he agreed. "After we parted this afternoon, I took Mr. Cheever's carriage back to Mr. Kittredge's livery as he had requested."

Bella's eyebrows arched. "Yes?"

"Mr. Kittredge asked if I'd mind delivering a message to Mr. Cheever before I returned home. Of course I told him I'd be happy to do so. After delivering the message to Mr. Cheever, he told me there had been important developments in regard to the little boy in Canterbury."

"David?"

Taylor nodded. "Yes. Perhaps it was a good thing we didn't gain custody of the boy. It seems he may not be Mrs. Cheever's blood relative after all. Mr. Cheever said the child might be the son of a well-known Bostonian. And if that's true, there's even concern the father would do the child harm."

Bella listened carefully as Taylor outlined the latest revelation, her mind reeling with the information. "Then it could be dangerous for David to live in Lowell?"

"Absolutely. Mr. Cheever asked that we keep this information between us. He said he wanted to share it with you and me since we had made the journey to Canterbury with Mrs. Cheever."

"And Mrs. Cheever? How did she take the news? Did she accept this information as truth?"

"Mr. Cheever said he's attempting to convince her to put the child out of her mind."

"I'm sure the poor woman is distraught—especially in her condition. I'm certain this news is very disturbing to her. We should both remember the Cheevers in our prayers."

Taylor gave her a sidelong glance. "I'm not much into praying yet, Bella. I'm just now becoming accustomed to actually listening in church."

Bella gave him a smile. "I'm pleased to hear you're beginning to find the services enlightening. As to the praying, just talk to

God as if you were talking to me. He doesn't require special words, Taylor."

"Seems a bit strange—just talking, that is—but I suppose I can give it a try," he said as he pulled open the door of the Mechanics Association meeting room. "Here we are. I'm looking forward to your class."

The class, Bella decided, might prove more difficult than anticipated. She'd never previously conducted a meeting where both men and women were in attendance. She now questioned her ability to teach such a group. And her idea of having the participants make a choice had been cause for great debate. The women's interests proved opposite to the men's. After much debate, they'd finally agreed upon Ivanhoe, deciding it would provide something for both the male and female readers. By meeting's end, she wanted nothing more than a quick retreat to the boardinghouse.

She had tied on her bonnet and had been waiting for at least fifteen minutes when Taylor finally approached. "Sorry for the delay, but I want to remain a little longer and visit with several of the men on another matter," he told her. "And incidentally, I think you may need to develop a higher level of skill in these combined meetings. Some of the men thought you gave more consideration to the women's requests."

His words punctured her already-wounded spirit. But instead of quietly retreating and reflecting upon his suggestion, she quickly rebutted.

"Consideration is obviously not at the top of your list, either. If it were, you would have advised me beforehand that you would be remaining late. I'm exhausted, and our meeting went much longer than I'd expected. I'd prefer to leave now."

"I'm sorry, Bella. It wasn't my intent to upset you. Surely you know by now that I'd not intentionally hurt your feelings. I promise to have you home by curfew. After all, I wouldn't want to tarnish the name of the woman I plan to marry."

Bella ignored his apology, unwilling to succumb to his charms. "That's unacceptable. I've already waited longer than necessary. All of the other girls have already left for home."

"I'll tell the men we need to move swiftly. Please sit down and wait in the main meeting room."

She didn't answer. Instead, she waited until he'd gone back to his meeting and then walked out the door. In any case, it wasn't as if she didn't know the way home by herself! Clutching her reticule in one hand and her paper work in the other, Bella strode off with purpose in her step. She realized it was later than she usually ventured out at night, especially unaccompanied, yet she was surprised to find the streets nearly deserted. Bella gave momentary consideration to Mr. Cheever's warning that the women of Lowell should not walk alone at night but quickly pushed the thought aside. She was weary. Besides, Taylor should be escorting her home!

A gust of wind whipped at her cape, and she clutched it more tightly around her. A puddle of crisp fallen leaves swirled around the hem of her dress, and the moon's light cast silhouettes of dancing tree branches in front of her. The breeze grew stronger and Bella glanced over her shoulder, certain that she'd heard something behind her. Probably the wind—or Taylor had realized she was gone and was following her. Her lips curved into a smile at the thought. He did care enough to leave the meeting. She gave thought to waiting for him but decided he could catch up quickly enough. However, she slowed her pace ever so slightly as she turned the corner. After all, she had spoken rather sharply, and differences were more easily resolved before they'd simmered for days on end.

Her heart quickened at the sound of the approaching foot- steps. She began to turn and greet Taylor when, without warning, a rough hand slammed over her face. Before she had opportunity to struggle, a cloth was stuffed into her mouth and two large hands were wrenching her arms behind her. She could feel a coarse rope being twisted around her wrists while another set of hands was pushing aside the hem of her dress and tying her ankles with such force that the cord was cutting deep into her flesh. It was impossible to fight against the brute force of the men as they rolled her into a carpet and then hoisted her up. Her body was now tightly wound in the rug, and she struggled to breathe. Horror engulfed her. Why hadn't she waited for Taylor? Instead of pushing her self-importance aside, she'd let emotion control her actions—and her life.

———————

Taylor's attempts to hasten the meeting proved futile, so it was nearing ten o'clock when the men finally decided to adjourn. Stealing a quick glimpse at the walnut case clock, he hurried from the meeting room. He could have Bella home by curfew if they hurried, and perhaps he'd still have time to set things aright. Rushing back to the small room where he'd left her, Taylor glanced in the doorway. Where was she? He pushed his way back through the sea of men exiting the building and momentarily felt as though he were swimming against a strong tidal wave that was going to suck him under. Finally making his way through the departing men, he hurried about the building, checking every nook and cranny, but Bella was nowhere to be found.

Taylor quickly realized it was going to take more than a few pleasant words to make amends, and there certainly wasn't time tonight. Her absence spoke volumes. Pondering the idea of whether a small gift might aid his cause, Taylor exited and locked the front door. After work tomorrow, he'd stop in town and find something Bella might like. Once again he chastised himself for not mentioning his need to remain late this evening. But he hadn't expected Bella's intense reaction. She had spunk—of that he was now certain. He went home, then thought better of the situation. It would be wise to at least go to the boardinghouse and make sure she'd returned safely. He turned the wagon around and headed back down the street. At least this would show Bella how much he cared. When he reached Miss Addie's house, however, he noted that all the lights had been extinguished. There was no sound coming from within—no doubt they had all retired. He couldn't disturb them now. With a sigh, he headed back to John's house.

"I'll see her tomorrow," he murmured as he made his way home.

With the sound of the first bell, Taylor groaned and rolled over. He hadn't slept well and now longed to remain abed for another hour or two, but such a luxury was impossible. Lifting the hand-painted pitcher of water, Taylor poured several inches into the matching china bowl and then splashed it on his face. Glancing into the mirror hanging above the oak chest, he shook his head in disgust. Dark circles rimmed his eyes, which gave him the appearance of a weary raccoon.

John stood near the bottom of the stairway, ready to leave for the mill. "You're looking none too chipper this morning."

"I didn't sleep well."

"That much is obvious. I'm wondering what caused your insomnia," John remarked as he pulled open the door, a smile playing on his lips. "Surely not problems with young Bella."

Taylor began recounting the evening's events as the men walked down the front steps. They had walked only a short distance when they turned toward the frantic sound of a young woman calling out their names.

Daughtie skidded to an abrupt halt only inches before plowing into Taylor's broad chest. Her eyes were panic-filled as she called out, "Where's Bella?"

"No need to scream, Daughtie. I'm right here." He gave her a guarded smile. "I haven't seen Bella since last night."

Daughtie grasped his arm, her fingers penetrating the thick wool of his jacket and digging into his flesh with a death grip. "She never came home!"

His terror merged with a surging panic before it actually plunged Daughtie's words into the depths of his consciousness. A choked guttural cry escaped his lips.

Taking hold of Taylor's shoulder, John said, "Calm yourself, boy! You've got to remain calm. Now tell me, when did you last see Bella?"

Moments passed before Taylor could quiet his jumbled thoughts. Finally he composed himself enough to speak coherently. "That's what I was beginning to tell you. I thought she was going to wait for me to escort her home after my second meeting, but she had already gone when we adjourned for the night. It was close to ten o'clock—she was angry with me. I thought she went home. Dear God in heaven, what have I done?" His mind reeled with possibilities. He turned and grasped John by the shoulders. "What if she's been abducted like those other girls?"

"Come on," John commanded. "We'll get over to the Appleton. Matthew can surely be of assistance. You've got to keep a level head, Taylor. Anything you can remember will surely help. Come along, Daughtie. Your supervisor won't excuse you if you're tardy."

The three of them rushed off toward the mill with Taylor taking the lead and Daughtie and John close on his heels. As they neared the mill yard, Daughtie grasped John's arm and begged him to send word of any news. When he had agreed, she bid the men farewell and scurried toward the stairwell.

Taylor spotted Lawrence Gault standing near the counting-house as they grew nearer and waved to the older gentleman. "Is Mr. Cheever in his office?"

"He is, but—"

"Good!" Taylor shouted in return, not waiting for any further information before bursting into Matthew Cheever's office. His mouth fell open at the sight. The outer room was already filled with several mill girls and Liam Donohue, and Miss Addie was sitting opposite Matthew's desk. Mr. Cheever's full attention was directed toward the older woman, but Taylor was undaunted by the sight. He strode past the others waiting in the outer office and into Matthew's office while saying, "I'm sorry, but this can't wait."

Matthew looked up as Taylor neared the desk. "Taylor, I'm—"

Miss Addie turned in her chair. "Oh, Taylor, I'm glad you're here. Where is Bella?"

"I don't know. That's why we've come. We need to organize a search party, and Uncle John thought this would be the place to get folks organized."

"Oh, John, this is terribly frightening," Addie said, rising from her chair. "I fear something dreadful has happened."

"Why don't you go on back home, Addie? You've done everything you can," John suggested. He took her arm and led her toward the door. "I'll keep you apprised of any news."

"Ask Liam to step in, would you, John?" Matthew requested.

Taylor turned his attention to Matthew. "What's Mr. Donohue got to do with Bella's disappearance? Do you think the Irish are involved in these abductions?"

"No, but Liam has furnished me with some helpful information regarding the abductions—or at least we're hoping it's going to be helpful," Matthew explained before turning his attention to Liam. "I'm sure you've heard enough of our conversation to realize we have another missing girl. I think we should get down to the canal. The locks begin operating at daybreak, and if they're going to attempt transporting the girls to Boston, we'll want to search any suspicious-looking boats or cargo."

John cleared his throat rather loudly. "I don't mean to be a spoiler, Matthew, but don't you think this is something the police should be called in on?"

"Absolutely. In fact, I've talked with them at some length, and they're aware of our concerns. However, since there are only two of them, it's impossible for them to lend much assistance. They requested our help at the waterway. I'll explain more fully if you like, but we'd best get down to the docks. Any of you on horseback?"

Liam gave a hearty laugh. "I don't think anyone in the Acre owns a horse."

"We're afoot, also. Taylor can fetch my horses from the livery if you think we'll need them," John offered. "It won't take long."

Matthew shook his head back and forth. "No. My horse is tied out back, so I'll ride ahead. The rest of you follow as quickly as possible," he said before moving to the outer office, where two girls still sat waiting. "Unless you have a missing person to report, you'll need to return later in the day. We've an emergency to tend to right now," Matthew told the mill girls as he opened the front door. He turned back toward the men. "I'll meet you near the loading dock by the millpond. It will probably take all four of us to inspect the boats preparing for departure."

Taylor was filled with a sense of mounting distress as they hurried off toward the wharf. He forced himself to take a deep calming breath. If he was going to find Bella, he needed clarity of thought, he decided as they finally approached the millpond. Without warning, he put voice to unbidden words that had mysteriously exploded in his mind. "I think we should pray."

The other three men stopped, turned, and stared at him as though he'd spoken in some unknown tongue.

He wondered if his words had been offensive. When none of them replied, he hastened to add, "If that would be all right with you."

John reached out and placed an arm around Taylor's shoulder. "You make me ashamed of myself, Taylor. I should have suggested prayer immediately. Yet it gives me great pleasure to know that you are beginning to place your trust in God rather than man. Gentlemen?"

Taylor silently communicated his own prayer for Bella as his uncle prayed aloud. The supplication took only a minute—it was a simple plea for help—yet Taylor felt more at peace. Bella's faith was strong, and surely she must be praying, too. Perhaps with the unification of their utterances, God would pause and assist them. A childish thought, perhaps, but it gave him added hope. He momentarily considered bartering with God but then decided God might frown upon such a concept. Bella would have an opinion on that idea. He'd discuss it with her once she was safely home.

"Taylor, you can go ahead and search this boat. Liam, you take that one," Matthew ordered while pointing where they were to go. "I'm going to talk to George West. He's in charge of the canal and locks this morning."

"Whadd'ya think you're doing? Get off this boat," a rough-looking man hollered as Taylor jumped aboard his boat.

"Nothing to be concerned about. We have permission to search all boats carrying cargo or passengers to Boston."

The man ran a dirty hand through his greasy unkempt hair before arching a stream of tobacco juice into the air that landed directly on Taylor's right shoe. "Since when?"

The other man working on the boat gave a snort.

Taylor looked down at his foot in disgust. Rolling his hand into a fist, he used his thumb to point toward Mr. West. "If you've got a problem, take it up with the man in charge. He says we've got permission, and so do the police. Now, you want to get out of my way? 'Cause if you don't, I'm going to guess it's because you've got something on this boat that ought not be here and you figure I'm going to find it. Could that be the problem, mister?"

"You talk mighty big. We'll see how big you are when you're alone in town someday."

Taylor knew the threat was intended to intimidate him, but it served only to make him angrier than he already was. "Why wait? You think you're man enough to take me on, then let's get to it."

"Taylor! We're not here for pugilistic entertainment," John called out. "Get busy and search that cargo. There are three more boats already loaded."

His uncle was right. They couldn't afford to waste time. Bella's life could be at risk, and he was acting like a schoolboy who needed to impress the other children in the play yard. He turned away from the man and began moving among the crates and barrels, moving them about and prying off lids while the two men spat curses in his direction.

The second man was following Taylor closely, hammering lids back down where needed and attempting to direct his path, or so it seemed to Taylor. Finally the man appeared to have lost all patience. "Look here, mate, you've gone through everything and found nothing out of order. Now get off the boat and let us be on our way."

Taylor surveyed the boat and glanced toward the center of the boat, where the one mast stood ready to hoist a sail when needed. "I've not gone through the goods stowed over there by your sail."

"Ain't nothing but some of the same what you've already seen."

Taylor gave the man an unswerving stare. "Then you've got nothing to be concerned about. The quicker we get done, the quicker you can be on your way," he said while tugging to move the deflated canvas sail.

Just then the first man rushed toward him. "Hey! Don't mess with that sail!" the man commanded as he shoved Taylor off balance, causing him to fall backward. He landed heavily on a row of rolled-up carpets, immediately thankful it hadn't been the pitchforks he'd found a short time earlier. He slowly began to lift himself up, then shook his head in wonder as two of the carpets appeared to wriggle back and forth.

"Seems to be a bit of turbulence in the water. Things is jostling about."

Taylor stared up at the man. "We're sitting dead still in a millpond. The only turbulence is right here in these carpets." He began to tug the edge of one of the rugs and heard a muffled noise.

"Uncle John! Over here!"

The scruffy boatman yanked at Taylor's arm. "Get away from there! You've got no right."

Taylor pulled free and yanked at the carpet. He saw two feet and then rope-bound ankles. Bella! It must be her. He looked up at his uncle, who was holding one of the men at bay while Liam held on to the other. Matthew rushed forward to help him. A torso appeared and then two bound arms—and then a face. But it wasn't Bella's face.

Working feverishly, they loosened the gag around the girl's head and then unbound her arms and legs. She flung about like a fish let loose on dry ground. "And for sure, I thought I was gonna die." The words spurted out in short gasps. "I could barely breathe with that carpet rolled about me." Her red hair flew about wildly as she lunged toward one of her abductors.

Matthew and Taylor let the other two men contend with the Irish girl and her temper. They unfurled carpet after carpet. They had now released seven girls, each one gasping for air and flailing for freedom as her bindings were loosed. Taylor stared down at the last roll of carpet. *Please, God, let it be Bella,* he silently prayed.

The two men tugged on the edge of the rug until they saw evidence of one more girl, whose feet and wrists were bound just as they had seen with the others. But this time the girl didn't shout with relief when her gag was loosened; this time the girl didn't flail about or jump to her feet. This time the girl lay perfectly still; this time the girl was Bella.

This time Taylor screamed in agony.

CHAPTER 36

Lilly Cheever grasped the fullness of her skirts, lifting the hem from the muck that lined the narrow winding path. She took careful steps, attempting to secure her footing in the slimy mess. Her walking boots were already covered with filth, and now a wiry-haired dog was yapping and nipping at her skirts as it circled her at a dizzying pace. Unfortunately, her attempts to shoo away the dog had only caused the animal to bark more incessantly.

A stooped old woman with a tattered shawl wrapped around her bent shoulders hoisted a bucketful of waste into the street, barely missing Lilly as she passed by. "What ya doin' in this part o' town?" The woman's voice was laced with a heavy Irish brogue. Piercing blue eyes that seemed strangely out of place were set deep in the ancient leathery face that had been marked with the countless creases of a hard life.

Lilly stopped and turned to face the woman, feeling out of place in her fur-collared mantle and morning dress of floral challis. "I'm looking for Noreen Gallagher's home. I was told it was down this path to the left. Is that correct?" She gave the woman a gentle smile. "I'd be willing to pay for the information."

The woman's eyes seemed to cut to her soul as she appraised Lilly for a moment before answering. "Hold to the left at the fork. Third door on the right," she replied and then held out her withered hand for payment.

Lilly dug into her lozenge-shaped velvet reticule and pulled out a coin. The woman's eyes brightened at the sight of the money as Lilly placed it in her hand. She clasped her bony fingers around the coin and then quickly disappeared behind her door as though she feared Lilly would snatch the money away from her.

The fork in the road was only a short distance away, and the mangy dog had now departed to chase after a wandering chicken rather than her skirts. She continued onward, picking her way through the litter-strewn pathway until she stood in front of Noreen Gallagher's door. *What kind of reception awaits me behind that dilapidated door?* she wondered. Fear would win if she remained there any longer.

She knocked—three firm raps—and waited. The door scraped open, the bottom of the board digging into the dirt floor before revealing an unkempt woman with matted hair and yellowed broken teeth. "Noreen Gallagher?" Lilly ventured.

"And who'd be wantin' to know?"

"I'm Lilly Cheever, and I wondered if I might have a word with you."

The woman fidgeted for a moment, running her fingers through her reddish-brown mass of greasy hair before answering. "What for? I ain't done nothin' to bring the likes of ya into the Acre."

"I've come to inquire about Kathryn O'Hanrahan's child."

Noreen's fingers immediately locked around Lilly's wrist. "Who says Kathryn ever had a child?" she hissed. The woman's eyes reflected a jittery mix of surprise, fear, and curiosity as she pulled Lilly forward into the hovel.

Lilly swallowed down her fear and croaked, "Liam Donohue."

"Liam!" The woman loosened her grip on Lilly's arm. "That traitorous man. Did he tell ya he wasn't possessed of enough manhood to tell me to me face that 'e was movin' out? And now it seems he's taken to spreadin' false rumors."

The smell inside was putrid, a farrago of every foul odor Lilly could imagine. She pulled a handkerchief from her pocket but then thought the better of placing it over her nose and mouth. Most likely the woman would take offense. "Your sister didn't have a child? Oh, please, this is very important."

Noreen held up an empty bottle. "How important?"

"I'm willing to pay for the information, and I promise no harm will come to you nor the child."

Noreen's lips curled into a wicked grin, her broken yellow teeth resembling the ruins of a city wall. "If I should be decidin' to tell ya anythin', there best be nothin' but good come from the use o' me words. Otherwise, I'll place a curse on ya that'll take the life of that child ya're carryin' in yar belly."

Lilly shivered at the threat. "If I tell you why I have an interest in the child, perhaps you'd be reconciled to helping me."

Noreen nodded and pointed at a broken-down wooden chair. "We'll see. Sit down."

Lilly carefully lowered herself into the chair, not certain it was capable of holding her weight without collapsing to the floor. Once seated and somewhat assured that the chair was stable, Lilly began to carefully explain the events surrounding her brother's untimely death. She told of his dying declaration concerning the existence of a child, a boy with a mushroom-shaped birthmark, and her determination to find the boy, although she remained silent regarding her journey to Canterbury.

"Yar brother's name?"

"Lewis. Lewis Armbruster."

Noreen slowly wagged her head back and forth. "Me sister never mentioned anyone by the name o' Armbruster to me. 'Course, that's not to say she didn't know 'im, 'cause I can't say that for sure. But Cullan is not yar brother's child. He was sired by William Thurston, and of that there is no doubt. For reasons I never understood, me sister believed that one day Thurston would leave 'is wife and marry 'er. Such nonsense! I told her so, too, but she wouldn't listen. William Thurston did nothin' but use her, and 'e was angry as a bull seein' red when Kathryn told 'im she was givin' him a babe—like he had nothin' to do with it."

"Did he accept the boy as his offspring?"

The Irish woman's lips curled in disgust. "He didn't like it none, but when he saw the birthmark, 'e knew. Besides, whether he wanted to admit it or not, he knew Kathryn hadn't been with other men. Kathryn said sometimes 'e was kind to the boy, but mostly not. I think Kathryn knew he'd never accept the lad. In fact, she told me should anything ever 'appen to her, she feared for the child's life. When she died, I figured Cullan would be safer outside of the Acre."

Lilly nodded. "And you took him to the Shaker Village in Canterbury."

Noreen jumped up from her chair and was leaning over Lilly. "How'd ya know that?"

"Purely coincidence, Mrs. Gallagher, but I've been to Canterbury to see the boy. They named him David but mentioned he had been known as Cullan."

Noreen's face softened slightly. "Is 'e well? How'd 'e look?"

"He appeared very well. He was neat and clean, obviously well nurtured—a fetching child," Lilly related. "I'm curious why you took him to Canterbury. You're obviously not of the same religious beliefs."

Noreen cackled and clapped her hands. "No. I doubt ya'll find many Irish among them Shakers. Odd sort of people, what little I saw of 'em, but I told Kathryn when the lad was born that if anything ever 'appened to her, I'd make certain the babe didn't come to any harm. I didn't think he'd be safe with me— figured if William Thurston heard tell I had a young boy living with me, he'd figure out soon enough the child was his and come after 'im."

Lilly remained silent, her gaze fixed upon Noreen's rough hands, the dirty fingers laced together as if in prayer. She didn't want to believe this woman's story. Lilly had fought against the idea the child could belong to anyone other than Lewis since she'd heard Liam Donohue's tale. But Matthew had willingly believed every word he'd been told. And as far as Lilly's husband was concerned, the matter was resolved—not that she hadn't attempted to resurrect the topic at every given opportunity. But Matthew always managed to change the subject. Today, she'd had no choice but to take matters into her own hands.

"Farfetched as my idea may seem, don't you think we should explore this matter more deeply? What if Lewis really is the boy's father? Wouldn't you want to know?"

"Me? I already know the truth. William Thurston's the boy's father, and there ain't nothin' ya can dig up that'll change that fact. I figure I could lie to ya. I might even make meself some money in the tellin'. Who would be the wiser? But the fact is Cullan might end up dead because of it. There ain't much I wouldn't do for a few coins, and folks here in the Acre would tell ya that's a fact. But I won't break a promise to me dead sister. If ya go and bring that lad back to Lowell, ya best be ready to accept the fact that yar actions will likely kill him. Are you so stubborn that ya're willing to see the lad die?"

"I'm stubborn enough to want him to have a better life, a life with his true family."

Noreen shook her head back and forth. "You ain't his kin, Mrs. Cheever. I don't know what else I can be sayin' to convince ya. But I'll tell ya this much—if ya have a speck of sense, ya'll leave this house and forget the lad."

Lilly knew she had been dismissed. There was, after all, nothing else to say. Reaching into her reticule, she pulled out several shiny coins and extended them to Noreen.

"Keep yar money. Just do as I've asked—forget the lad." Noreen's lips were set in a tight, hard line as she stood and looked down at Lilly. "Go back to yar fancy house, have a nice healthy baby of yar own, and pretend none of this ever 'appened."

Lilly stood, nodded, and dropped the coins into a metal cup as she slowly walked out of the shack. She remembered little of her journey out of the Acre. If there had been stares or whispered remarks, she'd been unaware. If there had been a yapping dog or an old woman pitching waste, it had gone unnoticed. So focused were her thoughts that she was surprised to find herself walking up the front steps to her home.

The first step was easy, but the second was halted as pain ripped through her abdomen and spread into her back. Gasping, Lilly put a hand to her stomach and tried to ignore the pain. In a moment it passed and she was able to reach the house. Drawing a deep breath, she knew her time had come. Now she would have to see about reaching Matthew and the doctor before the baby was born without them.

CHAPTER 37

Bella coughed, then sputtered, carpet fibers invading her airways as she strained to fill her lungs with fresh air. A voice somewhere in the distance instructed her to breathe slowly and relax. Yet she couldn't. Her body ached for oxygen. And so she fought for air—in short panicky gasps until her body finally responded and the distant voice became clearer, saying her name and instructing her to remain calm and open her eyes.

Fingers cradled her head, and she could feel the warmth of someone's breath on her face. She struggled to open her eyes. They felt heavy, as though a weight had been placed upon them, sealing them tight. Once again she heard someone calling her name in the distance. Her eyelids fluttered momentarily and then languidly opened to reveal a face that was nearly touching her own. Startled, Bella lurched upward and struck Taylor's forehead with her own. The force of the blow caused her to drop back onto the boat's deck.

Taylor moved to her side, his hand now rubbing his forehead. "Are you all right? I was so worried."

Bella focused upon Taylor's face and watched as a small bump began to rise on his brow. She gave him a faint smile. "I believe I've injured you."

"Don't concern yourself with me. Try to sit up," he encouraged, taking her hand. "How do you feel?"

Loosened strands of hair fell across her face as she lifted herself into a sitting position. Instinctively, she brushed the hair behind one ear. "I think I'm fine. The other girls, are they injured? Where is Ruth?"

Ruth moved closer, with the other girls following her lead. "I'm right here, Bella."

Bella glanced toward Hilda. "And you, Hilda, did they hurt you?"

Hilda gave her a bright smile. "I'll be fine once we get back home."

Turning her gaze to Taylor, Bella said, "Hilda works at the Hamilton. And poor Ruth, they've been holding her longer than any of us. We had given up all hope of being found."

Ruth nodded her head. "I was certain I'd never see my family again. Several times they said I was being sent to Boston."

"Where have you been all this time, Ruth?"

"I wish I could tell you, but I truly don't know. They blindfolded me and put me in the back of a wagon. I have no idea where we went, but I think it was somewhere out of town. I was kept in one room with no windows, and then they brought the other girls, one by one," Ruth explained, her gaze now shifting to Hilda and the Irish girls. "But they never brought Bella. We didn't see her until they moved us to the warehouse here at the millpond. Of course, we didn't know it was the millpond, but we could hear water and boats. We knew we were near water and that we were going to be shipped off somewhere."

Bella glanced toward Matthew and Liam. Both of them appeared to be listening intently as Ruth related her story. The two men in charge of the boat shifted about, obviously growing more and more uncomfortable as Matthew glared down at them. "I'm not going to waste much time on the two of you," Matthew growled. "You know we've already sent for the police. If you have any hopes of leniency, I suggest you cooperate and tell us everything you know about this illegal business you're conducting. Otherwise, I'm going to tell the police you both deserve as much punishment as can possibly be meted out by the judge."

"Now, wait a minute," one of them objected, "this wasn't our idea. We're being paid to haul cargo to Boston—nothing more."

Matthew grunted. "Don't lie to me. You two men kidnapped these girls and knew what was going to happen to them."

The other man stroked the bristly stubble along his jawline. "Well, yeah, that there is true, but we was following orders. It was them or us. If we didn't do what we was told, we'd find ourselves taking a bullet or floating in the river. I'm too young to die."

"Then you'd best tell us who put you up to this whole thing. I want names—all of them, starting with yours."

The two men exchanged a look before the second one continued. "My name is Jake Wilson and this here's Rafe Walton. But you ain't gonna believe me when I tell you who set this up."

"Try me. You may be surprised what I'll believe."

"William Thurston's the one in charge. Him and J. P. Green. They put us up to this whole thing, and they're the ones getting rich, not us. But I doubt you want to hear it's some of your fancy Associates dealing in human flesh. You don't believe me, do ya?"

"Unfortunately, I do. Have you left out any names? Is there anybody else involved?"

Rafe slowly moved his head back and forth. "If there is, they never told us. Thurston and Green are the only ones we ever met with, and I doubt they wanted to share their profits with anyone else."

"Me too. They wasn't paying us hardly anything," Jake said before turning his attention to the girls on the other side of the boat. "You tell 'em we never did you any harm."

Taylor jumped to his feet and took three long strides to where Jake was sitting and glared into the man's face. "What do you mean you didn't do them any harm? You tore them away from their homes against their will, kept them as prisoners—and you almost killed her," he shouted while pointing toward Bella. "And if we hadn't stopped you, they would be bound for the slave market in New Orleans. I'd say you did plenty of harm."

Bella gasped. "Slave market? They were going to sell us as slaves? Is that what you've discovered, Taylor?"

Her words brought him back to her side. "It's a long story, but Matthew discovered these men have gotten into the business of abducting girls when they are out alone at night. It appears as if they were waiting until they had a goodly number of you before making the journey to Boston."

The words struck fear in her heart. Foolish pride had nearly caused her ruin. She didn't want to imagine what would have happened had Taylor and the other men not arrived. Bella looked across the boat to where Matthew and Liam had now secured Rafe and Jake. "One of them said they were taking us to Boston and from there we would be taken south; he mentioned New Orleans. He said there was no need for concern— that we'd have lovely new homes. I inquired why he didn't advertise for girls to work in these homes if these were desirable positions, pointing out the fact that the Corporation advertises in the newspaper for mill girls. He quickly told me to shut up and labeled me a troublemaker. But the thought of slavery never entered my mind."

Taking her hands in his own, Taylor gently warmed her cold fingers. "It's best you don't dwell on what might have happened, Bella. You're safe and that's what really matters."

She couldn't believe his kindness. "After the way I acted, I'm surprised you would even bother to look for me."

"Don't be foolish. A few misspoken words can't drive me away from you, Bella. I realize my behavior last night upset you—and rightfully so. I should have told you I needed to remain for another meeting. I must admit I was surprised when I realized you'd left for home, but it wasn't until very early this morning that I discovered you had never arrived back at the boardinghouse. Miss Addie sent Daughtie to inquire about your whereabouts, and that's when our search began," he explained.

"I would have never stopped looking for you, Bella. I love you . . . and I never want to lose you again. It's my desire that one day you'll feel the same way. I can't make you trust me, but I hope you'll come to believe that I will never abandon you."

His words were filled with warmth and compassion. She wanted desperately to believe him, to once again feel the safety of another's love and protection. Yet dare she let him into her heart? Could she withstand rejection if he should one day decide she was no longer worthy of his love? Bella wasn't certain, yet she knew Taylor deserved a reply. Before she could form a response, Dr. Fontaine jumped onto the boat, his medical bag swinging from one hand.

"John tells me someone down here needs a doctor."

"Over here," Taylor called out. "Bella was having difficulty breathing. However, I believe she's much better now that she's gotten some fresh air."

Dr. Fontaine quickly moved to her side. "Let's take a look, young lady."

Bella held up a hand in protest. "I don't need a doctor. I'm fine. They've brought you down here unnecessarily."

The doctor gave her a paternal smile. "Since I'm the one with medical training, why don't you let me decide whether you need me or not?"

There was no sense in arguing; it was obvious she wouldn't win. "As you choose, but I'm certain you'll find me a healthy specimen."

All of them turned to look as a rider came galloping toward the dock, shouting and waving in their direction. "Doc, you're needed at the Cheever house. You'd best be coming, too, Matthew. I've been told your wife's about to have her baby." The rider jumped down from his horse. "You can take my horse, Doc," the man offered.

Matthew looked helplessly from Liam to Taylor. "I've got to go. John should be back with the police soon. Can you handle this?"

"For sure we can. Ya be gettin' yarself home," Liam said, giving Matthew a hearty laugh. "I've no doubt that yar wife might not be too forgivin' if ya don't get home to her right now."

"I'll return your horse once Uncle John gets back," Taylor promised as Matthew stepped out of the boat.

Matthew waved and called out over his shoulder, "And by that time, I hope to have a son or daughter to introduce."

Matthew's words brought a smile to Bella's face. "I pray that this baby will fill the void in Mrs. Cheever's life. I'm certain she's been distraught since hearing that the child in Canterbury isn't her nephew. I know this baby won't replace her parents or brother—or even the place she'd set aside for little Cullan—but certainly a new life will bring affirmation that her family lives on through the baby. Family is very important to her."

Taylor gazed into her eyes. "And to you, I believe."

A faint smile played upon Bella's lips as she stared into Taylor's intense blue eyes. "Yes, family is very important." At the sound of pounding horses' hooves, they both turned toward the road. "It appears your uncle John has arrived with the police."

"It seems to me that every time I'm able to engage you in a serious conversation, someone interrupts us," Taylor lamented. "Once we finally have this kidnapping issue resolved, I want time alone to discuss our future."

"Our future?"

Taylor put his arms around Bella and helped her to her feet. "Yes, our future . . . as Mr. and Mrs. Taylor Manning."

"I'm not sure—"

He placed a finger to her lips. "Wait until we have time to talk before you say anything more."

"Lilly!" Matthew called to his wife as he took the front porch steps two at a time. He knew the doctor would be on his heels and left the front door wide open as he bounded into the house. "Lilly!"

"I'm right here, dear," she said softly.

He found her sitting in the front room. "Why are you here? Why aren't you in bed?"

"I didn't feel like going to bed. Not yet, anyway. I sent for the doctor."

Matthew nodded. "I know. He was with me when the rider came."

"Why was the doctor with you?" she asked curiously.

"It's a long story. But it has a happy ending. We found many of the missing girls, Lilly. I'll tell you all about it after I help you to bed. The doctor should be here any minute." He knelt beside her and lifted her skirt slightly. "Here, let me take off your shoes. I'm sure—" He stopped in midsentence. "Your shoes are caked in mud . . . manure, too, from the smell of them. Where have you been?"

She gave him a weak smile. "I've been to see Noreen Gallagher."

Matthew momentarily forgot about his wife's labor and barely controlled his anger. "You went to the Acre?" He stared in silence for a moment before regaining his composure. "Surely my wife would not do such a thing. Tell me this is an ill-thought-out hoax, Lilly. Please."

"I'm sorry, Matthew, but it's true. I needed to talk with her, to somehow be convinced that the boy in Canterbury is not Lewis's child."

"And did you see her?"

Lilly nodded her head.

"And were you convinced?"

"Well . . ."

"I knew it!" he exclaimed. "What will it take to convince you, Lilly? Lewis is dead. The boy's mother is dead. Who is left that can make you see the truth?"

"I don't know."

"Obviously there is no one. You're even willing to bring on the premature birth of our child in this futile effort to convince yourself the boy is somehow related to you."

"That's not true. I would never harm our child. The baby may be coming a bit sooner than we expected, but that happens to a lot of women."

Matthew stopped pacing and leveled his gaze her way. "Lilly, you placed both yourself and our child in jeopardy the minute you walked into the Acre. I'm surprised you weren't knocked down and robbed. You certainly extended an invitation, dressed in fur and velvet and, if my guess is right, carrying a reticule in plain sight."

"How was I to know?"

"That's exactly my point, Lilly."

"I knew you'd refuse me. Every time I attempt to talk about the boy, you change the subject."

"Don't make this my fault, Lilly. I would have permitted a talk with Noreen. In fact, I had already mentioned the possibility to Liam Donohue. But I certainly wouldn't have sent you to the Acre. I would have brought Noreen here, to our home, where the possibility of danger would have been nonexistent."

Lilly lowered her head. "Nothing happened. We're both safe. I promise I'll not go back there again. Am I forgiven?" Her voice was little more than a whisper.

Matthew lowered himself into the chair opposite her and took her delicate hands into his own. "Of course you're forgiven, Lilly. I love you more than you can possibly imagine. It grieves me to know how deeply affected you've been by the boy and yet you believed I was unapproachable. Because I believed without doubt that the child was William Thurston's, I assumed that you, too, would be convinced. I was wrong."

"In my heart I know you're right. And even if I still harbored hope, Noreen has convinced me the boy's life would be in danger were he returned to Lowell. I can't take such a risk. I could never live with myself if he came to harm because of my selfish actions. Yet I maintain this deep longing for a continuation of my family."

He lifted her chin until their eyes met. "You do have a continuation of your family—the baby and me. God has blessed us, Lilly, and although your parents and brother are gone, they'll live on through you and our child."

"I know you're right, Matthew, but it's difficult letting go of the hope."

"You must never lose hope, Lilly. I'd never ask such a thing, but perhaps you could redirect your hope—reassign those dreams to the future of our child and our family."

She smiled up at him and whispered, "Perhaps I could." Her smile faded as she doubled in pain. "The baby!" she gasped.

"Did I hear tell there was a baby to be born today?" the doctor questioned as he came into the house.

Matthew lifted Lilly into his arms. "I was just getting her upstairs. She's the stubborn type, you know. Sometimes you just have to impose your will on her."

The doctor laughed and followed them upstairs. "No doubt the baby will impose his or her will on you both. Parenting is no easy chore."

After dealing with the police, Liam saw the Irish girls home while Taylor took care of Ruth and Bella and Hilda. Walking back to the boardinghouse, Bella glanced up hesitantly. "Why do you keep talking of marriage to me? You scarcely know me."

"I know enough," Taylor replied, grinning. "I know you're spirited and full of life. I know you believe in righting wrongs and standing your ground when you believe you're right." He paused on the walkway and took hold of her hands, turning her to face him. "I know that the thought of living without you is something I do not want to contemplate."

Bella swallowed hard, trying to push down the lump of emotion that had risen from within. "Taylor, you've been the most important person in your life for so long; why should I believe that would change now?"

"Because God can change anyone's heart. At least that's what Uncle John told me, and I believe you've said much the same. I did a great deal of thinking while searching for you, and I know I've been wrong to push God away. My mother brought me up to love the Scriptures and to esteem God. But losing her . . ." His voice grew soft. He straightened his shoulders and drew a deep breath. "It was so hard. I saw my father fail every day after her death. They were one in every sense, and when she died, he couldn't go on. That terrified me. I decided then and there I would never love a woman as my father had loved my mother."

"What changed your mind?"

He smiled. "You."

Bella shook her head. "Surely there was more."

"Oh, I suppose I was impressed with Uncle John and Miss Addie. I would come away from our meetings feeling emptiness in light of what they had. I would remind myself of Father's pain, but it didn't seem to matter." Taylor met Bella's gaze. "Then I came to realize it wasn't Miss Addie and Uncle John's situation that brought about this feeling, but rather you. When I first met you, I knew you were different . . . I knew you were unique."

"I'm not unique in any real sense," Bella replied. "I also know I'm not without my faults. I suppose I should thank you for bearing with my errors so graciously."

He laughed. "Bella, we are both troublesome creatures. We have much to learn and a long way to go toward a complete understanding of marriage and love, but I want to educate myself in those things with you by my side. I'm not asking you to marry me tomorrow—I'm just seeking a pledge that you will be my wife . . . someday."

Bella felt her knees tremble and fought to steady herself without giving notice to Taylor. During the entire ordeal of being kidnapped, Taylor had been all she could think of. She had already determined that she loved him—faults and all—but she wanted very much to be certain about this momentous step.

"I didn't come to Lowell with the thought of getting married."

He nodded. "I know, and that's what made you exactly the right woman for me. All the others threw themselves at me. I could give them a wink or a nod, and they were totally devoted to me."

"Yes, well," Bella said, feeling her anger ignite, "I witnessed enough of that to last me a lifetime." She pulled away from him and began walking again.

"Bella, those girls meant nothing to me then, and they mean nothing now. Don't you hear me? I know that toying with their affections was the wrong thing for me to do. I know I'm a sinful man, but, Bella . . . I love you."

She stopped and turned, seeing the sincerity in his expression. "We'll probably fight all the time," she murmured.

He grinned. "But then we can make up."

"I have a temper."

He walked slowly toward her. "So I've noticed."

Bella bit her lower lip. She felt a surge of excitement as he stopped only inches from her. "I find it difficult to trust—especially men."

"I don't care if you ever trust other men; just trust me. That's all I'm asking."

"I still believe in the equality of men and women. I still believe in education for females as well as males," she said, thinking it best to throw out everything and give him time to rethink his proposal.

"So do I, Bella," he said, taking hold of her shoulders. They stood there for several moments, neither one saying a word.

With a startling certainty, Bella knew her heart. She loved Taylor Manning and didn't want to go through life without him.

"And God must come first in our home," Bella finally added.

He pulled her into his arms. "Yes," he breathed against her lips.

"Yes," she murmured as he captured her mouth in a tender yet passionate kiss.

He pulled away. "Was that yes for me?"

She nodded.

He grinned in his self-assured manner. "Good. So long as we have that matter taken care of." He pulled her along toward the boardinghouse. "Now we must tell Miss Addie that you're safe and that Mrs. Cheever is having her baby."

Bella felt dazed but happy. "I suppose we might also tell her that we plan to marry in a few years."

Taylor stopped dead in his tracks. "A few years? I thought maybe next week."

Bella shook her head. "We need time, Taylor. Being engaged for, say . . . five years could be very prudent in our situation. You know that as well as I. We both need to reaffirm our hearts to God and to allow His guidance in this matter. Our love for each other will only grow stronger—if it's real."

Taylor shook his head and guided her up the walkway to Miss Addie's. "I've never known anything more real—and I never want to." He paused with a grin before opening the door and added, "And I'm not waiting five years."

EPILOGUE

Christmas 1831

"Lilly, she's positively perfect," Addie said as she beheld the newest member of the Cheever family.

"Her father certainly thinks so," Lilly replied. "Would you like to hold her?"

"Oh, please," Addie replied.

Lilly handed her daughter to Addie, then nodded to Bella. "You, too. You can share her for a moment, and then I'm going to put her down for her nap and we shall have our Christmas punch and exchange our gifts."

Addie cuddled the baby momentarily before giving her up. Bella thought her heart would melt into a puddle on the floor as she took the baby into her arms. Violet Cheever looked up at her with large dark eyes. She yawned a tiny baby yawn and made sucking noises as she closed her eyes.

Bella gently touched her downy soft hair and smiled. "She's perfect."

"You look very natural holding her. You and Taylor should have a whole houseful of children," Lilly said, reaching out to take Violet. "I'll be back momentarily. Why don't you both join the men in the music room?"

Addie linked her arm with Bella. As they crossed from the parlor to the music room, Addie stated, "I'd imagine holding Violet makes you want to speed up your wedding plans."

Bella grinned. "Just don't tell Taylor that or he'll start pestering me all over again."

"Don't tell Taylor what?"

Bella looked up to find Taylor at her side. "Never mind," she said. "Some things are better left unsaid."

"Since when? I've always known you to speak your mind and make certain that everyone knows your thoughts," Taylor teased.

Bella smiled as Miss Addie left her with Taylor and joined John and Matthew across the room by the fireplace. "You are purposefully trying my patience in the hope that I will tell you what I do not wish to share."

He laughed and pulled her close. "I can be most persuasive, Miss Newberry. Would you like me to show you how?" He gently caressed her cheek with his fingertips, then trailed the touch down to her lips.

Bella trembled. "Hmm, yes, actually . . . I think that might be a nice diversion."

Taylor roared with laughter and kissed her soundly. Bella wrapped her arms around his neck and sighed. Maybe putting the wedding off for five years would be too long. Maybe three would make better sense.

Their kiss deepened as they completely ignored the other people in the room. Maybe, Bella reconsidered, a year would be enough time to wait.

The Best Books
from Bestselling Authors

Her Pursuit of Justice Has Just Become Personal

Now a proven success as a lawyer, Kit Shannon has become a major force in the battle for justice in early 1900s Los Angeles. Her newest case is the cause of a society woman who fears her dark past will be exposed. At the same time Kit's fiancé is arrested for treason, and his life is now at stake. But Kit is left wondering how she'll defend a man who's betrayed both her love and country.

A Greater Glory by James Scott Bell

A Captivating Page-Turner with a Message of Hope!

Running from a bleak past and a terrifying present, Noelle St. Claire searches for sanctuary away from those who've betrayed her. On a horse ranch in the shadows of the Rocky Mountain, she finds herself escaping into a new life—until her worst fears are realized and her safe haven is torn apart.

A Rush of Wings by Kristen Heitzmann

The Leader in Christian Fiction!

◈ BETHANYHOUSE